A MORNING MOON

A MORNING MOON

Paula Reibel

WILLIAM MORROW AND COMPANY, INC.
NEW YORK

Library of Congress Cataloging in Publication Data

Reibel, Paula.
A morning moon.

I. Title.
PS3568.E47626M6   1984   813'.54   84-4666
ISBN 0-688-03972-3

Printed in the United States of America

First Edition

1 2 3 4 5 6 7 8 9 10

BOOK DESIGN BY JAMES UDELL

To my father,
who lived through all these worlds
and learned survival

ACKNOWLEDGMENTS

There are many people whose assistance and encouragement deserve my thanks. I hope they know how I feel. But I must express particular gratitude to those who made specific contributions to the work: to Zelda Blumberg, Arthur Harvith, Froma Lippmann, and Neil Moyer for sharing their expertise in Judaic lore and *Yiddishkeit;* to Maria Guarnaschelli for incisive, understanding editorial support; to Bruce Giffords for brilliant copy editing; to Hillel Black and Linda Healey for their backing at the early stages; to Victoria Pryor for her unflagging confidence in the work from its inception; and to Paula Klein, Ida Kline, Lyda Rochmis, and my unmatchable family for the support, advice, and encouragement that were my sustenance.

CONTENTS

Prologue, 1933
13

Part One: Mindel, 1895–1897
17

Part Two: Leib, 1904–1913
91

Part Three: Dov, 1913–1914
155

Part Four: Dvora, 1914–1919
179

Part Five: Dov, 1919–1928
239

Part Six: Yudi, 1926–1933
305

Part Seven: Avrum, 1933
361

*"And what have you laid up
for the cold weather?"
they asked a poor fellow.
"Shivering," he answered.*

—OLD YIDDISH FABLE

PROLOGUE

New York City
August, 1933

Sam—

I don't know even how to address you. I can't call you "my dearest one"
—not properly, that is—although I would like to. And if I called you "my
dear friend," you would only frown and say, "I'm not your friend and have no
wish to be." I've begun and thrown away a dozen letters to you since you left
me last night, but I can't find where to start. I want that you should under-
stand why I do what I do. Believe me, I know it's all my fault. I should never
have . . .

The young woman at the little kitchen table in front of the half-
opened window shook her head and sighed deeply. The words weren't
saying what she wanted. The pen shook in her fingers, clear evidence of
her weariness and frustration. She pushed back the hair from her forehead,
her thin, shaking fingers still unaccustomed to handling her recently cut
hair. "What can I say to him?" she asked herself in Yiddish.

She shut her eyes and lowered her head until it rested on the cold
rim of the enameled tabletop. She'd been at the task for hours and still
hadn't found a way to make clear to Sam why she had to go back. Maybe
if I didn't have to write to you in English, she thought, I could make
things clear. English is still so hard for me. But he wouldn't believe that.
He'd say that she couldn't write because her reasoning was too muddled.

A sudden breeze from the window tickled her ear. The smell combined the usual fumes of rotting garbage with a cool, moist freshness—

a morning smell contradicting the night blackness of the sky. She didn't have to look at a clock to know it was after four.

She ought to go to bed. There were still four days left before she would be embarking on the *Mauritania*. She had plenty of time to write the letter—there wasn't much she had to do in the meantime. She wouldn't be seeing Sam again; she'd told him she couldn't stand the arguing. Her mind was made up. In ten days she was sailing for Europe. "And despite you, Sam," she said aloud, "despite the arguments and the harangues and the wrenched feelings, I will be on board!"

But how, even if she had twice the time at her disposal, could she explain it all to him? Sam, the American born . . . how would he understand? What did Americans know of the pull of the past?

Americans. An amazing breed. They never spent a moment on yesterday. They knew only how to look forward. They were brought up to face front, to march straight and proud into their promising futures. They drank tomorrow in their bottled milk. The past was nothing to them but useless baggage, good only for weighing people down with regrets and guilts.

The breeze ruffled her bobbed hair more insistently, the feeling of wetness more noticeable in the aromatic air. By morning it would probably be raining. She lifted her head and looked up at the piece of sky she could see between the buildings across the street and caught a glimpse of the moon sliding behind a cloud. Was it a sign—a portent of her future? *Is it a symbol, Sam?*

It was Sam, who'd been her English teacher, who'd taught her about symbolism, but he'd laugh at her for seeing personal symbols in the movements of the moon. And he'd be right. To try to read one's future in daisy petals or palm wrinkles or the phases of the moon was foolishness. Old women's superstitious nonsense, not poetic symbolism.

She had a sudden flash of memory. She saw a child skipping along a dirt road, the road she used to take to school when she was . . . how old? Seven? Eight? Her sister, four years older, was hurrying ahead, pulling her by the hand. There were other children, too, four or five of them, all hurrying. And straight ahead, over the hill, the sun was coming up.

She didn't want to go to school that day. She dragged her feet, resisting the persistent tug of her sister's hand. Then she looked over her shoulder and saw, of all things, the *moon!* "Look, Dvora!" she cried in amazement, pulling free of her sister's grasp and pointing to the unearthly phenomenon that hung large and distinct behind them. "How can it be? The sun's up already, and there's the *moon!*"

Dvora and the others turned to stare at the apparition. The moon looked transparent, ghostly, with the blue sky seeming to shine right through where at night there would have been shadows. It seemed displaced . . . spectral . . . the stuff of fantasy.

But Dvora merely shrugged. "It's only a morning moon," she said. "Nothing to make a fuss about."

"That's right," one of the others agreed. "A morning moon. I've seen it lots of times."

"Come on, Yudi." Dvora yanked her arm impatiently. "You'll be late."

The others ran on, their eyes front to where the sun was brightening up with its red-gold pretentiousness. But she stumbled along the road, unable to take her eyes from the eerie presence behind her until she tripped and fell. Dvora pulled her to her feet by the collar of her blouse, whacked her ear, and dragged her off.

She blinked as the alien shapes of Essex Street reasserted themselves on her consciousness, a fascinating insight bursting on her. It was a shock to recognize that she and her entire family were very like that little child. They all went stumbling through their lives, bumping into things, tripping and wounding themselves at every turn, because their eyes were fixed on what was behind them. On Avrum. Avrum, their past . . . hanging over all their shoulders like that pale, distracting, fantastic phenomenon, the morning moon.

It's a truly poetic symbol, Sam, she thought, smiling a little. Even you would have to agree.

The smile lingered as she sat down at the table again. "No, not a symbol," Sam would say. "A metaphor."

But symbol or metaphor, there was a kind of truth in the image. If only she could make Sam see it. She wasn't the least bit sleepy . . . she might as well start her letter again. With renewed determination, she tore a new page from her pad, brushed back her unruly hair, and picked up the pen.

Dear, dear Sam . . .

Part One

MINDEL
1895–1897

1

I suppose, Sam, that the root of all the trouble was that my father was a lemeshkeh, a true shlemiel. All right, no Yiddish. In American, then, he was a nothing. At least that was the way my mother and the others in our shtetl—sorry, our little town—evaluated him. It was my mother who—

But this isn't how to explain myself to you. To tell the story I ought to start with my mother. It is she you must understand first. So I have to go back before my father even came into it . . . before my mother even married her first husband. The true beginning would have to be 1895, in a little town called Solitava in the northeast corner of what was then the Austro-Hungarian Empire. If only I had the words to make you see the way it happened, the way I see it. And I do see it, you know, just as if I lived through it myself—all of it, right from the time the trouble began, the week my mother, Mindel Rossner the Proud One, became sixteen. . . .

Mindel the Proud One was scrubbing the pots. She was banging them against the basin with a great deal more noise than was necessary.

Her mother glared at her. "Don't think you'll drown me out with that clatter, you mule! If your uncle Nathan, who has always made so much of you, who praised you and petted you and even taught you the Gemara—which he didn't do for any other girl in the world—summons you to a *din Torah,* you must've done something terrible. Tell me what it is!"

"Ask Uncle Nathan, if you're so curious," Mindel responded rudely, her mouth set tightly and her eyes fixed on the pot she was scouring with undue vigor.

"Is this how a girl talks to her mother, you shrew? Have you the impudence to suggest that I go to your uncle, who is more than an uncle, more than a rabbi—a Tzaddik, that's what he is, a Tzaddik of renown!—and shame myself before him by admitting that I don't know what goes on under my own roof?"

Raizel, Mindel's younger sister, who was listening with wide-eyed attention to the altercation from her perch on the windowsill, attempted to placate her irate mother with a mild interjection. "You could ask Aunt Chana, couldn't you?"

Their mother, Etel Fruma the Short-tempered, threw the younger girl a dagger look. "Keep still, Miss Stirring Spoon! This is not your pudding to mix. Besides, I already asked Chana, and she knows nothing but that your sister has earned her uncle's deepest anger. It's something serious, I can tell. So will you tell me what you've done, troublemaker, or will you keep defying me?"

"You'll know soon enough," Mindel muttered. "The whole town will soon know."

"They all know already that you've made some sort of trouble. They must have seen Zaleh when he came here with the message."

"Maybe no one saw Zaleh," Raizel suggested hopefully. "It's raining very hard, you know. Maybe no one was outside."

"Someone saw, don't worry. I never knew rain to stop the spread of gossip. The whole town's probably talking about it already." She took a step closer to Mindel and peered into her face. "It's about the match, isn't it? A match blessed by two holy men! You've done something to spoil things, haven't you?"

Mindel pressed her lips tightly together and continued to scrub the pots.

Etel Fruma knew she would get no further word from the girl, but her frustration and fury drove her on. "An old maid, that's what you'll be, may God forgive me for saying so. An old maid!" She dropped into a chair, shut her eyes, and began to rock herself back and forth in perturbation. "I told your father he was wrong to raise you so much like a boy. It was pride. Too much pride in your cleverness. He and my brother, both. I told your father he'd be sorry. First pride comes, then shame comes—isn't that what is written?"

" 'When pride cometh, then cometh shame,' " Mindel and Raizel intoned in chorus.

Their mother opened her eyes and looked from one to the other in disgust. "Isn't that what I said? Shame—that's what we'll have now. A daughter who knows the Gemara but doesn't know how to find a husband. Prospects ruined already, and you not yet sixteen." She blinked in sudden confusion. "Or are you sixteen already?"

Etel Fruma shut her eyes again and resumed her rocking. She was distraught, but it was not her distraction that confused her about her daughter's birthday. It was common for females' births to go unrecorded and unremembered. In her recollection of such matters, she was as accurate as anyone in Solitava. She wasn't entirely sure whether Mindel had been born two days before Purim or three, but that the obstinate girl was to be sixteen sometime this week was more or less a certainty. If Mindel had been born a boy, of course, Etel Fruma would have known the exact date of the birth—after all, a boy had to have his *bar mitzvah* at the proper time. But a girl's birthday was a matter of small importance. And with this one, it might be better to forget the birthday entirely. If Mindel was going to be as difficult to marry off as her stiff-necked behavior seemed to indicate, it would be better if the world didn't know how old she was.

The disgusted woman got up from the chair and crossed the room to the door, reaching for a large, fringed shawl that hung from a hook on the wall. "An old maid, may my tongue wither for saying such a thing about my own daughter, but that's what you'll be. I've known it from the first. Even as a baby you were headstrong and willful. I told your father so, but he would not pay attention. 'Women's bickerings,' he said. Now he'll know." She shook out the shawl and held it out to her daughter. "Well, why are you standing there like a piece of wood? It's time to go. Dry your hands and put this on."

Mindel expelled a breath, dried her hands, and took the shawl from her mother. She felt a hammering in her chest, but in her mind she was not afraid. It would only be a reprimand—what else could her uncle do to her, even if he was the renowned Tzaddik of Solitava? There was nothing to be afraid of. She threw the shawl over her shoulder defiantly and reached for the doorknob.

"Put it *on*!" Etel Fruma ordered furiously. "Don't you see how it's raining? Put it on, I tell you! Can't you do anything you're told? It's not bad enough you've shamed us all with your craziness, but do you have to stand before your uncle with rain dripping from your hair?"

Mindel ignored the tirade and marched out the door. She set off down the muddy street without a backward look at the faces of her mother and sister, who watched her worriedly from the front window. Two neighbor women, hurrying up the street from the opposite direction, stopped and clucked their tongues as they watched her walk by. They knew where she was going. They'd already heard that the Tzaddik's niece—his favorite, like a daughter to him!—had done something unspeakable. But Mindel passed by the curious women with complete unconcern, her chin up, her arm swinging from the pace of her stride, and her heavy braid slapping against her back.

Someone had once said to Mindel that she walked like a queen. She'd laughed. "Queen, eh? Queen of what—the *shtetl*?" She'd found the comment ludicrous. After all, didn't she walk through the same spring mud and kick up the same summer dust as everyone else in the town? Didn't she wear the same shabby, ugly shoes as the rest of them? Queen, indeed!

But deep inside, she felt like an aristocrat. Her uncle and her father had always made her feel privileged. And she'd seen in the mirror beside her bed that she had a strong face—a wide forehead, deep gray eyes whose color was unusual in a town of dark-eyed girls, a slightly protruding but well-chiseled chin, and thick brown hair which she wore in one long heavy braid. Even the braid was unlike the other girls'; theirs grew narrower and narrower as they lengthened, but hers remained just as thick at the bottom as it was at the top. She enjoyed feeling the weight of it when it struck her back as she strode along the street.

She knew that people found her arrogant, that there was something about the set of her shoulders, the swing of her skirts and her braid, the expression on her face, that made her different. Aloof, they said. But they treated her with respect. No one pinched her cheeks or teased her about her prettiness or said the silly things to her that they said to other girls her age.

. . . *Don't ask me why, Sam, for I don't understand myself why people always treated my mother with deference. I don't think she deserved it. Her education may have been better than the other village girls' (for her uncle, the Tzaddik himself, had supervised her education, and her brother, my uncle Shmuel, was a dealer in used books, and she always had her nose in one of them). But she wasn't kind or gracious; she didn't take from her mouth to give to the poor; she didn't heal the sick, or tell stories, or bring ease to the oppressed or joy to those in misery. Can people command respect just by their manner? . . .*

As she walked through the streets, chin high, ignoring the pelting rain, others who passed paused to glance at her curiously. Though the heart in her breast was beating ever more fearfully as she grew closer to the angry confrontation with her uncle, there was no sign of it in her face. She noticed the stares of the passersby—did they have gleams of satisfaction in their eyes?—before they scurried on their way, huddled under their shawls or hunched over to keep the wetness more on their backs than on their faces. But she didn't care about their stares. She didn't care about the wet. She kept her bare head up, her shoulders straight, and her eyes fixed ahead of her, as if the sun were shining. The pointed end of her shawl (as negligently hung from one shoulder as if she had a dozen more at home) dragged in the mud behind her.

She cut diagonally across the town square, which only yesterday had been the scene of hectic activity, for it had been Market Day, when all the peasants from the surrounding countryside came in to barter for the needles, soap, kerchiefs, candy, dried herring, and dozens of other items that the Jews of Solitava managed to fabricate. The square had been crowded with stalls and wagons of every size and description, and she would have found it difficult to make her way through the press of noisy people intent on their bargaining. Today, however, there was not a soul on the street, even at the well in the far corner of the square.

Only two men, lounging in the doorway of the hardware store opposite the well, gave evidence that the shops in the square were open for business. One was Mottel Kutner, the owner of the shop. The other was Leib Weisenberg, a young *shlemiel* of nineteen, who looked as if God had put him together with leftover parts. Nothing seemed to belong together: his beak of a nose was too large for his hollow-cheeked face and his large hands flapped at the ends of a pair of skinny arms. He spent his days swapping tales and jokes with anyone who had the time to waste with him.

. . . Aunt Raizel told me how she and Mama used to laugh at poor Leib Weisenberg. They called him a shlimazl, *Sam—a person who is always having a streak of bad luck. Leib himself acknowledged he was a* shlimazl. *He used to sing an old twelfth-century song, claiming it had been written just for him:*

> *If I sold shrouds, no one would die;*
> *If I sold lamps, then in the sky*
> *The sun, for spite,*
> *Would shine by night.*

He was wonderful at telling jokes, but at making a living, well, not so wonderful. But the whole town knew that ever since he was fourteen years old, he'd been infatuated with my mother. . . .

As Mindel crossed the square, Leib and Mottel Kutner watched her with interest. She returned their looks with cool dispassion. Mottel's expression suggested to her mind the face of someone enjoying a hanging. "Good afternoon, Mindele," he shouted at her with a leer. "Where are you off to in this downpour?"

He followed the question with a hooting laugh that told her he knew quite well where she was going. Leib Weisenberg, also watching with his doglike eyes, gave Mottel a poke. "Shut up," he growled. "Leave the girl alone."

Mindel pretended not to hear them. She knew Leib's eyes would follow her until she was out of sight, so she raised her chin to an angle that fully expressed her scorn and turned without a backward look into the street where the gate into the Tzaddik's court was located.

. . . The court ruled by Nathan Baer, the Tzaddik of Solitava, was not as grand as it had been three generations before when my great-great-great-grandfather, Rabbi Israel of Ruzhin, escaped from Russian persecution and established his Hasidic court on the Austrian side of the border. You—so American, Sam—won't easily understand about the shtetl *Jews and what the Tzaddikim were to us. In Europe we were—and are—a people unwanted by the governments of the countries where we lived, despised, ignored, or tormented. So we had our own government and our own laws, the rabbis becoming not only religious leaders but rulers over civil matters as well. Oh, in the large cities like Vienna and Berlin the more modern rabbis did less governing and left civil matters to the state authorities. But in Solitava, as in many small towns throughout Austria-Hungary, Poland, and Russia, the Tzaddikim—the "wonder rabbis"—ruled over all phases of Jewish life.*

Our ancestor, Rabbi Israel of Ruzhin, had been a very great Tzaddik. Religious leaders from all over had gathered in his court. But by the time the title had come down to his sons and then their sons, their reputations, as well as their wealth, had been dissipated. My great-uncle Nathan was still like a king to the Jews of Solitava, but his reputation was not as wide nor his scholarship as noteworthy as his ancestors' had been. Nevertheless, his word was law to my mother's family and to the Jews of the town. Absolute law. That's why what my mother had done was so shocking. . . .

Uncle Nathan's "court" was actually a compound of buildings occupying most of the land on the north side of the square. The synagogue was the largest of the buildings and directly accessible from the street, but the others—the Tzaddik's house, the study house, the summer house, the guest house, the barns, and the other outbuildings—were all situated within a wooden fence and accessible only through one wide, white-washed gate. Mindel had pushed open that gate every day of her life without a moment's trepidation, for her father, the Tzaddik's brother-in-law, was Uncle Nathan's right-hand man, his number one *gabbe*, and Mindel herself had been Uncle Nathan's particular pet. She had always received a warm welcome within this gate. But today she hesitated before pushing it open.

She took the path to her uncle's house. On the doorstep she wiped her shoes on the mat, took a deep breath and knocked. Instead of the servant, it was her Aunt Chana who admitted her. Aunt Chana gave no greeting but shook her head disapprovingly at the girl's wet hair. She put out her hand for Mindel's shawl.

"Where's Beine? Why are *you* answering the door, Aunt?" Mindel asked.

"Lower your voice. Do you want him to hear us?" Aunt Chana, tall and angular, was always nervous and habitually expected the worst. Uncle Nathan couldn't possibly have heard them from his study all the way down the hall. "He's in a terrible mood," Chana whispered. "What have you done?"

"Didn't he tell you?"

"No. He says it's only an example of 'female nonsense,' but I could tell that you've angered him greatly. He didn't even tell your father. He sent him to the study house so that he'd be out of the way when you went in."

Mindel's stomach lurched. Not even Papa would be present to help her. "Oh," she said.

"So?" Aunt Chana couldn't contain her curiosity. "Tell me already."

"I'd better not. It's late."

Aunt Chana threw her a narrow-eyed look. "All right, if you don't want to tell me, don't. So go ahead, go already. I'll take your shawl to the kitchen to dry. Shake off the wet from your hair, *meshuggeneh.* You look like a drowned cat." She shook her head once more, sighed, shrugged, and turned toward the kitchen. "You'd better watch your tongue, Miss High-and-Mighty, or this will be a *din Torah* you won't forget."

Mindel made a cursory attempt to brush the droplets from her forehead and turned to the long, dark hallway that led to Uncle Nathan's study-office, where much of the business of his calling was conducted. It was in that room at the end of the corridor that he wrote his commentaries on the holy books, held meetings, received visitors, and adjudicated disputes. It was the largest room in the house; the huge double-doors at the end of the hallway (made of heavy oak, ornately carved and gleaming with polish) seemed to announce the room's importance like the visual equivalent of a flourish of trumpets. Mindel could almost hear the sound as she lifted her hand to knock.

She had denied to herself any feelings of fear—she'd done what she'd done, and she was glad!—but she paused before knocking. Her heart had begun to pound uncomfortably, and she needed another moment to collect herself. She wondered how many people would be present in that room this afternoon to witness her disgrace. There was usually a crowd gathered in the study; besides Uncle Nathan enthroned on a high-backed chair, one could count on seeing Mindel's father, two assistants to her father, a scribe, Zaleh the Beadle, a few students, some complainants, some defendants, and any number of assorted visitors. Could she bear to face them all?

But she couldn't just stand there. Squaring her shoulders she knocked firmly. She would not cower or falter. What she'd done was right, and no one, not even the Tzaddik of Solitava, would make her feel ashamed.

The door was opened by Zaleh, who looked her over pityingly with his rheumy, old woman's eyes. But the pity was superficial; she could see beneath the surface the signs of eagerness—the eagerness of an old gossip to witness someone else's humiliation. She brushed by him disdainfully, crossed the threshold, and looked quickly around the room. To her surprise she saw that it was almost empty. The chairs, the sofas, the benches near the fire, they were all unoccupied. But sitting on his high-backed chair behind his long table was Uncle Nathan, watching her with eyes that seemed to burn.

Mindel stopped just inside the doorway, taking in every detail of the scene before her. She noted the fire crackling in the hearth and giving a warm glow to the whitewashed walls. She noted Zaleh scurrying to his place on a stool in the far corner. She noted how the room's two high windows (which faced the grounds at the back and through which, in better weather, one could see the orchard) framed the Tzaddik's table and how his chair was so perfectly centered behind it. Today there was not much light streaming in from the windows. The wizened, almost-budding trees of the orchard were barely visible through the rivulets of rain that trailed down the outer casements. It was too bad that the day was so dark—she'd have to strain to read her uncle's face.

She stepped farther into the room and peered at him. Her uncle, Nathan Baer, the Tzaddik of Solitava, was leaning forward, one hand on his cluttered table and the other stroking his curly, red-brown beard. His eyes glittered darkly. Mindel was convinced that people were fooled by those black eyes into believing that Uncle Nathan had enormous depth of soul. She herself was not so sure.

Before she was able to measure the degree of anger emanating from those eyes, her attention was distracted by a sudden awareness of another presence in the room. One of the easy chairs had been pushed from its place in the corner to the far end of the table. In it sat a heavily bearded man she'd never before laid eyes on. The stranger's hair was dark, but his beard was shot with gray. His eyebrows, also heavily gray, almost met at the bridge of his nose and made his expression seem gloweringly forbidding. But as she looked at him, he withdrew from his pocket a pair of rimless spectacles and put them on, and she thought she saw him give her the merest suggestion of a smile. It warmed her through.

Her uncle, however, was not smiling at all. He glared at her and cleared his throat threateningly. "So, Mindel, you are here."

"Yes, Uncle. You sent for me, no?" The moment the words left her lips she wished she could unsay them. They sounded insolent—as if she'd meant them as a reproach to his meaningless greeting. And Aunt Chana had warned her to watch her tongue.

But the Tzaddik pretended not to notice any insolence in her words. He had a larger offense on his mind. "Sit down," he said, waving his fingers toward the low bench near the fire. "Yes, there. Good. Now then, do you know who this is?"

The girl turned her gray eyes to the face of the stranger. "No, Uncle, but I can guess."

"Naturally you can guess. And you are right. This is the illustrious Rabbi Mayer Gentz from Ilinghovka, to whom, I understand, you had the temerity to write this letter." And he picked up from amid a chaos of books, papers, and scrolls that littered his table a folded sheet of paper. Holding it up with thumb and forefinger, as if the touch of the paper would contaminate him, he asked with judicial thoroughness, "Is this the document?"

"Yes, Uncle."

"And it was you, and only you, who wrote this . . . this abomination?"

"Yes."

The Tzaddik put the paper down in front of him and rummaged about for his spectacles. Zaleh the Beadle got up and began to help in the search by lifting and putting down books in a useless bustle of energy, but the Tzaddik waved him away.

"In your pocket, Uncle," Mindel suggested.

There they were. Without a word of thanks, he adjusted the wire earpieces with deliberation and picked up the paper again. Then, his mouth pursed and his nose wrinkled as if he held a piece of spoiled fish, he began to read. " 'Dear Rabbi Gentz, I suppose I ought to begin by thanking you for the honor you have done me by proposing to my father and uncle an alliance between your son and me. So I thank you.' " He looked up at her over the rimless glasses, his mouth twisted in a sarcastic grimace. "Very generous of you. I'm surprised you troubled yourself to thank him at all."

Mindel lifted her chin belligerently. "It *was* generous of me. I don't believe I have anything to thank him *for*."

"Mindele!" Zaleh cautioned in an alarmed whisper.

Her uncle, startled at her intractability, glared at her. He was seething. "It doesn't occur to you to be *flattered* that Mayer Gentz chose you, of all the girls he could have found, for his firstborn son?"

"Why flattered? He doesn't even know me."

The Tzaddik turned his eyes up to heaven, shaking his head in disgust. "The good Lord give me patience," he muttered. Then, looking back at her, he growled, "Not only should you have been grateful to my friend, the illustrious Rabbi of Ilinghovka, but you should have thanked the good Lord for His generosity in providing such a worthy, upright, learned young man for an arrogant, selfish, disobedient creature as yourself! But let us go on." He looked down at the paper to find his place. " 'So I thank you. But I think it best to inform you, before matters proceed further . . .' " Another glare told her what he thought of her temerity in taking it upon herself to so inform him. " '. . . before matters proceed further and get out of hand, that I do not intend to enter into wedlock at this time or in the foreseeable future.' "

Zaleh tsk-tsked his disapproval.

The Tzaddik frowned at the beadle, a distinct signal that the old man was to refrain from any comment, and turned his attention back to Mindel. "Since when is it a female's place to entertain intentions not to enter into wedlock?" he demanded.

The girl drew in her breath and leaned forward to speak, but the Tzaddik raised a restraining hand.

"No, no," he said, his voice dripping with scorn, "we must finish this . . . this literary exhibition before we discuss it further." He adjusted his glasses, found his place, and proceeded. " '. . . or in the foreseeable future. Thank you again for your flattering attention to my existence . . .' " Another withering glance here. " '. . . and please convey to your son my best wishes for his future happiness with another young woman. Very sincerely yours, Mindel Rossner.' Beautiful. A beautiful piece of writing from a young girl to a man of learning—and her elder and better!"

"I meant no disrespect," Mindel muttered sullenly, her gray eyes flashing rebelliously at him for a moment. "I was only trying to . . . to . . ."

He waited, but she only pressed her lips together. "Well?"

"Never mind," she murmured, her lashes lowered so that he couldn't read her expression.

"Go on! You have my permission to say what is in your mind," he said with impatient condescension. "You've always done so before."

"I've *never* done so before."

The Tzaddik felt his face redden in anger. Her words cut him. She was like some creature he'd never met before. He was infuriated that a respected colleague should hear her address him with such disrespect . . . should see him floundering in his handling of a mere girl. For years he'd personally overseen her tutelage and had felt a particular pride in her cleverness and aptitude for scholarship. A man in his position had taken the time to interest himself in a mere female, and this was her gratitude! How was it possible that such a one should dare to flout the traditions of her people, the rules of behavior for girls, and even his own explicit orders—the orders of the Tzaddik? And now she was shaming him before an admired friend! "If you've never spoken your mind before," he said tightly, trying to decide how best to squelch her unforgivable pride, "then now is the time to do so."

She fixed her eyes on his face. "Do you really wish me to speak my mind?"

"I've already said so."

She hesitated. Then, lowering her eyes to her hands, she said quietly, "The reason I wrote the letter was to try . . . to try to take command of . . . of my life."

"Take command of your life?" He gaped at her. "What nonsense is this?"

Her head shot up again. "Isn't it my life we're speaking of? Why shouldn't I have some authority over the very small dominion that is my own future?"

"*Authority?*" Almost choking, the Tzaddik rose from his chair. "What kind of foolishness is this? Never have I heard a child of intellectual promise babble such meaningless nonsense! Authority! Your parents and your elders are your authority! Your Tzaddik is your authority! We know better than you how to plan your future!"

She met his furious gaze with courage. "You asked me to speak my mind. In my mind, these ideas are relics of . . . of, if you'll forgive me, the Dark Ages. Don't you see that we're living in changing times? I've read that in America the girls—"

"Don't tell me about America! What do you think is America—the new Eden? The Goldeneh Medina, eh? The lazy and the cowardly—they say goodbye and go to America! In America they trample on tradition . . . on everything sacred. And besides, this isn't America. This is Solitava. In Solitava the girls marry *whom* their elders choose, *when* their elders choose!"

Biting her lip, Mindel cast a quick glance at the stranger who'd been listening to the exchange without a flicker of emotion in his face. Then she lowered her eyelids. "I don't wish to get married," she insisted with quiet stubbornness.

"What have your wishes to do with anything? It is *our* wish that you marry! Have you forgotten your scripture? It is written, 'Therefore shall a man leave his father and his mother, and shall cleave unto his wife, and they shall be one flesh.' "

She shrugged. "Yes, for a *man* that is good advice."

The Tzaddik pressed the flat of his hands on the table and, leaning toward her threateningly, enunciated each word carefully in spite of the angry rigidity of his jaw. " 'Unto the *woman* He said . . . thy desire shall be to thy husband, and he shall rule over thee.' "

There was another brief flash of her rebellious eyes, and then she lowered her glance to her hands. "I do not desire to be ruled over," she said flatly.

"*Again* with your wishes and desires?" he roared. "Do you think of nothing else? Have you forgotten the three things that are sacred in our faith?"

"No, Uncle, I haven't forgotten. Study of the Holy Law, marriage, and good deeds." She'd recited the response in a quiet voice that was nevertheless tinged with contempt.

"Don't you *dare* take that tone with me! What have I here in front of me in place of my niece? Has a *dybbuk* possessed you? Some demon who has made you blaspheme against our sacred traditions of wedlock?"

"I do not blaspheme against wedlock just because I don't wish to enter into it, do I?"

"Yes, you do. Your manner blasphemes, your tone blasphemes, and *this* blasphemes!" He held up her letter again, waving it in the air.

"I only said that I didn't want to enter into wedlock now. Someday, I suppose, I—"

"*Be still!* Your tongue only drives you deeper into the mire of sin."

He sat down heavily and lowered his head onto his hand, which trembled with the emotion he was attempting to bring under control. That a mere girl could speak so vilely to him was bad enough, but that the girl was Mindel—Mindel, his gem, the girl whom he'd written to Mayer Gentz was a prize among females!—filled him with unspeakable shame. "I never knew I'd spent my efforts and affections on so willful and unregenerate a girl." Then, lifting his head, he looked at the letter still in his hand and crumpled it with angry deliberation.

Mindel watched him with a set face. She had, for once, spoken her true feelings. If she were sinful, then so be it. She was ready to face her punishment.

The Tzaddik rose majestically and walked to the hearth. He tossed the crumpled note into the fire with a dramatic finality. "I had intended, *meshuggeneh maidel*, to permit you to apologize to my friend, Rabbi Gentz, for that monstrous letter. I was misguided enough to hope that you could convince him that it was only girlish anxiety that caused you to write it. But obviously it is too late for apologies. My friend has seen you, as I have, for what you are. The issue is now closed. So go home."

"What?" Her eyes widened in astonishment. She'd imagined herself as Joan of Arc before the inquisitors, and *that* story had ended with Joan's being dragged to the stake and burned alive. Was this all that would happen to her? "G-go home?"

"Yes. The matter of your punishment I will discuss with your father as soon as possible. I needn't embarrass Rabbi Gentz further by making him witness to any more of this."

Zaleh, chewing his underlip and shaking his head like a reproachful brood hen, scurried to the door and held it open. Mindel rose from the low seat and shrugged. Let him devise whatever punishment he wished; she didn't care. She nodded to her uncle curtly and then did the same to Rabbi Gentz. Finally, with one last lightning-bolt look at her uncle, she turned and walked proudly from the room, Zaleh following her out.

The Tzaddik took due note of her additional insolence, fury rising in his throat again. But he restrained himself from shouting out her name and forced himself to sit down. For a while, an awkward silence prevailed while he got himself in hand. Then he turned to his visitor. "I'm sorry, my friend," he sighed in chagrin, "that I misled you about my niece's character. I knew that the girl was strong-willed, but I didn't dream she had such rebelliousness in her."

Rabbi Gentz threw his head back and laughed. "Yes, she's a fighter, isn't she?" he remarked cheerfully.

Nathan Baer's eyebrows rose. "It's good of you to take it so well," he said, studying his black-haired friend in surprise. "Another man would have felt strongly offended."

"Offended? Why?"

"To have been so insulted! The letter . . . her manner . . . everything. And worst of all, to have come all this way for nothing."

Rabbi Gentz grinned and got to his feet. "Believe me, Rabbi, I took no offense."

The Tzaddik nodded gratefully. "Call me Nathan, my friend. We're alone here, after all."

"Then, Nathan, let me assure you that I don't feel my time was wasted. I wanted to see the girl, to be certain she'd be the right one for my son. Well, I've seen. Will you object to taking on the task of getting her into line?"

The Tzaddik was now completely astonished. "Getting her into line? What are you *saying*?"

Rabbi Gentz's grin broadened as he walked to the door. "I'm saying that I'd like the wedding to be held right after Pesach. Is that all right with you?"

"A *wedding*? *Pesach*? You mean you *want* such a termagant for your remarkable son?"

"No question I want her." He turned from the door. "*Oy,* Nathan, Nathan," he chortled, rubbing his hands together gleefully, "what wonderful babies they will make!"

2

*So you see, Sam, whether my mother wanted it or no, there
was going to be a wedding. But through a quirk of history (for across the Russian border, life for Jews was not the same as in Austria-Hungary) the wedding had to be postponed. And during that postponement, Avrum Gentz, my
mother's intended, further complicated the course of our future lives by becoming a hero. . . .*

They all—the Gentz family, their relatives, and a few good friends
—had every intention of leaving for the wedding on the Sunday after
Passover. In fact, there was growing excitement in the Russian town of
Ilinghovka during the weeks before the appointed time arrived. A carriage had been hired to transport the family, and a wagon belonging to
Reb Eiger, the town's most successful businessman, had been borrowed
to carry the rest of the wedding guests from Ilinghovka across the border
to Solitava. As soon as the best clothing could be readied, as soon as the
gifts could be collected and crated (the family had already packed up an
oak rocking chair, a pair of silver candlesticks, a mirror whose silvering
was streaked and spotted but whose deficiencies were more than compen-
sated for by a marvelously rococo gilt frame, and an almost brand-new
set of the Gemara, bound in tooled leather), as soon as Mayer Gentz could
conclude his obligations to his congregation for the celebration of Passover, they would be ready to depart.

Though the Jews of Ilinghovka were all excited about the wedding
plans, not everyone felt joyful about them. A number of young girls, who
had nurtured in their bosoms dreams that the dark-eyed, broad-shoul-

dered, brilliant, and promising Avrum Gentz would look in their direction, were crushingly disappointed in the arrangements the Rabbi had made. Even more bitter than these girls was Avrum's mother, Hinde Sarah. "Give me one good reason," Hinde Sarah would harangue her husband daily, "why you had to choose a girl from another town—another *country*? And a shrew, yet, who had the gall to write and say she doesn't want my Avrum! What has she got that more than a dozen girls here haven't got, I ask you? A fine dowry, maybe? A tin box full of rubles? Or maybe she has the character of a saint, is that it? Gentle and good and hardworking? But she's not a bit like that, am I right? They say that not only is she a shrew but, in spite of having barely a kopek to bring to her husband, she keeps her nose in the air and spits on anyone who speaks to her!"

"Stop yammering, woman," her husband would respond in disgust. "She's a fine young woman, the niece of a Tzaddik, and so clever she reads like a scholar. The girl's a prize, I tell you. Stop repeating malicious gossip and wait until you see her for yourself."

"Some prize! What could be so wonderful about a scholar, even if her uncle is a Tzaddik? Why better than Freyda Eiger, for instance? Such a sweet, gentle, smiling girl I've never seen! And her father would even have given them that little house right next to his. It would hurt you to see your son with a house of his own? And right here in Ilinghovka, where I could have brought him sugar cookies every day and enjoyed my grandchildren, if God would be so good to us!"

"Hinde Sarah, *enough*! Freyda Eiger smiles all the time because she's never held a serious thought in her silly head. I don't wish to speak of this again. The match is arranged. There's nothing more to be said on the subject!" And he would take himself off to his study and shut the door on her.

Avrum Gentz, the groom-to-be, had misgivings of his own about the arranged match. Although his broad shoulders and the beginnings of a thick growth of black beard made him look older, he was only seventeen and not at all sure he was ready for so radical a change in his life. Besides, his father's timing couldn't have been worse, for it was only during the past winter that he'd discovered the unfathomable pleasures of sin. There was a magnificently *zaftig* Gentile peasant girl who lived not more than two miles down the road from town with whom he'd had a number of memorable experiences. For a young man whose entire life had been spent poring over heavy tomes written in ancient Hebrew, the hours he'd snatched to hide away with her in the loft of her father's barn had been both a release and a revelation.

Donya was two years older than he, good-natured, simple, and cheerfully sensual. She was engaged to be married to the son of a neighbor, but since her betrothed was serving in the army, she welcomed the attentions of the Jewish youth. He helped to ease her boredom, while at the same time, his need for secrecy perfectly suited hers. Each wanted nothing from the other but a few hours of stolen pleasure.

Avrum's discovery of the compliant peasant girl had occurred at a fortuitous moment for him—right after his father had informed him that he was *not* being sent to the *yeshiva* at Volozhin, the center of Talmudic studies where the best Jewish scholars in Russia were gathered. Avrum had been devastated. "Am I not good enough?" he'd asked, his voice trembling in chagrin.

"More than good enough," his father had assured him. "I should have told you long ago that the *yeshiva* is not my goal for you." And slowly, with many pauses during which he sighed with deep pain, he explained his feelings to his son. Ever since 1881, when the terrible *pogroms* against the Jews had broken out, Rabbi Gentz had been disillusioned with the quality of the *yeshiva* scholars. In the years directly preceding the horrible massacres, a great number of those scholars, who had been sent to the school at the expense of the entire Jewish community to study the Holy Law, had instead imported and studied secular literature and revolutionary political philosophy. Their bond to the Lord was forgotten, and they grew heady with modern ideas. They wanted to remake the world, to break down the barrier between Jew and Gentile and build a new society for workers of all faiths.

"What's wrong with that?" Avrum had asked. "I myself often feel—"

"They soon found out what was wrong!" his father had cut in angrily. "When the Jews were butchered in fifty towns in the region of Kiev fourteen years ago—and I don't have to tell you in how many places since!—did a single Russian 'liberal' lift a finger? Those so-called liberals were the *heroes* of the scholars in the *yeshiva*. Fine heroes! They had written all those revolutionary tomes, inflamed the Jewish youth with their supposed idealism, and then failed to write one word to stop the massacres! Not one of them raised a voice in the Jews' behalf. The *yeshiva buchers* learned a hard lesson. They found out that the Jews are alone in the world. No one will save us but ourselves!"

Avrum had heard much of this before, and it failed to console him. The massacres had occurred in distant towns and had little reality to a young man who'd never himself been a witness of the destruction. To him, the *pogroms* were associated with the wail in the old men's voices as they said the prayers for the dead, with the keening of the women when the news of a new massacre came to them. Old people tended to harp on the tragedies of the past. But he was young. He wanted to think of the future, of life, of adventure, of new challenges, new triumphs, and new surroundings. The *yeshiva* had seemed to him a door to a world of new possibilities.

He'd argued with his father for hours on the subject. "What has all that—the happenings of fourteen years ago—to do with the scholars there *now*?" he'd asked. "Surely after that experience, they've learned better than to follow the radical—"

But his father had silenced him. "Better for you to study on your own. To keep your mind on God's Law, and to push aside the distractions of daily life and the outside world—that is the task of the scholar. A true scholar needs no intermediaries between himself and the scriptures. At Volozhin you'd face distractions at every turn—dangerous distractions. No, you don't need the *yeshiva*. You'll do very well without it."

Avrum had fallen into despair. His studies, which earlier had given him feelings of real excitement—for every discovery, every new interpretation that burst on him, had seemed to bring him a step closer to a new life—now seemed to be a dead end. Where would his hours over his books lead but to more hours over the same books?

When the studies had become unbearable, he'd taken to stealing away from the study house and roaming the countryside. It was during these rambles that he'd encountered the voluptuous Donya. She'd followed him down a darkening road, laughing and taunting him about the clumsiness of his long gabardine coat. He'd finally lost his temper and seized her by the shoulders to give her a good shaking. But she'd only giggled, reached out with both her hands, and grasped him by his genitals. The thrilling shock of that touch almost made him jump out of his shoes. Within ten minutes he'd followed her to her father's barn.

He was aware that the girl was ignorant and coarse, but she charmed him nevertheless. It was delightfully relaxing to be with someone who was so outspoken, so direct in expressing her sexual desires, so untroubled by guilt, so completely uninterested in the problems of ethical standards, so unconcerned about religious retribution.

From her embraces he discovered the amazing satisfactions of sheer physicality, and in his all-consuming efforts to experience those satisfactions over and over again, he forgot his disappointment over not being able to go to Volozhin. After years of dedication to the Holy Law, life had suddenly offered him this new, engrossing, and forbidden wine, and, to his shame, he was enjoying it in frequent, dizzying gulps. In her arms he learned that his developing manhood had provided him with an unexpected asset, and he felt a new, heady self-confidence. His usual round-shouldered, studentlike slouch gave way to a stride that could have almost been called a swagger. Although mired in a deep and secret shame, he was at the same time very proud of himself.

Thus his father's announcement that he was to be married found Avrum quite unprepared and understandably reluctant to face the impending change. He didn't want to leave Ilinghovka now. He didn't want to change what had become a life of stimulating and sinful adventure. During one long and sleepless night, he marshaled in his mind all the arguments he could devise to persuade his father to cancel—or at least postpone—the forthcoming nuptials.

But by morning he changed his mind. He decided to say nothing, to voice no objection to his father's plans for him. He had three reasons for his decision. The first was guilt. He had the deepest affection for and feeling of loyalty to his father, and he knew that his behavior with a peasant girl would be abhorrent in his father's eyes. It was sometimes abhorrent in his own. Only when his lust built up to the bursting point did he lose his sense of shame. At those times, no amount of self-hate, no recollection of his father's wise, suffering eyes, no awareness of the restrictions in the holy writings, could deter him from making off down the road to Donya's arms. But marriage was a cure for such sinning, wasn't it? Once married, he told himself, a man didn't need to steal off to find sexual gratification in illicit ways.

The second reason for his silence was his revulsion toward his mother's alternative suggestion for his future. If his mother had her way, he would find himself with Freyda Eiger for a bride. Freyda Eiger was everything his mother said she was—and more. The more was a pair of overly ample hips. Above the waist, Freyda Eiger was a delight to look upon, but even in her early girlhood she'd been cursed with a backside much too wide for the rest of her. The lack of proportion made her waddle when she walked, and the boys had named her Duckie. Imitating the waddling gait of Duckie Eiger had been a favorite pastime during recess at *cheder;* it was an easy way to elicit howls of laughter from an audience of derisive boys. Despite the fact that her father was the most prosperous Jew in Ilinghovka and that he'd offered a house as part of a generous dowry, Avrum did not want Freyda Eiger for a wife. Even the added inducement of proximity to his mother and her sugar cookies did not tempt him.

But there was a third reason for his acquiescence to his father's plan—the letter that his father had shown him from the unknown girl in Solitava. What sort of girl was it who could pen such a letter? What sort of girl would reject marriage so summarily, especially a marriage to the son of a respected rabbi of excellent family who was an outstanding scholar in his own right and a young man of promise? It was unheard of. She was a challenge to his manhood. He was fascinated, intrigued, consumed with curiosity about her.

So, by his silence, he gave tacit agreement to his father's plans for him. But to say that he was eager for time to pass, for Passover to come and go, would not be true. His misgivings were many. Would he like living in another town, another country? Would he be content with a woman who might turn out to be a shrew? Was he ready for the responsibility of marriage and fatherhood? He didn't know any of the answers, but he kept his own counsel and waited.

So plans for the wedding proceeded apace, and Passover came. It was a holiday that was usually celebrated with great joy, but in Russia during the years since the massacres of 1881, the Jews watched its approach with ambivalent feelings. The holiday usually coincided with the Christian celebration of Easter, and it was at Easter time that many of the *pogroms* had broken out. Ilinghovka had never experienced an outbreak of violence, but the Russian Jews had learned from childhood to hope for the best while expecting the worst.

It was with alarm, therefore, if not with surprise, that the Ilinghovka Jews heard the first intimations of trouble brewing. There had been anti-Jewish talk in the tavern. A drunk had been shouting about ridding the world of Christ killers. During Easter week, this sort of thing was not unusual, but there were other ominous signs. A number of the Gentiles of the town had put icons in their windows or crosses on their doors. "It's only for the Easter celebration," some of the Jews explained to their nervous fellows. "It doesn't mean anything." But there seemed to be more crosses than on previous Easters, and it certainly *could* mean that the Gentiles in question were signaling any potential rioters that the houses with the crosses were exempt and should not be touched.

Passover ended on the Wednesday before Easter Sunday, and the Gentz family and their friends began to ready themselves for the trip to Solitava. But on Thursday, after evening prayers, Yossel, the itinerant tailor, gathered a few of the men around him in the vestibule of the synagogue and gave them a warning. Yossel did sewing at the homes of the peasants in the nearby rural districts. He spoke fluent Russian, had a stock of jokes to tell the women who hired him to make them holiday attire or to sew christening dresses for their babies, and kept a pocketful of hard candies to distribute to their children. The Russian peasants liked him. During his travels (for he only came home on Fridays in time to celebrate the Sabbath) they let him sleep on the shelves over their ovens or in their barns. They even confided to him their intimate family troubles. He was a good listener. "But they're up to something this year," he said to the crowd around him. "I've heard whisperings."

"Nonsense," Reb Eiger declared emphatically. "Every year at this time someone brings us such stories. Has it ever happened yet?"

"Because it never happened *yet* doesn't mean it won't happen *now*," Yossel the Tailor insisted.

The men argued the pros and cons of the likelihood of an attack. "Nothing out of the way has happened to set tempers flaring," Akiva the Water-carrier pointed out.

"So what?" countered Big Yankel the Carpenter. His business depended on the coffins he made for the dead of the district, Jew or Gentile, and his trade made him gloomy. "Did anything out of the way happen at Elisavetgrad? At Chernigov? At Nizhni Novgorod?"

"But we've all gotten along for *years* in this district," Reb Eiger argued. "Every Market Day they come and trade, they laugh, they drink with us . . ."

"Didn't they say the same in Kiev?"

The argument had no solution—they talked round and round until they realized they were at an impasse. So they took the problem to the Rabbi. He was found, as usual, in his study. He listened to their arguments for a while, his mouth growing tight. "Tell me, Yossel," he asked at last, "what *exactly* did you hear?"

There was nothing *specific* that Yossel could report. Just a feeling. He'd noticed a few sly glances; sometimes a group of peasant men would stop talking when he approached; they didn't meet his eye when he greeted them. Nothing specific. "But I know them, Rabbi. They're acting funny. Something's up, for sure."

Avrum, who'd been sitting with his father, watched the Rabbi's face, his own heart beginning to hammer. What would his father decide to do? He knew what *he* would do—he'd band the men together to *defend* themselves. He'd heard stories of Jewish men—young groups, mostly— who'd fought back at Berdichev and Odessa and other places. Here, too, at Ilinghovka, they could fight back. All they needed were some wooden planks, some iron kettles, anything—

"There is no real evidence of impending violence," Rabbi Gentz said after several minutes of consideration. "I think you're all worrying about nothing. Go home in peace. God will watch over us."

Avrum almost groaned aloud, but he couldn't argue with his father before his congregants. It was not until they were alone that he spoke his mind. "What's wrong with preparing ourselves just in case?" he argued hotly. "Is it better to stand like sheep and let them butcher us?"

Rabbi Gentz lowered his head, resting his forehead on a hand that suddenly seemed to the son to be frail and old. "In what way can we prepare ourselves? A handful against a mob. We aren't fighters." Rabbi Gentz's voice was dull, hoarse.

Avrum squinted at his father's face in the dim lamplight. "Then you *do* think Yossel is right? My *God,* Papa, why did you tell them not to worry?"

"What good would it do to alarm them? Let's hope for the best. If the worst comes, we'll put our faith in God to protect us." He lowered his eyes, unable to face the burning accusation in Avrum's. "God is all the defense we have."

Avrum ached to retort, but he held his tongue. His father had always seemed to him a man of infinite wisdom. He was accustomed to thinking of his father as a man of decision, not someone who spoke foolish platitudes.

His father sighed deeply and looked up at his son. "I'll have to write to the Tzaddik in Solitava that the wedding must be put off. We can't leave on Sunday while the atmosphere is so unsettled. I hope you won't mind too much."

Avrum shrugged. "The wedding is not of concern to me, Papa. Not now, with the threat of a massacre hanging over us."

The Rabbi got up, put an arm over his son's shoulder and tried to smile. "I've heard these alarums a dozen times, my son. But Ilinghovka has not yet suffered from a *pogrom.* Go to bed and don't worry. In Russia at this season, all Jews tremble at shadows."

The following day, word spread through the town that the Rabbi's party was not going to leave on Sunday for the wedding after all. If his words to the men in his study the night before had been at all comforting, the effect of this latest news nullified the benefits. People were more ill at ease than ever. Wherever they gathered, they argued in whispers. Was a *pogrom* coming or wasn't it?

The Sabbath came and went, leaving the question unresolved. The peace that the Sabbath was supposed to bring was not felt anywhere in

Ilinghovka. That night, Avrum stole out of the window of his tiny bedroom and ran down the road to Donya. If anything was brewing, the peasant girl would surely tell him. But she'd heard nothing. She'd worked in the fields all week and had spoken to no one but her family. But she promised to learn what she could and to send him word.

Later, in his bed, Avrum tossed and turned for half the night. Shortly after he'd fallen into a stuporous sleep, just before dawn, he was awakened by a scratching at his window. Dazed, his mind thick and lingering vaguely in some distant place where a now-forgotten dream had taken him, he blinked at the face of a little boy peering at him through the lowest pane. He shook himself awake and, with a start of alarm, recognized the child. He'd noticed the boy from time to time when he'd looked down from the hayloft of Donya's father's barn. With the breath frozen in his chest, he got out of bed and opened the window. "Who are you?" he whispered. "What do you want?"

The boy's eyes, just above the level of the sill, peered past Avrum into the room. "Why do you whisper? There's no one else in there with you, is there?"

"People are sleeping nearby. What do you want?"

"Are you Avrum Gentz?" The boy's whisper was exaggerated and mocking, and his eyes gleamed conspiratorially.

"Yes. So?"

"I'm Grisha. Donya's brother."

"Oh."

The boy could not have been more than eight or nine, but he grinned up at Avrum with a knowing leer. "I seen you going into the barn with her."

Avrum reached out of the window. With one hand grasping the neckband of the boy's peasant shirt and the other clutching him under the arm, he lifted him up so that their faces were level. "You've never seen me before in your life," he said with quiet menace.

The boy was not a bit intimidated. "I seen you, all right. If my papa ever finds out, he'll take his ax to you."

"You'd like that, I suppose, you little cockroach!" With a look of scorn he let the child fall with a thud.

The boy toppled over on his backside and, without a moment's pause, turned a somersault and leaped to his feet, grinning up at Avrum with perfect friendliness. "Wouldn't matter to me one way or the other," he said frankly. "Don't you want to know why I come? Donya sent me."

"So?" With a start, Avrum remembered that Donya had promised to send him news. But to the child he pretended complete unconcern.

"She said I was to tell you four words." He paused, studying Avrum with shrewd blue eyes.

"Well, then, *tell* them to me!"

"She said you would give me a kopek."

"All right, I will. Tell me first."

"Show me the kopek first."

Avrum reached out to grab the little rogue again, but this time Grisha hopped backward out of reach. Avrum, muttering angrily to himself, turned away from the window to hunt impatiently through the pockets of his gabardine for a coin. "Here. I'll give you *two* of these when you've told me the words and given me your promise to keep your mouth shut about ever having seen me."

"All right. The words are 'church,' 'yes,' 'today' . . .'"

"That's only three. What's the fourth?"

The boy blinked, his grin fading. "Oh, shit, I can't remember."

Avrum would have liked to wring his neck. "*Think,* you idiot! 'Church,' 'yes,' 'today' . . . what else?"

The boy looked sincerely troubled. He put a hand to his brow and screwed up his face in deep concentration. " 'Church,' 'yes,' 'today' . . . those were the most important. The other was just an . . . an in-between word."

"An in-between word? I don't understand. Did she give you the words in that order?"

"She said the order didn't matter. She said you'd figure out the order."

Avrum gave his head a shake. He'd been too groggy with sleep and too annoyed by Grisha's manner to think. But the message Donya had sent was quite clear as soon as he stopped himself from being distracted by other things. "Yes" meant that a *pogrom* was indeed being planned. Good God! *Today!* He stared at the boy, his face whitening. "Was the fourth word 'after'?"

Grisha's face cleared. "Yeah, that was it! 'After.' Can I have my two kopeks now?"

Avrum tossed the coins out the window, his mind too preoccupied to pay attention to the grace of the boy's leap to catch them and the speed with which he scampered off and disappeared into the morning mist. Avrum's mind was spinning. The *pogrom* was *on—after church today*! In only a few hours, disaster would strike, and they'd made no preparations to stave it off. Quickly, his hands shaking, he tore off his nightshirt and dressed himself.

He ran out of the room with the intention of waking his father, but he saw a light under the study door. His father was awake already! Avrum burst in without knocking. "Papa, there *is* a *pogrom* com—"

Two visitors were standing beside the study table—Big Yankel the Carpenter, looking white-faced and disheveled, and his son, Zev Moishe, a lanky youth just Avrum's age with whom Avrum had been friends for a lifetime. "See? Even Avrum knows!" Big Yankel declared.

"How did *you*—?" Avrum asked the carpenter.

"I was just about to ask you the same question," his father put in. "You've been in bed, haven't you? Did you have a vision in a dream?"

"No, Papa. A . . . little boy brought me a message from . . . from a friend of mine."

The Rabbi's brows knit in suspicion. "What friend?"

Avrum felt his neck grow red. He wasn't accustomed to lying. "A . . . a peasant fellow . . . that I met on my . . . my walks."

He could see, from a certain pain that flared up in his father's eyes, that the man knew he was lying. But Big Yankel was speaking again, and Rabbi Gentz forced himself to turn from his son and concentrate on the more pressing problem looming up before him.

Big Yankel was retelling his tale for Avrum's benefit. "As I told the Rabbi, I had to deliver a coffin out toward Drubno, and on my way back I came upon Stephanov's wife driving her wagon toward the church. Well, I know that Stephanov has a nice little buckboard he uses for church, so I asked her where was Stephanov and why wasn't she driving the buckboard? So she says—and I give you her very words, for they're burned in my brain, believe me!—'I have nothing against you Jews,' she says, 'but if there's going to be looting, I may as well have my share, so I drove the wagon to take the stuff home in.' "

" 'Looting'? She actually said the word *'looting'*?" the Rabbi asked, his voice hollow.

"Her very word. 'Looting.' "

"And you, Avrum?" His father, pale and tight-lipped, turned to him again. "What did your *friend* tell you?"

"That something is afoot for today, after church."

Rabbi Gentz sank down on his chair and shut his eyes in pain. "May the Lord have mercy on us! Our Armageddon is at hand."

There was a horrified silence. For Avrum, all the stories he'd heard from survivors, all the rumors, the tearful reminiscences that he'd associated in his mind with the old, the maimed, and the pathetic—the slaughtered babies they'd told about . . . the women raped . . . the men whose heads they'd seen split open . . . the windows bashed in . . . the wreckage and destruction that had been described in repeated and hideous detail—now came flooding into his mind with a sinister reality. "Papa! You aren't going to sit there and do nothing!" he cried hoarsely. "We can't bow our heads and pray to God while they slaughter us!"

"What else can we do?" He looked up at his son with an expression of utter helplessness. "We'll lock our doors and pray for the best."

Pray! Avrum felt sickened. The look on his father's face pierced him to the bone. Last time he'd given his father the benefit of the doubt, but this time he saw his father as inadequate to the demands of a situation that needed leadership. Prayer would have been the answer of any old, feeble Jew. Surely they could find a better answer than that!

"We could send a committee," Big Yankel suggested. "Reb Eiger, and Yossel and a few others, like me, who deal with them." He looked at his son for support, but Zev Moishe lowered his eyes. "Maybe they'd listen," the huge man urged without conviction.

Avrum saw Zev Moishe wince. His friend felt just as he did—the same angry impotence. The two young men exchanged glances of complete understanding. In the eyes of both was the unquenchable urge to fight back. The Rabbi raised his eyes and looked from one to the other. "No," he said, reading their thoughts. "Violence is not the Jewish way."

Old men's words, Avrum thought. May the Lord take me before I become old and fearful in my thoughts.

His glance again met Zev Moishe's, and again he read the same accord. Zev Moishe had always been a courageous fellow. Avrum remembered that when they were boys they used to play in Big Yankel's carpentry shop. Zev Moishe would lie down in the newly made coffins as if they were nothing more fearful than benches in the schoolroom. He would laugh gleefully from within the box while the other boys cowered in superstitious fear. But Zev Moishe knew that a coffin was not forbidding. It was only a box his father had fashioned out of wood and nails.

Suddenly Avrum gasped. His untimely and irrelevant thoughts about Zev Moishe's boyhood games had led to an inspired idea! "Wait a minute!" he cried, eagerly leaning across the table to his father. "I think there's something . . ." And he began to talk.

Less than two hours later, some thirty-odd men and women were grouped in front of the synagogue, rehearsed and ready. The rest of the Jews of Ilinghovka were barricaded behind their doors, waiting in terrified suspense. They could already hear, down the road at the outskirts of the town, the shouting and raucous laughter of an unruly mob. Nervously, Avrum and the other three men chosen to carry the coffin in which Zev Moishe had hidden himself lifted it to their shoulders. The Rabbi signaled the rest to fall in behind.

They formed a typical funeral procession, with the Rabbi following the coffin, the men grouped behind him, and the women bringing up the rear. As they began their slow parade toward the cemetery, the women began their ritual wailing. Rabbi Gentz, keeping his pace measured and slow, followed the coffin toward the peasant mob. Although this was not in the direction of the Jewish cemetery, the route could easily be explained to a challenger; it was not unusual for funeral processions to circle the town. They could only hope that the peasants would not find the circuitous route to be grounds for suspicion.

Soon the Jews, making sounds of mourning but looking ahead from beneath lowered eyes, could see what they were up against. They couldn't estimate the exact number, but there seemed to be at least two hundred people—men, women, and children—massed in the road ahead. It was a chilling sight. Most of the rioters had come on foot, and it seemed that almost every man among them carried a shovel or pickax. Several wagons were trundling along right in the midst of the crowd, one of them loaded with men carrying rough-hewn clubs. They came on with a deafening noise, at first sounding like a strange sort of thunderous rumble, but soon sounds could be differentiated—there was hooting and singing, many were shouting obscenities against the "kikes" and several were roaring slogans about Russia for the Russians.

Avrum, at the head of the procession (bearing the right-front corner of the coffin on his shoulder with Akiva the Water-carrier beside him on the left), was stunned by the size of the mob. But if he'd felt a twinge of misgiving at the sight of them, the sounds of their curses and their Russia-for-the-Russians slogans ended it. The bitterness of the Jew forever alienated from the land in which he lived welled up in his throat, tightened his jaw, and made him wild for a chance to bash in a few heads himself. But he had to behave according to plan, so he kept his eyes lowered and his feet inching forward.

Already some of the rioters had broken into two houses situated just at the end of the town's principal street. An elderly Jewish woman was screaming in the front yard of one of them as the glass from her front window came flying out, followed by a wooden chair. The crowd howled and cheered. At the back of the second house, Hershel Wolf, his wife, and their three children huddled in terror.

A table followed the chair through the broken window, but the cheer that followed its crash to the yard was not as loud, for the rioters at the head of the mob had taken note of the approaching procession. "Someone *died,*" a Russian child exclaimed, pointing.

"Good! One kike less in the world," a rough voice responded.

A shout of laughter and cheers greeted this sally, and the mob surged forward. The funeral procession continued to move inexorably toward them, loud sounds of woe rising from the Jewish mourners. In another moment the procession confronted the rabble thronging the street and could progress no further.

Avrum and Akiva maneuvered the coffin so that they stood directly before two of the largest men at the front of the mob. There they paused, waiting for a passageway. This was the crucial moment for the success of their scheme. If the Russians showed no respect for a funeral and trampled their way through the procession, all would be lost.

The Jewish men lined up behind the coffin began to chant in their deepest, most solemn tones the words of the prayer for the dead, and the women began to keen in earnest. The two burly peasants who faced the coffin, awed by the solemnity of funereal customs with which they were unfamiliar, fell back a step. This was enough of an excuse for their followers, cowed by a superstitious discomfort in the presence of death, to withdraw a few steps also. The Russian words "Let them through" were murmured through the mob. A passageway was cleared, and the coffin began its progress through the press, the Rabbi and the "mourners" following closely behind.

They had not gone more than ten steps into the crowd when the coffin lid fluttered. The "widow" screamed shrilly.

"What? What *is* it?" came voices from the crowd.

The "widow" pointed a trembling finger at the coffin. "A *spirit*! A spirit is trying to escape!" she shrilled.

At that moment a peasant threw open a window on the upper floor of the second house and thrust a thick featherbed on the sill. "Look what I found," he shouted, and with a knife slit a great gash into the covering, releasing a cloud of goosedown. Laughing, he looked down at the crowd below, expecting a cheer. Only then did he notice the black-garbed file of Jews among the throng below him. "Hey, what's going on down there?" he asked, annoyed.

But everyone's eyes were riveted on the coffin resting on the shoulders of four tall men. The lid began to lift again. There was a gasp from the crowd, and the Jewish women shrieked piercingly. "A *dybbuk,* a *dybbuk*!" they screamed hysterically, lifting their arms over their heads as if to ward off something.

The spectators near the procession pushed back nervously, but to those in the back it seemed as if the Jewish women were trying to ward off the goosedown. "What's the matter with them?" they shouted in Russian. "Are they afraid of a few feathers?" And there was a loud, derisive jeer.

Avrum cursed under his breath. The damned feathers might cause the destruction of their plan. Feathers! What a ludicrous instrument to bring about their downfall. He tapped quietly at the bottom of the coffin. The lid lifted again, this time higher than before, and it dropped closed with a heavy thud. Cries of "Evil spirit! A *dybbuk*!" now came not only from the Jewish women but from the mourning men, who also began to hold up their arms as if to protect themselves from an attacking bat.

"It's an evil spirit looking for a new body!" someone shouted in Russian. In the confusion and alarm that spread among the rioters pressed close to the coffin, no one noticed that the shout came from Yossel the Tailor, standing with the mourners.

"An *evil spirit*?" The peasants near the coffin pushed away in alarm. This caused a crush among those crowding in behind, and they began to scream and squirm about for breathing room.

"He's swooping this way!" shrieked one of the Jewish women at the back of the procession, and all those near her, Jew and Gentile alike, ducked and shrieked as if the evil spirit would attack their heads.

Confusion and indecision made the mob forget the purpose for which they'd assembled. Avrum, watching the crowd for signs of panic, caught sight of Donya in the crowd. He gave her a meaningful glance, making a small movement suggesting the covering of the head. The girl nodded. She uttered a shrill, resounding scream, ducking and clutching at her kerchief as she did so. "The evil thing! I *felt* it!" she yelled. "Let me *out of here*!" The women near her, already on the verge of panic, began to shriek and duck.

"Now it's *here*!" shouted Avrum, and he snatched off his black hat and began to swing it in the air as if to swat away the invisible attacker. While he did so, he caught a glimpse of his father, gazing at him with a strangely arrested stare. Had he caught a glimpse of the look Avrum had exchanged with Donya? But there was no time to pursue the thought. The other three coffin-bearers began to shout, to swing their arms about in their attempts to shield their heads. The coffin swung crazily, tilted, and dropped to the ground.

The sound of the crash echoed above the shrieks and noise with the hideous crack of splintering wood, and, suddenly, those standing nearby could see the arm of the "corpse," enveloped in its white shroud, the hand tearing through and its skin looking bloodlessly greenish-white.

There was a great gasp. "The *hand*! The dead one's *hand*!"

A child began to blubber loudly, and another screamed in Russian, "Take me *away* from here! *Mama, Mama,* take me *away*!"

The pushing and shoving in the crowd now brought on screams of pain and fear. "Let me *out* of here!"

"Stop shoving!"

"I can't *breathe*!"

Confusion and panic had set in, with some people trying to push their way out while others pressed forward to get a better view of the corpse. The noise became deafening and heightened the hysteria. Those who were trapped in the thickest of the press began to shriek for their very lives.

The man in the window leaned far out over the split featherbed to see what was happening, forcing out of the opening another cloud of goosedown, which spurted high in the air. He saw women running down the road away from the town, waving their arms in the air, but whether to ward off the evil spirit or to protect themselves from flying feathers he couldn't tell. "Where are you running?" he shouted scornfully. "We've just *begun* to—"

But Hershel Wolf, who had stolen back into his house when he'd realized that the rioters' attention had been distracted, crept up behind him and, with one shove, pushed the vandal and the featherbed from the window.

The man landed in the yard with a terrible screech of pain, completely obscured in a cloud of feathers. He seemed to the onlookers to be a feathered apparition of terrifying aspect, adding further to their panic. They began to disperse in earnest, stumbling over each other in their desperate haste to get away.

The drivers of the wagons, attempting to turn the vehicles around amid the fleeing, shrieking throng, were shouting hysterical warnings to the panicky runners who blocked their way. The wagon loaded with peasants with clubs made a precipitous turn and toppled over. The riders, falling on top of one another, yelled and groaned, but as soon as they could regain their footing they scrambled away, leaving the wrecked wagon behind, its remaining wheel spinning aimlessly in the air.

The Jews in the funeral procession watched in silence as the rioters made off down the road. When the last feather had settled on the ground, only one peasant—a poor fellow whose leg had been crushed in the wagon incident—could still be seen hobbling off in the distance.

Big Yankel opened his mouth to cheer, but a sign from the Rabbi silenced him. "Hush, someone might be watching," he cautioned. He motioned the bearers to lift the coffin. Cracked though it was, they managed to keep it together and they carried it back to the synagogue, the procession following after. Its numbers swelled as the occupants of each house they passed came out to join the crowd. The women continued their pretended wailing, but underneath there was a good deal of giggling, and as soon as they entered the synagogue the laughter and cheering burst forth unrestrained.

The entire Jewish population turned out to celebrate. From nowhere, kegs of cider appeared, mounds of raisin pudding, bottles of *shnaps,* and trays of little rolled cakes. The laughter rang through the synagogue for hours; the backslapping and the self-congratulations were repeated as the story was told and retold until well into the night. The woman who had played the widow glowed with the praises heaped on her for her performance. Zev Moishe, only slightly bruised by the crash of the coffin (for he had prepared for it by carefully padding the inside of the box), was embraced and lauded for his daring. But it was Avrum who was the most honored, the most adored, and the most petted, for it was he who had conceived and executed the plan that had saved them all. He was their hero.

It wasn't until the festivities ended and he was on his way to bed that his father's voice cut through the glow of success that filled his being. "So, Avrum," he asked curtly, "so, Mr. Hero of the Hour, who was the girl?"

3

On the day that Avrum Gentz and his family were finally due to arrive in Solitava for the wedding, the whole village stirred, buzzing with excitement. Everyone had heard the tale of his heroic deed. Everyone wanted to get a glimpse of this well-favored, noble young man. Everyone except Mindel.

The more they told her how lucky she was to be betrothed to a young man of character, learning, and good family—and a hero in the bargain!—the more she closed her mind to him. *Can you understand, Sam, why my mother didn't care to marry a noble youth and bask in his reflected glory? She had dreams of glory for herself. She, too, was young, with her own dreams. Why couldn't she have the chance to achieve her own nobility? . . .*

Mindel's mouth would tighten at the mere mention of the name of her betrothed. She showed not the slightest interest in hearing about him, not the least desire to speak of him. She avoided all casual conversation, for she knew that sooner or later the subject of Avrum Gentz would be brought up. She didn't care to hear his name.

Her sister Raizel couldn't understand it. "Aren't you curious about what sort of man you're going to marry? Don't you care if he's handsome?"

They were on their knees, mopping the kitchen floor in preparation for the Sabbath meal at which the prospective bridegroom was to be a guest. "What difference does his appearance make?" Mindel flipped back the braid that had fallen over her shoulder with an arrogant toss of her head. But at the same moment she brushed the back of her hand across her forehead in a gesture that revealed the tension and inner despair she tried to keep hidden under the cover of her contempt.

"His looks would make a difference to me." Raizel, ceasing her labors, threw the washrag into the bucket and sat back on her heels, regarding her sister in wonder. "I don't think I could bear to share a bed with someone ugly—like Leib Weisenberg or that *behayma* peasant Josef who works in Uncle Nathan's orchard."

"You're the *behayma*. It's stupid to believe that sharing a bed with a man is made any easier if he's good-looking. I'm revolted by the entire prospect, no matter what the man's face is like."

"I'm not," Raizel grinned. "Itzik Kramer kissed me five times already, and I liked it quite a lot." Raizel, only fourteen, was high-spirited and lively, with a face too round and eyes too small to be called a beauty. But her cheerfulness was contagious; people liked to be with her. Good-natured and conventional, she didn't yearn for excitement or adventure. But she observed the dramatic vicissitudes of her sister's life with a kind of vicarious involvement, as if through her sister she would at least *taste* the flavor of romance.

Mindel swished her rag in the bucket, wrung it out with her hands, and slapped it on the floor in disgust. "You're a fool!" On hands and knees she scrubbed away at the floor angrily. "With all that kissing, before you know it you'll get yourself a bad name—or Itzik Kramer for a husband."

"What's wrong with that? He's going to be a *shochet.*"

"Wonderful," the older girl said with bitter sarcasm. "What more can a girl ask from life?"

"What do you mean by that? A slaughterer has respect ... and a good living. If he's only lucky enough to be accepted as an apprentice, and if he stays interested in me, and if his family doesn't ask too large a dowry, we can be very happy one day."

"And if his grandmother had wheels, she'd be a wagon," Mindel mocked.

"Is that so? Well, listen, Lady Testy Tongue, just because Itzik isn't a hero like your Avrum Gentz—"

"Shut your mouth and push your rag! Talking isn't going to get the floor clean," Mindel ordered, and she wouldn't say another word.

Later, after the table had been set, the chicken left simmering on the stove, and their clothes changed to Sabbath best, their mother announced they would all three go to the synagogue for the evening service. "Everyone will be there to see the Gentzes arrive. Even the women."

"We never go for the evening service. I'm not going!" Mindel declared.

But her mother would not permit her to remain behind. "How can I greet his mother without you at my side? What excuse could I give? Have you no consideration for me at all? Have you no manners?" And she pushed the reluctant girl out the door.

Their arrival at the synagogue caused a stir among the women and girls who loitered about outside. While the men went in to take their places in the sanctuary, the women crowded about Mindel's mother eagerly. "So . . . tonight is the night, eh? The bridegroom comes to meet his bride!" cooed Esther Perl.

"Such a blessing, to have so honored a son-in-law." Bella Yusling, the most notorious gossip in the town, spoke in so exaggeratedly honeyed a voice that her envy was apparent.

"Will you make me known to him personally, Etel Fruma, dear?" the sycophantic Gussie Berg begged. "I want to shake his hand. I have a cousin in Ilinghovka, you know. The boy saved her life!"

"There's a dust cloud down the road," a child shouted. "Is it—?"

"No, it's nothing. But don't worry, they'll be here. A man doesn't want to be late for his first look at his intended, eh, Mindele?" said Bella Yusling with a leer.

The remarks were more than Mindel could bear. She pulled at her mother's arm to urge her inside. It would be worse than anything to be discovered, on the arrival of the Gentz family, standing by the roadside gaping with the rest of the gossips. Her mother, perhaps feeling some of the same discomfort, succumbed to the pressure of her grasp and let herself be drawn into the synagogue, her two daughters at her sides.

As soon as Mindel, Raizel, and their mother had passed out of hearing, the women's heads came together and the whispering commenced. Gussie Berg got the first word. "They say the Gentz boy is a brilliant scholar, besides being so brave and heroic."

"What a pity for him to be stuck with Her Haughtiness, Mindel Rossner," Bella Yusling muttered bitterly.

"If only my Sheine could have such a chance," sighed Esther Perl.

"Your Sheine is not the niece of the Tzaddik."

"Do you see them coming? Nothing seems to be moving on the road."

"Do you think the Gentzes changed their minds?"

Bella Yusling smiled with venomous glee at the prospect. "Maybe someone warned them that Mindel is a stuck-up bitch."

That was the last word, for the sounds from within indicated that it was time for gossip to end and prayer to begin.

There was still no sign of the party from Ilinghovka. The gossips had to take their places in the women's section of the synagogue without having had a glimpse of the celebrated Avrum Gentz. Mindel smiled to herself at their frustration. The women's section was separated from the rest of the sanctuary by a partition—a screen of thick, woven cloth that blocked their view of the activities in the sanctuary below. Now the *yentas* would have a good, long wait before they could gape at Avrum Gentz.

Usually, the screen that walled off the women's section was a source of irritation to Mindel. When she was quite a little girl, only nine or ten, she'd expressed to her father her intuitive feeling that the entire arrangement was an insult to females. That the women's area had to be cut off from the rest of the sanctuary by a screen had seemed to her to be an affront. Her father had patiently explained that, on the contrary, the fact of the screen was complimentary to females. It signified that the males needed the protection of the screen to keep from being distracted from their devotions by the sight of the female form. Even back then Mindel had not been placated. And in all the years since, she'd not been able to accept the tradition. It seemed to her that the dividing screen belittled a woman's prayers.

On this evening, however, she was glad for the screen. It served those harpies right to have their view blocked. Of course, if they were curious enough, they could always get up and peep through The Crack. The Crack was a two-inch-wide gap between the screen and the outer wall, and if a woman peered through it with her head at the proper angle, she could manage to see a good part of the area below. It was a very useful opening indeed, for although the women were usually content to sit and listen to the services and read their prayer books, they occasionally had good reason to want to view the proceedings below: the *bar mitzvah* of a son, or a husband's reading of a portion of the Torah, for instance. At such times, a woman could position herself behind The Crack, tilt her head a little to the right, and get a passable view of the goings-on. Mindel wondered how many of the women would have the effrontery to look out of The Crack this evening in order to sate their curiosity about Avrum Gentz.

She was soon to see. Just as the service was about to begin, the Gentzes arrived. The women knew by the sound of footsteps down below. There was no time for the men in the congregation to give verbal greetings, but there was an obvious, murmured undercurrent of excitement. The women could hear the shuffling of feet and the swoosh of cloth as the men turned on their benches to look at the newcomers.

As the service commenced below, the women turned as one to the doorway of the women's section, but the females of the Gentz party failed to appear. Hinde Sarah Gentz and the other women in her party, not expecting to see any women at evening services, had gone directly to the guest house in the Tzaddik's compound.

As soon as they understood that the Gentz females would not appear, a dozen women rose and rushed to The Crack. Bella was the first to reach it. "Ah, there they are, sitting down right in front. The one with the gray beard must be the father. Very dignified. A very dignified man."

She had to keep her voice to a whisper, so the word "dignified" was repeated as the news was passed from one woman to the next.

"Do you see the son?"

"I think so, but only the back."

"Is he tall?"

"What is he doing?"

"Is he sitting beside the father?"

"What color is his hair?"

Bella Yusling was enjoying her position of importance and kept them all dangling in suspense. "Wait till he turns his head, so I can get a good look. Dark hair I see. Good, manly shoulders . . ."

The word "manly" circulated through the crowd. One or two heads turned toward Mindel, the expressions leering. She could feel herself redden.

"Wait, wait! Yacob Nissen has tapped him on the shoulder! I think he's going to turn. . . . Yes, he's turning around—! Oh, *no*! He's turning the other way."

"Move away, Bella, and give someone else a chance."

"Yes, move away."

"Who gave you the lease on the space? Move aside."

"Give Mindel a chance to look." Esther Perl turned to Mindel and waved her arm. "Come here, girl," she said in a hissing whisper, "and take your first look at your intended." A ripple of giggles stirred the air.

Mindel, seething in embarrassment and irritation, jumped to her feet. It was infuriating to realize that her private life had become the subject of public entertainment. With a look of withering scorn directed at them all—at the women crowded around The Crack, at the more restrained ones who'd kept their seats, at her sister, her mother, all of them—she strode out the door without a word.

Her mother ran out after her, catching up with her a few yards down the road from the synagogue. "I'm sorry, Mindele. I didn't think those hens would try so hard to embarrass you. Come, we'll go home and get things ready for dinner." She put a comforting arm about her daughter's waist and peered into her face. "Are you all right?"

Mindel nodded. She had an urge to cry, "No, I'm *not* all right," and throw herself weeping into her mother's arms. Her mother had rarely revealed feelings of tenderness toward her recalcitrant daughter, and this unexpected gentleness softened Mindel's defenses. She would have liked to sit right down with her mother at the roadside, bury her head in the older woman's lap and pour out all her fears, her misgivings, her regrets about the course her life was about to take. But she said nothing. There would be no use in trying to explain—her mother could never understand. They were too different. They had different dreams. So she merely accepted the weight of her mother's arm about her waist with an obedient inclination of her head, and the two women walked silently down the road through the deepening dark.

Half an hour later, Raizel burst in the door. "I *saw* him! He's *beautiful!*"

"Who? The young Gentz?" asked their mother, coming into the front room from the kitchen, her face lighting eagerly.

Mindel, who'd been crossing from the kitchen to the dining room carrying the braided *challa* on a board, didn't even glance in her sister's direction. She continued on her way to the dining room and set the bread down.

"Did you hear me, Mindel?" Raizel persisted, following her sister to the door of the dining room. "He's tall and broad-shouldered, and his hair is as thick as yours, but curly, and—"

"Who cares?" Mindel brushed by her sister and returned to the kitchen. "Beautiful!" she snorted as she passed. "Who needs beautiful?"

But Raizel only grinned. Her sister had heard all that was necessary. And from the way Mindel had swung her hips as she walked away, Raizel knew her sister felt relieved. However much Mindel might deny it, she was certain to be, deep down, happy to learn that Avrum was good to look at. Raizel couldn't be wrong about that. It *had* to be better to go to bed with a handsome man than an ugly one.

Mindel, in the kitchen, heard the sound of male voices outside the door and felt sick. There they were, back from the synagogue. She felt trapped like an animal. She heard her father's laugh as the three men came in: her father, her older brother, and the guest. Her father's laugh sounded nervous and uncomfortable. Poor Papa. She'd put him through torture these past weeks. Ephraim Rossner was not like his brother-in-law, the Tzaddik. When Uncle Nathan made up his mind, no one could change it, but Papa was Ephraim the Irresolute. A vacillator. When Uncle Nathan had first decided that Mindel must marry Avrum Gentz, Ephraim had run back and forth between the Tzaddik's study and his house, trying first to convince his daughter that Nathan was right and then to convince the Tzaddik that his daughter might have a point—that maybe she *was* too young for marriage.

But in the end, the Tzaddik had prevailed. Sixteen was not too young; everybody knew that. And Avrum Gentz was the catch of all catches. Mindel was behaving like a stubborn lunatic, Nathan had insisted, and it was Ephraim's place to pull her into line. Thus the Tzaddik gave the order, and Ephraim had to trot home and work on his daughter. Poor Papa.

She could hear her mother's exchange of Sabbath greetings with the guest, her tone tinged with awe. Then Raizel giggled. Avrum must have paid the girl a compliment. Even Shmuel, her brother, the sophisticate who'd left home to open his own used-book shop in Czernowitz, was laughing at the Gentz boy's witticisms. Shmuel had come from Czernowitz for the wedding, and Mindel had hoped she could rally him to her side. But there he was, laughing and chatting with the young Gentz as if they were old friends. If Gentz had won him over, she was completely alone. Poor Mindel.

There was a call from the other room. "Mindel, come here at *once*!" The tremor in her father's voice told her everything the man was feeling. The tone had in it both a command and an entreaty: "Don't make a scene," it said. "Come and meet your groom-to-be like a nice, normal girl. Don't make trouble for me!"

Well, she would go. She would join the family at the table. She would even marry Gentz on Sunday—she had no other choice. But tonight she would neither look at nor speak to the man they were forcing her to wed. Let him know the extent of her unwillingness!

She stood framed in the kitchen doorway, her eyes lowered as the chatter in the front room died away. There was an awkward exchange of Sabbath greetings, and then her father said, too heartily, "Well, Avrum, there she is, the bride-to-be. What do you think of her, eh?"

She was not going to look at him, she was *not*. But eyes are not like hands. You can keep hands locked at your sides or clutched behind your back—they obey the orders of the mind. But it's difficult to make the eyes obey the brain's commands, and before she quite realized what she was doing, she found herself staring at him.

. . . She told me years later, Sam, that her first thought was that Raizel's word "beautiful" was not the right one. "Beautiful" is the symmetry in a marble bust of a young Greek god. Avrum was not like that. She saw at once that his lips were too thick and had a slight lopsided twist, giving him a look of suppressed mischief. And his chin was too square and too heavily emphasized by the short growth of black beard. But his eyes, a very light brown, were intently intelligent—she liked them at once. And his cheekbones were high in lean cheeks, his hair abundantly, luxuriously curly and gleaming black. And he was taller than she . . . taller even than the average shtetl *youth. I realize now that he wasn't tall by your American standards, but this was another time and another place.*

He had the stooped shoulders of scholars who spend too much time hunched over books—like you, Sam—but my mother said she didn't find the slouch unappealing. I think the slight stoop gave a welcome air of humility to a personality my mother might otherwise have found too arrogant.

Are you amazed that I can describe in such detail the appearance of a man I couldn't have seen, not having yet been born? It's because my mother told the tale so often that even now, after all that's happened, I can still see the young Avrum in my dreams. And I recognize him at once, just as if he were someone with whom I was intimately acquainted. . . .

"So, tell us already! What do you think?" Ephraim repeated when the silence had gone on too long, and the fixed stares of the betrothed couple were beginning to make everyone uncomfortable.

"Pretty, isn't she?" Shmuel chortled, amused by the appreciative gleam in Avrum's eyes. "I don't think you could look a year and find a bride who's prettier than that."

Avrum forced himself to look away from her. "Very pretty," he said, his lopsided, mischievous smile making a tentative appearance. "But don't you think she talks too much?"

Everyone but Mindel and Avrum burst into guffaws. Shmuel clapped the young fellow on the shoulder with enthusiasm. There was nothing he liked more than a good laugh. "Ha, ha! A regular chatterbox you're stuck with," he bellowed. "But why are we hanging about here looking at each other like pop-eyed fish in a bowl? There's a Shabbes dinner waiting to be eaten!" And he took Avrum's arm and propelled him toward the dining room.

Mindel watched as Avrum threw her one last glance before Shmuel took him from the room. His eyes seemed to be asking her something, but she turned coldly away.

Ephraim waited until Raizel and Etel Fruma had followed the others to the dining room. Then he seized Mindel by the shoulders. "Behave yourself, girl," he whispered nervously. "Don't make things hard for him. He's sitting down at a table full of strangers. Not a familiar face to smile at him. So be nice. *Talk* to him!"

Mindel didn't respond, but she accompanied her father into the dining room without balking. All during the soup course, Ephraim tried to draw her into the conversation, but she said not a word. Her mother, trying valiantly to bridge the silences, began to chatter compulsively, apologizing over and over for the blandness of the soup. Her husband and their guest repeatedly assured her that it was delicious, but the poor woman, unable to think of another subject, kept uttering apologies. "I was so rushed today, I probably cooked it too quick," she muttered.

"My mother," Shmuel said, grinning at Avrum, "may not be a thorough cook, but she's a thorough worrier."

Avrum laughed. "I think that most mothers work quickly and worry slowly."

"A nice way to put it," Shmuel approved. "You see, Papa, how a scholar knows how to turn a phrase?"

Ephraim smiled and began to relax. He reached for the wine bottle and refilled Avrum's glass. "Yes, a scholar," he said, beaming at the young man with pride. "In the Yomah it is written, 'To treat a scholar to wine is like offering a libation to God.' "

"You make too much of me, Reb Rossner," Avrum demurred. "It is written in the Yesod Mora that some scholars are like camels loaded with silk—the silk is of no use to the camel, and the camel is of no use to the silk."

"Aha!" Shmuel crowed. "He's modest, too!"

Ephraim questioned his son-in-law-to-be about his studies as the women cleared the soup bowls from the table and went to fetch the chicken and the various side dishes that would make the dinner special. "My soup maybe wasn't the best," Etel Fruma declared as they returned laden with platters, "but wait till you taste my *tsimmes*. If I say so who shouldn't, and may the Lord forgive me for the sin of self-praise, when you eat my *tsimmes* you'll taste something wonderful."

Her *tsimmes*—a side dish of cooked carrots sweetened with raisins and other dried fruits—drew an avalanche of praise from everyone but the stubbornly silent Mindel.

Ephraim was growing irritated with the implacable silence of his daughter. After the table had been cleared, he refilled the wineglasses and got to his feet. "To my prospective son-in-law," he said proudly, trying by his enthusiasm to make up for Mindel's lack of it. He lifted his glass high. "He's a young man of learning and wit whom I'm proud to welcome into this house and this family."

Shmuel cried, "Amen to that!" and Avrum bowed his head in acknowledgment of the toast. Then he rose and looked directly across the table at his bride-to-be.

"If I may be permitted to make a toast," he said with his easy confidence, "I would like to drink to my bride, a young woman of unusual loveliness and learning."

Her father snorted. The girl should have been given a box on the ears, not a complimentary toast. "Lovely, maybe," he muttered sourly, "but why do you say 'learning'? The girl hasn't said a word tonight. How can you, young Gentz from across the border, know anything about her learning?"

"Her reputation precedes her," Avrum answered promptly, his mischievous grin making another appearance. "Besides, I read a bit of her writing."

Since the tale of her arrogant letter to Rabbi Gentz had spread throughout the village, everyone at the table was aware of what piece of writing the young man spoke of. They burst into peals of laughter, Shmuel chortling the loudest as he pounded on the table in his glee.

Mindel lifted her eyes to Avrum's face—her first direct look at him since they had taken their places at the table—with an expression that combined a sense of betrayal with withering scorn. But Avrum merely smiled back at her while he drained his wineglass, his eyes seeming to say, "This is all nonsense. There are in this world only two creatures who count—you and I."

4

They were to be married on Sunday. In the meantime Avrum, his family, and the other visitors from Ilinghovka stayed at the compound as guests of the Tzaddik. There was a festive air about the town during the Sabbath. It was apparent that there was something special about these nuptials. A match arranged not by a matchmaker but by their Tzaddik and a rabbi from Russia had about it an air of being blessed. Almost everyone approved.

Avrum's mother was one who did not. Hinde Sarah Gentz said openly and freely to anyone who'd lend an ear that Mindel Rossner was too proud and cold to deserve for a husband a boy as handsome, brilliant, and brave as her son. "Oh, the girl's good-looking enough," she'd mutter, "but it's character that counts in the long run. And this stubborn, *farbis-seneh* female is not the equal of my son."

Bella Yusling lost no time in repeating to Etel Fruma what Hinde Sarah had said, and Mindel's mother, in her turn, let it be known to all and sundry that she was a direct descendent of the Baal Shem and that therefore it was her daughter who was doing the stooping in this match!

But for most of the inhabitants of Solitava, the wedding was a welcome event. It was an honor to the village to have the hero of the Ilinghovka *pogrom* marry one of their girls—the Tzaddik's niece, no less! —and take a place in their midst. Despite the scratchings and backbitings of the mothers of the betrothed couple, the wedding plans proceeded happily.

Ephraim had been expecting some sort of rebellious explosion from the bride-to-be, but he began to relax by the time the Sabbath ended and there had been no incident. The girl had evidently accepted the inevitable and had decided to submit to their wishes without making trouble. "I knew she would want him when she saw him," the Tzaddik chuckled to his brother-in-law on the night before the wedding. "All women are alike. They melt before a handsome face."

Ephraim shook his head dubiously. "I don't know, Nathan. I can't tell what the girl is thinking. I'll feel content only when the wedding is over."

On the wedding day, Mindel was escorted to the ritual bath and dressed in her wedding finery. She was quiet and complaisant. Even the nervous Ephraim admitted to the Tzaddik that he was beginning to be convinced the worst was over. "Maybe things will go well after all."

Within an hour of that remark, the rebellion came. It happened over the ritual of the haircutting. The haircutting ceremony was a *shtetl* tradition. Based on the reasoning that a wife must not be beautiful to the eyes of men other than her husband (and even to the *husband* her female allurements should not be so great that they distract him from his holy thoughts), the bride's hair was shorn off before the wedding ceremony. In Solitava the tradition was observed with a formal, solemn rite. The unmarried girls of the village came to the bride's room and, each with a candle held aloft, made a ring around the bride. While one was chosen to shear off the girl's hair, the others chanted ritual prayers and bade the bride say goodbye to her maidenhood. It was during this ceremony that Sheine Perl came running out of Mindel's room to tell Raizel to tell her mother to tell the *gabbe* to tell the Tzaddik that Mindel was refusing to let them cut her hair.

Rabbi Gentz, Ephraim Rossner, and Shmuel gathered in the Tzaddik's study for a hurried meeting. The Tzaddik sent Ephraim first, and then each of the others, to stand outside Mindel's door and reason with the girl. All to no avail. Mindel would not permit anyone near her with a scissors.

There is a saying among Jews that what three know is no secret. More than three had heard that Mindel was rebelling, and before very long, Avrum heard what was happening. Already dressed in his wedding clothes, he ran to the Tzaddik's house from the guest house and found the other men in the study, conferring helplessly.

"Why must she be forced to cut her hair at all?" Avrum asked them.

"Why?" Ephraim shouted, his nerves frayed beyond reason. "Why? Because it is *done*!"

"But where is it *written*?"

The two rabbis exchanged puzzled looks. The Tzaddik shrugged. "It is custom. From ancient times it's been done."

"No doubt we could find relevant sources if we searched a bit," Rabbi Gentz added.

"But in the Midrash it is told that the Lord, before presenting Eve to Adam, gave her pleasing, flowing tresses," the bridegroom argued.

Shmuel snorted. "Yes, and look what happened to her!"

Avrum would not be daunted. "And in the Talmud doesn't it say that in ancient times the brides appeared for their nuptials 'unbraided'? Doesn't that mean they had their hair?"

Rabbi Gentz frowned at his son. "I think the word is 'disheveled.' "

" 'Disheveled,' then. How can a girl have disheveled hair if it's cut off?"

The Tzaddik smiled at the youth in admiration. "What do you think, Mayer, of the validity of this interpretation?"

Rabbi Gentz was regarding his son with a speculative gleam. "I think we might accept 'unbraided' as a valid translation. The purpose was to keep the evil spirits from weaving 'binding spells' in the braid."

"Stupid superstitions," muttered Shmuel.

"Not at all," said his Uncle Nathan sternly.

"Nevertheless," Rabbi Gentz mused thoughtfully, "doesn't it give us a precedent to let the girl have her way in this?"

The Tzaddik, although eager to grasp at this sophistical reasoning as a way out of the predicament, was more conventional in his thinking than his colleague from across the border. He pursed his lips in hesitation. "It will be a source of gossip and dissension among the women as long as she walks among us with her own hair on her head."

"She will keep it covered with a kerchief after she's wed, just as the other women do, I promise you," Avrum said confidently.

"Only *you* will see it, eh, little brother?" Shmuel mocked, nudging Avrum in the ribs with his elbow. "When you're alone in the bedroom, right?"

Avrum colored but said nothing.

Ephraim sighed. His daughter Mindel had always been both his pride and his shame. He'd always made excuses for her excesses, so why should he stop now? "With a kerchief," he suggested diffidently, looking pleadingly at his brother-in-law, "she will look no different from the other women with their *shaytls.* "

The Tzaddik leaned back in his chair and shook his head. "She'll *always* look different, whether she wears a wig or her own hair," he said with a tinge of bitterness. "But very well, let her have her way in this. Maybe then she'll let herself be wed, and we can drop her and her rebellions into the lap of this silver-tongued young Solomon."

Shmuel laughed. "And may you have joy of her, poor fellow," he said, clapping Avrum on the back.

And so Mindel Rossner went to her wedding with her hair, if not disheveled, at least unbraided. It hung down over her shoulders like a shimmering mantle. The older women clucked in disapproval, the younger ones gaped in envy, but the men all enjoyed the unusual sight of such unfettered loveliness, and they danced all the merrier because of it.

5

My mother told me that she fell in love with him that night. She insisted that her collapse from independence to submission had nothing to do with his face, his mind, or his heroic reputation, but I suspect that all those attributes must have made him hard to resist. You, with your devotion to the theories of Dr. Freud, will probably say that, since love is often envy turned inside out, she reached out for the luster that emanated from him and, by loving him, made that luster her own. I don't know. Maybe so. . . .

Mindel did nothing else to interfere with the smooth functioning of the wedding rituals. She donned her white dress, sat obediently through the ceremony of the veiling, accepted the ring that Avrum placed on her finger under the *chuppa* without a grimace, and danced the handkerchief dance with appropriate grace. There was only one time she did anything inappropriate, and that was done so quietly that no one but Avrum took any notice of it. It happened after the feasting, when all the gifts were formally presented. It was a custom for the Rossner and the Baer brides to present their grooms with a gold watch. When the Tzaddik gave the nod, and Etel Fruma poked her in the back, Mindel rose, glided gracefully across the floor, and handed the watch to her husband, her cheeks coloring becomingly. Avrum accepted the gift with a warm smile. "Thank you with all my heart," he said with sincere gratitude. "I shall wear this all my life."

"Don't thank me," Mindel muttered under her breath, barely moving her lips. "They made me give it to you, as they made me do everything else today."

Avrum restrained his surprise, and the onlookers, impressed by the beauty and elegance of the newlyweds, were cheering too loudly to hear what was said. The spirit of the guests was high, and the celebration continued on its noisy, joyful way. If the bride appeared to some to be less than ecstatic, well, it only went to prove what they'd always known: Mindel Rossner, now Gentz, was a young woman of innate dignity. By the time the wedding was over, everyone agreed that it had been one of the happiest and most lavish ceremonies of recent memory.

The couple were to live in Mindel's father's house, in the room vacated by Shmuel. Avrum was not expected to take his wife to a home of their own or even to earn a living. He was a scholar, and a scholar had to spend his time in study. It was considered a high honor for the Rossner family to support him, with his wife and progeny, until such time as those studies led to enough remuneration for the couple to be independent. "If you must," says the Talmud, "sell everything and marry your daughter to a scholar."

Thus, when the festivities of the wedding had been concluded, Ephraim beamed with pride as the newly wedded pair were led to their room. The door closed on them, the other Gentzes piled into the carriage and the wagon and departed for Ilinghovka, and the local wedding guests went home to their respective beds. Even Shmuel declined to spend an extra night bunking on the shelf over the oven in the kitchen; he hitched a ride with the Gentzes, whose route would take him close enough to Czernowitz to permit him to arrive at his lodgings in time for a few hours' sleep before he had to open his bookshop the following morning.

The town grew silent. Within the room that used to be Shmuel's, Mindel sat stiffly on the edge of one of the beds looking around at what would be her home for the next few years. The room was not much changed from what it had been when Shmuel occupied it. Most of her brother's clothes and possessions had been removed, and a second bed installed, but for the rest it was very much the same. The worn, rickety table that had stood under the window for as long as she could remember would now be used for Avrum's studies, and the chest of drawers in the corner would now hold their clothes and the linens she'd received as wedding gifts (which were stacked with the other gifts in a pile near the door), but the room still felt more like her brother's than her own. She had to fight the urge to run out of there, to dash across the passageway to the front room where she used to sleep with Raizel, to jump into the bed that Raizel now had for herself and hide under the covers.

Avrum stood at the foot of the bed watching her. They had never before been alone together, nor had they exchanged a private word.

"Why don't you like me?" he asked, suddenly breaking the long silence. "Everyone else likes me."

"Who's everyone?" Mindel retorted coldly. "Your mother?"

He laughed. "She especially. But *your* mother likes me, too. And so does your father, your brother, your sister, your uncle, my father, my aunt Yussie, my aunt Faygel, my cousin—"

"Too bad you couldn't marry one of them."

He came and sat down beside her. "No, seriously. What's wrong with me?"

"Nothing. If you weren't my husband, I'd like you, too."

"Aha! Then we're back to that letter again. That was quite a piece of writing, that was. 'I do not intend to enter into wedlock at this time or in the foreseeable future.' Why did you say that?"

"Because I meant it. I don't want to be married."

"Why not?"

"I've spent all these years washing floors for my parents. Now they expect me to wash floors for my husband. Can't a girl wish for something else from life?"

He stared at her in considerable astonishment. "You think that married life is only washing floors?"

She shrugged. "More or less. Floors, shirts, pots. Then, for excitement, there's kneading dough. It's not a life to cheer about, is it?"

"No, I don't suppose it is," he said, remembering with sudden shame the number of times he and his friends had chanted, "Thank the Lord I wasn't born a girl." He took her chin in his hand and turned her face up. "When we have a house of our own, I'll get you a servant to do the washing."

"A servant?" For the first time, she gave him a smile. "Promises! I know you're the hero of Ilinghovka, but don't let pride carry you away. You're only a student, after all. How will a mere student have a house of his own . . . and a servant?"

"Give me time. First I'll be a *melamed* . . . then maybe a rabbi . . . then to a fine, rich congregation . . ."

"And if you fail?"

"Fail? The savior of Ilinghovka *fail*?"

"It's possible, even for the savior of Ilinghovka."

"I won't fail. But if I do, I promise to make no complaints if you leave the floors dirty. So there. Whatever happens, you will live like a queen. No floors to wash. Will that make you happy?"

"No."

He dropped his hand from her chin and looked at her in mock horror. "Ah, yes. They *said* you were a malcontent. But I wouldn't listen."

"You should have. I *am* a malcontent."

He leaned back against the bedpost and surveyed her brazenly from head to toe. "But such a beautiful one," he murmured, sighing. He reached out a hand and grasped a handful of her hair, letting the soft, gleaming strands sift through his fingers. "I saved your hair for you, you know."

"For me, or for you?" she retorted, pulling the tresses from his hand.

He grinned. "All right, for me. But doesn't it prove that I can do the impossible? What other bride do you know has come to her wedding night with her sinfully lovely hair intact?"

She looked at him scornfully. "So if you can do the impossible, do it for *me*. Make me free."

He reached for her hair again. Playing with it absently, he said with his lopsided smile, "There's the impossible, and then there's the impossible. Who is free? What do you want to be free to do?"

"I want to be free to see the world. To learn things. To have experiences like the people in the books I've read."

"We'll do it together. We'll travel some day. We'll see the world. And meanwhile, instead of washing the floor, you can study Talmud with me."

She blinked at him. "Would you really let me study with you?"

He took the handful of hair to his lips and kissed it. "Only if you'd bind up your hair and cover it with a kerchief. I couldn't concentrate on studies if you sat near me looking like this."

He was very close, and she could feel his breath on her ear. His words had revealed a sweetness and warmth that she'd never felt in those around her. She had an urge to let her head fall on his shoulder. But he moved his arm to her back, and his hand, too quickly, began to caress her side, and she stiffened. Snatching her hair away again, she jumped to her feet. "Liar!" she spat at him. "You'll say anything to . . . to . . ."

"To?"

"To coax me into bed with you!"

He looked up at her complacently. "Why should I coax. Don't you want to?"

"No, I *don't* want to. Why should I? I hardly know you."

"You're *afraid*!" he exclaimed, surprised. "That's the reason for all this talk, isn't it? I've heard that some girls are too shy to . . . but you seemed so sure of yourself—"

"Brilliant! So that's a sample of the brilliant analytical mind of

Avrum Gentz, prize know-it-all! He so ingeniously comes to the outstanding conclusion that some girls are shy. Brilliant!"

He seemed not even to notice her outburst. He grasped her hand and pulled her down beside him. "Don't be afraid of me, Mindel," he said softly. "Marriage can be a joy, I promise you. And its consummation . . . well, it's a blessing from God to rich and poor alike."

"Thank you, Rabbi," she said nastily. "Now, of course, I am completely reassured."

They sat for a moment in silence. "I'll never force you," he said gently, stroking the hand he still held.

"Won't you?"

"No. But lovemaking is a pleasure, you know. It's not like washing floors."

She threw him a quick, narrow-eyed look. "How do you know? From your books?"

"Never mind. I know."

"Well, I don't." She lowered her head. "I don't know *anything* about—"

"I'm aware of that. I didn't think I'd married a *corve*. But *you* married a *melamed*. I'll teach you. Of all your experiences, it will be the best."

She had to laugh at his remarkable self-confidence. "A *maven* I've married. An expert on everything!"

He grinned and pulled her into his arms. "On everything. If you don't believe me, ask my mother."

She let herself be kissed. It was a sensation not unpleasant, and she felt herself relax against him. "You said you wouldn't force me. . . ."

"Never," he murmured, kissing her eyes, her hair. "Even though I've been going mad for the past two days, waiting for this night. Burning for it, to tell the truth."

"Promise me," she whispered, feeling breathless and a little dizzy and not a little terrified, "that you're telling the truth. Promise me that you'll do it only when I say."

"I'll promise anything . . . everything . . . if only you'll say one word!"

"What word?"

" 'Now'! Oh, God, say 'now'!"

Amazingly, a giggle sounded in her throat. Her terror seemed to disappear in the swirl of other sensations bombarding her. Even when she fell back against the pillows, with Avrum lying across her, his lips against her ear, her throat, his hands caressing her breasts, her thighs, she was not aware of fear. She felt, instead, a wave of heat, and the strangest sensation that combined an urgent tension with a melting lassitude. She barely noticed that her own hands were clutching at his back as if to press him closer to her. Suddenly, her back arched up in an acrobatic reach of her body to his. She heard herself cry out his name in pleased surprise. *"Now!"* she breathed.

6

Some people who knew my mother in those days later denied that there had been any change in her during the two years of her marriage to Avrum Gentz. She had been proud and aloof before and would be worse afterward, so it's only to be expected, I suppose, that they would forget the two years in which she had her luxuriant bloom. Most of the change was internal, anyway. A tendency to laugh easily, a shine of the eyes, a turn of the corners of the mouth to indicate an inner, secret glow. You told me once, Sam, that love is like an instant psychic adjustment—a medicine to heal the infirmities of the soul, you said. Well, my mother was in love, and her angers and resentments melted away. She was, Aunt Raizel said, like a creature reborn. . . .

Raizel often heard them laughing behind the closed door of their room. They delighted in each other—in the curves of the other's body, the quirks of the other's mind. When they sat down with the family at the table, even though they were at opposite sides, their eyes sent secret little messages, excluding the rest of the family altogether. Avrum watched Mindel when she got up to go to the kitchen, and she always felt his eyes on her.

Life was unhurried, unpressured, almost sybaritic. When he came from the study house to read at home, Avrum often drifted from the table to the bed. Daily he told himself that he should spend more time at the study house where Mindel wouldn't be able to distract him, but daily she reminded him of his promise to let her study with him, and with good intentions they would sit down together at the books. But daily the study session gave way to the love session.

There was also another distraction that kept Avrum from his studies. On a visit to Shmuel's bookstore in Czernowitz, he discovered a German translation of a book by an American, James Fenimore Cooper. *The Deerslayer* so fascinated him that he began to read everything about America that he could find. Every time he discovered something new about the brawling country across the sea, he read it aloud to Mindel. The pair began to fashion dreams of going to America. They didn't know when or how, but someday, somehow, he promised her, he would find a way. It was their secret goal, and as their pile of books about America grew (crowding the little niche behind Avrum's worktable), so did their determination.

When Rabbi Gentz paid a visit after several months, expecting to be able to celebrate a *siyum*—the completion of the scholarly assignment Avrum had set for himself before his marriage—he found that Avrum's progress had not been nearly as great as he'd expected. Avrum's work was nowhere near completion. "Too much marriage?" the father queried, half teasing and half scolding. "They say where there is too much, something is missing."

Avrum grinned. "In my marriage, nothing is missing."

Rabbi Gentz was too pleased to see his son happy to voice further misgivings. "See, didn't I tell you it would be so?" he bragged, clapping his son on the back. "Better than having a peasant girl in a hayloft, isn't it?"

Avrum winced. "Don't, Papa." How could his father ask such a question, even as a joke? With Donya he had sinned. With Mindel he was obeying Holy Law. His life with Mindel was too blessed to permit it to be the subject of such jokes.

As if heaven were seconding the notion that the marriage was blessed, Mindel, in little more than a year, gave birth to a boy. The infant Dovid was perfect. He had huge, light, dark-lashed eyes like his father's, a shapely mouth like his mother's, and a gurgling, happy disposition all his own. Even Avrum's mother had to admit that her daughter-in-law had done this one thing well. The baby was a universal favorite.

But of all the child's admirers, none was more taken with him than Mindel herself. Her labor to deliver him had been more painful than she'd anticipated; she'd lain on her bed, the midwife and her mother in attendance, and had screamed in agony for seven hours. It had been a nightmare. She'd felt like an animal—degraded, debased. But when they'd placed the child in her arms, she'd forgotten the pain. It had all been worth it. The tiny fingers had curled round her thumb, the little mouth had suckled at her breasts, and she'd felt a surge of love so powerful she thought she'd burst with it. Because her heart had been so filled with Avrum, she hadn't believed that there would be any room in it for a child—especially not for a baby, who would tie her down even more to the mundane household chores that she'd never learned to enjoy. But little Dov showed her how a woman's capacity for love could expand.

. . . They say she was obnoxious in her pride. No baby was so beautiful or gifted, no couple in the world so blessed. "If pride were an art," Aunt Raizel told me, "your mother would have been a prodigy." Why then didn't someone warn her that pride in prosperity is misery in adversity? . . .

Mindel's pride in her baby caused endless tongue clacking among the women. "Something terrible will come of it," Bella Yusling predicted. It was not wise to praise a newborn baby, for in the first days of life an infant was at its most vulnerable to the evil eye. Didn't Mindel know that?

Mindel alone among the women had no belief in the evil eye. She lay on her bed for the week after the birth of her son, surrounded, as was customary, by a constant court of female visitors, and smiled down at the child adoringly. "Isn't he magnificent?" she murmured.

There was an immediate reaction among the guests. They averted their eyes, spat three times, and muttered, "No evil eye! No evil eye!"

Mindel only laughed.

On the eighth day after his birth, little Dov had to be circumcised. An elaborate *bris* was held, with the paternal grandparents traveling all the way from Ilinghovka for the ceremony, accompanied by an entourage as large as that for the wedding. Hinde Sarah Gentz took her first look at her first grandchild and beamed with delight. "Such a *shayneh*," she murmured. "May the Lord keep away the evil eye, but he is the image of his father!"

The other women spat three times and muttered, "No evil eye!" But they felt in their hearts that their incantations would not suffice. Even the grandmother showed too much pride.

Rabbi Gentz was revolted by the superstitious women and walked out of the room. The members of his congregation were pious but not riddled with antiquated fears of *dybbuks* and devils. He wondered how his Avrum could bear to be surrounded by such nonsense.

On the day of the *bris,* the Tzaddik left the compound with his entire retinue following behind and paid a visit to the Rossner house to celebrate the occasion. With much ceremony he was ushered into the bedroom, where he examined the infant with a warm smile. But while Rabbi

Gentz watched in horrified fascination, the Tzaddik, too, like the superstitious women of his village, turned and spat three times to ward off evil.

Rabbi Gentz observed these chantings and spittings with growing distaste. He belonged to that group of philosophers who leaned toward a more rationalistic view of the world. He had little admiration for the superstitious practices of Hasidic Jews. He was not comfortable with mysticism, with belief in demons, or with the idea that the Tzaddikim were "wonder rabbis." Since his last visit, he'd felt a growing concern that the atmosphere in Solitava, under the leadership of Nathan Baer, was more mystical than intellectual. It was not an atmosphere he liked.

When he'd first met the Tzaddik of Solitava, he'd had the impression that Nathan Baer was a man of character and intellect. That was why he'd urged a union between his son and the Tzaddik's niece. Avrum had a tendency to be too progressive, too intrigued by secular matters, too attracted to things of the world. He'd hoped that, away from the seminary at Volozhin and immersed in the Hasidic world of Solitava, the boy would stick to his Judaic scholarship and would not be faced with the temptations of modernism. But each time Rabbi Gentz had visited Solitava in the months since Avrum's marriage, he'd found Nathan Baer and his flock to be less and less admirable. Had he made a mistake in his earlier judgment?

When the Tzaddik and his followers had left the room to take refreshment in the dining room and perform their joyous dances in the street to express their delight, Rabbi Gentz remained with the women in the bedroom. Spitting, chanting, dancing, he thought . . . what place did such behavior have in the world of the twentieth century? He stood at the window, brooding. He hadn't wished his son to assimilate into the secular world, but he hadn't wanted him dragged back into medievalism either.

After a while he turned from the window, hoping that the sight of the new baby would lift his spirits. He leaned over the cradle and smiled down. This simple act produced a new flurry of spittings and a new chorus of "No evil eye."

He looked around at them and frowned. "Never mind the evil eye," he growled. "Just keep the child away from drafts. Cold air will bring more harm than all the evil spirits you can conjure."

This made the women all the more certain that the evil eye would have a disastrous effect on the inhabitants of this house.

Rabbi Gentz returned to Ilinghovka from the *bris* with a troubled mind. His son's studies were not progressing, the boy's responsibilities were growing, and he was surrounded by people who failed to provide adequate challenges to his intellect. He had not meant for his son to study among backward, superstitious mystics. "I wish we could arrange to have Avrum return with his family to us," he confided to his wife.

Hinde Sarah snorted. "Impossible. I would be overjoyed to have Avrum and the baby under my roof, God knows, but to have that Mindel in my kitchen would be the end of me."

Rabbi Gentz didn't worry about his wife's comments. The scratching and squabbles of women in the kitchen were not subjects worthy of his attention. If he could have found a way to move Avrum and his family to Ilinghovka, the affairs in the kitchen could go hang. But there was no way. The present arrangement had been agreed to in the marriage contract, and unless the Rossner family requested such a change—because of financial need or other upheaval in the family situation—it would be an offense to suggest it.

So the Ilinghovka Rabbi stewed and fretted, feeling irritably helpless. The matter was still very much on his mind a few months later when the renowned scholar Rabbi Nahum Solman, traveling from Bershad to Lemberg, stopped for a few days at Ilinghovka to visit his old friend Mayer Gentz. The warmth of their reunion was so soothing to Rabbi Gentz that, in a moment of confidentiality, he revealed to Nahum Solman his disappointment in the quality of the Tzaddik Nathan Baer's scholarship and his misgivings about his son's new surroundings. Rabbi Solman, stopping next on the other side of the border at Sniatin, told the Sniatin Rabbi (in a moment of warm confidentiality) what he'd heard about the Tzaddik of Solitava. This account, with certain embellishments, was then promptly reported by the Sniatin Rabbi to one of the rabbis of Czernowitz. This last gentleman was well acquainted with Shmuel Rossner, Shmuel's little bookstore being quite close to his synagogue. He therefore hurried over to repeat the story to Shmuel before he could forget any of the details—telling it in the strictest confidence, of course, and adding a few embellishments of his own.

Shmuel, completely forgetting that he himself disliked the superstitious practices in which his uncle indulged, fell into a fury. He closed the bookstore and hopped on the back of a wagon whose driver was on his way to Solitava to deliver a load of cut lumber. On his arrival at his father's house, and without bothering with a word of greeting, he pulled his father from the table where the poor man was just digging into his evening meal, and dragged him across the square to his uncle's compound. There he requested a private interview with his uncle, the Tzaddik, and when it was granted, told his uncle and his father what he'd heard. "They say that Mayer Gentz is telling everyone who will listen that you, Uncle Nathan, are nothing but a mediocrity who encourages his followers in the practice of medieval nonsense, and that the rest of the family is nothing more than a collection of superstitious fools!"

Ephraim gasped, and the Tzaddik turned white. "Mayer Gentz is saying these things?" Nathan cried. *"Mayer Gentz?"*

"I can't believe such a thing of him," Ephraim exclaimed.

"He said I was a mediocre scholar? *Mediocre?"* Nathan's voice took on an unmistakable quiver.

"He said *we* are superstitious fools?" Ephraim asked, horrified.

Shmuel repeated what he'd heard to his disbelieving father and uncle until, after the third rendering, they began to accept the authenticity of the tale. After all, when such a report comes from a member of one's own family, and when that member had it from so reputable a person as the Czernowitz Rabbi, who had it from the Sniatin Rabbi, who had it from no less a personage than Nahum Solman himself, one could scarcely question the source.

The three men conferred at great length, with Shmuel adding painful details to the sketchy summary he'd given earlier. There was no question that the Tzaddik and his family had been grossly, malignantly insulted. Their intelligence and abilities had been slandered and their reputations sullied. But what were they to do about it?

"First, of course, we must keep this among ourselves. No use making things worse by repeating the insults," Ephraim suggested.

"Very well," the Tzaddik agreed. "And second, I'll write to Mayer Gentz a letter he'll not soon forget!"

Shmuel nodded in firm support. "Yes, that's it. Tell him what we think of his arrogance! If you ask me, we should demand an immediate retraction and a public apology!"

The letter was dictated, discussed, revised by all three, and sent. Shmuel returned to Czernowitz, and Nathan and Ephraim awaited a reply. While they waited, they stewed in anger. They found that their resentment was so strong they could barely look at Avrum. They avoided him whenever possible and were barely civil to him when a meeting was unavoidable. But Avrum, happily absorbed in his own concerns, took no notice.

In Ilinghovka, Rabbi Gentz read the letter from his colleague-kinsman with a simmering anger. His innocent remarks had been blown up out of all proportion, he told himself. Couldn't that fool, the Solitava Tzaddik, see that the story had been exaggerated?

A MORNING MOON

The more he read the letter, the more his anger heated, driven almost to the boiling point by his own shame for having said what he had to Nahum Solman. He should never have said anything to anyone about his secret misgivings. But he was able to push his guilt to the deep recesses of his mind by logical argument; after all, his remarks to Nahum Solman had been reasonably circumspect. He'd merely said that Nathan Baer had too conventional a mind. Was that so terrible a thing to have said? Only a fool would fail to see that the story had been distorted by gossip. The more he thought about it, the more he blamed Nathan for misjudging him in favor of rumor-mongers. This entire incident was just more evidence that Nathan Baer was, at bottom, a nincompoop.

Retract? Make a public apology? Over his dead body! Whatever he'd said to Nahum Solman (ill advised though it had been) was nothing but the truth, and he'd burn in Gehenna for eternity before he'd retract a single word. In a bitter, vituperative response, he wrote that the Tzaddik's reaction to malicious gossip "only serves to illustrate further your lack of perspicacity."

When the response reached Solitava, it caused an explosion of outrage from Nathan. He sent for Avrum at once and ranted at him with such animosity that the young man turned pale. "Wait a *minute,* Uncle Nathan," he declared when he could manage to fit a word in. "I'd like to remind you that I'm only the son, not the man himself. I had nothing to do with this episode. This is the first I've heard of it."

The Tzaddik had to admit that this was true, and though Avrum's declaration of innocence did little to alleviate his feelings of affront, it did put an end to his tirade.

Avrum, considerably upset by what looked like the start of a family feud, told his mother-in-law what had happened. Etel Fruma had already suspected, from Ephraim's moodiness, that something was wrong. She scurried out to the compound to confer with her sister-in-law, Chana. Chana, too, had just learned from an overwrought Nathan the details of the quarrel. The women put their heads together and decided, with perfect female logic, that what was needed to put matters right was a good dinner. "We'll have it at your house," Chana said, "so that it will be just the family. At our house is always such a crowd."

"Yes, good idea," Etel Fruma agreed, already making mental notes on what would make a suitable menu.

"But Nathan won't come. I feel it in my bones that he won't come," Chana the Pessimist declared.

"*Make* him come. You're his wife."

"*You* make him come. You're his sister."

"Never mind that now. We won't say anything until we're sure the Gentzes will be here."

Thus, without discussing their plans with their husbands, they sent an invitation to the Gentz family asking them to come to a festive dinner at the conclusion of the celebration of the holiday of Simchas Torah.

The message they received in return was a refusal. Rabbi Gentz wrote that (a) the trip was too long, (b) his wife was not in the best of health, and (c) his duties at home were too heavy.

"One excuse I might have believed," Chana grumbled to her sister-in-law, "but three makes two too many."

"Right," Etel Fruma agreed. "It's time to get Avrum into this."

Avrum sent a persuasive plea to his parents to attend the dinner, and Rabbi Gentz succumbed. On the appointed day, he and his wife arrived in Solitava and presented themselves at the home of Ephraim Rossner, their faces set and unsmiling. The stiffness of their expressions was more than matched by that of their host. When the Tzaddik arrived with his wife, the greetings were formal to the point of iciness. Nathan and Ephraim had both refused to take any part in the festivities until, at the very last moment, Chana and Etel Fruma predicted that an apology would surely be forthcoming from the visitor. Only with that expectation had the Tzaddik deigned to attend, and until he heard that apology with his own ears, he would not unbend.

They all entered Etel Fruma's modest dining room. Avrum and Mindel were also present, and even the baby, cooing up at everyone from his little wooden cradle, had a place near the table. It was the baby's presence that helped to ease the tension of the first few minutes, for Hinde Sarah and Mayer Gentz were able to focus their attention on him instead of on their offended relatives.

While they took their seats, Etel Fruma and Chana exchanged satisfied smiles. It would all work out well. Over a plate of good food, who could quarrel?

"You'll say the blessing, of course," Ephraim said to his brother-in-law as he settled into his chair.

"Me? No, no, I'm too stupid," Nathan answered bitterly. "I might mispronounce the words. Let *him* say it!"

Mayer Gentz stiffened, his wife glared, and everyone else looked nervous. "Come, come, Uncle," Avrum said placatingly, "let's not be foolish—"

"Foolish? *Foolish?*" the Tzaddik roared, lifting himself from his chair. "Are you, too, joined in maligning me?"

"Oh, be still, Nathan," Chana hissed, "and say the blessing. Do you want the soup to get cold?"

She accompanied her whisper with an angry nudge under the table, and the Tzaddik swallowed his ire and resumed his seat. After a tense pause, he said the blessing, and the soup course passed without further incident, with Raizel, Mindel, their aunt, and their mother making all the conversation.

Over the main course, Etel Fruma smiled with valiant effort at her sister-in-law. "Your chicken is especially delicious tonight, Chana." She smiled at the others. "She prepared the chicken herself and sent it over. It has a different flavoring, I think. Very special, don't you think so, Hinde Sarah?"

"A very nice flavor," Hinde Sarah said impassively. "Very nice."

"Delicious," Mayer Gentz ventured, feeling certain that the one word could not possibly be misinterpreted and cause dissension.

"Sure," growled Nathan, "delicious! My own wife makes chicken for my enemies better than she makes for me."

"Nathan!" Chana warned.

"Enemies? What enemies?" Mayer Gentz asked, putting down his knife and trying to be reasonable. "What gives you the idea—?"

"You disparaged me before half the rabbis of the region, no? And for that I'm *not* supposed to think of you as an enemy? That's supposed to be the act of a *friend?*"

"Nathan," Chana murmured, "don't yell."

"Don't yell, she says! Why shouldn't I yell? First he insults me, then you wheedle me into dining with him, and you don't want me to yell? What should I do, *sing?*"

"My dear Nathan," Rabbi Gentz said quietly, "I never disparaged you before half the rabbis of the region. Let's try to discuss calmly what—"

"Calmly? Oh, that's fine, coming from you! Let *me* tell the world that *you're* an incompetent and a simpleton, and we'll see how calmly—"

"I never called you an incompetent or a—"

"No, that's too *good* a version of what you called me! I *heard* what you called me. I'm ashamed to say before my family what you—"

"Uncle," Mindel interrupted gently, "let Mayer Gentz say a word. Perhaps he can explain—"

"Mindel, keep out of this!" Ephraim ordered. "What can he explain, now that the damage is done?"

"Damage?" Mayer Gentz echoed with a shrug of disparagement. "What's the terrible damage?"

"A man's reputation is ruined before his associates, and you don't think it's *damage*?" Nathan shouted.

"Stop shouting at me," Mayer said angrily. "I'm not a student in your *cheder*. I only said to Nahum Solman, in strict confidence, that I'd found your thinking . . . er . . . unoriginal. Is that so terri—?"

"Oh, *you* found my thinking unoriginal, did you? And who are you, Mr. Philosopher, to pass judgments on my thinking? Another Akiva? Another Rashi? Another Moses Mendelssohn?"

"I did not pass judgment," Mayer insisted, a tremor creeping into his voice. "I only expressed to a personal friend and scholar that I was somewhat worried about the quality of my son's studies in Solitava, that's all."

"But, Papa, I never complained—" Avrum began.

"Oh, you were worried about your so-wonderful son, eh? I'm not good enough to oversee the studies of the hero of Ilinghovka, is that it? Well, if you ask me, I don't see much evidence of the brilliance you've been bragging about—"

"*Uncle!*" Mindel cried out, wounded.

"*My son* has been judged brilliant by the best minds in Russia!" Hinde Sarah declared loudly.

"Your son is a lazy good-for-nothing," Nathan shouted back.

Ephraim began to feel that things were going too far. "Nathan, that's not fair. You don't mean—"

The Solitava Tzaddik, quite beside himself, swung on his brother-in-law. "Don't *you* start! Are you forgetting that he called you and yours a bunch of superstitious fools?"

"Who, *us*?" asked Etel Fruma, turning to Mayer Gentz in offense.

"Mama, please," Mindel whispered urgently.

"Even if it's true, Mayer wouldn't say it," Hinde Sarah said grandly.

"What do you mean, 'even if it's true'?" Chana asked icily.

"It's true, all right," Hinde Sarah said, pleased to be able to exact a revenge for the slur on her son. "Ask Mayer to be honest. He'll tell you."

"Mama, *please*!" Avrum cried in consternation.

"Sure, let's ask Mayer!" Nathan rose, leaned over the table and thrust his face into Rabbi Gentz's. "You haven't said enough yet about our failings. Let's hear some *more* from the great thinker of Ilinghovka. Let's hear how backward and superstitious we are around here!"

Mayer Gentz ground his teeth in fury. "You don't have to be a great thinker to come to that conclusion!"

"Oh, is that so!"

"All that spitting three times, and the throwing the salt over the shoulder, and the screaming to look out for the evil eye when we were here for the *bris*—I suppose that never happened, eh? I never saw such things?"

"And you never saw such things at Ilinghovka either? Ilinghovka is such a modern, worldly metropolis, is that it? Arrogant snob!"

"Nathan!"

"Are you calling *me* names now?"

"Papa, sit down. He didn't mean—"

"Yes, I did. I'm calling you names. Arrogant snob! There!"

"Then *you* are a babbling simpleton!"

"Stop shouting! The baby is crying already."

"And *you* are a slanderer!"

"Uncle, I *beg* you—!"

"Look out! What are you trying to do? You'll knock over the table!"

"Medieval hocus-pocuser!"

"Vilifier! *Liar!*"

The tea service on the sideboard got in the way of a waving arm and came tumbling down with a terrible crash, tray, teapot, dishes, and all.

"Oh, my *God!*"

For a moment they all stared at the wreckage, aghast. Then Nathan, almost purple in fury, made a threatening move toward Mayer. Ephraim held him back. "Don't, Nathan. What *good* will come of this?"

"Meshuggenehs!" Mayer Gentz spat out. "I'm sorry I ever let my son marry into such a family of lunatics!"

"And I'm *more* sorry I encouraged it! Ephraim, let me at him!"

"Avrum, let me at him!"

Nathan swung wildly from under Ephraim's arm, connecting with Mayer's nose. Mayer howled in pain, Hinde Sarah screamed, the baby wailed in terror at the unaccustomed noise, and everyone else shouted at once. Mayer, putting a hand up to his aching nose, discovered blood. Enraged, he made a fist and swung clumsily but furiously at Nathan's face, knocking his son aside and smashing Nathan in the eye. Nathan tottered back and fell, dazed, to the floor, overturning a chair as he dropped. The women shrieked.

"Throw them out of here!" Nathan demanded, clapping both hands to his eye.

"Don't bother. We're getting out of this crazy place, this madhouse, this lunatic asylum!" Mayer Gentz declared, wiping the blood from his nose with a linen napkin while his wife hovered over him in distraught solicitude. "Avrum, come with me. You'll not remain with these *farbis-seneh* ignoramuses another minute!"

"But, *Papa*—!"

Ephraim, kneeling beside his brother-in-law, looked up in startled indecision. But the Tzaddik made the decision for him. "Yes, go!" he said to Avrum. "None of us will permit a Gentz into this house after today. Not even you."

"*Uncle!*" Mindel gasped. "Papa, you can't—! This is *crazy*!"

"Hush, Mindele," Avrum said, trying to think calmly in the midst of the chaos. "We'll take the baby with us to Ilinghovka for a few weeks, till this blows over."

Etel Fruma snatched the squalling baby from the cradle and hugged it to her bosom, while Ephraim jumped up and grabbed hold of Mindel. "No, Mindel will not go with the baby to such a home!"

"I should say she won't," Hinde Sarah snapped.

"Come, Avrum!" his father ordered, taking his arm.

"*My God! Avrum!*" Mindel gasped.

Avrum's parents, one on each arm, were dragging him out the door. He hitched himself around to look back at her, unaware that in the struggle his gold watch had broken from the chain and fallen to the floor. "Don't be frightened, love," he shouted back over his shoulder as they pulled him out to the street. "I'll calm them down and be back in a day. Don't worry!"

Mindel snatched her baby from her mother and stared at the door in horror while the others in the family followed the Gentzes down the hall and out into the street, shouting curses and threats. "If you ever step foot on this ground, may you grow like a beet with your head in the earth!"

"May a *kazarnya* fall on your heads!" Hinde Sarah flung back.

"May your name be besmirched as you besmirched ours!"

"May you and yours have a dark year!"

"May your name return without your body!"

Mayer Gentz pushed his wife and son into the rented carriage and, pausing before climbing up, he looked back at the others crowded in the doorway. Neighbors had long been listening to the commotion and were gathered in the middle of the street staring at all of them. Rabbi Gentz took a last swipe at his still-bleeding nose and threw the bloody napkin, like a gauntlet, to the ground. "A curse on all your forebears back to Adam," he croaked in a voice of doom, "and on your progeny all the way ahead to infinity!" And with that philosophical, modern, superstition-free declaration, he climbed into the vehicle and turned the horse toward home.

Alone with her baby in the dining room, Mindel felt the chill of foreboding. Shivering, she clutched the baby tightly to her breast and wept.

7

Days, and then weeks, went by without bringing solace to the parted lovers. Avrum tried without success to prevail on his parents to let Mindel and the baby come to Ilinghovka. Mindel suffered an equal failure in her attempt to coax her parents to agree to let Avrum return. The bitterness between the two families showed no signs of abating.

Avrum, in a depression unlike anything he'd ever experienced, moped about his parents' house unable to decide on what to do next. To continue to live separate from his wife and child was unthinkable, but he didn't know what course to take to bring them together. He suspected that the Tzaddik of Solitava had been too deeply offended to listen to reason, and he knew that the Rossners would do nothing about taking Avrum back without his permission. His only hope was to convince his father to let Mindel come to live with them in Ilinghovka, but thus far his pleas had fallen on deaf ears. What Avrum most wished to do was to run off with his wife and child to America, but he had no money of his own and no skills with which to earn some. His pain and frustration were boundless; never before had he felt so inadequate, so unequal to his problems. Spoiled, praised, and pampered all his life, the hero of Ilinghovka had not learned tolerance for failure.

His depression was so great that he found himself unable to sleep. He would lie awake wondering what time it was, but his gold watch—the symbol of his marriage—had disappeared in the confusion of the quarrel. When the waiting in the dark hours of the night became unbearable, he stole from his bed and prowled the lonely roads, trying to shake himself free of his devils. But the walking did no good. He ached for the feel of his wife with an obsessive need, and walking was a completely inadequate substitute. The autumn wind whistled through the tall grass, seeming to emphasize the emptiness around him. By the time he returned to his bedroom, he was always shivering with cold and agonized with grief.

But still he walked the nights away. On one such walk, he heard the crack of a twig in the grass alongside the road. "Who's there?" he asked nervously.

There was a giggle. "Is that the timid voice of young Gentz who saved his town from being sacked?" came a female voice.

"Donya? Is that you?"

She came out from behind a shrub. "I've been following you for ten minutes. If I'd been a robber, you'd be a plucked goose by now," she said, coming up beside him. "What are you doing here? I thought you lived in another country."

"I'm . . . visiting my parents," he explained awkwardly. "And you? Have you married your soldier?"

"Yes, last year," she said, making a face.

"What's the matter," he teased, "doesn't he treat you well?"

"He's all right when he's home. But he's still in the army, you know."

"Poor Donya. Didn't he leave you a baby to keep you busy?"

"Not yet." She rubbed her stomach fretfully. "One is cooking."

"Good, then. Don't pout. Once he's born you won't be so lonely."

"Once he's born he'll be a great nuisance!" She walked ahead a few steps, her peasant skirt swishing with the irritated swing of her step. Abruptly, she wheeled around. "Are *you* lonely?" she asked.

He sighed and nodded. "We have a saying: even in paradise, it's not good to be alone."

"And this is far from paradise," she muttered.

"Yes. Very far."

She came back and took his arm. "Let's go to the barn, then. We'll both feel better."

He shook his head. "I can't. I'm married now, you know."

"So what? She's not here, is she? She's not waiting for you back at your father's house?"

"No, but—"

She threw her arms about his neck and pressed herself against him. "Why not? Wasn't it fun before?"

"Yes. Great fun."

"Then don't be such a prude." Kittenlike, she wriggled against him and put her lips to his ear. "Come!" she whispered softly. "We'll make a little bit of paradise for ourselves."

Her breath on his ear set him trembling. Why not? he asked himself. He'd be a fool to refuse a bit of paradise. He let her take his hand and lead him across the field. The soughing wind, which on so many nights had pierced his heart with its lonely sound, now excited him. It blew up her skirts and billowed under his gabardine. Breaking into an eager laugh, he tightened his grip on her hand and broke into a run.

They climbed up to the hayloft. Directly in front of the wide opening, Donya began to strip off her clothing, gasping in the wind. The light was so dim that Avrum could almost imagine she looked like his wife. But this wasn't his wife. A clear image of Mindel, naked beside him on their bed, rose before his eyes and filled him with a painful yearning. "Donya, I . . . I can't." He took off his coat and covered her with it. "Forgive me."

She kept her eyes fixed on his face as he wrapped the coat closely about her. "You're a fool," she whispered with an ironic smile, "but I like you. I've always liked you."

"And I you."

A gust of wind chilled them both. "Well, you won't object only to holding me, will you?" she asked, moving close.

He backed away. "I'd better not."

"Then at least lie down on the hay with me. It's too cold to stand about like this. Let's lie down and cover ourselves, and you can tell me all about this wife of yours who's so wonderful that you can't be unfaithful to her even a little."

They covered themselves with the hay. It scratched, but it was warm and sweet smelling, and Avrum let himself speak of Mindel, the baby, his dreams of going to America, the quarrel, everything that was pent up in him. He talked and talked until a little snore told him that Donya had drowsed off into her own dreams. He grinned, snuggled deeper into the hay, and drowsed off, too.

Donya's gasp woke him with a start. He opened his eyes and saw, horrified, that Grisha's face was leering at them from the top of the ladder that connected the loft to the barn and that a light from below seemed to be rising. He had an instant recollection of the boy's mocking voice saying, "If my papa ever finds out, he'll take his ax to you." Before he could sit up and reach for his clothes, a torch appeared . . . an arm . . . and then the glaring eyes of a heavyset, grizzled, oxlike man. But he had no ax.

A MORNING MOON

Donya's father, uttering a stream of Russian curses that stung like whips, boxed Donya's ears and ordered her to dress. He threw Avrum's coat at him and, giving Grisha a smart cuff, he ordered the boy off to bed. Then, keeping an iron grip on Avrum's arm with one hand and holding the torch aloft with the other, he pulled the young man down the ladder, across the field, and down the road, the sobbing Donya following close behind. When they came to the town, the clatter of the man's boots on the cobbles and the light of his torch woke some of the sleepers in the houses along the way, and Avrum could see the windows lighting up and faces peering at them through the gloom.

The irate farmer pounded on the door of Rabbi Gentz's house, his shouts of "Wake up in there!" ringing through the street. Hinde Sarah, wide-eyed with fear, opened the door to him. "What is it? *Avrum? What—?*"

But Mayer Gentz came up behind her. "Go back to bed, woman," he ordered, his eyes darkly pained in his white face. And he led the others to his study.

Avrum and Donya were not permitted to say a word. The farmer shouted; Rabbi Gentz placated him. Their dialogue lasted more than an hour. Finally, a sum of money was exchanged, and in the first light of dawn, the farmer dragged his daughter back down the road toward their home.

When they'd gone, Mayer sank into his chair and put a trembling hand to his forehead. "So, the *hero* of Ilinghovka becomes the *adulterer* of Ilinghovka. My pride becomes my shame."

"Papa, it was not as it appeared. Please let me ex—"

"Be still! Don't take me for a fool. Lies will only belittle you more. I feared before that you had a streak of the sensualist in you, but those months with those vulgarians in Solitava have completely corrupted your character. The son I once knew could never have been so despicable . . . so deceitful as to sin with a wanton by night while he begged to be reunited with a wife he called beloved by day."

"Damn it, I haven't been deceitful," Avrum said furiously. "My wife *is* beloved. But if you won't believe me, there's no use going on. This would never have happened if you'd permitted me to bring Mindel here."

His father lifted his head and glared at him. "Must you cut up my soul with this last iniquity? Must you make your sins *my* fault?" He rose from his chair and turned his back on his son. "May God forgive you . . . but I cannot. You are no longer the son I knew. Go from my sight. Go to Solitava. There they are more your family than here." His voice trembled, but the meaning was clear: "You are no longer a son of mine."

It took Avrum, who had only a few kopeks in his pocket, almost a week to make his way back to Solitava. But the story of his indiscretion flew on wings. It spread throughout the town and reached the ears of Mindel and her family days before Avrum himself arrived. To the Tzaddik, the news was the final evidence he needed to conclude that the marriage had been a terrible mistake. "The father is false, and the son is an adulterer," he declared. "The claims made about the character of the man and the quality of his family were lies from the start. We must arrange to sever the marriage at once."

Ephraim the Irresolute did not argue with his brother-in-law. The Tzaddik was their leader; if he decreed that divorce was the best course for his daughter, so be it. But he knew it would not be easy to inform the girl of the Tzaddik's decision. Ever since Avrum had been torn from her, she'd moved about the house like a distracted creature. Her eyes were dazed, and she had an air of listlessness, as if someone had torn the spirit from her. The news of his unfaithfulness had been an additional blow. She sat by the window for hours on end, not saying a word. Even the baby's gurglings failed to distract her from what her father could see was an overwhelming sorrow.

He shuffled into the house and drew up a chair alongside hers near the window. "Nathan has sent for a special scholar," he said, taking her listless hand in his and patting it gently. "One who is expert in arranging divorces."

She made no response.

"Do you hear me, Mindele? The boy is not worthy of you. You were right from the first—we never should have forced you to wed him. But we'll end it now. We will have a proper *get,* and before you know it you will be free of him. Don't look like that, my sweet one! You'll be happy again one day. You're still young and beautiful. Not even eighteen. We'll find you someone who knows respect . . . who knows how to be faithful. You'll forget all about this—"

She turned her head and stared her father into silence. He shrank back at the coldness of her eyes. Then, without a word, she got up and walked from the room, shutting the door of her bedroom behind her with a vicious slam.

When Avrum appeared at the outskirts of the village, Bella Yusling saw him and sent her youngest boy racing to the Tzaddik's house to inform him of the news. Ephraim, with Zaleh the Beadle on one side of him and the second *gabbe* on the other, ran down the road and intercepted

Avrum before he could get to Mindel. Avrum was starving, frozen, and weary to the bone. When he was seized so near his goal, he howled in rage like an animal. And through all his misery, his mind kept asking him how he'd declined so abruptly from an honored, enviable youth to a beggarly, despised outcast.

They dragged him to the Tzaddik's house, where they let him wash and eat. When that was done, he was brought to the study. There, waiting for him, was an entire tribunal. Behind the long table, enthroned at its center, was Nathan Baer, the Tzaddik. Beside him sat Reb Handelman, a scholar whose specialty was the complicated Jewish divorce law. On Nathan's other side sat his number one *gabbe*, Ephraim, and the second *gabbe*. Near the fire, wiping tears from her eyes, was Etel Fruma. And at the window, staring out into the orchard, her face completely drained of color, was Avrum's wife. "Mindel!" he croaked.

She didn't turn, but she began to tremble from head to foot.

"Mindel, ask them to leave us for a minute. Let me talk to you!"

She wouldn't turn her head.

Reb Handelman, the divorce scholar, cleared his throat. "It has been found by this council that the woman, Mindel Gentz, has good and valid grounds for the *get*—divorce. We ask you to sign this divorce contract."

Avrum looked from one face to another for a sign of friendliness, a crumb of support, but there was none. "No, I won't sign," he said angrily. "I know the law. If the man does not wish to initiate the divorce, there can *be* none. And I don't wish it."

"Adulterer!" Nathan Baer roared. "Offspring of defamers! Your wishes don't concern us. Sign the paper and go on your way!"

"Never! I am not an adulterer. I won't do it!"

"You will! There is no other choice for you. Tell him, Reb Handelman."

Reb Handelman cleared his throat again. "I must inform you, Avrum Gentz, that it is the right of the divorce court to *compel* you to sign if the woman's request for the severing of the marriage has been found to be valid."

Avrum felt his blood run cold. "*Did* you request this divorce, Mindel?" he asked in disbelief.

The divorce scholar had been leafing through a heavy tome to find the source for his pronouncement. "Here it is. From Maimonides: 'If one who is obligated by law to divorce his wife refuses to do so, a Jewish court at any place and at any time may beat him until he says, "I am willing." ' You may come and read it for yourself, if you wish."

Avrum ignored him. "Answer me, Mindel! Did you ask for this divorce?"

"You may not speak to her!" Ephraim cautioned, rising and placing himself before Avrum and blocking the desperate fellow's view of his wife. "Did you hear what Reb Handelman said? Do you want to be beaten?"

"Beat me all you like. I won't sign anything!"

Nathan made a motion of his head toward Zaleh the Beadle. The old man came up behind Avrum's chair, grasped his two hands, and, pulling them behind the chair's back, tried to tie them together. When Avrum realized what the old man was about, he shook himself free. Zaleh was immediately joined by Ephraim and the second *gabbe*. The three of them were able, despite Avrum's wild struggles, to tie his hands behind his back. Then Nathan picked up from his table a long, evil-looking leather horsewhip. Etel Fruma gasped.

Ephraim went to the Tzaddik's side and leaned over him. "Nathan," he muttered miserably, "must we go so far—?"

Nathan glared his brother-in-law back to his seat, raised the whip over his head, and made a snapping movement. The crack of sound that shot through the room as the leather whip slapped, knifelike, across Avrum's chest coincided with Mindel's piercing scream. *"No!"* she shrieked, wheeling about and dashing across the room.

She pushed the startled Zaleh aside, flung herself down on her knees before Avrum, and threw her arms about his waist. "I never asked for this," she sobbed. "Never! Oh, God, Avrum, my own, don't you know how my heart is breaking?"

"Mindel, go back to your place!" the Tzaddik roared furiously. "This is an official proceeding!"

Avrum struggled to free his tied wrists. He couldn't even hold her now, much less defend her against them all. "Why are you letting them do this to us?" he asked her desperately. "Is it what they say I did . . . in Ilinghovka? I didn't! You must believe me!"

"I don't care about that. It is a thing of no importance." Her arms dropped from around him, and she put her hands to her face. "What does it matter? They won't let us remain together anyway. We are helpless."

"Mindel, I *beg* you, don't listen to them! They are like . . . like mastodons—relics of the past that live on beyond their time. We are the *future!*"

She looked up at him, the tears coursing down her cheeks. "There's nothing we can do, nowhere we can go. There's no money. . . . There's the baby. . . . We're trapped. I tried to fight them before and could not. What's the good of letting them beat you? You'll only have to sign the contract in the end."

He stared at her, the blood draining from his face, his lips white. It was true. He was unable to save them. He was nothing—a scholar who couldn't think of one rabbinical argument to fight them with. Only a short while ago he'd thought he was like a prince—the pride of his people. But as soon as they'd withdrawn that pride, he was nothing. At last he understood. And in her eyes he could see that she understood, too.

The second *gabbe* lifted her to her feet, and the Tzaddik ordered her mother to take her in charge. Reb Handelman approached Avrum with the divorce contract in one hand and a pen in the other. Zaleh untied his hands, and Reb Handelman thrust the pen in his shaking right hand. The second *gabbe* gripped his wrist and forced his hand to the paper, while Mindel sobbed bitterly in her mother's arms.

Avrum signed. The rest of the ritual was conducted with dispatch. Mindel shook with sobs, and Avrum sat motionless, slumped in his chair. Finally, the Tzaddik rose and faced the company. "It's over," he announced coldly. "The marriage has been severed."

Mindel, with a sharp intake of breath, slipped to the floor in a faint. Avrum started up from his chair to go to her, but Ephraim, the second *gabbe,* and Zaleh seized him by the arms and pulled him from the room.

"Mindel!" he screamed. The hopeless, drawn-out cry hung in the air long after they'd dragged him down the hallway and thrown him from the house.

. . . *So the marriage of my mother to Avrum Gentz ended, less than two years after their wedding day. And three months after the signing of the divorce decree, the Tzaddik forced his once favorite niece, my mother, into marriage with the* lemeshkeh *who was to be my father.*

Part Two
LEIB
1904-1913

1

It was Leib Weisenberg they chose for her, and everyone knew that he was, in my aunt Raizel's phrase, no bargain. Even if you loved him—as we children did—you'd have to admit he was awkward, homely, and cursed with a foolish, embarrassed grin that accented his sad eyes.

He was a maikler. *I don't think you have them in America, Sam. A cattle agent. If someone in Solitava wants to sell a cow, he goes to the* maikler *to find him a buyer. The work isn't steady, and even for a schemer with a golden tongue the remuneration wouldn't be adequate for a family of five. But Papa wasn't in any way a schemer. He barely brought home enough money to keep bread on the table. If it hadn't been for the help of my grandmother and my uncle Shmuel, we would have had many hungry nights.*

My mother bore him two children (my sister Dvora two years after they were married, and me, Yahudis, four years after that), but we never understood how it was done. We never saw her show him a moment of affection. Dov and Dvora hated her for that, but I felt sorry for Mama. I knew she'd suffered some sort of tragedy (although for years I didn't know its nature), and I grieved for her. Especially when I'd wake up in the black of night and hear her stifled sobs.

That sound haunted our childhood years. For a decade or more after Avrum Gentz disappeared from her life, Mama cried for him at night. I used to assume, when I was very small, that crying at night was something all women did. I even asked Dvora how old one had to be before one wept in one's sleep.

Sometimes Mama would wake up from a dream and scream, "Avrum!" The sound would chill my bones. Avrum! *The name was a dark specter hanging over our childhood. Now that I understand, I suppose it was not possible for*

*her to love anyone else like that. Except my brother, of course. Every-
one could see that Mama adored Dov with every fiber of what was left of her
heart. . . .*

Dov Gentz, his mother's darling, returned her affection most reluc-
tantly even on good days. But today, standing at the fence of the
Czernowitz boy's school with his ankle throbbing, he almost hated her.
It was her fault that he faced the prospect of a four-mile walk home from
school. On ordinary days the four-mile walk seemed to the eight-year-
old boy a difficult enough chore, but today the prospect was impossible.
The walk to his home on the outskirts of the city usually took an hour;
today it would last an eternity. He leaned against the schoolyard fence
and screwed the muscles of his little face tight in an attempt to squeeze
out the pain and squeeze in the tears. He'd never make it home, never.

On ordinary days he managed it well enough. He'd make the walk
bearable by dividing up the route in his mind. He'd cut it into five
sections, uneven ones to be sure (like Mama dividing up the noodle
pudding into five clumsy pieces and trying to pretend that everyone was
getting an equal amount) but more acceptable to the mind than the
prospect of one long, unbroken journey. The first section stretched from
the schoolyard to the town hall on the Hauptstrasse. This was the shortest
and most interesting of the sections because of all the store windows one
could look into. Then came the part along the cobbles of the Hauptstrasse
to the city park. The third section was the walk along the edge of the
park to the bridge, a good part because the bridge, which spanned the
river Prut, was a midway point where one could pause, climb up on
the railing, and look down into the clouded, brown-green water flowing underneath. The fourth and longest stretch (where there was nothing
much to look at but fields, shrubbery, and shabby houses) ran between
the river and what Dov had named the Big Bend—the turning marked
by a misshapen oak tree where the road veered off to the left and changed
from cobbles to packed-down dirt. That was the dangerous section,
because sometimes the Gentile boys who lived there would set their dogs
on him. And finally, the stretch from the oak tree to his house.

He usually made up games to pass the time. He'd recite Schiller's
Bergshaft (his favorite poem, the story of the remarkable friendship of
Damon and Pythias, which always tightened his throat at the end) very
quickly under his breath; if he could finish the whole poem—every one
of the twenty stanzas—between the town hall and the bridge, he would
award himself two points. If he could manage to hop on one foot between
the schoolyard and the Hauptstrasse, three points. If he glimpsed a real

live fish under the murky surface of the river from his perch on the bridge within the count of fifty, five points. Ten points meant that Papa would be home for supper, or something else lucky.

But nothing would be lucky today. He wouldn't make a single point. Not with a broken ankle. How could he have been so stupid? He'd let the loathsome Itche Kettler goad him into shinnying up the pole at recess. When he came sliding down, having lost his grip only three feet from the top, Kettler hooted with laughter. Dov picked himself up and walked away with his head up, giving no sign that he'd been hurt. He didn't let himself stumble or limp. And he remained hidden in the coat closet after school until all the boys had dispersed. He didn't want anyone to know the fall had injured him.

At first he'd felt an all-over pain—head dizzy, hands burning from the friction of the pole during his downward slide, right knee bruised. But by now the other pains were trivial when compared to the throbbing agony of his ankle. From the way the swollen flesh was pressing against the leather of his high shoe he knew the injury was serious. His left ankle had become a presence, an alien spirit that had invaded his leg. With every step it seemed to give out a cry of its own, as if it were a unique, separate entity that was demanding attention.

Dov began to move slowly along the fence, holding on to it with both hands to ease the pressure on the foot. The fence helped, but it ran only the length of one street. When he came to the corner, then what?

It was all his mother's fault. If she hadn't insisted on moving to Czernowitz, he would still be going to *cheder* in Solitava, where the study house and everything else was a hop and a jump from home. But just because Mama wanted to have bigger rooms, they'd been forced to move to the outskirts of this city, and he had to attend a government school where they spoke German and where the boys looked on him as a country bumpkin.

It had been a bad move for Papa, too. Papa, who was a *maikler* and had no connections here in Czernowitz, had to travel constantly between here and Solitava. The trip was long, especially when one had to rely on begged rides from passing wagons, and thus Papa was often away for days at a time. Who knew where he ate or slept? All Mama's fault, too.

. . . Oh, my dear Sam, how little we children sympathized with my mother's wish to better our existence. When Uncle Shmuel inherited a piece of land outside Czernowitz with a four-room house on it and offered it to Mama, she saw it as an opportunity to move up in the world—away from Solitava and its stifling closeness, its backward folkways (she called them medieval), its (to

*her) unbearable memories. But even I, who always took Mama's part, disliked
the move to Czernowitz. To us the move was a rift, a cruel separation from
the rest of the family and the only life we knew, and we resented her for
it. . . .*

Whenever Dov thought about his mother he felt a bad place in his
chest. He didn't like to think about her . . . about her grief for the father
he never knew, about Papa's not being his real father, about his being only
a half brother to his sisters and having the name Gentz while the others
were Weisenberg. But thoughts of her crowded into his mind unbidden,
even now when every step he took was an agony.

Dov liked things to be neatly balanced, to be symmetrical, to add up.
He didn't like the arrangements in the household Mama had set up; there
was something unbalanced about it. He knew his mother adored him
above all the others in the family, and sometimes he felt warmed inside
by the intensity of her affection. But her adoration of him made her
coldness to Papa even more obvious. She didn't really like Papa, and Dov
hated her for that. Papa was so *good.* If Mama had been really good, she
wouldn't have insisted on moving here and making life so hard for Papa.

It was terrible to carry, in some hidden place in one's chest, a suspicion
that one's mother was not a good person. Mothers were supposed to be
good—like angels. But there was nothing angelic about *his* mother if she
could speak to Papa in a voice of barely hidden contempt and always stop
just short of calling him a fool.

In fact Dov remembered quite clearly a time she *had* called Papa a
fool. It had been at a family gathering at the home of Great-uncle Nathan,
the Tzaddik, where they always went to celebrate Hanukkah. After
dinner, the younger children were excused from the table and sat on the
floor in a corner of the room twirling their *dreidels* while the adults
remained at the table talking and singing. As usual, Mama sat a little apart
from the rest and stared absently out the window. Papa was, also as usual,
keeping in the background, as if he was ashamed to take part in the talk
of the rest of the family. It was as if Papa didn't feel important enough
or wise enough to participate in the conversation exchanged by the Baers
and the Rossners. He would always take a seat somewhere behind Mama,
smiling but silent, leaning forward only to ask Mama if she wanted a glass
of tea or something to eat. For this he would get nothing from Mama
but a disdainful wave of the hand and a look of scorn.

Uncle Shmuel knew that Papa was a good storyteller, and he would
often try to draw him out. Whenever he succeeded, Papa would tell a
story in a too quiet voice and with a shy, self-deprecating smile that
would give Dov a pain in the chest, for Dov knew that Papa, when he

told stories to the children or to his cronies, was able to speak up with the best. But when Mama was listening, something inside him seemed to change . . . to stiffen into self-consciousness.

On this particular evening, Uncle Shmuel was regaling the family with the latest gossip from Czernowitz. One of his neighbors had recently become a father, he related with a chortle, "just *three months* after the wedding!"

"Three months? Ha!" Grandma Etel Fruma gave a hoot.

"Shocking!" muttered Great-aunt Chana.

The men all laughed, but Aunt Raizel shook her head. "The poor bride," she said with sympathy, bouncing her own baby, little Yossele, on her knee and letting him suck honey from her finger. "It must be hard to pretend to the world that a nine-month process can be squeezed into three."

"Not so hard," Papa offered, coming a step forward from his place near the window. "Even a fool from Chelm . . ." But he glanced at Mama, and his voice died away.

Uncle Shmuel looked across at him eagerly. "One of your Chelm stories, eh, Leib? Well, go on."

"Yes, Leib," Grandma Etel Fruma urged. "I love your stories about the town of fools."

But Papa had retreated shyly back to his chair. "No, no, never mind."

"But I want to hear, Leib," Uncle Shmuel urged.

"Come on, Leib, we all want to hear," said Great-uncle Nathan. "I insist."

Aunt Raizel looked at Papa challengingly. "Besides, I don't believe that even one of your fools from Chelm can convince us that three months could become nine."

"By the logic of the town of fools," Papa said, coming forward again, "it's quite simple." He faced Uncle Shmuel and asked, "The bridegroom in question, how many months has he lived as husband to this woman?"

"Three," Uncle Shmuel answered, grinning in anticipation.

"And how many months has the woman lived as wife to this man?"

"Three."

"And how many months have they lived together?"

"Three, of course."

Papa nodded. "There, you see? Three months he's lived with her, three months she's lived with him, and three months they've lived together. Three and three and three makes—"

"Nine!" everyone shouted and roared with laughter.

Everyone except Mama.

"Mindel," Uncle Shmuel exclaimed, coming up to her chair, "your Leib has just made everyone howl with his fool-from-Chelm logic. Why aren't you laughing?"

Mama gave her brother an unreadable look. "If he weren't *my* fool, I'd be laughing, too."

Dov remembered the knot that had formed in his stomach when he'd seen Papa's face stiffen at his mother's retort. He could feel the pain of it even now.

But the pain in his ankle was at this moment even worse. It seemed to the injured boy that hours had passed, and still he hadn't reached the town hall. He could barely stand the pain. How could he make it the rest of the way?

At a snail's pace, and with excruciating effort, he passed the town hall and began the passage along the edge of the park. He could see the bridge, but it seemed a long way off. He couldn't go a step farther—the pain was too much for him. He sat down clumsily on the cold ground of the park. He was done for. He would simply stay here and wait for death.

The sky was growing dark. He wondered how long one could remain alive in the cold night with a terrible injury. Perhaps, he thought, I should lie down and try to sleep. If the Angel of Death comes while I sleep I won't be frightened.

He shifted to his side to prepare his deathbed. The wool muffler his mother always tied about his neck would do for a pillow. He pulled it off, shivered a bit, and readied the spot for sleep. His last resting place. He hoped someone would find his body before he moldered into dust. He sat up and took a last look at the world . . . at the sky, at the almost barren trees, at the bridge where, beyond its stanchions, the last of the daylight still lit the horizon. He blinked in surprise—there was someone crossing the bridge from the other side. The silhouetted figure of a man. There was something familiar about the man's way of walking. That half shuffle, half run . . . could it be—?

But of course it couldn't. Papa was in Solitava. He hardly ever came home in the middle of the week. If it were Friday . . . but this was Wednesday. He rubbed his eyes and squinted at the figure intently. Who else would walk in quite that funny way? His heart began to race with wild hope. "Papa?" he shouted into the wind. He sat up and waved frantically. *"Papa?"*

The man on the bridge paused, peered into the dimness, and then waved both hands high above his head in excitement. *"Dov—?"* He gave a clumsy little jump and broke into a run. *"Doviddle,* is that you?"

In a few moments he was kneeling beside Dov on the ground. "Dov, my son, what happened? What's the matter? Why are you sitting here like this?"

Dov, enveloped in his tight embrace, burst into tears. "My ankle, Papa. I think I . . . broke it."

"Broke it? Let me see." The man lifted the leg tenderly and tried to undo the shoe. Dov gasped. Leib shook his head. "We'd better wait till we get home to take the shoe off. Come, my little one, my imp, my troublemaker, let's go home."

Dov bit his lip. "It hurts so much, Papa. Do you think I can walk on it?"

"Who said anything about walking? You'll ride. Like a prince of all the Russias."

"Ride?"

"On my back."

"Oh, Papa!" Dov threw his arm around his rescuer's neck. "It's a miracle you're here!"

Leib hugged the boy to his chest for a long moment. Then he placed him gently on the ground, fiddled in the pocket of his shabby coat for a dirty handkerchief, and blew his nose. "Miracle? What are you talking about? What's such a miracle?" He knelt down, tied the muffler around the boy's neck and helped him to climb upon his back. "But there was a rabbi once, in the town where I was born—*he* could perform miracles."

Dov, clasping his papa tightly about the neck, giggled. He'd heard the miracle-rabbi story dozens of times before. "You don't say," he answered in the way they always enacted the story. "What sort of miracles?"

Leib, with a little heave, lifted himself to his feet (the burden on his back causing only a slight stumble) and set off down the road. "Well, when a poor woman complained that she had only one small fish in her pot to feed her five children, he waved his hand over the pot. And when the poor woman opened it, lo and behold, there were five fish in the pot."

"Five?" Dov asked with the proper touch of suspicion.

"Five."

"That's not such a miracle," Dov said, as prescribed. "I've heard of a rabbi who turned a dish of dried peas that a poor woman had on her table into five live chickens."

"Five live chickens?"

"That's what I said. Five."

"I'll tell you what," Leib offered. "Let's make a deal. You take away one chicken from your poor woman's table, and I'll—"

"—you'll take away one fish from your poor woman's pot!" Dov finished, joining in so that they said the last phrase in unison. They both laughed uproariously until they reached the bridge. It was one of several little comedy routines they'd developed for their own amusement.

"Feeling better, little klutz?" Leib asked, reaching up a hand and giving the face leaning on his shoulder an affectionate pat.

"Yes, Papa, a whole lot better. But it *was* a miracle, you know."

"What was?"

"Your coming just when I needed you. It's not Friday. You're supposed to be in Solitava, yet here you are, just in time to save my life. A miracle brought you."

"Miracle, shmiracle," Leib snorted, hoisting his burden a little higher on his back. "A *wagon* brought me. A man I know told me he was coming to Czernowitz with a wagonload of cattle feed. I had no business anyway, so I came along with him."

"Really, Papa? Imagine that! What luck! And I didn't make a single point today."

"Point? What point? What are you babbling about? Has your broken ankle made you light-headed?"

Dov laughed. "No, I'm all right. It's only a game I play."

"Oh, is that all? I was afraid for a minute that you'd lost your wits. We can't have that, you know. One witless one in the family is enough."

"Oh, Papa!" The boy turned his face into his stepfather's shoulder and nuzzled his neck like a puppy. "Do you want to know a secret, Papa?"

"Yes, sure. Nothing I like better than secrets."

"Do you know who I love better than . . . than almonds?"

They had reached the Big Bend. The malformed oak, looking in the shadows like an old witch with wild hair, waved after them with what the boy would earlier have found to be eerie menace. But now neither the boy nor the man took notice.

"Better than *almonds*?"

"Better even than apple strudel with cream. Guess who."

The stepfather grinned. "No one. It's impossible. You can't love anyone in the world better than apple strudel with cream."

Down the road a light shone through the darkness—the light from the kitchen of their house. But the boy, no longer in a hurry to get home, didn't look at it. "Yes, I can. I love someone better."

"Unbelievable. Who?"

The boy rubbed his cheek against his papa's ear. "You. That's who."

2

The gossips of Solitava predicted that the move to Czernowitz wouldn't improve Mama's disposition one whit. And they were probably right. Everyone noticed that Mindel Rossner Gentz Weisenberg always wore an expression of—how did you put it once, Sam?—stoically endured unhappiness. She attended to her household chores and to our physical needs with a silent efficiency, but whenever anyone caught a glimpse of her in her occasional moments of repose, one would notice that her eyes were staring at something far away and that her facial muscles were slack—like someone who'd just heard tragic news and hadn't yet taken it fully into consciousness.

In the days of our childhood, Dov, Dvora, and I would be smitten with a sense of tragic awe when we saw that look. But Dov and Dvora changed as they grew older. They began to feel irritation . . . even disgust. "How long should one be permitted to indulge in suffering over the past?" they asked themselves. Childlike, they felt that there ought to be a time limit to tragedy. There was only so much sympathy they were capable of. Enough was enough. . . .

The three children noticed that, behind their backs, people called their mother Mindel the Silent. It was an apt epithet. Mindel spoke rarely, even to her children. Sometimes she made an attempt to communicate with Dov, but the boy was embarrassed by her obvious favoritism and avoided her attempts at closeness by responding in monosyllables and edging away. When she said something to the others, it was usually to give orders in only the most necessary words. Her tone was flat, unemotional, not conducive to either response or argument.

Her manner was the same to her husband, but to him her tone held an edge of contempt, as if she couldn't bear to let a soul believe that she harbored any tender feelings toward this man she'd married. Despite the fact that he'd fathered her two daughters, she seemed determined never to permit anyone—especially Leib himself—to forget that the marriage had been forced on her.

Leib endured her scorn with a humble acceptance. He was convinced that his marriage to Mindel was the greatest blessing God had ever bestowed on him. The daily disdain to which she subjected him he ignored. When she became angry with him—and those scenes grew more frequent as the children grew and his income did not—he withstood her invective with lowered eyes and a bent head. His feelings for her were permeated with an overwhelming gratitude. He never forgot that when he'd applied to the Tzaddik for her hand, he'd had no expectation that his request would be granted. That the Tzaddik had granted it was the miracle of his life. To his mind she was a proud goddess, and he an unworthy nobody. To have won her hand was enough; her heart was beyond his aspirations.

The day he brought home the cow was typical. The animal should have gone to Mottel, the owner of the Solitava hardware store, who had asked Leib to buy him a cow as a surprise for his wife. After Leib had made the purchase, however, Mottel changed his mind and refused to take it. The seller, a dairyman named Rashower, with Leib's money safely in his pocket, quite understandably rejected the suggestion that he take the cow back. Poor Leib, having no idea of what else to do, rented a wagon, laboriously pushed the cow upon it, tied her up, and took her home with him to Czernowitz.

When the wagon arrived at the house, the children ran out to greet the new addition to the family with cries of delight. Dov, now twelve, Dvora, nine, and little Yahudis, five, had never known the joy of keeping a pet. They climbed up on the wagon and crowded around the cow, Dvora touching her hide, Dov peering into her eyes, and Yahudis tugging at her tail and gaping at her udder, which seemed to her quite strange and huge. "Papa, Papa," they cried, jumping up and down excitedly, "is she ours to *keep*?"

But Leib was already entangled in a labored explanation to his wife, who stood in the doorway glaring at him furiously. "I couldn't force Mottel to take her if he didn't want to, could I? He didn't give me a deposit, you see—I took his word when he asked me to buy—and Rashower said that a bargain is a bargain, and he wouldn't take her back. So I thought that . . . for the time being . . . I might as well take her home with me."

Mindel listened with disgust. To her this fiasco was but another example of the man's monumental ineptitude. "*Koptzen!* Good-for-nothing! You've lost a small fortune on this transaction, haven't you? Is this how you conduct your business? Any simpleton could tell you that you're supposed to get the money first, and *then* you buy!"

"But Mottel is an old friend. I couldn't ask him—"

"No, of course you couldn't. But you *could* let him make an ass of you. That was quite all right with you, eh?"

She didn't wait for an answer but swung around and went into the house, slamming the door behind her in a fury. The children, who ordinarily would have watched this scene with tearful eyes, were this time too absorbed in the cow to take full notice of their father's humiliation. As soon as their mother was out of sight, they ran up to him, grasped his hands, pulled at his coat, and pelted him with eager questions. "Shall we keep her?" "Where will she sleep?" "Can we name her Butter Belly?"

The beaten look faded from his eyes. "Butter Belly?" He smiled down at them and hoisted Yahudis to his shoulder. "Is that a name for such a beauty as this? Come, Dov, help me untie her. And you, Dvora, run up the road to the widow Falz and see if she'll give you a bundle of hay. Tell her we'll give her some fresh milk in return. Well, my little Yudi, is Butter Belly the best name you can think of for so sweet an animal as this?"

So Tzickerl (for Yudi promptly picked up her father's word "sweet" and decided to call her Sugar) came into the family. Mama ignored her existence at first, while Papa kept promising her to find a buyer for the animal. But the children's prayers were answered—a month went by without Leib's getting an offer. In that month Mindel and the children learned to milk her, and Mindel decided to keep her. Besides the obvious advantage of not having to buy milk (and having more cream and butter on their table than they'd ever had before), Mindel was able to make a few extra kreuzers each day by selling the excess to the neighbors. By the end of the month it was apparent to the children that even Mindel found Tzickerl a welcome addition to the household, although as far as they knew, she never apologized to Leib for her earlier vituperation.

It became Dvora's task to take the cow across the road every day to graze. Their road marked the far edge of a military reservation whose vast acreage was mostly in disuse. The land was used for cavalry maneuvers, but the *caserne,* the barracks that housed the dragoons, was situated miles away to the north, and the soldiers were rarely seen at this far corner of their reservation. Although it was probably illegal to use the land for grazing, Mindel knew that it was extremely unlikely that anyone would object—or even take notice.

But one day the cow was missing when Dvora went to lead her home. She and Dov spent over an hour tracking her down. They found her two miles away, on the other side of a patch of woods. They couldn't imagine what had caused the placid Tzickerl to make such an arduous trek, but they brought her back unharmed.

A few days later she disappeared again. This time Dvora and Dov didn't find her until dark. The search had been worrisome, and they were very puzzled by Tzickerl's uncowlike behavior. When it happened a third time, Dov decided to set up watch. He, Dvora, and Yudi took turns keeping an eye on her at all times. It was little Yudi who made the discovery: a group of Gentile boys, with much amusement over the "Yid cow," were driving her off through the woods with sticks.

The children conferred. They agreed not to tell Mama, "because," Dvora pointed out, "she'll say she knew all along that the cow would cause trouble, and she'll make Papa sell her."

"I don't want Papa to sell my lovely Tzickerl," Yudi whimpered, eyes filling with tears.

"I suppose I ought to fight those boys," Dov suggested dubiously.

"Fight them? All three?" Dvora laughed scornfully. "They'd murder you."

"Yes, I know. I just don't know what else to do."

"But I don't *want* you to b-be murdered," Yudi blubbered.

"Oh, be still, stupid," Dvora snapped. "No one will be murdered but you, if you don't stop crying. There's only one thing to do, Dov. Let's talk to Papa."

At the end of the week, when Leib returned from Solitava, the children joined him in cleaning out Tzickerl's shed and told him what had happened. Leib listened to the children, as he always did, with the sort of concentration that made them feel important. "What do *you* think we ought to do?" he asked Dov.

"Me? I don't know. Maybe we could reason with those boys."

"Ah, yes. Dov the Logician," Leib murmured, smiling at the boy admiringly.

Dov looked down at his feet sheepishly. Leib had a habit of concocting little epithets for everybody—Ische the Arguer, Shmuel of the Knit Eyebrows, Widow Falz the Weeper.

"Some logic," Dvora said scornfully. "If those *am ha-aretzim* were reasonable, would they have driven poor Tzickerl into the woods in the first place?"

"Then what do you suggest, my beauty?" Leib asked her.

Dvora raised two fists. "What I'd like to do is punch them all on their damn *goyishe* noses!"

Leib laughed. "Just what I expected from Dvora the Impetuous."

Yudi tugged at his coat. "Maybe we could give them a few pennies if they promise to stay away," she suggested hopefully.

Leib picked her up and swung her through the air. "That's my sweet little baby for you! Yudi the Giver."

"Yes, Papa, but bribing them won't do any good," Dov pointed out. "They'll take the money and come back again for more."

Leib nodded in agreement, put Yudi down, and then stood for a while leaning on his rake, thinking. At last his brow cleared. Motioning for the children to sit down beside him, he perched himself on a pile of hay.

"Have you thought of something, then?" Dov asked, eyes alight with expectation as his sisters seated themselves on the hay.

"Did I ever tell you the story of Velvel the Tailor?"

"A *story*? *Now*?" Dvora eyed her father in annoyance. "Papa, this matter is serious."

"Shut up, Dvora," Dov said. "Sometimes a story can teach you something." And he sat down on the ground before his stepfather and folded his legs under him. "Go ahead, Papa. What about Velvel the Tailor?"

"Well, he lived in the city of Minsk, where, I don't have to tell you, Jews don't have an easy time of it. And every day, three peasant boys would pass by the little house where he did his tailoring, and they would stand outside his door and shout, 'Velvel the Tailor is a kike! Velvel the Tailor is a lousy Yid!'"

"That was very mean," Yudi murmured, her underlip beginning to tremble.

"Yes, my little Yudi, that was very mean. And they did it every day without fail until the poor tailor could stand it no more. So, one day, when he heard them shouting, he thought of a trick. He went outside and greeted them. 'Good day, little boys,' he said. 'I see you've come to visit me again. How nice to see you. From now on, every day you come by and call me Yid and kike and lousy Jew, I'll give you two kopeks.' And he put his hand in his pocket and gave each of the boys two coins."

"Two kopeks each?" Dvora grimaced in disgust. "Crazy!"

"Is a kopek like our kreuzer?" Yudi asked, wide-eyed. "He *must* have been crazy."

"Just wait a minute," Dov said, his eyes fixed on Leib's face. "Let Papa finish."

They listened to the rest of the tale with rapt attention. When it was done, they stared at their father openmouthed. Even Yudi could see how the story might apply to the boys who were molesting their cow. "Do you really think it'll work?" Dvora asked doubtfully.

"It's worth a try," Leib answered.

"But it will cost . . . let me see . . . nine kreuzers at the very least," Dov calculated.

"I think we can spare nine kreuzers to keep Tzickerl safe. But who's going to play Velvel the Tailor?"

Dvora was working out the plot in her mind. "Dov, of course. He's the one to deal with those ruffians."

"No," Dov said with a wink at his stepfather. "I think Dvora should do it."

"Me?" Dvora blinked in surprise. "Why me?"

"Because you're so pretty. The plan might work even better with a pretty girl than it did with Velvel the Tailor."

They went back to the house in high spirits, Leib because he'd set in motion a plan to solve a knotty problem, Dvora because she'd heard, for the first time in her life, that she was a pretty girl, and Yudi because everyone else was happy. But Dov itched with impatience. He could hardly wait for those boys to come back.

They came back three days later. Yudi, who'd been watching for them while hidden in the shadows of the shrubbery in front of their house, ran in to alert her sister.

Dvora walked calmly across the road, while Dov joined Yudi behind the bushes to watch developments. His fists were tightly clenched, ready to go into action if his sister needed him.

"Hey, there," Dvora called out as she approached the vandals, "are you the boys who've been driving our cow through the woods?"

The boys looked her over brazenly. Then the largest of them spoke up. "What if we are? What're you gonna do about it, eh?"

"We want to thank you. It's good exercise for her. In fact, my father said I could give you each two pennies every time you do it."

The boys looked at each other suspiciously. "She's joking," one of them said.

"She's cracked," said the first.

Dvora held out her hand. "Do you want to take these or don't you?"

The boys stared at the copper coins in disbelief. Then the large one grinned. "Sure. Why not?" he said, helping himself to his share. The others followed suit. As soon as they'd taken the money, Dvora turned to go. The boys, with much hooting, picked up their sticks and began to prod Tzickerl toward the wood. "Do you want us to do it again tomorrow?" the large fellow asked.

Dvora looked back at him over her shoulder. "No hurry. Whenever you're in the neighborhood."

They were back again the next day, barely able to contain their snickers. Dvora crossed the road again. "I'm sorry," she said, holding out her hand. I can only give you one kreuzer each today. Papa had a bad day."

The boys exchanged looks, obviously disappointed. Then the big one shrugged. "Oh, well, better than nothing," he muttered, and they each took a coin.

When they next appeared, Dvora approached them with hands behind her back and head lowered. "Sorry," she said. "Papa says we can't afford it anymore."

"Not even one penny each?" the youngest asked with a pout.

"No. I'm sorry."

"But a few days ago you gave us each two!"

"I know. But times are hard with us, you see."

"Yeah? Well, times are no better with us," said the middle one. "We don't come all the way from the other side of the Prut just for our health."

"You don't think," the big one added threateningly, "that we're going to drive your damn Jew cow through the woods for nothing, do you?"

Dvora looked up and met his eye. "So don't."

"So we won't!"

And off they stalked, leaving Tzickerl to graze in peace. Dvora waited till they were out of sight and then ran, laughing, to where Yudi and Dov were waiting. They hugged each other gleefully and danced about in wild elation. "Can you believe it?" Dvora chortled. "It really *worked*! Just like in Papa's story. Oh, blessings on you, Velvel the Tailor, wherever you are."

Dov's face sobered. "You know who really deserves the blessings, don't you?"

"*I* know," Yudi piped up. "Papa!"

Dov picked her up in his arms and whirled her around in a dizzying embrace. "Yes, you little smarty, you're absolutely right. Papa!"

3

*A*s it turned out, there was one major benefit for Dov in the move to Czernowitz—the proximity to Uncle Shmuel and the bookstore. As he grew older, Dov spent more and more time there, ostensibly to help out but, more accurately, to sit near the window and read. Books were his addiction. The time spent in the store was never enough. Shmuel could only marvel at the boy's omnivorous appetite for the printed page. It was the boy, rather than the store owner, who knew the substance of the product being peddled in the shop. Shmuel spent his time either working on his accounts or playing chess with Chaim the Capmaker, who had a tiny shop next door.

It was Dov who pored over every book that came in. Soon it was Dov who could find what a customer wanted, who could recommend a title to a doubtful client, who could identify an author's name from the merest of clues, and who could find where the most insignificant volume was hiding on the overcrowded shelves.

Shmuel didn't pay him. He broached the subject once, but the boy shook his head. "Pay me for reading, Uncle Shmuel? Don't be silly."

Shmuel understood the boy's reluctance. Taking payment would change the character of Dov's relationship to him and the store. It would impose an element of coercion into what had been freely and eagerly offered. So, instead, Shmuel gave regular "gifts" to his sister Mindel, to ease the strain caused by Leib's inability to eke out an adequate living.

At first Mindel hesitated to accept the gifts, embarrassed by her need for help and too proud to accept largesse even from her brother. But

Shmuel told her flatly that the gifts were payments for her son's services, "and worth every penny."

It didn't occur to Mindel to question her brother's statement. His judgment of Dov matched her own. To her the boy was worth his weight in gold. But only to Shmuel would she reveal her inner conviction that Dov was special. "Yes, he has a remarkable head on him, hasn't he?" she'd say, pocketing the money and turning to stare out the window. There would follow a moment of silence and a sigh. "Like his father," she would murmur at last.

Six months before Dov's thirteenth birthday, Leib brought a letter to Mindel from her father. Ephraim wrote to invite Dov to stay with his grandparents in Solitava until the time of his *bar mitzvah:* "Your uncle Nathan has offered to supervise the boy's preparatory studies, which is a very great condescension on his part under the circumstances. It was when he heard of the boy's scholarly gifts that he kindly made the offer. I hope you will be equally forgiving and let the boy come. Your mother says to assure you that she will look after him with all her grandmotherly devotion. She is already preparing your old room for the boy."

Mindel read the letter with a tense, angry face. "What's this? Why didn't you tell him that Dov's studies here in Czernowitz are quite satisfactory?"

Leib shifted his weight from one foot to the other in a guilty shuffle. "I don't know how satisfactory they are."

"Well, *I* know." She flicked a glaring look at him. "They are good enough. How did Nathan hear of Dov's scholarly gifts? If Shmuel has been bragging to him, I'll give my brother a piece of my mind!"

"Not only Shmuel. The Czernowitz Rabbi, too. And me, also."

"You? How *could* you? I told you I don't want him trained in Nathan's backward ways!"

"Backward or not, your Uncle Nathan is a Tzaddik. Who is the Czernowitz Rabbi to compare with him in scholarship? Besides, don't you think Dov deserves the honor of studying under his eye?"

"Such an honor we don't need. Dov is *my* son, not yours. I'll make the decisions."

Dov, listening outside the door, wanted to hit his mother. He came into the room ready to do battle on the side of his stepfather. "You're talking about me, aren't you? Have I nothing to say?"

Leib put an arm about the boy's shoulder. "He's right. Why shouldn't he have a say in this?"

Mindel expelled a breath of annoyance. "All right, we'll let him have a say. So, Dov, speak up. There's nothing wrong with your teacher here in Czernowitz, is there?"

"No, but—"

"But? Are you trying to say that you'd rather have your *bar mitzvah* in Solitava than right here as we always planned?"

"Yes. I'd rather have it in Solitava," the boy answered promptly, eager to show Papa that he was as much *his* son as Mama's.

Mindel's eyes blazed from her son's face to her husband's and back again. "All right, go! Do what you want! But if your mind is warped by the experience, it won't be any fault of mine."

So Dov went to his great-uncle Nathan's town to prepare for his *bar mitzvah*. The six months in Solitava proved to be an eye-opening experience for him. He lived in the home of his grandparents and studied in the Tzaddik's study house, sometimes under Great-uncle Nathan's own eye. He hoped to find the work exciting, to prove that his mother was wrong, but with a newly developing adult awareness, he saw for himself what his mother had tried to describe—the antiquated, superstitious narrowness of the Tzaddik's court. He didn't like it.

There were other things he learned during his short stay at the place of his mother's birth, things that had nothing to do with Judaic studies. He learned a great deal about his father. On several occasions he paid visits to his aunt Raizel's little house. Her husband, Itzik Kramer, the slaughterer, liked to spend evenings at the tavern, and when she felt deserted, Raizel often invited the boy to take supper with her. She would tuck her two children into bed and then sit with Dov near the stove in the kitchen and tell him stories about the past. Dov told himself that he didn't want to hear them, but he was fascinated in spite of himself. He felt that his curiosity about his father was somehow disloyal to his stepfather, but he rationalized his fascination with Raizel's stories by telling himself that he couldn't avoid listening without giving his aunt offense.

He discovered that his father was not only an admired scholar but "the hero of Ilinghovka" and an adulterer. After the evenings in Raizel's kitchen, he would go back to his bed in his grandmother's house and lie awake for hours, trying to picture his father, but he couldn't get a coherent image in his mind. There were too many conflicting impressions. Scholar, hero, adulterer, deserter . . . what sort of man *was* Avrum Gentz? There was only one clear impression that inched its way into his mind despite all his efforts to keep it out—Avrum Gentz seemed to be a much more magnetic personality than Leib Weisenberg.

The thought made him feel sick. Papa was such a *good* person. *He* would never leave home and forget all about the family he'd left behind, as Avrum Gentz had done. It was disgusting that Mama and Aunt Raizel still thought so highly of Avrum Gentz. Dov told himself that he hated Avrum Gentz more than ever.

At the end of one of those evenings in his aunt's kitchen, Raizel handed Dov a parcel. It was wrapped in soft paper, and the way she presented it to him signified that she felt it was something important. He opened it with a feeling of breathlessness. Inside was a gold watch with its face smashed. "It was your father's," Aunt Raizel said solemnly, her eyes moist. "I've saved it all these years. It doesn't work, but I thought you'd like to have it."

Dov didn't want it at all. But, he told himself, Aunt Raizel was sentimental, and he didn't want to hurt her by refusing it. He took it, promising himself that he would throw it away later.

His *bar mitzvah* was a great success, but he was glad to return to Czernowitz, to his home, his family, and the bookstore. And to the new school he was soon to start—the German *Handeln-schule*. While waiting to take the entrance examinations, he spent all his days at the bookstore. A few years earlier, at the age of ten or eleven, he'd read mostly stories—Herman Hesse and Hofmannsthal, *Four Feathers, The Sea Wolf, The Invisible Man,* Conrad's *Lord Jim,* and all of Sternow's many volumes about the American West. But now he found his interest in fiction waning. He began to read history and biography. A particular turning point in his intellectual growth occurred with his discovery (in an old packing crate in the back of the store) of a yellowing old volume by Christian Wilhelm Dohm called *Über die bürgerliche Verbesserung der Juden* (Concerning the Civil Improvement of the Jews). The book had been written more than a hundred years before but dealt with a subject that was still hotly debated in German politics: the place of Jews in German society. The author, evidently a "liberal" thinker of his time, argued that the Jews should indeed be given full citizenship, but in return they would be expected to improve their "debased" character, give up their tendency toward "separatism," and learn to control what other writers had described as their "extraordinary inclination for commerce, theft, fraud, and usury."

Dov was appalled. That the Jewish character was "debased," he suddenly realized, was an assumption underlying most of the books he'd read. Where had such an assumption come from? There was nothing in the characters of the people around him to account for such a description. When he'd been younger, he'd noted that, in fiction, the Jew was depicted, if at all, as a peripheral character—strange, ignorant, or ludicrous at best, threatening or villainous at worst. In his hunger to pursue the stories, he'd pushed his awareness of these insulting portraits to the back of his mind. After all, they'd been only works of fiction and, he supposed, had little to do with the real world. But Dohm's book dealt with historical *fact*. This was an evaluation of Dov's own people by an educated, worldly man. It was deeply troubling.

He had a need to discuss the matter with someone. Uncle Shmuel was the first one he tried, but the older man didn't even look up from his chessboard. "It's an old story," he said with a dismissive shrug. "The *goyim* hate us, so they say we're debased. You may as well get used to it."

This was not a satisfactory response. As Dov walked home through the late evening shadows with his coat collar up around his ears and his head lowered against the wind, he yearned for someone with whom to discuss the matter. If only his sisters had been a bit older. Dvora, at ten, had a native shrewdness and a rebellious, original way of thinking; in a few years she might be a good person to talk to. And Yudi, so eager and good-hearted that she would listen to Dov read aloud with rapt attention even if she didn't understand a word, would one day make a good sounding board for his ideas. But now she was only six.

When he got home he discovered that he'd had a stroke of luck— Papa was home a day early. Leib (who looked to Dov thinner and more bent every time he saw him after a week's absence) was just heading down to the cellar to bring up a load of firewood. Dov threw off his coat and muffler and followed his stepfather down the stairs. As the two of them sorted through the wood for stove-length pieces, Dov revealed the problem that was troubling him.

Leib didn't even pause in the act of stacking the wood. "So this German, whoever he is, says we're debased. This is big news?"

"It's news to me. Why does he think we're debased? I don't understand what's *debased* in practicing a different religion."

"What's to understand? It comes from hatred. Isn't it written somewhere that one can't find virtue where there's hatred? In the Book of Proverbs or somewhere?"

Dov was conscious of a stab of disappointment. Papa was not going to be any more helpful than Uncle Shmuel had been. He lowered his eyes. "Yes, Papa, but not in Proverbs. In the Shirat Yisrael."

Leib looked around, his face lighting up in pride. "See? I knew there was a saying somewhere. But I probably didn't say it right. How does it go, Dov?"

" 'Love blinds us to faults, but hatred blinds us to virtues.' " The boy dropped his eyes and took the load of logs from his stepfather's arms.

Leib gazed at his stepson with adoration. "That's it! Just so!" He started up the steps, shaking his head in wonder. "I don't know how you keep so much in that head of yours. It's a marvel."

Dov looked after him, depressed. Neither Papa nor Uncle Shmuel seemed capable of seeing the complexities of the subject, Shmuel because he'd probably argued the matter too frequently in his youth and Papa because—Dov hated to think it!—because Papa's mind worked only on the level of jokes and platitudes. Papa believed there was truth in the little proverbs and parables he'd collected in his head, but Dov was beginning to see that truth was too intricate and convoluted to be captured in clichés. Even the saying that he'd just quoted, which sounded so neat and so right, wasn't true. *Love blinds us to faults.* He loved Papa with all his heart, yet he could see with painful clarity that Papa's mind was not capable of depth. It occurred to him that perhaps Avrum Gentz might have been able . . . but no. He would not permit himself to think along those lines. He would not make unfair and unfavorable comparisons in his mind between his beloved Papa and the hated Avrum.

Later than night, just before going to bed, he came upon his mother seated at the now-cleared kitchen table, her head resting on her hand and that familiar, faraway look in her eyes. On an impulse he asked her, "Have you every heard of a book called *Über die bürgerliche Verbesserung der Juden?*"

Mindel blinked at her son in surprise. "The one by Dohm?"

A twinge of delight shot through him. "Yes, that's the one." He took an eager step toward her. "You *have* heard of it."

"Oh, yes. Your father used to speak of it."

Your father. Those words created a dark shadow in his chest and instantly dampened his excitement. Why did his mother always have that *ghost* on her mind? "I . . . I see," he said, falling back on his habitual way of avoiding her by taking a step in retreat.

She raised a hand toward him, as if to hold him there. "Why do you ask about it?" she inquired, surprised by this rare opportunity to share in the concerns of her son's mind and unwilling to let the moment slip away.

"No special reason." The boy edged to the door. "I just wondered if . . . if it was well known."

"Very well known." In desperation, she forced her mind to remember enough about the book to keep the conversation going. "That book made a mark on every German-speaking Jew in Europe."

"Did it?" Dov couldn't resist coming back to the table. "Why?"

"Because some of them tried to take Dohm's strictures to heart and change themselves, while the others—"

"*Change* themselves?" He dropped into the chair opposite hers. "Why would they want to change themselves?"

"Oh, there are a thousand reasons. It's hard to be a species apart, you see. Very hard, as you'll have to learn for yourself soon enough."

Dov made an impatient gesture. "I've learned enough already. I've read about the Beilis case in Russia, and I know about the Kishinev massacre, about Schönerer, and about Karl Lueger in Vienna. I've even had my own bouts with Jew-haters."

Her eyes searched his face. "Have you, my son?"

"Of course. How many times have I had to fight off their dogs? But I don't want to *change* because of it. It's the last thing I'd want to do."

"Well," she said, sighing, "many do want to change. Some want to do it for reasons of finance . . . to be able to do business in the world. Some want to enter into society, or civil service, or politics. Some want to go to universities. And some suffer from such self-hatred that they yearn to be something else."

Dov was silent, trying to digest all this. "Yes, I can see that. But . . ."

"But?"

He looked at her as if making an accusation. "But they are all—no matter what their reasons—*beneath contempt*!"

"Are they?" She shook her head at him, and her lips curled in amusement, as if she both disapproved of and was charmed by his boyish vehemence. "Are you saying that it's a sin to wish to change . . . to try to improve oneself or one's lot?"

"Isn't it? It's like agreeing with Dohm—like saying we *are* debased."

"No, it's not saying that at all. But there are many—and yes, perhaps I'm among them—who believe that we Jews have saddled ourselves with a weight of medieval customs, traditions, and beliefs that make a troublesome burden in modern times."

Dov stared at her with knit brows and then leaped to his feet angrily. "And you think we should dispose of our customs just because a Gentile government, offering us the bone of enfranchisement, wants us to sit up and beg for it?"

"I didn't say that." Her smile was now more pronounced and her eyes, fixed on his face, were gleaming. "Come now, Dov, sit down. When you fire up like that, you remind me of your father."

Again the shadow crossed his chest, this time with a chilling coldness. But he sat down. "What *are* you saying, then?"

"I'm only pointing out that it's possible—and forgivable—to believe that as a people we're not perfect. Not debased, but not perfect either."

He turned his eyes away from hers. It was her uncle, the autocratic, narrow-minded, antiquated Tzaddik of Solitava, who'd driven her to these thoughts, he realized. It was her Uncle Nathan and his court whom she considered medieval. Her beliefs were shaped by her experiences, by the tragedy of her past. Dov's immediate reaction was to reject what she'd said as ideas distorted by her personal prejudices, ideas formed in her mind by the father he'd never seen—Avrum, whose very name he'd come to hate. Yet of all the people around him, his mother was the only one who'd been able to stimulate his mind, the only one who's shown any depth at all. How could he dislike her and admire her at the same time? "Maybe we're not perfect," he said grudgingly, "but if I want to change *myself*, that's one thing. If someone *compels* me to change, that's quite another."

"Yes, my dear, I'll have to agree to that."

Dov rose from the chair. "Well, thank you, Mama," he said, turning to the door. "You've given me a lot to think about."

Mindel's fingers twisted together as she watched him go. It had been the most satisfying exchange she'd ever had with her son, and she hated to have it end. "Dov?"

He paused in the doorway. "Yes, Mama?"

"Have you ever read Moses Mendelssohn?"

He turned around and shook his head.

"You should read him. One of our greatest philosophers. He argued for Jews to move into the Enlightenment. But he also said that the state has no right to demand that Jews barter their religion in return for emancipation."

Dov stared at his mother in amazement. This entire conversation had been an unsettling surprise. "How did you learn all this, Mama?" he asked almost in spite of himself.

She gave a throaty, unexpected laugh. "Did you think me an unlettered fool? I'll have you know, my son, that I was the best student of scriptures in all of Solitava. Not that it was so great a feat. Solitava, despite our great Tzaddik, is only a little pond. But your father was a noted scholar, you know, and I used to study with him."

Your father again. Something in the boy's chest clenched. His whole body stiffened. "You've said 'your father' three times. I don't know whom you mean. Leib Weisenberg is my father."

Her breath caught in her throat. "But Dov, don't you want to know about—?"

"No, I don't." His heart seemed to have jumped up, palpitating, into his throat. He'd never spoken to her like this. But he felt he had to say what he was thinking. He made his voice cold, to mask any outward sign of weakness or emotion. "Your husband—your present husband—is all the father I need. I wish you'd remember that. Good night, Mama."

"Dov, wait!" She started from her seat. *"Dov!"*

But down the hall, his door slammed shut. She was too late.

She leaned back in her chair and put a shaking hand to her mouth. She'd had a chance, a rare chance, and she'd bungled it. A few moments ago she'd been congratulating herself on her erudition, her cleverness. But she'd been unbelievably stupid. She'd concentrated on impressing his mind, but she'd forgotten his heart. While trying to win him with one hand, she'd lost him with the other.

---------------- **4** ----------------

It was a strange childhood. We watched Mama grow more bitter and remote with each passing day. Dvora, resentful of Mama's unloving attitude, needled her constantly. Dov stayed away from home as much as possible, but we could all see how Mama hovered over him or devoured him with her eyes when he was home. Yes, Sam, I can hear you ask, "What about you?" Well, as for me, I was coddled and petted by Papa, indulged by Dov, and teased by Dvora, but Mama hardly seemed to notice me at all. But that was soon to change.

Papa was aware of the tensions of our household, but he tried to turn everything into a joke. We lived together in the small house in entirely separate worlds. The only thing we did together was read aloud at night. Mama made us. We had to take turns, every evening, reading aloud from books in English. Mama insisted on it, because, she said, someday we would go to America. Someday . . . when we had money . . .

Dov had done well on the exams. He entered his new school with more self-confidence and open-mindedness than he'd had when he first came to Czernowitz. He began to make good friends. He became particularly close to two other Jewish boys in his class because they, too, were addicted to reading: Hershel Waksman (familiarly known as Hersh the Fresser because he loved to eat and showed it in his protruding belly and double chin) and Eliezer "Squinty Eli" Reiss, who, gangly and bespectacled, lived more in a dream world than in the real one. Early in their friendship, the three boys took to meeting after school at the bookstore, where they spent long hours in the late afternoons discussing life, Zionism, and the Mystery of Girls.

The locale suited them perfectly. There was no interference from bothersome parents at the bookstore. Shmuel was rarely there, for as soon as Dov arrived after school, Shmuel took off to play chess next door with Chaim the Capmaker. The boys, blissful in their privacy (which was only occasionally interrupted by the entrance of a customer), drank tea that Dov brewed for them on the pot-bellied stove that warmed the store, ate their fill of sticky buns or cream pastry provided for them by Hersh the Fresser (whose father, the owner of the Waksman Glassworks, was well-to-do and supplied his son with plenty of pocket money), and talked.

They had plenty to talk about. The state of European Jews in those years was chaotic. In eastern Europe, under the influence of a cruelly anti-Semitic government, most of the Russian Jews had been driven into the Pale, where they lived in abject poverty and were subjected to periodic massacres, riots, and humiliations, like the Beilis case of 1911. The boys talked for weeks about that.

In western Europe, the German government, while according its Jewish population certain civil rights, demanded in return an assimilation into the German culture so extreme that it amounted to the surrendering of all Jewishness. This Dov found particularly offensive, and he ranted to his friends against it with great vehemence. "All those Jews who try to blend into the mainstream haven't done themselves or us any good at all," he pointed out. "Did it prevent the popularity of Schönerer or Vergani? Did it prevent Karl Lueger, that Jew-hater, from becoming Mayor of Vienna?"

The almost fanatical nationalism that was pervading Europe had a disturbing effect on Jewish boys. They sensed that the various crusades toward a "united Germany for all Germans" or a "separate Serbia for all the Serbs" were not movements that would help Jews. In fact, those nationalistic urges that were dominating the European political scene only strengthened the boys' feeling that they would be alien wherever they lived.

Dov found a letter in a German-language periodical in which an intellectual Jew, who had tried to convert, expressed his despair. Dov read it to his friends. The man had written: "We are so tired, oh, so tired of our Judaism which separates us from our [German] people. The precious possession, which natures bestows on the infant in the cradle, *peoplehood*, is denied us. Into Germanism we cannot enter, to Judaism we do not wish to return. We continue to walk our hopeless road alone. The great crime of the crucifixion is punished to the thousandth generation."

Such bitter rejection of Jewishness was extreme, Dov admitted, but the conditions that encouraged it were reprehensible to the idealistic youth and his friends. They were beginning to see that, for Jews, there was only one of four possible choices for their future: they could try to blend into the surrounding culture by assimilating its values, as the poor fellow who had written the letter had done; they could try to escape to America; they could dream of founding a new nation of the Jews themselves—in other words, turn to Zionism; or they could hold on to the medieval ways of their Jewish ancestors with a stubborn, desperate tenacity, as if to a life belt.

During the next few years the three boys shared everything—their thoughts, their books, their worldly goods and their time. Under Dov's influence, they read everything they could find on the subject of the establishment of a Jewish state. They read Moses Hess, the socialist who said that Jews would "always remain strangers among nations." They read Rabbi Kalischer and the brilliant Leo Pinsker, who bitterly wrote that the Jews of Europe were worse than aliens—that they were regarded by their governments as merely ghosts. And they read the best of all, Theodor Herzl, who made the dream of a Jewish state in Palestine seem a real possibility. Dov kept a copy of *Der Judenstaat* always at hand for inspiration and to settle arguments.

And argue they did. Hours on end. In spite of their reading the same books, each one of the three had a different position on the subject. Squinty Eli, the dreamer, believed that the European governments could be made more enlightened and could learn to accept Jews into the mainstream. Hersh, the more practical one, was head over heels in love with America. That big, brawling land across the Atlantic held the best hope for a Jew, he believed. "In America," he'd say, licking the remains of powdered sugar from his fingers, "everyone worships God as he pleases and gets rich in the bargain. Who can ask for more than that?"

"America!" Dov would say in a tone of sardonic disparagement. "Everyone always talks of going to America. Why is it always *there* that Jews want to run?" He had little patience for discussing America. America was the place to which everyone assumed his father had gone. The cursed Avrum. Dov had no intention of following those footsteps. He believed he had become a disciple of Theodor Herzl because of the intellectual soundness of his arguments. But in the back of his mind he knew that he'd become a Zionist more in rebellion against his unknown father than because of Herzl's arguments. If Avrum Gentz had chosen America over Palestine, then he, Dov, would choose Palestine over America.

In the next few years, he didn't let a day go by without trying to bring his friends around to his position. It was Theodor Herzl who had the answer, he repeated daily. Palestine was the rightful place for the Jews.

By the time Dov reached his sixteenth year, he'd grown in size and mind. He liked school; he liked his friends; he enjoyed his days. He was big and strong, his head was bursting with ideas for the future, and he believed he had firm control of his destiny. If only his mother hadn't been so strange—so fixated on her past and so depressing to the spirits of those around her—he might have considered himself content.

But then came the year 1913.

. . . That was a crucial time for us, Sam . . . a year in which we suffered a series of shocks. Nineteen thirteen—the year I was ten. By the end of it, our lives had changed so abruptly that we still carry the scars. . . .

The first surprise of 1913 was Uncle Shmuel's marriage. After almost forty years of contented bachelorhood, Shmuel decided to take a wife. The girl he chose was half his age and so shy that when Shmuel brought her to Mindel's house for Sabbath dinner early that spring, the girl never lifted her eyes from her plate. Leib promptly dubbed her Temele of the Lowered Eyes. But before the name had had time to take hold, the shy Temele blossomed out. With marriage, Temele's entire personality seemed to change. She began to walk with a strut, to carry her head high, and to cast sly looks about her. And playing about her lips was a decided cat-who-ate-the-canary smile.

Uncle Shmuel, too, underwent a change. From the moment his bride moved into the suite of rooms he'd fixed up for her over the bookstore, his hitherto simple life was altered. There was nothing he wouldn't do for his young bride. Her every whim had to be indulged. And Temele's whims were many. One day it was a new scarf she had to have, the next a set of dishes, the following day a pair of silver combs. Shmuel, who'd always managed to make enough money to satisfy his needs, suddenly found himself short. The revenue from his little bookstore was not enough to keep Temele's desires satisfied.

The obvious solution for Shmuel was to hire a clerk to take care of the bookstore all day while he, Shmuel, took a position somewhere else. In that way he could retain a portion of the store's income while supplementing it with a new salary. He was a trained bookkeeper; he had no doubt he could find work.

But before this could be accomplished, the second shock of the year took place. Leib, while dragging a mule to a prospective buyer in Solitava, was stricken with a seizure in his chest and collapsed unconscious on the ground. He was taken to the home of his father-in-law, Ephraim Rossner, and a message was sent to his family in Czernowitz.

As soon as he got the news, Dov raced to Hersh's house and borrowed the Waksman buckboard and one of their horses. He drove to Solitava at breakneck speed, reaching his grandparents' house late at night. His grandmother, Etel Fruma, advised him not to disturb the patient, but Leib heard their voices in the hall. "Dov, is that you?" he asked feebly.

Dov entered the room where Leib lay. To Dov's stricken eyes the man looked emaciated, and the skin of his face seemed blue. Dov knelt beside the bed and took Leib's hand. The older man's eyes filled with tears.

"Don't cry, Papa," Dov whispered, choked. "It'll be all right."

"You'll take me home?" Leib asked pathetically. "Now?"

"Well, I . . ." He looked up at his grandmother, standing worriedly in the doorway. "I don't know if . . ."

"Not now," Etel Fruma said decisively. "Plenty of time tomorrow to talk about going home."

"Can't we go now?" Leib pleaded, his eyes fixed on Dov's with a look of helpless pain, like a stricken animal.

Dov couldn't bear that look. He squared his shoulders. He could make the decision as well as his grandmother. "If you want to go now, Papa, we will," he said and lifted his stepfather into his arms. It was like lifting a bag of bones.

Leib gripped the boy tightly around the neck. "I'm being carried like . . . like . . ."

"Like a prince of all the Russias," Dov said, trying not to let the agony in his chest show in his voice.

Leib gave him a ghostly smile. "You remember? The day I found you with the broken ankle?"

"Of course I remember."

Tears filled his eyes again. "Now *you* have to carry *me*."

Dov tried to fight his own tears. He smiled shakily and shrugged. "It's only fair."

But Leib was aware of the young man's tears. "There, you see? It's like the old saying—when a father helps a son, both smile; but when a son must help a father, both cry."

. . . We didn't send for a doctor, Sam. Only in America do the poor go to doctors. We never saw a doctor in all our lives. But when we saw Papa that night, we didn't need a doctor to tell us that his heart had been affected.

After a week he insisted on getting out of bed. Mama permitted it, but she knew that Papa would no longer be able to travel back and forth to Solitava. He could try to do some business in Czernowitz, but if we were to be certain of having food on the table, the money would have to come from somewhere else. . . .

Dov knew what had to be done. He had to stop his schooling and take a job. And the obvious one was in the bookstore. Uncle Shmuel needed a full-time clerk. Dov would be that clerk, at a fixed salary.

Uncle Shmuel found work at the Waksman Glassworks before Leib rose from his sickbed. Before the week was out, Dov had resigned from school and begun to take over the full running of the bookstore.

Leaving school was no great tragedy. He was sixteen, after all. How many years could he expect to spend without gainful employment? And besides, the bookstore was as appealing a place as the classroom. At least that was what Dov tried to tell himself.

Although Hersh and Eli continued to come to the store after school, helping Dov to pretend to himself that life was not so different from what it had been, the reality was that things had changed. Papa was home permanently now, looking gray of cheek and helpless of eye. And something had changed deep within Dov's soul. His sense of having a grip on the future had been shaken.

And 1913 wasn't half over yet.

5

The three boys continued to discuss life, Zionism, and the Mystery of Girls at the bookstore, but the order of importance had changed. More and more, the mysterious nature of women began to occupy the young men's thoughts. In varying degrees of urgency, all three were becoming aware of the potency of manhood. The subject of females came most readily to their tongues because it was now uppermost in their minds. "It's even pervading my dreams," Eli despondently admitted.

Fat Hersh was the first of the three to experience in actuality what all three were dreaming of. His mother employed a household staff of two: an elderly housekeeper-cook and a young country girl named Gerda to assist the elder. The youthful housemaid did not struggle for long against Hersh's passionately whispered entreaties, and on the afternoon following his Big Breakthrough he appeared at the bookstore glowing with triumph. The experience had been, he assured them, more thrilling than they had dared to dream.

Hersh's succeeding encounters with his housemaid—in his mother's sewing room, on a pile of flour sacks in the pantry, in the stable, and on Gerda's rickety bed in a tiny attic room—soon became regular occurrences. After each act of copulation Hersh told his friends all about it, completely unimpeded by shyness or modesty. If any instincts for manly reticence asserted themselves, his feeling of closeness toward his friends overcame them. His generosity in sharing the details drove Dov and Eli mad with envy.

But generosity was a large part of Hersh's character. He was almost as eager for his friends to experience what he was experiencing as they were themselves, and he took it upon himself to find a pair of suitable *tsatskelehs* for his friends. He asked his Gerda if she had any young friends in the vicinity, but she had not yet made any. Undeterred, he canvassed the shops near the bookstore to see if a couple of young shopgirls might be enlisted in the cause. He got his face slapped twice for his pains. He even suggested to his friends that they pay a visit to a certain *bordel* he'd heard of, with all costs on him. But by this time Dov and Eli had had enough of his officiousness and ordered him to mind his own business. "You're acting like the Procurer in a Roman comedy," Dov told him. "Enough already."

Nonetheless, Hersh kept his eyes open. With his superior sophistication, he reasoned, he would be the one to recognize any promising prospects. Thus it was he who first drew Eli's attention to the slim, dark-eyed young vixen who stopped in at the bookshop one rainy afternoon. At first Hersh gaped at her in amazement. In all the years he'd spent in the store he'd never imagined that a creature so appealing would wander inside.

The girl's magnificent long hair and fringed shawl were spattered with droplets of icy rain. While she struggled to close her umbrella— an antiquated, almost useless contraption—Hersh looked her over with a detachment made possible only because he had a sweetheart of his own. "Now *there*," he whispered to Eli with enthusiasm, "is a juicy pullet if ever I saw one."

Eli turned and squinted at her. The girl was very young—too young to be considered a candidate for their nefarious purposes—but she was indeed appetizing. Eli's eyes bulged behind his thick spectacles. The girl pulled off her shawl to shake the raindrops from it and thus was open to their enraptured scrutiny. Her hair was tied carelessly back at the nape of her neck with a bit of satin ribbon, revealing a lustrously pale face with strong cheekbones (made ruddy by a wind unusually icy for September) and a full-lipped, sensuous mouth. She wore a schoolgirlish middy blouse and a long blue skirt, but the legs and a pair of shapely ankles that could be seen beneath the hem were anything but schoolgirlish. Her waist was tiny, and above it, a pair of remarkably conical, firm breasts caught Eli's fascinated gaze. He was, from that moment, a lost man.

Dov, who hadn't heard Hersh's whispered comment, came out from behind the cashbox and approached the newcomer in annoyance. "What are you doing here, Dvora?" he asked belligerently. "Mama doesn't want you walking about the city alone."

"It was Mama who sent me, Mr. Know-it-all," she answered waspishly.

"Oh, damn," Hersh muttered in disappointment, "she's his sister."

"Mama told me to bring you these," Dvora was saying. "You forgot them this morning." And from a crocheted pouch that hung from her elbow she withdrew a pair of shabby overshoes.

"I didn't forget them. I didn't want them," Dov muttered in disgust, taking them anyway. "A little wetness on my shoes won't hurt me."

"Then take the matter up with Mama. Don't squabble with me over it." While she spoke, her eyes roved over the store, taking in the two young men who still gaped at her in speechless admiration. "Customers?" she inquired in the tone of heavy irony that had become her customary way of speaking, meanwhile meeting Hersh's eyes and looking him over with an expression of unmistakable disparagement.

"They're my friends. This is Hershel Waksman, and the tall one behind him is Eliezer Reiss."

Hersh made a formal, Germanic bow. "How do you do, Miss Gentz?"

"Weisenberg," Dvora corrected. "I'm his half sister."

"Ah, yes, I forgot. Miss Weisenberg, then." He edged closer to Eli, elbowed him in the ribs and muttered under his breath, "Say hello, you nincompoop!"

"H-hello," Eli stuttered, flushing.

Dvora's eyes flicked over him with no more approval than she'd shown Hersh. "Well, I'd better be going," she said after a moment. She gave her shawl another shake and prepared to toss it over her shoulders.

Hersh stepped forward with gentlemanly aplomb. "Allow me," he said, and with a superior smirk at Eli, took the shawl from her hands and dropped it carefully over her.

Dvora threw him a glance that indicated clearly that his exaggerated gallantry did not impress her. "Thank you," she said in her sarcastic style.

But Eli was impressed by Hersh's self-assurance. If Hersh (who was certainly not an imposing figure, with his lack of stature and his rotundity) could conduct himself with women with such aplomb, then perhaps he, Eli, could do as well. With awkward determination, he stepped in front of Dvora, blocking her path to the door. "M-may I s-see you home, Miss Weisenberg?" he stammered.

Dvora looked up at him again, her eyes coolly speculative. Then she shrugged. Wordlessly, she handed him her umbrella, flipped the corner of her shawl over her shoulder, brushed by him, and marched to the door.

Eli gave Hersh and Dov a look that was half-ecstatic, half-triumphant, and scurried in long-legged clumsiness after the departing girl, attempting to open her umbrella as he ran. Dov and Hersh gaped at each other in astonishment and dashed to the door to watch. By the time Eli had opened the umbrella, Dvora was several yards ahead of him and not so much as glancing back. The two watchers observed in fascinated silence as Dvora turned the corner and was lost to their view, but their last glimpse of Eli made them hoot. With his coat flapping behind him in the wind, he was running after the disappearing girl with all the speed his ungainly legs would allow, splashing heedlessly through the puddles and holding the umbrella out ahead of him uselessly as the rain pelted down on the heads of both of them.

After that encounter, it was useless for Hersh to try to interest Eli in anyone else. Eli was in love. However long it took, he declared, he would save himself for Dvora. The dreamer now had something new to dream of. No reality that Hersh could propose interested Eli half so much as the dream of consummation with Dvora.

But, Hersh consoled himself, there was still Dov. Dov was no foolish dreamer but a man of action. If anyone needed the experience of having a woman, it was Dov. And it didn't matter that Dov pretended to indifference. Hersh knew better.

Dov couldn't have said, later, whether it had begun as a figment of Hersh's sexually fevered imagination or whether Temele had intended it herself from the first. But certainly it was Hersh who put the idea into Dov's head. Temele had always—since the first month of her marriage—been known to slip down from her upstairs apartment to visit the store when she was bored with her housekeeping or with herself. She would appear without warning at the doorway that led to the back stairs and look around. If there was a customer present, she would go upstairs again. If not, she would wander about aimlessly, fingering a book or looking over Dov's shoulder to see what he was reading. Then she would give him a smile and disappear as silently as she'd come. Dov thought nothing of it.

But then she began to appear more regularly. She would make an appearance several afternoons during the week, even when Eli and Hersh were present. She would stand in the doorway, a mysterious smile on her lips and a dish of strudel in her hand. "I thought you and your friends might be hungry," she'd say, her eyes on Dov's face.

"She's after you," Hersh decided, chortling with glee. "She married an old man and now she's itching for a young one."

"Don't be a fool," Dov retorted. "Uncle Shmuel's not so old."

"No? He's your mother's older brother, isn't he? He could be a grandfather."

"Shut up, Hersh. You're so active with your lower parts, I think your upper ones are getting stale."

"Is that so? Well, they're not so stale that they can't figure out women better than yours can. I tell you, Dov, she's after you, like it or not. And if I were you, I'd like it." He threw his friend an expression that was supposed to be an evil leer, but his face was so openly pleasant and plump that the leer only looked silly. "After all, you don't want *your* 'lower parts' to atrophy from disuse, do you?"

Dov responded by stuffing a large piece of strudel into his friend's mouth and pushing him, sputtering loudly, into an empty crate.

But the next time Temele came downstairs, he felt himself redden to the ears and couldn't meet her eyes.

One day she came down when he was alone. He hunched over his book and took no notice of her. She came up behind him and stroked his shoulder. "What strong arms you have, Dov," she murmured.

"Mmmmph," he grunted, pretending complete absorption in his reading, and she went away.

It's nothing, he told himself. Hersh is making me crazy.

Not long afterward, on a morning when business had been completely stalled by heavy rain, he heard her call his name from upstairs. He was unpacking a large shipment of *Der Tunnel* (a new novel that was selling very well) when he heard her voice. Puzzled, he went to the foot of the stairs. "Temele, did you call me?"

"Yes, Dov. Can you come upstairs for a minute?"

Dov felt real discomfort. "Upstairs?"

"Yes, please."

His heart began to pound. "But . . . the store . . ."

"Never mind the store, *dumkopf*. No one will come in this weather."

He mounted the stairs slowly, his hands sweaty and the organs in his chest frozen in fear. "What do you need me for?" he asked at the top.

"I'm in here," came her voice from the next room. "Come on."

She was sitting on the edge of the bed, wearing a thin wrapper over what was obviously her naked body, and her lips were curled in her sly, enigmatic smile. Deliberately, she shook the wrapper from her left shoulder. She was lovely.

His knees were shaking, and he could hardly breathe. He leaned on the doorframe for support.

"Come and sit down," she said softly, smoothing the coverlet beside her.

"Temele, I . . . *can't.* He's my uncle!"

"Don't be a *narr.* You'll be doing him a favor."

"A favor?"

"Yes. His wife won't have to make those annoying demands on him so often."

Dov reddened. "That's some favor."

"It is. You can take my word." And she pulled the wrapper from her other shoulder.

Later he hated himself for it. He was an adulterer, like his despised father. Like Avrum. He loathed himself. But every time she called him, he went.

He suffered hours of agonizing guilt for every one of the brief moments of exquisite pleasure. The thought that he could be like his father sickened him. But worse, he despised his disloyalty to his uncle. He was very fond of Uncle Shmuel. How could he permit himself to cuckold so good and kind a man?

He was haunted by the fear that his uncle would come home one day and find them squirming together in their nakedness. Sooner or later, he knew, there was bound to be a confrontation. Fate . . . God . . . *justice* demanded it! Every work of literature dealing with adultery had prepared him for it. Confrontation was inevitable.

At night he lived the scene in dreams. He'd be kissing Temele's soft flesh and look up to find his uncle's face looming over him. Shmuel's expression would be terrible, and he'd raise a knife threateningly over Dov's head. Dov would wake up sweating in terror, the sound of Temele's screams ringing in his ears.

But he continued to go up to her whenever she called. And Uncle Shmuel never did discover them.

6

By this time Dvora had had all the schooling that Jewish girls without wealth could expect. She had nothing to look forward to but marriage to someone her parents would find for her, and until that marriage was arranged, she had no choice but to help her mother with the household duties. Since her relationship with her mother was completely antagonistic, Dvora was far from content with her lot.

... That antagonism, Sam, was of long standing. From the time that Dvora was old enough to understand that Mama held fast to an attachment to a man other than her husband, Dvora resented her. A woman was supposed to care for her husband, not for some stranger from the past. Mama, therefore, was bad. Dov concurred in that judgment, which only reinforced Dvora's conviction that she was right. If Mama had tried to reach Dvora—to confide in her, or to attempt in any way to come close to her—Dvora would have rejected the approach. But Mama never even made the attempt. ...

Having to spend her days in the same house with her mother was very irritating to Dvora. In addition, her chores bored her. Mindel had turned the cow's fecundity into a small business by supplying a few of the neighbors with butter and cream on a regular basis, and it became Dvora's task to do the milking, the churning, and the delivering. She was also expected to help clean the kitchen, do some of the cooking, and walk ten-year-old Yudi to and from school. It was, she told herself daily, a rotten life.

The entrance of Eli Reiss into her life was the only source of distraction she had. True, Eli was not the sort of romantic figure of whom girls weave their dreams, but he was better than nothing. When he began to wait outside Yudi's school and follow them home, Dvora was amused. First she pretended not to notice him, but after a while she nodded to him, then smiled, and then allowed him to walk beside her. The walk home began to take longer and longer as Dvora indulged herself in the pleasure of teasing and tormenting her admirer.

Yudi liked the tall, gangling young man who was courting her sister with such patient devotion, and therefore, when the three of them dallied along the road, the little girl did nothing to disturb their flirtation. She didn't try to hurry her sister along or interrupt the conversation. She merely watched the goings-on with her bright, observant eyes and made herself inconspicuous.

But their mother grew irritated at their later and later arrivals. "What's been taking you so long?" she demanded of the girls one day.

Dvora merely shrugged, but Yudi innocently volunteered the information that they'd been talking to Eli.

"Eli? Who's Eli?"

"Nobody," Dvora answered, throwing Yudi a dagger look. "A friend of Dov's."

Mindel's eyebrows rose suspiciously. "A friend of Dov's? You just happened to meet him?"

Dvora gave her little sister a surreptitious, warning pinch. "Yes. By accident."

"But you've been coming late for days. Have you met him 'by accident' often?"

"No."

Mindel looked at Yudi for corroboration, but the little girl bit her lip and lowered her eyes. Their mother gave them both a look of disgust. "Well, don't let it happen again. I want no more 'accidental' meetings."

Dvora glared at her mother. "Is it my fault if people come along the road? Can't I even *talk* to anybody if I want to?"

"Mind your tone, Miss Vinegar Tongue. If a young man wants to talk to you, let him come here and call on you properly."

"What do you mean, 'call on you'?" Dvora shot back. "Who am I, the Queen of Sheba, that I have to be 'called on'?"

"You're a direct descendent of Rabbi Israel of Ruzhin, that's who you are, not some tart of the streets who takes up with every he-goat who passes by and tips his hat."

"Eli isn't a he-goat, Mama," Yudi corrected gently. "He's very nice. He gives me peppermints, and—"

"And you, Miss Yahudis Weisenberg," Mindel cut in sharply, "are old enough to know better than to take candy from strangers!"

"But he's not a str—" But another, much crueler pinch from her sister stilled Yudi's tongue.

Mindel looked from one to the other sternly. "All right, enough. I've said what needs to be said. I expect you home tomorrow on time, and that's all."

But that wasn't all. Dvora was too much like her mother in instinctive rebelliousness to accept the decree. She continued to dawdle with Eli, causing a state of near war between herself and her mother.

Leib tended to avoid situations of this sort, firmly believing that a man, when coming upon two women arguing, should reach for his hat. But one day a scene between Mindel and Dvora was enacted before his eyes, and he couldn't avoid it. Dvora had come in later than usual, and Mindel had had to prepare supper without any help. "That's it!" she said furiously when Dvora and Yudi at last made their appearance. "That's the last time! It's been dark outside for two hours. If you can't be trusted to bring Yudi straight home—"

"Come, come, Mindele," Leib placated. "So they're a little late." He gave Yudi an affectionate pat on her backside and tried to lighten the atmosphere. "Even Adam was sometimes late for dinner, eh, Yudi, my little one? And what did Eve do when Adam was late?"

Yudi giggled, glad to join in the attempt to distract Mama. "She counted his ribs."

Leib chortled loudly. "Right!" He poked his wife gently on her side. "You hear, Mindele? Isn't that a howl? Why aren't you laughing?"

His wife gave him one of her icy looks. "Go ahead, joke. Make jokes while your daughter destroys her reputation."

"Who cares about my reputation?" Dvora muttered.

"I care. So you can stay home in the afternoons from now on," her mother shot back.

"So what?" Dvora taunted. "I can meet him other times . . . and other places."

"And I can lock you up in your room!" Mindel's hands were clenched in fury.

Leib tried again to ease the tension. "What's all this about?" he asked his wife. "Who is this boy, anyway? Do we know him?"

"He's nobody important," Dvora said in disgust. "She's making a *tsimmes* over nothing. It's only Dov's friend."

"If he's Dov's friend, let him come and talk to you here in the house in the proper way," Mindel ordered.

"I don't *want* him to come to the house. Do you want to give him the idea that . . . that I'm going to *marry* him or something?"

131

"Well, if you don't want to marry him, why do you have to see him at all?" her mother asked in exasperation.

"Because he's a *change*!"

"A change?" Leib looked from his daughter to his wife bewilderedly. "What does she mean, a change?"

"I mean a change from all this. From having to spend the whole day long with nobody to talk to but Mama. A change from being caged inside the walls of this *stupid house*!" And she stalked off to the bedroom she shared with Yudi and slammed the door.

"Dvora Weisenberg, come back here!" Mindel ordered.

Leib put a restraining hand on her shoulder. "Let her be," he said softly. "Why make so much of this? If the boy's a friend of Dov's, I don't see what harm there is in letting her talk to him a little."

"Oh, you don't see the harm, eh?" She shook off his hand with a snort of scorn. "Another gem from the lips of the sage of the house. Why don't you take a good look at your daughter? Can't you see what's right in front of your eyes? She has the ways of a *corve*. Is that the future you want for your daughter? You want a whore?"

Leib shook his head. "Maybe I'm not a sage, but I have eyes. I look at my daughter all the time, but that's not what I see."

"No? All right, my sage, tell me what *you* see."

"I see a young woman who looks . . ."

"Yes? So? Who looks how?"

Leib looked with a strange, intent sadness at his wife's face. ". . . who looks very much like her mother used to look at that age," he said and turned away.

Dvora, her ear at the door, was surprised by her mother's word for her—*corve*. She'd never in her life even kissed a boy, yet her mother thought of her as loose and wanton. In her heart she wondered if her mother might be right. She was full of strange feelings that she couldn't interpret—burnings and yearnings that she was certain were sinful. She noticed how boys looked at her, and she liked the gleam in their eyes. It made her want to walk with a swagger, to hold her chest out, to entice their attention even more. Were those the signs of a wanton?

The next day she decided to try an experiment. It was a very warm day for fall. When Eli joined her and Yudi on the way home, she was unusually sweet to him. She told him she wanted to speak to him alone and sent Yudi on ahead. "Come, let's walk through the woods," she requested, her eyes mischievous and inviting.

But the woods were on the military grounds where, even now, they could see in the distance a platoon of dragoons putting their horses through their paces. "I don't think—" Eli demurred, his eyes on the hazy, distant figures.

She followed his glance. "Don't be ridiculous. They never come here. And even if one of them should wander in this direction, he'd never see us in the woods. Come on."

She led him into the trees until they stood in the deepest part, where the daylight barely penetrated the thick, goldening leaves of the beeches and the dense, dark firs. "Put your coat on the ground," she said softly, and when he did so, she sat down on it and pulled him down beside her. "Now kiss me, Eli," she murmured in his ear.

His skin tingled from the feel of her breath, but he couldn't quite believe what he'd heard. "What?"

"Kiss me. You want to, don't you?"

"Yes, more than anything. But—"

She frowned in disgust. "If someone offered *me* something I wanted 'more than anything,' I wouldn't waste time with buts."

Eli, his long legs trembling, leaned over and kissed her cheek. But Dvora turned her head, put her hand up to his face, and kissed him squarely on the mouth. Eli was terrified. In all the daydreams in which he'd kissed her, he'd never imagined the scene like this. It had always been in a bedroom, on their wedding night. Their first kiss, he believed, should be sanctified, holy, blessed by the spirit of God and the approbation of their people. Here, hiding in the woods, was not the way he'd dreamed it.

It was not what she'd dreamed either. She withdrew her face and stared at him, obviously disappointed. "You're afraid, aren't you?" she accused. "That's what's wrong. Why must you be such a coward?"

"Well, you see, I never—"

"I know you never. I never did either. But you don't see me shivering like a rabbit. Come, Eli, be a man. I'll give you another chance if you put some spirit in it."

Eli tried to comply. The situation was a dream come true, even if the circumstances and the surroundings were not what he'd envisioned. He put his arms around her and kissed her with a desperate earnestness.

She remained in his embrace for a long while, but when at last she broke from it, the disappointed expression still remained in her eyes. She studied him thoughtfully. "I don't know . . ." she muttered, shaking her head in confusion.

"Is s-something wrong?" Eli stammered, the blood coursing through him with frightening urgency. "I'm full of s-spirit, really I am." He couldn't let her believe him cowardly. He reached out for her. "Let me try again."

She regarded him with a measuring stare. "Wait a minute," she said, holding him off. Slowly she put both hands to her hair, lifting up the tresses in a stretching movement that made him dizzy to watch. Then, without warning, she lay down on the ground. Her hair spread out around her face and rested on the dead leaves that matted the ground. She lifted her arms to him. "All right, let's try again."

He leaned over her, heart beating. A large part of his mind didn't want him to be doing this. It was a defilement, a corruption of the purity of his dreams of her. He loved her, despite this tendency of hers to be impetuous and headstrong, and the dreamer in him wanted to restrain her, to urge her to wait for the beautiful, sanctified day when all would be pure. But another part of him wanted urgently to seize the moment. Reality might not be as beautiful as the dream, but it was *here.* Her real arms were reaching up, her cool fingers were touching his throat in *actuality,* and the presence of reality proved too strong for him to keep his dreams intact. With a groan of surrender he fell upon her and let his instincts take over, kissing her with an abandon completely unfamiliar to him. His dreams were forgotten, the trees above him and the ground beneath seemed to recede from his consciousness; he was aware only of the thrilling presence of the girl beneath him and the mad tumult of his own blood.

But all at once she made a violent movement, and he found himself being pushed away. He rolled over clumsily, emitting a bewildered cry, while Dvora jumped up and strode away through the trees. "Dvora, wait—!" he shouted, his voice choked with blocked passion. "What's the *matter? Wait* for me!" But he could no longer see even the blue flash of her skirt through the trees. She was gone.

Dvora slowed her stride as she neared home. She wanted a few more moments to think before entering the house. She had to make sense of the confusion in her mind. One thing was clear, however; she hadn't enjoyed the short bout of lovemaking she'd just indulged in. She didn't know why, but it had not been at all what she'd expected. Maybe she wasn't a wanton after all. She smiled to herself in relief. It might have been troublesome to be a wanton.

The smile still lingered on her lips as she stepped in the door. Her mother and Yudi were already setting the plates on the table for supper. "So," her mother said coldly, not looking up, "now you don't even care enough to bring your sister home."

"Oh, Mama, I'm old enough to come home by myself," Yudi declared.

"Be still!" Mindel snapped. "I'm not talking to you." She wheeled on Dvora. "And where have you been all—?" The words died on her lips.

Dvora didn't understand her mother's suddenly frozen expression. "I haven't been anywhere," she said.

Mindel walked toward her slowly, lifted a hand and pulled a dead leaf from Dvora's hair. She held it before her daughter's eyes in silent accusation and then, shockingly, struck the girl across the face.

Yudi cried out, but Dvora made no sound. She put her hand to her stinging cheek, gave her mother a look of loathing, and walked out of the room.

. . . *After that day, Dvora took me home from school promptly. She no longer dawdled on the road nor gave Eli a moment's attention. But she never spoke a direct word to Mama again.*

7

Dov and Eli were sitting on a pair of packing cases in the rear of the bookstore, each with a book open on his lap. But neither was reading. Eli was staring glumly out into space, agonizing over his failure to persuade Dvora to speak to him, while Dov was listening intently to the footsteps overhead. Temele's footsteps. Temele was pacing back and forth aimlessly, and he wondered if she would dare call downstairs while Eli was with him. Only this morning he'd refused, for the first time, to answer her summons, and he had yet to discover just what she intended to do about it.

The bell over the door tinkled. They looked up to see Hersh posed in the doorway, one hand on his hip, the other raised over his head like a dancer waiting for the music to begin.

"Hersh? What—?" Dov began.

"Ya-*tat*-ta-*tat*-ta-*ta*!" Hersh sang as he danced up to them. "You'll *ne*ver, *ne*ver *guess* . . ."

Eli and Dov exchanged curious glances. "I guess the bakery has his favorite lemon cookies today," Eli suggested with amused sarcasm.

Hersh kept dancing, flicking away Eli's suggestion with a wave of his upraised hand.

"No, something more thrilling," Dov offered. "He picked up that new coat of his from the tailor."

Hersh kept singing and prancing about, knocking over Dov's carefully arranged display of an interesting new novel called *Death in Venice*.

Eli tried again. "He passed the German grammar exam."

"Impossible," Dov chuckled. "Not grammar." He watched for a moment as Hersh blissfully dipped and glided around the boxes and piles of books, and then he snorted. "Ah, I have it. His mother's hired another housemaid!"

Eli broke into a roar of laughter, but Hersh stopped in his tracks. "As a matter of fact, she did. After they sent poor Gerda back to the country."

The grins faded from the faces of his friends. "They sent her back?"

"Yes. We were caught *in flagrante delicto,* as the lawyers say."

"That's why you're *singing*?" Eli asked in disbelief.

"No. It's my *punishment* that has me singing. You'll never believe it!"

"Then tell us already."

Hersh paused dramatically. "Papa is banishing me. To . . . guess where?" And he began his song and dance again.

Realization burst on Dov like a blow. "My God! *America?*"

Hersh beamed at him. "That's it! At the end of the month. Did you ever hear of such luck? My father thinks he's punishing me, my mother sits all day crying into a towel, and I feel like dancing in the streets!"

While his friends gaped at him speechlessly, Hersh sat down and related the story in full detail. His father, in a fury of activity, was arranging everything—booking his passage, arranging for him to stay with cousins in Vienna and Berlin, contacting his brothers in New York for whom Hersh would go to work, everything. Hersh had never been so overjoyed. The parting from his sweetheart meant nothing when compared with this enormous stroke of luck.

Dov and Eli listened, sobered. Dov was again beset with the feeling that his grip on the future had weakened. Hersh was going out of his life without a bit of warning. He'd probably never see his friend again. Life was full of these unexpected twists and turns. How could one plan for anything?

Eli shook his head, confused. "But . . . you're almost eighteen, Hersh," he said, unwilling to believe that such an event could occur so quickly. "I thought they weren't issuing passports to men of military age."

"Aha!" Hersh beamed. "That's the best part. Papa gave me an envelope of Russian rubles and sent me to a man he knows who deals in Turkish passports. It's the only thing Papa let me do for myself. What Papa doesn't know is how clever I can be at bargaining when I want to be. Look!" And with great ceremony he removed a packet from inside his coat. Like a pirate unfolding a treasure map, he undid the string and held out the contents for his friends' inspection.

"My God!" Eli gasped. "He's got *three*!"

Hersh chuckled delightedly. "Three for the price of one. How do you like that, eh? Am I a bargainer or am I a bargainer?"

"Hersh?" Dov felt his throat tighten. "For *us*?"

"No, for the Emperor Franz Josef and his wife. Of *course* for you. You can both come with me."

"Hersh, you're crazy," Eli said in an awed whisper. "He's crazy, isn't he, Dov?"

"As a loon." Dov shook his head. "A prince of a fellow, but definitely with a screw loose."

Hersh's moon face grew pink with pleasure and triumph. "So? Can you be ready to go by the end of the month?"

Eli's eyes were fixed on the open packet. "How could we—?"

"You mean money? You could do it without much money. You could stop with cousins hither and yon until you got there. A Jew can find cousins in every major city in the world," Hersh answered promptly.

His two friends eyed the passports hungrily. The little booklets with their gold letters on the covers seemed to exude emanations of romance, excitement, and the promise of high adventure. America! Their eyes shone with visions of the distant land whose air of freedom had been a siren song for years. What a prospect for three young men who'd spent all their lives in bondage to tight family groups, to repressive religious restrictions, and to a country that held them fast while at the same time making them feel despised and alien! If they could only reach out and pick up the passports, they might find themselves in a world where they could *belong*. For a long moment, they let themselves imagine all the thrilling possibilities. *America!*

Eli was the first to turn away. "Thanks, Hersh. I wish I could. I know I've always argued that we can build ourselves a future right here in Austria . . . but who can really resist America? But I can't go away. Not now. My father isn't well, you know, and I've already promised my mother that I'd leave school and find work by the end of term."

Dov, meanwhile, got up and began to restack the pile of Thomas Mann novels that Hersh had knocked over. What weakness was it in him that had made him, even momentarily, yearn for America? Even assuming he could have managed to gather together enough money to pay for the passage—which alone was impossible—he wouldn't have gone to America. Not there, where the despised Avrum had gone. He had no intention of following those footsteps. At least he had enough control over the future to prevent *that*! "I thank you, too, Hersh," he said quietly. "It was such a good, Hersh-like thing to do. But you know what I've always said. When I go away from here, it won't be to America. It's Palestine for me."

Hersh nodded, deflated. "I was afraid it wouldn't work out. Too much to hope for, the three of us in America together."

But he insisted that his friends take the passports anyway. He had no use for them, he pointed out, and if Dov and Eli took them, he could hold on to the hope that they might some day put them to use. Who could foretell? Some unexpected wind of fate might blow one of them—or both—to America one day.

So Dov and Eli pocketed the passports with silent solemnity. Later, when his friends had left the store, Dov slipped the passport under his shirt and prepared to close the shop.

But Temele appeared in the back doorway. "Don't go yet," she said imperiously. "Shmuel won't be home for another hour."

"I told you," Dov said, eyes down. "No more."

She gave a sarcastic smile. "How heroic!"

"I don't mean to be heroic—"

"No? Just idiotic, eh?"

Dov closed the cash drawer and went to the door. "Good night, *Aunt* Temele," he said firmly. "Lock up for me."

When he got home, before he joined the family at the table, he went to his bedroom, closed the door, and pried loose his windowsill. Below the sill was a small, dry cavity in which he'd hidden a sheaf of gloomy poems he'd written, a yellowing sketch of a lovely naked lady he'd once cut from an old book he'd discovered discarded in Uncle Shmuel's storeroom, and a broken gold watch. Into this cavity he carefully placed the passport, hiding it away with his other secret belongings—the precious impedimenta of his youth. They were things that he felt were of no real use at all but that, despite a number of attempts, he somehow found impossible to throw away.

8

*O*ctober turned unusually chilly, but Dvora and Yudi, on their return walks from Yudi's school, could still see the dragoons on their maneuvers on the far side of the military reservation. In spite of the weather the cavalry continued its rigorous outdoor training. From a distance the officers appeared to the girls to cut impressive figures in their colorful uniforms and astride their shapely, well-groomed mounts. But one wintry afternoon, when two of the dragoons suddenly appeared close at hand in the road ahead of them, directly in their path, their figures were more than impressive—they were terrifying. Their horses were huge, with steam issuing from their nostrils, and the mustachioed men sitting on their backs looked foreign and sinister. "What shall we do, Dvora?" Yudi whispered, clutching her sister's hand tightly.

"Nothing. Just keep on walking and don't look at them," Dvora muttered through barely moving lips.

The girls walked bravely on, but the riders slowed and took a good look at the older girl. "Nice," one of them said distinctly.

Dvora tossed her head and pulled Yudi along faster. As the riders and the girls passed each other, Dvora could feel their eyes on her. A tremor passed through her chest, but as the sound of the horses' hooves receded, she was able to breathe a sigh of relief. Then she heard them pause. She threw a quick look over her shoulder, and her chest clenched again. They were turning back! "Yudi," she hissed, eyes on the returning officers, "*run*!"

Yudi's eyes widened in horror. "But, Dvora—!"

"Do as I say! Cut through the woods. *Quick!*" And she gave the little girl a shove.

The urgency of her sister's command froze Yudi's heart. But she did as she was told and ran off the dirt path, floundering through the dry grasses that fringed the roadway and stumbling into the woods. She ran almost blindly, tripping over roots and blundering into branches until she thought her breast would tear apart. When she couldn't run any longer, she stopped and leaned on a tree. Let them catch me, she thought; I'm dying anyway.

But there wasn't a sound behind her. The dragoons hadn't followed her into the woods. She was safe. But where was Dvora? She couldn't go home and leave her sister to the mercies of those ominous strangers. Slowly and as silently as she could, Yudi retraced her steps. She was almost back where she'd started when she heard a horse neighing. She paused, not breathing, and peered through the trees. There on the road were the two horses, but neither one carried a rider. One of the dragoons was standing beside them, holding the reins and grinning at something to his left. Yudi turned to look.

At the edge of the woods, leaning against a tree, stood Dvora. The other dragoon stood before her, his arms outstretched and his hands pressed against the treetrunk, one on each side of Dvora's head. And both of them were smiling! It was clear to Yudi that her sister was engaging in a flirtation and enjoying herself hugely. Yudi wanted to laugh. She'd imagined she would find her sister lying dead on the road. Releasing a long sigh of relief, she turned and tiptoed stealthily back through the woods again. Dvora could take care of herself. She didn't need any assistance from her little sister.

It wasn't until Yudi was almost home that it occurred to her to wonder if her mother would be angry. She didn't know why, but she knew instinctively that Mama would disapprove of what Dvora was doing. She wondered if she'd done wrong by not showing herself when she'd come back through the woods and seen Dvora safe. Should she have come forward, taken Dvora's hand, and pulled her away from the flirting officer?

She decided to say nothing to anyone about what had happened on the road. So long as Dvora was safe, there was no point in making trouble. Why be a tattletale for nothing? When she entered the house, and her mother asked where Dvora was, Yudi only shrugged. "She's coming," was all she said.

Dvora came home, and the day passed without further incident. Yudi had put the experience almost completely out of her mind when, a few days later, the officer who'd flirted with Dvora at the tree appeared on the road again. This time Dvora showed no signs of fear. "Go home, Yudi," she said as soon as the officer rode into sight.

Yudi, obeying that basic instinct that had made her uncomfortable before, pulled at her sister's hand. "You, too," she insisted.

"Go home, I said!" Dvora pushed her sister on her way with a shove on her back. "I'll follow in a little."

Yudi shook her head mulishly and tried to stand firm, but another shove from Dvora told her that it was useless to argue.

Soon the officer was appearing on the road every day, and Dvora was taking longer and longer to get home. "Mama is asking questions," Yudi warned when she spotted the dragoon's horse approaching for the fourth day in a row. "I don't know what to say to her."

"Just say what you've been saying all along," Dvora answered carelessly, her eyes fixed on the soldier and shining with mysterious anticipation.

"I haven't been saying anything."

"Good. That's just as it should be. Now, go home like a good girl and keep your mouth shut."

Yudi strode away annoyed, her usually sweet nature soured by the strain of keeping her sister's trysts secret. She marched off down the road muttering under her breath. How could she say nothing if Mama should decide to ask a direct question? Yudi had no talent for lying. Dvora had no right to put her in this uncomfortable position.

The more she thought about it, the angrier she became. Dvora was a selfish beast to expect Yudi to be her shield. She was too young and unskilled at subterfuge to be asked to cover over her sister's behavior. In a sudden burst of courage, she turned around and retraced her steps, determined to face her sister and demand her rights. Dvora, not she, had to be the one to confront Mama. Yudi would not go home without Dvora by her side. Her mind was made up.

When she returned to the place where she and Dvora had parted company, she didn't see Dvora at first. Only the horse was there, tied by his reins to a tree and quietly nuzzling about in the grass. She could see no one else. But a strange sound—a sort of grunt—drew her attention to the woods beyond. There, a few paces into the trees, she saw something moving on the ground. Puzzled, with her heart pounding in fright, she crept closer. It was the officer, lying on top of her sister. Little Yudi stared, appalled. The officer was doing something dreadful to her sister!

She had to do something to save Dvora from this monstrous attack. She glanced around desperately, picked up a stone and stole closer, ready to clout the officer on the head. But as she raised her weapon, she caught a glimpse of Dvora's face. Dvora's eyes were shut and her mouth slightly open. The expression was not that of a girl who wanted help. Although gasping for breath, Dvora was clearly in a state of peculiar, inexplicable, awe-inspiring bliss.

Yudi lowered her arm and backed away in confusion. She knew she'd blundered on a scene that Dvora would not have wanted her to see. She knew, too, that whatever it was the officer was doing was with Dvora's consent. In some deeply felt, instinctual way, she understood something else—that what her sister and the officer were doing together was bad. She didn't understand exactly what they were doing or why it was bad, nor did she wish to discover the answers. She couldn't explain to herself what it was she'd read in her sister's face. She couldn't account for the painful turmoil in her own breast. She wanted only to get away from there . . . to get away unseen and as fast as could be. And then to try to forget everything about it.

She ran all the way home. She stopped just outside the door and struggled to catch her breath. Her mother mustn't see that she was in any way perturbed. But her chest was heaving, and she couldn't seem to get it to stop. And her hands were trembling uncontrollably. Maybe, she thought, I shouldn't go in at all. I can hide in the shed with Tzickerl until I'm feeling better.

She went down the steps and around to the back. But as she was about to push open the shed door, she heard the sound of milk being squirted into a pail. Papa was doing the milking. She didn't want to face Papa either just now. He'd start to make jokes, and she didn't think she could laugh very convincingly in her present mood.

She decided to go inside the house after all. If she was very quiet and nonchalant, her mother might not ask her anything, and she could escape to her room. She needn't worry too much, she told herself. Her mother rarely took any particular notice of her.

She tried again to gain control of her breathing as she returned to the front door. With an assumed casualness, she pushed it open and went in. Mama was standing over the kitchen table near the window, vigorously kneading dough. She threw a quick look over her shoulder. "Where's Dvora?" she asked almost automatically.

"She's coming," Yudi mumbled, her pulse racing as she edged toward the little hallway that led to the bedrooms.

But her mother had paused in her work and was looking at her searchingly. "What's the matter with *you*? You look . . . funny."

Yudi clenched her trembling fingers behind her back. "Funny? M-me?"

Mindel wiped her hands on her apron and crossed the room. "You're pale as a ghost. What's happened?"

"Nothing, Mama."

The kitchen door opened, and Leib came in carrying the pail of milk. "Yudi!" he greeted, his face brightening. "My little Yudele. How was school?"

"Never mind school," Mindel cut in. "I see you did the milking for Dvora again. I told you not to—"

"You told me, you told me. You tell me so much, how can I remember it all?"

As he turned to place the pail on the table, and Mindel continued to glare at him, Yudi backed noiselessly toward the hallway. But Papa's voice stopped her. "So, my clever little diamond, my shining star, tell me something. If I were Rothschild, why would I be even richer than Rothschild?"

"Wh-what, Papa?" She could feel her lips trembling like her fingers.

But her father didn't seem to notice her anxiety. "If I were Rothschild, I'd be even richer than he, wouldn't I?" he prodded, giving her a broad wink.

"Yes, Papa."

"But how? How could I be richer than Rothschild?"

Yudi forced her mouth to smile. "Easy, Papa. You'd be doing a little m-milking on the side."

Leib crowed with laughter and slapped at his leg in delight. "You hear her, Mindel? Your baby never misses!"

But Mindel was peering at her youngest child suspiciously. "My baby has something on her mind more important than jokes. What is it, Yudi? What's the matter?"

"N-nothing, Mama."

"Don't tell me nothing! Your eyes say *something*."

"But there's . . . nothing to say, Mama. Really."

"Has this anything to do with your sister?"

The recollection of the dragoon lying upon Dvora flashed before her eyes. "N-no, Mama," she whimpered, urgently fighting to hold in the tears that gathered just behind her eyelids.

"*No,* Mama, *nothing,* Mama," Mindel mocked. "That's why you're twisting your fingers behind your back? That's why you're standing on one foot with the other foot curled around your ankle? That's why you're shaking like a leaf?"

Dvora's face appeared in Yudi's mind—the eyes shut, the lips parted, the breath coming in gasps. The strange, terrifying expression of rapture . . . what did it all mean? Yudi's heart beat against her ribs with great, pounding thuds.

"Look at her," Mindel said in disgust. "Some nothing!"

"Let her be, Mindel," Leib said gently. "If she says it's nothing, then it's nothing. Trust her."

"*Trust* her? Fools trust. If you never trust, you're never deceived. Will you *talk*, Yudi, for God's sake? I asked you a question!"

Yudi glanced up at her mother, but all she saw was Dvora's face. Dvora's ecstatic face. Helplessly, she began to sob.

Leib, alarmed, knelt down beside her and took her in his arms. "Yudi, my baby, what it is?"

"Nothing, P-Papa," the child wept.

"Again, nothing?" Mindel demanded, at the end of her patience.

Yudi glanced fearfully up at her mother. "I . . . I don't feel very well."

"You'll feel a lot worse in a minute," her mother threatened, "if I don't get an answer to my question. Where's your sister?"

Yudi shivered and sobbed more vehemently. Leib lifted her up in his arms. "Let the child be," he pleaded. "Why make her a tattletale? You'll ask Dvora herself when she comes home. Let me put Yudi to bed."

Mindel, about to make her customary, disparaging retort to her husband, suddenly paused. She gave a shrug and walked back to her kneading board without another word. Leib placed a kiss on his little daughter's brow and carried her to bed. "There now, my little one, calm yourself. Everything will be all right."

Yudi tried to wipe her eyes. "Y-yes, Papa."

"Do you want to talk to your silly old papa about anything?"

She gave him a tremulous hug but shook her head. "No, thank you, Papa, not n-now."

"All right, then, I'll leave you alone. Take a nice rest. And no more crying, please. Do you promise?"

"Yes, Papa. I love you, Papa."

After he'd gone and closed the door behind him, Yudi curled up like a little ball and tried to sleep. But troublesome thoughts crowded her mind and didn't let her rest. After a short while, she heard Dvora come home. The shouting from the kitchen was not unexpected, but she put her hands to her ears to stifle the sounds. She didn't want to hear Dvora's lies and her mother's curses. But no matter how tightly she pressed her hands to her ears, she couldn't completely muffle the sounds. She could hear her father's placating tones, her mother's shrill abuse, Dvora's strangely calm responses; and, once or twice, she made out Dov's voice. And one word came out loud and clear: *corve,* whore.

Silence fell at last, and she was called to the table by her father. They ate the evening meal in absolute silence, Papa with nervous speed, Dov with his eyes fixed on his plate, Mama in white-lipped fury (moving things around on her plate but not eating a bite), and Dvora trying to be casual and pretending that nothing whatever was wrong.

Later that night the two sisters lay side by side in the bed they shared, neither able to sleep. "I . . . I didn't say anything," Yudi whispered after a long silence.

"I know." Dvora leaned over and kissed her sister's cheek. "Go to sleep."

"Dvora, may I ask you a question?"

"Sure."

"Are you a *corve*?"

There was a long pause. "I don't know. I'm not even sure what it means."

Yudi sat up and peered at her sister in the dark. "It's a girl who's . . . bad with men."

Dvora snorted. "Do you know what it means to be bad with men?"

"I think so. I saw you and the dragoon today."

Dvora turned on her side and stared at her sister for a moment. Then she lay back and looked up at the ceiling. "His name is Franz," she said quietly. "I love him."

"Oh," Yudi said, struggling to understand.

"I love him. Do you know what I'm saying? I love him."

"Better than you love Mama and Papa?"

"I hate Mama."

"Papa, then. Do you love him better than Papa? And Dov? And . . . me?"

"Oh, Yudi!" Her sister took the child in a tight embrace. "You don't understand. How can I explain it? It's a different sort of love, you see."

"How is it different?"

"I don't know how to put it into words. You'll learn for yourself, one day."

. . . And I did, Sam. But it took a very long time. Years and years. I never understood till now. But I mustn't let myself digress on that subject. Back to the night when my sister confided in me that the dragoon, her Franz, was soon to be transferred and wanted to take her with him. I couldn't understand what she was trying to tell me. I was only ten. The love I felt for Papa, for Dov, for Dvora, and, yes, for Mama, too . . . I thought that was the only kind of love there was. . . .

"Dvora?" Yudi asked after Dvora had talked herself out. The two sisters were sitting up against the pillows, Yudi curled in the crook of the older girl's arm.

"Yes, my sweet?" Dvora prodded gently, made tender by the unexpected pleasure of sisterly intimacy.

"If you love your dragoon—"

"Franz. His name is Franz. You can say it; it's not a curse."

"Franz. If you love him . . ."

"Yes? Ask. Don't be afraid."

"If you love him, does that . . . make it all right?"

"Make what all right?"

"What you . . . did this afternoon."

Dvora stroked her sister's hair slowly, with a steady, womanly affection. "What I did this afternoon," she said after a long while, "was wonderful."

"Wonderful?"

She sighed. "Terrible, too."

"Terrible, Dvora? What do you mean? Do you mean . . . bad?"

Yudi felt a tear fall on her forehead. "Oh, Yudi," her sister whispered in a voice of agony, "I wish I knew."

Less than two weeks later, Yudi woke up earlier than usual. Daylight was just breaking, and the mist outside the window was so thick that Yudi couldn't even see the trees in the yard. "Dvora," she said sleepily, throwing off the covers, "look at the fog."

There was no answer.

"Dvora?" She turned to look at the place in the bed where Dvora should have been. No head rested on the pillow. Dvora was gone.

9

When Mama realized that Dvora was gone, she let out one anguished curse and then said no more. She pretended to herself and to us that Dvora's disappearance was no more than she'd expected from so disobedient and whorish a girl. But Papa was beside himself. He couldn't let his daughter go so easily. . . .

As soon as he learned the news, Leib quietly left the house to see if he could find her. He didn't return all day. Dov, meanwhile, had gone to work. When he came home and learned that his father had not yet returned, he went out to look for him. He found Leib sitting on the side of the road, weeping. "The regiment's gone," he told his son brokenly. "I went to the *caserne*. There was hardly anyone there—the new batch of soldiers aren't due till later this week."

"And . . . Dvora?"

"No sign of her. She must have gone with them."

Dov helped Leib to his feet. "Then why are you sitting here in the cold? Why didn't you come home?"

Leib wiped his eyes with the back of his large hands, hands that were too shaky and gnarled for a man his age. "I felt so . . . so tired."

. . . By the end of the week, Sam, the new regiment was installed in the caserne, and Papa was bedridden. Dvora's disappearance, which none of us spoke of again, had been more than his weakened heart could stand. He was dying, and we all knew it. . . .

Mama sat at his bedside while Dov was at work and Yudi at school, but as soon as they came home, she surrendered her place to them. They held his hand and smiled at him, pretending that they weren't worried and that everything would be all right again before the next day dawned. When he had the strength, he smiled back at them and even made jokes. "Tell me, Rabbi," he'd say to Dov with a ghost of his comical smile, "do you really believe that those who are poor in this world will be rich in the next?"

Dov would make a face of rabbinical seriousness and nod with mock dignity. "Yes, that is most certainly what I believe."

"Then, Rabbi, in that case, will you lend me a hundred florins? When I collect my riches in heaven, I'll return them to you."

"Certainly, my good man," Dov would say, counting out a hundred pretend florins from his pocket. "What do you plan to do with this money?"

"I'll buy a new stock of merchandise," Leib would answer promptly, "and sell it around town."

"Do you expect to make a profit?"

"Of course I expect to make a profit."

"In that case," Dov would say with finality, putting the pretend florins back in his pocket, "the deal's off. If you get rich here, you'll be poor in heaven, and then how will I get my money back?"

Yudi would giggle as if she'd never heard the joke before, and Leib would cackle with pleasure until a coughing fit stopped him.

Yudi was alone with him when he told his last joke. She had taken her mother's place on the chair at his bedside and was watching him sleep, but soon his breathing changed. It was labored and irregular. "Papa, Papa!" the girl cried in alarm, shaking him by the shoulders.

His eyes flickered open. "Ah, Yudi . . . my . . . love . . ." he managed.

"Papa? Papa, don't go back to sleep! Papa, can you hear me?"

A suggestion of a smile appeared on his lips. "I'm trying to hear you, Doctor," he whispered hoarsely. "You're telling me that if I want my hearing back . . . I'll have to give up . . . *shnaps.*"

Yudi recognized the words as a cue for an old joke, but she couldn't bring herself to say the expected line. "No jokes, Papa," she murmured, feeling her throat tighten.

Leib opened his eyes and peered at her as if through a mist. "Why not?"

"You're too t-tired," she said, wiping his forehead.

He made a negative motion of his hand. "So, Doctor, you're say-ing—?"

Yudi's mouth trembled. "I'm saying that too much d-drink will make you deaf. I told you that before. So did you stop drinking?"

Leib's smile widened. "Yes, for a . . . while."

"Only for a while?" Yudi clenched her fingers and tried to throw herself into her performance. "I told you no drinking, ever, if you . . . if you . . ." She couldn't go on.

Leib reached for her hand. The icy touch of his fingers made her shiver. "But, Doctor—" he muttered with an effort, his breath coming in irregular gasps.

"Papa, don't," Yudi begged, putting a hand gently over his mouth.

"Go on," he insisted.

She tried to stiffen her trembling lips. "No drinking, ever, if you want to hear what p-people say to you."

"Believe me, Doctor," Leib said, his voice a mere breath, "nothing I heard . . . was worth . . . one good *shnaps.*"

"Oh, Papa," Yudi whispered, letting her head fall on his shoulder and throwing an arm around his neck. She couldn't prevent the escape of an agonized sob.

He lifted his arm with an effort and patted her shoulder. "My sweet little . . . silly," he whispered, "you're . . . supposed to be . . . laughing. . . ."

He died very quietly the next morning. Yudi hid in a corner of her bedroom and wept inconsolably. Mindel sat in the kitchen, silent and unmoving, and stared out the window at the bleak November sky. Dov, who had never been faced with death before, suffered both pain and bewilderment. Was he the one to manage affairs from now on? Did he have to arrange the details necessary for the funeral? The thought was terrifying.

After sitting with Yudi in his arms until the little girl had cried herself dry, he told his mother he was going into town for a short while to notify Uncle Shmuel. To himself he thanked God that there was still Uncle Shmuel on whom he could call for help.

It wasn't until he ran breathlessly into the bookstore that he realized Uncle Shmuel would not yet be back from work. Well, he thought quickly, he could leave word with Temele. He ran to the back stairs and shouted up, "Temele, where are you?"

There was no answer. In impatient irritation, he dashed up the stairs. "Temele, something terrible's happened. I have to—" He burst unceremoniously into her bedroom and stood stock still. Chaim, the skinny capmaker from the shop next door, Uncle Shmuel's longtime chess partner, was trying to crawl under the bed, the coverlet wrapped around his naked waist. Temele, with cheeks flushed and eyes startled, sat upright on the bed trying to cover herself with the sheet.

"Oh, my God!" the capmaker moaned.

Temele and Dov stared at each other speechlessly. Then Temele shrugged. "You don't have to look at me like that. What did you expect? It's your own fault. And who asked you to come barging in?"

Dov turned his back on the scene. "Tell Uncle Shmuel to come to us as soon as he can. My father died this morning." And he strode from the room, down the stairs, and out into the dank street. He was never to enter the store again.

Late that night Uncle Shmuel and Temele drew up before the house in a hired carriage in which they'd brought a newly made coffin. While Mindel and the red-eyed Yudi joined Temele (ostentatiously dressed for the funeral in a black silk dress, a wide-brimmed hat, and a voluminous black veil) in the carriage, which would carry them to Solitava, Shmuel carried a shroud into the house. Dov helped him drape Leib's thin body with the white garment. When Shmuel started to draw the covering over Leib's head, Dov raised a restraining hand. He couldn't take his eyes from the gray face of his beloved father. Shmuel stepped aside and let the boy cry. Through his tears, Dov studied the lifeless, sightless face. It was wrinkled deeply about the mouth and eyes, and the fringes of hair that framed the face were scrawny and mottled with streaks of white. It was an elderly man he stared at. Leib was forty-two.

Dov, his heart seeming to burst within his chest, ran from the room. In his bedroom he leaned his forehead against the glass of his window and wept like a baby. Like a weak little girl. Like Yudi. In the midst of his grief he felt ashamed of his lack of strength. He should be able to hold back his tears, as his mother was doing. He hadn't seen her shed a tear in all the days Papa lay dying.

His head came up slowly. Was it strength that had kept the tears from his mother's eyes . . . or was it coldness? Did she care for Papa at all? Did she care for anybody but her cursed Avrum? In a kind of trembling fury, he pried up the windowsill and pulled out from his secret hiding place the gold watch that Aunt Raizel had given him. Avrum Gentz's legacy. He opened the window and threw the watch out into the darkness as far as he could, with every ounce of strength his arm possessed. "It should be *you*, Avrum Gentz, we're putting into the ground," he sobbed.

When he got hold of himself, he began to replace the windowsill. His eyes fell on the packet that held the Turkish passport. Not quite sure why, he pulled it out and stuffed it into the inner pocket of his coat. Then he replaced the sill, closed the window, and, wiping the wetness from his cheeks, went out to rejoin his uncle.

Nathan the Tzaddik performed the ritual service in the Solitava synagogue. The mourners were not numerous, but there was much weeping. Dov didn't find the service satisfactory. The words Great-uncle Nathan said about the deceased were the ritual ones: he had been a good and pious man. They could have been said about anyone. They provided not an ounce of comfort to Dov's soul.

At the side of the open grave, his mother stood beside him, dry-eyed and cold as a stone. On his other side, Yudi clutched his hand. The little girl was taking quick, open-mouthed gasps of breath as she shivered in confusion. But his mother never for a moment lost her dry-eyed dignity. All day and well into the night, Dov watched her as she received the ritual words of sympathy from the entire population of Solitava. Not once did she shed a tear. Dov, who'd struggled all day to keep his sister and himself from losing control of their emotions, felt a corrosive bitterness growing within him. Hadn't his mother cared *at all* for the man she'd lived with all these years? Had she no feeling of regret for having withheld love, for having failed to fill the emptiness of his life, for having humiliated him both publicly and privately? Had she no pity in her heart for the failures of his life and the pathetic lack of grandeur in the manner of his dying?

For the week of mourning, the group from Czernowitz would be housed with the Rossners. Shmuel and his wife were assigned Shmuel's old room (where once Mindel had spent a wedding night and the two happy years of her life), and Mindel and her two children (for Dvora's name was not mentioned, Shmuel having reported the entire tale to Nathan as soon as it had occurred) were given the room she'd slept in as a girl. "You and Yahudis can share the bed," Etel Fruma said to her daughter, "and Dov can sleep on these cushions in the corner."

Mindel nodded and herded her children down the hall. "Wait a minute," Etel Fruma added, pulling Mindel back into the dining room. "I want to talk to you. You should give some thought to moving in with me again. You can't afford to keep that house in Czernowitz now that Leib is gone. With only the three of you left, you don't need—"

"I'll think about it, Mama," Mindel said and followed her children into the bedroom.

Yudi was sitting on the edge of the bed, looking lost, while Dov stood gazing out of the window at nothing. "So why aren't you getting ready for bed?" their mother asked.

Dov turned around slowly. "What kind of woman are you?" he asked, his voice thick with revulsion.

Mindel's face grew stiff. "What?"

"Was he such a nothing to you that you can't even mourn for him?" The words seemed to choke him, but he spat them out anyway. There was a taste in his throat like bile. It was so strong, his eyes burned.

"That is not a way I will ever permit you to speak to me," she said coldly.

"You don't *care* that he's dead!"

"Dov!" Yudi winced in horror, her already pale face turning ashen.

Dov didn't even hear his sister. "You don't care a bit, do you?"

Mindel stood up straight and eyed him with a face carefully impassive. "I don't need an arrogant son to tell me how to grieve."

"Grieve? I don't see you grieving at *all.*" He turned back to the window, clenching his shaking hands. "He deserved better from you. Much better. He was a good man."

Mindel stared at her son's back. "I never said he wasn't."

Dov wheeled around. "You never said he *was*! He was only a fool to you, a poor incompetent fool. You could hardly keep from saying the word to his face!"

"Dov, *stop*!" Yudi cried, running to her mother and clasping both arms around her waist in protection against her brother's attack.

"I won't stop. Let her hear what her children really think, for once. Our mother has been crying for years over a man that left her, but when the one who stayed—who worked for her and worshiped her and raised her children and ... and died for her—" The tears began to fall unheeded from his eyes. "—when that one dies, she can't shed a tear for him!"

Mindel shut her eyes and swayed slightly on her feet. But when she spoke her voice was calm. "All right, Dov, that's enough. This is not a night to talk." She unclasped Yudi's arms from about her and went up to him. She lifted a hand and tried to brush the tears from his cheeks. "Let's try to get some sleep—"

He thrust her hand away. "Don't touch me! And I don't want to sleep. I'm getting out of here."

"Don't speak nonsense. Do as I say and go to bed."

"No. Not me. I'm going." With a sudden rush of movement, he ran, stumbling, to the door. "And I'm not coming back."

"Dov, what are you saying?" She started after him, her face a study in bewilderment. "You can't leave now!"

"No? Just watch me." He flung open the door and ran into the hallway.

"Dov!" Yudi screeched.

"Dov, come back here. I won't have this foolishness at such a time!" Her voice cracked. "Dov, I . . . I *need* you."

He paused and turned back to look at her, trying to speak calmly. "You don't need me. You'll manage well enough if you move in here with Grandma."

"Again you dare to tell me what to do?"

His face hardened. "Goodbye, Mama."

"For God's sake, Dov, be sensible! Where will you go at this time of night? Back to Czernowitz? To the store? The house?"

He threw her a sneering laugh as he ran down the narrow hallway to the front door. "Somewhere a little farther away than that."

The commotion brought Etel Fruma and Temele to their doors. "What's going on?" Temele asked.

But Mindel brushed by her and ran down the hallway after her son. "Dov, wait! Where—?"

He pulled open the door. "To *Palestine,* that's where!" And the door slammed shut behind him.

"Dov!" The cry rang through the house, reminding Etel Fruma of another cry that had broken from her daughter's throat so many years before.

Mindel fell heavily against the door and slowly, slowly slid down to the floor. "Dov . . ." she wept, her hand groping uselessly for the doorknob that she couldn't see. "Oh, my *God . . . not Dov, too!"*

. . . I stayed huddled on the bed, not knowing what to do. In little more than a month I had lost almost everyone I loved. I was too shaken, Sam, too shocked to be capable of action. I heard the commotion in the hall . . . Uncle Shmuel's voice . . . Grandma's. I heard Mama's sobs slowly subside. And then she came back into the room, closed the door, and stared at me. "Well, Yudi," she said in a strange, low voice, "we seem to be the only ones left. Just you and me."

Mama had taken notice of me at last.

Part Three

DOV
1913-1914

1

I mourned a lot for the family I had lost, even if those losses were not unique. I don't have to tell you, Sam, that it was commonplace at that time in Europe for Jewish families to disintegrate. The young, the adventurous, the hunted, the desperately needy, the persecuted—they had been running off and leaving their families behind in the shtetls *for a quarter of a century. And Solitava was no exception. There was not a family in our town that had remained completely intact.*

But knowing that our situation was not unique was no comfort to me at all. I had lost almost everyone I held dear, and I was miserable. What good did it do me to know that everyone else around me had suffered similar losses? That old proverb, misery loves company, isn't true. Misery is misery, with company or without it.

I used to lie in bed at night trying to imagine where Dov and Dvora were and what they were doing. But none of my childish imaginings came anywhere near the truth. . . .

Dov was sitting on the back of a hay wagon making its way through the late-afternoon twilight toward a little village he'd never heard of. It was only two days after he'd left his mother's side, and already he was regretting his rashness. For one thing, he could still hear her cries ringing in his ears, and he couldn't shake the cloud of guilt that hung over him. For another, he was exhausted and hungry; he hadn't had food or sleep since his Papa's funeral. Worst of all, he didn't have a kreuzer to his name. He'd been a fool, he told himself, to run away without first making plans.

If he'd had any sense at all, he wouldn't have thrown away Avrum

Gentz's watch. Broken though it was, that watch would have been of some value to him now. He could have traded it for something. It had been gold, after all. Now all he had in his possession were his good coat (which was spoiled by the little cut on the lapel to indicate mourning), his rapidly disintegrating shoes, and the Turkish passport in his pocket. How was he to get to Palestine on those?

His plan (such as it was) was to get to Warsaw and find work. He knew how to run a bookstore, and since Warsaw was large enough to have many such establishments, he had optimistic expectations of securing a position as a clerk and saving enough of his wages to pay for passage to Palestine. But getting to Warsaw had proved more difficult than he'd expected. He'd thought, when he first started out, that he could last a week without food or sleep, but now, only forty-eight hours later, he was so hungry and tired that he doubted he could survive another day. He leaned back wearily against a bale of hay behind him and pulled out a piece of straw on which to chew, wondering glumly if there was any hope of getting anything else to eat before nightfall.

The wagon was heading toward the village of Teplik. The driver had picked Dov up at the border, and they'd crossed over without so much as a nod of the head from the border guards. The passport in Dov's pocket wasn't even needed.

Dov had learned from the driver that Teplik was a *shtetl* of only a few hundred Jewish families. He wondered what he would do when he got there. He remembered hearing his friend Hersh say that a Jew could find a cousin in every major city in the world. "But what about Teplik, eh, Hersh?" he asked aloud. "What are my chances of finding a cousin there?"

It would be nice to find a relative in Teplik, he thought longingly— someone who, because of the tie of blood, would feel impelled to feed him and offer him a bed. For Jews, hospitality was a blessed deed. He recalled an incident that had occurred when he was staying in Great-uncle Nathan's compound during the months before his *bar mitzvah*. The Tzaddik had regularly welcomed visitors to his court, and one day a young man had come and said he was a cousin from Minsk. The fellow had lived on the Tzaddik's hospitality for weeks before it was discovered that no family relationship really existed. Even then, Great-uncle Nathan hadn't sent the fellow away. "The Talmud says that hospitality to strangers shows reverence for the name of the Lord," he'd declared.

As the wagon trundled along into the deepening gloom of twilight, a wicked idea crossed Dov's hunger-sharpened brain. If that *shnorrer* in the Tzaddik's court could invent a relationship that didn't really exist, then why couldn't he do the same thing? "Besides, who's to say that I *haven't* got a cousin in Teplik?" he asked himself, laughing aloud.

By the time the driver dropped him off at the well in the center of the village, Dov had a plan. He approached a neat little house with a light in the window and tapped at the door. It was opened by a stooped woman with fearful eyes. "Yes? What do you want?"

He took off his cap and smiled at her. "Good evening. I'm Dov, your cousin from Cracow."

The woman cocked her head suspiciously. "From Cracow? I have no cousins in Cracow. Who are you, boy? What's your name?"

Dov's mind raced around to find a commonplace Jewish name. "Levy," he said promptly. "Don't you know your cousins, the Levys from Cracow?"

"You've made a mistake," the woman said flatly. "You have the wrong house. You must want the Bersons down the road. Getzel, the wife, was a Levy."

"The Bersons, yes. I thought this was the Berson house. Where—?"

"Down the road, on the other side. With the beech tree in front. You can't miss it."

Dov thanked her and ran off. The Bersons' house was indeed easy to find. He knocked at the door with assurance. This time a man answered. "Reb Berson? Good evening. I'm your wife's cousin Dov, from Cracow. Dov Levy."

The man peered at him. "Dov Levy? From Cracow?" He shook his head bewilderedly. Then his brow cleared. "Oh, of course! Froike's son, right? The older one, who goes to the university."

Dov was too shrewd to answer yes. If he had, he'd have found himself caught up in a tangle of lies too thick to wriggle out of. "No, not Froike's son. Froike's nephew."

"Really? You don't say. I didn't know his brother had a son your age. But come in, come in. My wife will scold me if I keep her cousin standing in the cold. Getzele, come quick! You'll never guess who's here!"

Dov stood silently near the door, hat in hand, and let Reb Berson explain his background to his wife. Getzel Berson looked bewildered by the explanation, but one glance at Dov's face won her over. He appeared to be innocent, sincere, and mannerly, and she warmed to him at once. Besides, she had two daughters to marry off. Why should she be suspicious when God had sent such a fine specimen right to her doorstep?

"Welcome to our home," she said with a shy smile. Then she went to an inner doorway and called out eagerly, "Perele, Esther, come quickly. I want you to meet your cousin Dov from Cracow."

He was fed, fussed over, and given a bed for the night. And when he left the next morning, it was despite their repeated urgings that he remain longer. Better still, he was given the address of another cousin of theirs in a town about a day's ride away. "Cousin Getzel" even wiped away a tear as she waved goodbye from the doorstep.

He refined his Cousin-from-Cracow technique as he traveled from town to town. He learned to find the houses with marriageable daughters on the premises. He learned not to name specific places or to make himself closer than "your second cousin once removed." When he was asked how Uncle Moishe was doing in his business, or how Aunt Sarah was coping with her "problem," he learned to say with a shrug, "Oh, very fine . . . considering." The questioner would usually nod knowingly and let the matter pass.

By this means he arrived in Warsaw well rested and well fed. But it had taken him closer to a month than a week. He still hadn't a groschen in his pocket, but he had a new self-confidence—a deep conviction that he would be able to overcome any obstacle in his path. With this feeling showing in the jauntiness of his stride, he set out to look for work.

It didn't take him long to learn about his surroundings. He soon discovered that Sigismund Square marked the center of the city, that the Saski Ogrod was Warsaw's most beautiful public park but that the Jews promenaded in the Krasinski Gardens, and that the Jewish quarter was located in the Old City just north of the square. After walking the streets of Warsaw for hours without luck, he came upon a bookstore that seemed to beckon him. It was on a busy commercial street but it exuded an air of quiet prosperity in every detail of its facade, from the sparkling-clean mullioned windows that flanked its wide doorway to the fancy gilt lettering over the door, which read FINE BOOKS BOUGHT AND SOLD—M. GOLDBLUM, PROP.

He peered in the window and sighed with yearning. There was a look inside of mellow peacefulness. The oak bookshelves were trimmed with brass and stocked with quality wares. A number of polished wood tables in the center of the store held neat piles of current books, which were well lit by hanging brass lamps with green glass shades. This was the sort of shop he had dreamed of finding.

He pushed open the door and walked in. It took a moment for his eyes to adjust to the dimmer light, but when they did he peered about with interest. There were two clerks in evidence. One had taken off his coat, donned an apron and sleeve protectors, and was dusting shelves. The other approached Dov. "May I help you, sir?" he asked.

"Is this the establishment of Mr. Goldblum?" Dov asked, sizing up the clerk as an easy fellow to draw out. "Mr. M.-for-Maurice Goldblum?"

"The M. is for Mendel," the clerk answered promptly.

"Yes, of course. Mendel. May I see him, please?"

The clerk looked Dov over suspiciously. "Why? Do you want to sell him something?"

Dov smiled. "In a way."

"He's over there," the clerk said with a shrug, "but he won't buy it. Mr. Goldblum's a hard man to sell to." And he pointed to a platform at the rear.

The platform was a sort of office area, set off from the rest of the shop by a wood railing. On the platform, standing behind a high desk shaped like a lectern, was a short, wiry, swarthy man whose nose was buried in a ledger book. It was lowered so far that it almost touched the page he was studying through his spectacles with evident disgust. Dov, taking a stance below the platform right before him, could barely see his face. He cleared his throat to get the man's attention.

"Yes?" Mr. Goldblum didn't even look up.

"Mr. Goldblum? I'm your cousin Dov, from Cracow."

"What?" Goldblum glanced up quickly, barely lifting his head. He frowned, blinked, and looked back down at his ledger. "Just a moment, please. I'm having a problem balancing these figures."

Dov, in a burst of enterprise, courageously opened a little gate in the railing, climbed up the two steps of the platform, and came up behind the abstracted Goldblum. Looking over Goldblum's shoulder, he studied the ledger and added the column quickly. "That's a seventeen," he said, pointing. "The crossbar just extended too far. You're taking it for a seventy-seven."

"What? Where—?"

"Right here."

"Good God, that's it! You're absolutely *right*!" He cast Dov another quick glance, adjusted his totals, and put down his pen. "Thank you very much indeed. That was very clever of you. It might have taken me hours to . . ." He stared at Dov with sudden interest. "Who did you say you were?"

Dov pulled off his cap. "Your cousin Dov. From Cracow." Dov

could feel his heart pounding in embarrassment and tension. That clerk had been right; Mr. Goldblum's face was not that of a man who could be easily hoodwinked. His eyes were too shrewd, and he had a pair of distended nostrils that gave his face an expression of congenital suspicion. Perhaps he shouldn't have tried the Cousin-from-Cracow ploy with this man. He might have been able to get work here on the basis of his experience alone, without resorting to subterfuge.

But it was too late to backtrack. He had to go on with the trickery. He resorted to one of the refinements he'd developed in his travels. "My mother said you'd remember meeting her."

"Meeting her where? In Cracow? I haven't been there in . . . seventeen, eighteen years."

"Yes, I know. I wasn't yet born, of course, but Mama said . . ." He let his voice die out awkwardly. Whenever he'd tried the Dying Voice ploy before, the victim would feel impelled to say something to cover the silence and would usually give away some useful information.

Goldblum took off his spectacles and peered at him. "Wait a minute. Don't tell me you're Berele Simke's son."

Dov expelled a relieved breath. Despite Goldblum's reputed shrewdness and his look of innate suspicion, he was swallowing the story. "Not Berele's son," Dov said smoothly. "Berele's nephew."

Goldblum's eyes narrowed. The bookseller, though not as suspicious as his wide nostrils led people to believe, was nobody's fool. Anyone could walk in off the street and claim to be a relation. But this boy had a nice face and a quick mind. And he *could* be a relation. Goldblum didn't remember his cousin Berele very well, had no recollection of her married name, and wasn't even sure of the names of her brothers or sisters. He didn't even remember how many brothers and sisters there were. "Whose boy *are* you?" he asked.

Dov was well practiced and knew how to avoid a direct question. "So you *don't* remember my mother. I *told* her it was foolish to—"

The man took out a handkerchief and polished his glasses, keeping his eyes fixed on Dov's face. "I'm sorry, but it's been so many years. It's hard to keep up, now that the family's spread out all over the world."

"Yes, that's what I said to Mama. 'How can you expect Cousin Mendel to remember?' I asked her. 'He hasn't seen you in almost twenty years, and I'm a complete stranger to him,' I said. 'You can't expect him, even if he's a cousin, to hire someone who's a complete stranger—' "

"You came to me for *work*?" Goldblum asked.

"Yes, sir. I worked in a bookstore in Cracow, you see, but it isn't doing very well. So Mama thought—"

Goldblum's suspicious expression seemed to soften as a gleam lit his eyes. All the fellow wanted from him was work. The bookseller was already wishing for a clerk like this one. Even the better of his two clerks, Pinhas Pinofsky, had never had an idea worth a groat. From the little he'd seen of *this* boy, he'd already deduced that "Cousin Dov" was quicker-witted than both his clerks put together. Neither one of those idiots would have been able to find that error in the ledger book. Not even with a week of effort. He would be happy to give the boy a position no matter who he was. And if he was a cousin, so much the better.

Mendel Goldblum put on his spectacles and studied the boy carefully. Dov from Cracow had not come to Warsaw well prepared. His clothes were ragged and his shoes a shambles, but his face was clean-cut and honest. Very good-looking, too. Goldblum's wife would undoubtedly applaud his decision to hire the boy; in fact, she'd probably like to have him home for dinner, so that Chava, their daughter, could meet him.

With his mind made up, Goldblum removed his glasses again and smiled at the boy with unexpected warmth. "Your mama was quite right," he said, clapping an arm about Dov's shoulders. "If we can't help our families, what good are we, eh?"

"You mean . . . you're going to hire me?" Dov asked, astonished. "Just like that?"

"Why not just like that? You're my cousin, no?"

"Yes, but . . ." Dov's conscience smote him a hard blow. This man, despite his shrewd expression, was so *trusting*. Dov wished he'd never uttered that Cousin-from-Cracow lie. "Listen, Cousin Mendel, you . . . you don't even remember my name."

"True, I don't. So what is it?"

"My name is—" Dov's mind suddenly balked. What name should he give? Should he choose a common name like Levy and live with a daily reminder of his falsehood? He didn't want to do it. If he was going to work for this man, he wanted to be honest and fair. He wanted to be known by his real name. But what *was* his real name? Was he Dov Gentz? In this, the start of a new life, did he want to carry the surname that meant so little to him? Why should he be forever tied by name to the father he'd never known and had always despised? The name Gentz was their only link. Avrum Gentz had never been a father to him. The only father he'd known was buried in the ground in a little cemetery in Solitava.

He met the eyes of his new employer with a sincere directness. "My name," he said aloud, putting out his hand, "is Weisenberg. Dov Weisenberg." He knew that at last he'd spoken nothing but the truth.

2

That very evening, Mr. Goldblum took his new clerk to his house in the Jewish quarter for dinner. They found Mrs. Goldblum standing in the kitchen, up to her elbows in flour. "You mustn't mind my wife," Mr. Goldblum said to Dov. "She's always baking. Taube Goldblum lives in constant terror that an army of guests will descend upon us unexpectedly and she will not have enough *challa* or *mandel* bread to feed them. Taube, my love, come away from your mixing bowl and say hello to Dov Weisenberg. He's my cousin from Cracow."

Taube Goldblum was as plump as her husband was thin, and her face was as round and pasty as the dough she was mixing. She had strong, motherly instincts, made even stronger by the frustration of having had only one child in her two decades of marriage, so she looked up at Dov's boyish face, looked down at his shabby clothes, and melted at once. Before Dov could catch his breath, he was installed in an attic bedroom, provided with a hot bath and a clean shirt, and led down to the dinner table.

It was there that he was introduced to the daughter of the household. Chava was a pretty girl, despite the fact that her face had the same round, pastry-dough quality as her mother's. It was obvious that she, also like her mother, took to Dov at once, for she blushed and simpered every time he looked at her. Taube took due note of Chava's coy behavior and beamed at both the young people all through the meal. And when dinner was over she made it quite clear that Dov was welcome to stay in the attic bedroom for as long as he wished.

Dov began work the very next day. After a few weeks, he realized that he liked his job very much. The shop was well patronized, and Dov was able to put to use everything he'd learned in his years of being surrounded by books in Shmuel's little store. Here, however, everything was so much grander. Every idea he'd ever had about merchandizing or cataloging (if Goldblum hadn't thought of it already) could be put into practice. In fact, Goldblum was delighted with all Dov's suggestions. Pinhas Pinofsky, the senior clerk, was consumed with jealousy at Mr. Goldblum's obvious favoritism. Dov tried to make light of it in his conversations with his co-workers, but he could see that Goldblum was fond of him.

Working for Mendel Goldblum was an education, for there was nothing about books that the man didn't know. Not only was he familiar with the authors and their works, but he knew all about publishers' costs, the process of printing and binding books, the way to recognize a rare book, and how to put a value on everything that came into his shop. He soon gave Dov special assignments that in the past he'd only trusted himself to do, like the bookkeeping. Dov learned so much so quickly that he felt he could set up a business for himself as soon as he got to Palestine.

Sometimes, during their walks to and from the store, "Cousin Mendel" would argue with Dov about his plans for the future. "Why would a bright young man like you want to go to so undeveloped a land? If I were young and promising I know where I would go. America. That's where the world's future resides."

"But what about the Jewish future?" Dov would retort.

"In America, the Jewish future is the same as anyone else's. That's the beauty of America."

But Dov remained committed to his original plan. He was not going to go to America, as Avrum Gentz had done. He was going to carve his own path in life. As much as he admired Mendel Goldblum, he was not going to let the man change his mind about Palestine.

Life in the Goldblum household was not as comfortable for Dov as it was in the bookstore. Taube Goldblum always made too much of a fuss over him at the dinner table, waxing so effusive about his progress in the store that it made him blush. "Mendel tells me he's put you in charge of all the English and German books," she'd gush.

"That's because I'm so weak in Russian and Polish," he'd respond.

But she would not let him deprecate himself. "Nonsense," she'd say. "You're wonderful in all languages. Mendel always tells me so, don't you, my dear?"

And since Mendel was usually deep in his newspaper, the response would be a grunt of agreement, and Dov would have to accept the fulsome compliment without further remonstrance.

Another source of discomfort for Dov was his proximity to the pampered, empty-eyed Chava. He didn't know what to make of the girl. Except for her simpering smile whenever she took notice of him, she seemed completely turned inward. But what went on in her head he couldn't guess. He'd never seen the girl read a book or heard her enter into a serious conversation. Nor did he ever discover her *doing* anything. She never helped her mother with the housework; she never cooked or sewed; she never, as far as he could see, did a smidgen of useful work. The few times Dov heard her speak were when she gave orders to the maid who came in daily to do the heavy cleaning or when she spoke to her mother. Even the communication with her mother was brief and utilitarian: "I'm taking this skirt to the dressmaker's, Mama," or, "We're not having chicken again, are we?" And the few words she spoke were never in Yiddish but in Polish. Dov suspected that Chava was one of those affected creatures who found Yiddish too vulgar for their tastes. To speak in Polish seemed to her more genteel.

Dov instinctively felt that the girl lacked depth and sensitivity, but he didn't exactly dislike her. In truth, he was attracted to her prettiness. But he couldn't bear to be left alone in a room with her. When such a circumstance occurred, he couldn't think of a thing to say to the girl. She was no help at all at such times. She merely giggled, smirked, or threw him covert glances. In desperation, he would mumble some excuse and back out of the room.

After living with the Goldblums for more than three months, matters with Chava came to a crisis. The situation began most unexpectedly, late one night after he'd returned from delivering a parcel to a customer who lived in a suburb called Wola. He'd never been there before, so on his return he got lost. He spent the entire evening wandering about the streets of Warsaw in a bewildered search for a familiar landmark, like the memorial in Sigismund Square. He enjoyed the experience, however. He felt deliciously free, and he viewed his wanderings as a sort of unguided tour; he discovered a number of parks and palaces he hadn't seen before.

But when he at last found his way home, it was very late. Everyone had retired for the night. The only light still shining was the dim glow of the little gas jet on the turning of the stairs on the second floor. He was just approaching the landing when Chava, dressed only in a wrapper and slippers, tiptoed out of her room. "We were all worried about you," she whispered.

"I'm sorry," he whispered back. "I got lost."

"You missed dinner."

"Yes."

"Are you hungry? There's plenty to eat in the pantry—"

"No, thank you. It's all right." He twisted his cap awkwardly in his hand. "Well . . . good night, Chava."

She didn't answer but stood there peering at him in the dim light. Then, without warning, she threw herself headlong into his arms. "Oh, Dov," she breathed, clutching his neck and pressing herself close to him. "Oh, Dov!"

He was almost thrown off balance by the precipitousness of this unexpected encounter. He froze in bewilderment, unable to move or say a word. The girl was pressing her breasts against him too closely for sanity, and the overpowering aroma of the lavender water with which she too liberally doused herself was making him nauseous. Before he could decide whether he wanted to hold her close or push her away, she lifted her head from his shoulder. "Oh, Dov," she whispered again, kissing him with a kind of fervent madness, "I love you!"

As abruptly as she'd come, she fled back to the door of her room, threw him one last, imploring look, and disappeared inside.

Dov wondered if he should follow her. It had been a very long time since he'd kissed a woman, and his body's response had been immediate, in spite of his twinge of revulsion. But some instinct of self-preservation, stronger than the urge toward copulation, made him climb the stairs to his own room. Something told him that the consequences of entangling himself with Chava Goldblum would be worse than those he'd expected from his liaison with Aunt Temele. He'd better keep his trousers buttoned this time.

The next day, however, Chava made it very clear to Dov—by throwing him a number of reproachful looks—that he'd let her down. Across the dinner table, her round black eyes fastened themselves on his face with unmistakable umbrage. As the numbers of these looks increased, they raised prodigiously the level of his discomfort. But Chava, though not a creature of words, proved herself to be a girl of action when the motivation was strong enough. Before the week was out, she confronted Dov in his bedroom with a second, and even more emotional, demonstration of her ardor.

At first Dov tried to reject her advances, but Chava became so hysterical he felt constrained to reciprocate. He decided that acquiescence might be the better part of valor, and he took her in his arms feeling a strange mixture of eagerness and self-disgust.

So began a series of clandestine meetings held after midnight in her bedroom. They met, always at her instigation, two or three nights a week. The coupling was always wordless except for Chava's giggles, gasps, and groans, all of which were so loud that they kept Dov in a perpetual state of nervous terror. It was not until their meetings became routine that Chava began to speak. "Do you love me, Dov, sweetie?" she'd whisper in her affected Polish, just when his passion was reaching its peak. "Tell me that you love me."

"I love you," Dov would gasp, telling himself that the words were not as significant in Polish as they were in Yiddish. In Polish, one "loved" everything, even custard pudding.

But the words were evidently quite significant to Chava, for one night in mid-June she made a shocking statement at the dinner table. The evening had begun like any ordinary evening, with Taube plying Dov with food, Mendel reading his newspaper, and Chava throwing Dov enigmatic looks from across the table. But suddenly Mendel looked up. "I've been thinking, Dov," he said, pushing away his plate, "that it might be a good idea to expand our English book department. We've done better than I expected with *Sons and Lovers,* and the books by H. G. Wells always sell. And there's been a good bit of interest in that Irishman— what's his name, Joyce?"

"Yes, James Joyce. I think we've already run out of copies of *Dubliners.*"

"That's just what I've been mulling over. Maybe we ought to buy directly from England. What would you say to going over on a buying trip?"

Dov gaped at him. "Me? You want to send *me?*"

"Who else? I should send Pinhas, maybe? He can't even speak well in Polish."

Dov dropped his fork in excitement. "You mean it? You want to send me to England?"

"I was thinking we might arrange something for next week. June and July are usually slow in the store. You could take your time, look around, learn whom to contact—"

"No," Chava said distinctly.

Every head came up in astonishment. Chava never before had participated in the dinnertime conversation. "What?" her father asked, bemused.

"Dov can't go away in June. We'll be too busy making plans for our wedding."

"Wedding?" Her mother gasped out the word like a joyful scream. "Did you say *wedding*?"

"What are you babbling about?" her father said, his natural sneer more pronounced than usual.

"I'm going to wed Dov this summer." Chava calmly ladled a generous spoonful of gravy on her chicken and popped a piece of the white meat into her mouth, completely disregarding her mother's elation, Dov's sudden pallor, and the large droplet of gravy that dribbled down her chin. "I've just decided that July'd be a good time."

Taube leaped from her chair and smothered Dov in an ecstatic embrace. "Dov, you darling boy," she cooed. "I didn't *dream*—"

Dov felt the blood drain from his face. How could Chava have done such a thing? Never had the word "wedding" been mentioned in the exchanges that passed for conversation between them. Marriage was the furthest thing from Dov's mind. He was not yet eighteen. And even if he *had* been ready for marriage, Chava would have been the last girl in the world he'd have chosen. Yet now that she'd made the announcement, he realized he was trapped. There was no way he could think of to get out of it. Her parents would never believe that she'd make such an announcement without his prior agreement. And if he stood up now and denied that he'd ever ask her to marry him, she might well tell them about what had been going on upstairs in her bedroom . . . and then it wouldn't matter whether he'd proposed to her or not.

Dazed, he endured Taube's kisses and effusions. Stupified, he met Mendel's enigmatic stare. He felt sick. His stomach was bouncing around inside him like a rat imprisoned in a cage. When Taube let him go, he looked across the table at the girl who was to be his wife. She sat calmly chewing away at her chicken breast, the drop of gravy still on her chin. He wondered how he'd ever found her physically enticing. She now seemed to be as repulsive as a pink sow. She was absorbed only in herself, her own feelings, and her own comfort while blissfully unaware of anyone else's. It was more than that she lacked sensitivity. It seemed to him now that she was completely lacking in character itself.

Taube began to prattle on about wedding plans—suggesting possible dates, a guest list, arrangements with dressmakers—while Chava either nodded in agreement or muttered a definitive negative. Dov, meanwhile, sat miserably in his place, his eyes fixed on his plate. After a while, feeling someone's eyes on him, he looked up. Mendel was still studying him with an unreadable expression in his eyes. Dov was stricken with a sense that he'd betrayed the man who'd befriended him. Reddening in guilt, his eyes fell away from his employer's gaze. But don't hate me, Dov begged in silent penitence. I'm going to marry her. That's sufficient atonement for my sin, isn't it?

The next morning, as Dov and his employer walked along the Senator's Street on their way to the bookshop, Mendel broke their silence. "I'll arrange for your trip to England today. You'll be on your way by Thursday."

Dov's heart began to pound. "Do you still—? But . . . the wedding—"

Mendel's mouth twisted into a wry smile. "You don't really want to marry my empty-headed daughter, do you? If you do, you certainly hid it well last night. You looked more like a hooked fish struggling on a line than a happy bridegroom."

"I'm sorry. I . . . I mean to do my best to . . . to make her a good husband."

"Don't talk like a *narr*. You wouldn't suit each other at all. Listen, Cousin Dov, I like you, so I'll talk to you like a father. Whatever happened between you and Chava I don't want to know. But whatever it was, marriage with her you don't deserve. So I'll send you to England for a couple of months, and I'll bring Pinhas Pinofsky home to dinner a few times while you're gone. By the time you get back, Chava will have landed a fish more her style."

Dov could scarcely believe his ears. "Do you mean it?" He gave his benefactor a piercing glance. "You're not just saying this, are you? Testing me or something? Because I fully intended to go through with the marriage plans."

"You'll sacrifice yourself, eh? Listen, boy, it's a long time since mankind practiced human sacrifice. Do me a favor and take the chance I'm giving you. To tell you the truth, if it had been me in your place last night, I would have packed my things as soon as everyone was asleep and made off. I'd have been on my way to America by now."

Dov laughed. "America! Is that all you think about?"

"If I was your age, that *would* be all I thought about. So I take it you'll go on that book-buying trip?"

Dov's face sobered. "Yes, with much gratitude. I don't know what to say. You've been a good friend to me, Mendel Goldblum. I wish I could say I've done as well by you."

"If you're talking about Chava, don't feel so bad. I was young once myself. As for the rest, you've been the best clerk I ever had in the store —honest, hardworking, always thinking of new ideas for the business. I have no complaints."

"Yes, but . . . there's something else. I've been wanting to tell you from the first. I lied to you, Goldblum. I'm not your cousin."

Mendel laughed. "You don't say. Listen, Weisenberg, you should know by now that I'm no pigeon. I knew from the first day that you weren't my cousin. I remembered, the very night you came, that Berele Simke had no sisters or brothers, so I knew you couldn't be her nephew."

Dov was dumbfounded. "You knew? Then why—?"

"Who knows why. Maybe because you were such a good liar. Maybe because your shoes were so shabby. Maybe because I never had a son."

They walked on in silence. Dov felt too choked to speak. Mendel had just admitted something that Dov had suspected from the first—that he looked on Dov as the son he'd never had. But if that was the case, why had he given him this chance to escape from the commitment of marriage? If Mendel had forced Dov to wed his daughter, he would have had him as a son in actuality. But instead, he was helping him to get away. It was a puzzle.

It took Dov a while before he worked out the answer, but by the time Mendel put him on the train to Calais, he'd figured it out. Mendel had a basic understanding of the nature of love that his mother didn't have: the knowledge that you can't force a loved one to stay at your side. Mendel knew that nothing works to hold a loved one when circumstance or lack of feeling drives him away—not guilt, not passion, not even trickery. If you really love, you learn to let go.

3

The day after Dov arrived in London the news vendors screamed the news that the Archduke of Austria had been shot at Sarajevo. The world seemed in a turmoil. If the shooting proved to be a Serbian plot, the Emperor of Austria-Hungary might well declare war. Dov, just trying to acclimate himself to a strange room in a strange lodging house in a strange country, sat on his bed reading a newspaper in a strange language and tried to determine what was happening and what he should do next. Would the Emperor declare war against Serbia? If he did, would Germany join? Would the Russians then go to the aid of Serbia as treaty required? And if all that occurred, where did *his* duty lie? Should he go home to Solitava and let himself be conscripted into the Austrian army? Should he return to Warsaw and possibly find himself in the Russian army fighting the Austrians? His situation was utterly bewildering.

It seemed wise, before anything further happened, to arrange for his return to Warsaw. Once he was back there, if war did break out, he would have Mendel Goldblum to advise him. But before he was able to arrange passage, a letter arrived from Goldblum that Dov found very reassuring. There would be no war, Mendel wrote. Messages were being exchanged between Austria and Serbia, and the heat generated by the incident was already cooling. Dov was to stay where he was and conduct business as usual. Besides, Mendel added, Pinhas Pinofsky had already come to dinner, and Chava had definitely acted playful. If a romance between them was to be permitted to develop, this was not the time for Dov to come home.

Thus set at ease, Dov began to explore his new surroundings. London was a revelation to him. It wasn't the bigness or the bustle—Warsaw had also been large and busy. But Warsaw had not seemed foreign to Dov. He hadn't felt displaced in it. Everywhere he'd gone in Warsaw he'd found Jews very much like himself. He could talk Yiddish to them, and therefore he hadn't felt alien. But here in London everything was strange. The signs on the roadways and in the store windows had to be carefully read and mentally translated. In London even the Jews (who were not nearly as numerous as they'd been everywhere else he'd lived) seemed foreign. They spoke English, dressed in the English style and lived like the English. They were prosperous, bourgeois, *modern.*

It was the modernity of London that impressed him. For the first time in his life he felt a part of the twentieth century. He'd moved into the modern world, and it excited him. He loved leaping on the backs of the two-storied, open-topped, motorized omnibuses; he loved walking down busy Oxford Street and gazing at the shop windows glittering with wares he'd never seen before; he loved mingling with the crowds in Piccadilly. In the afternoons he loved to wander over to Trafalgar Square, seat himself on a stone balustrade, and gaze up at the enormous monument while the sounds of spoken English surrounded him. That was one of the things he liked best about London—to hear English spoken so casually on the streets. *English,* which until that time had been the awe-inspiring language of Shakespeare and Keats and the other writers whom his mother had forced the family to read on cold winter evenings.

So the days of July slipped by, with Dov doing a little business and a great deal of exploring, until, on July 28, the news broke that Austria had declared war. Germany soon followed, with Russia promptly retaliating. The news was shocking. The four weeks of negotiations had lulled everyone into complacency about the aftermath of the Sarajevo shooting. In the soothing warmth of the European summer, war was the last thing anyone expected.

Dov immediately tried to arrange passage home, but every foreign traveler on English soil was attempting to do the same thing. Train stations, shipping lines, booking offices, and travel agencies were scenes of wild hysteria. Dov spent the next few days in fruitless efforts to make arrangements.

He was still trying on the fourth of August, when England declared war on Germany. With a swiftness that shook everyone, the nation began to gear up for war. Overnight, everyone German became suspect, and everything German became despicable. People of German ancestry, even if they'd been British citizens for years, began to change their names. Innocuous little German words were suddenly banished from English mouths. Sausage and sauerkraut became "good English viands."

Everyone with a foreign accent was suspected of spying, and the government, in response to public hysteria, moved quickly and ordered all foreign nationals to register with the police. The owner of Dov's lodging house informed him coldly that he'd better register at once, "if y'know whut's good fer you." And he added, "Ye'd better take along yer passport, too."

Dov was astounded. In all his travels since leaving Solitava, not once had he been asked to produce a passport. But now, of course, things were different. The world was at war. A passport had suddenly become the most important document one could own. Fortunately, he'd taken Hersh's Turkish passport with him when he'd left Warsaw. He dug it out of the worn travel bag Mendel had given him and went to the neighborhood police station to register.

The police station, like the travel bureaus, was a scene of hysterical confusion. Travelers, unable to make arrangements to leave the country, were standing about in forlorn groups. While Dov waited on a queue to register, a German woman bedecked in a flowered hat came storming in. "Where can I change my passport?" she demanded loudly in German.

The police sergeant on duty didn't understand her. "Is there some'un 'ere oo knows whut's eatin' this lady?" he asked the crowd.

Though the place was crowded with Germans, no one volunteered. At last Dov stepped forward. "She says she wants to change her passport," he told the sergeant.

"Whut's she jawin' about? Change 'er passport 'ow?" the sergeant asked impatiently.

Dov turned to the woman. "What is it you want to do with your passport?"

"I want to change it for an English one," she explained, holding it out for him to see.

"But it's German."

"Of course it is. That's why I want it changed. When people see it, they treat me like a leper."

The Germans in the queue all laughed as Dov tried to explain that one's passport couldn't be changed. The woman wouldn't believe him. "Stupid Jew," she snapped, tossing her head so violently that her flowered hat shook, "if I can't get an English passport, ask the officer where I can get a Russian one."

"Go to the Russian embassy," one of the other Germans in the line said to her while the others roared. "Maybe they'll accommodate you."

After she swept out, Dov and the others in the line were handed registration forms to fill out. Without giving it much thought, Dov filled out his name and the address of his lodging house. The queue moved slowly toward a desk at the rear of the room at which two khaki-clad officers were seated. Dov noticed that some people were sent into an inner room while others merely handed in their forms and were excused. He wondered what it was all about.

When he reached the front of the queue, he handed the paper to one of the officers. "Is this your name?" the officer asked.

"Yes," he replied. "Dov Weisenberg."

"May I see your passport, please?" The officer was polite, but there was an undercurrent of impatience in his tone.

When he handed over his passport, Dov could see at once that things would not go well. The officer looked at it, showed it to his second-in-command, and they both frowned. "This is Turkish," the officer remarked accusingly.

Dov's heart began to pound in alarm. "Yes," he said.

"But you're no Turk. Your accent is German, isn't it?"

"I was born in Austria," Dov said, suddenly remembering that Hersh had bought the passport illegally. How on earth could he explain? "I . . . I moved to Turkey, you see." The explanation sounded lame even to his own ears.

"Turkish *and* Austrian," the officer muttered to his associate. "Double trouble, if you ask me." He looked down at the registration form. "What are you doing in England, Mr. Weisenberg?"

"I work in a bookstore in . . . er . . . Turkey. I'm here on a book-buying trip."

The second officer had been examining the passport. He suddenly touched his superior's arm. "Look at this. The names. They don't match."

The first officer studied the passport, his brow rising. "The name on this is Gentz," he said to Dov suspiciously.

Dov winced in self-disgust. How could he have been so stupid as to forget what name he'd put on the passport? "Yes," he said, trying to sound casual, "Gentz is my legal name."

"Then why did you write Weisenberg on the registration form?"

Dov felt like an utter fool. Why hadn't he *thought* before filling out the blasted form? "Weisenberg is my stepfather's name. I prefer it."

"Oh, you do, do you? Well, Mr. Gentz or Weisenberg, or whatever your name is, will you please step inside that door? I'm afraid you'll have to be detained for a while."

"Detained? I don't understand. Why? And for how long?"

"Just step inside, if you please. Your questions will be answered in due course."

In the other room there were about twenty men standing about in silent aloofness or huddled together in small groups. Dov noticed that they were all between the ages of eighteen and forty-five. Military age. Some of them were whispering among themselves, expressing their fears, their alarm, their confusion. "Do they think we're spies?" someone asked in German.

"They think all Germans are spies," another responded.

"They call me an enemy alien," said an English voice, pitched nervously high. "I've lived in Spitalfields fer thirty years. 'Ow can they say I'm an enemy alien?"

"Internment camp, that's where we're going," another voice said in the cultivated German accent known as *Hochdeutsch*. "Internment camp. We may well be stuck there for the whole war."

"I'm not worried," said his companion. "Even if you're right, the war won't last past Christmas."

A thin young man about Dov's own age, who'd been standing by himself near the window coughing into a handkerchief, looked up at this and groaned. "Oh, God, I can't stay cooped up till Christmas. What am I doing here? I was only on vacation, sketching. See?" He held up some drawings for Dov to look at. "The great houses of England. Every architectural student draws the great houses of England. I'm no spy."

Dov tried to murmur words of encouragement, but he felt too depressed to be convincing. After a while, everyone lapsed into silence, and a short time later Dov and the others were led out and loaded into a bus, which took them to an internment camp for enemy aliens in Upper Holloway, north London. They were kept there for four weeks. Spirits were not hopeless, because it was rumored that the Upper Holloway camp was a facility for temporary incarceration. As soon as the government investigated properly, rumor had it, the authorities would learn that none of them was a spy. They convinced themselves and each other that they would soon be freed.

But early one fall morning, several hundred of the Upper Holloway prisoners were lined up in fours and marched through the streets of the town to the train, Dov among them. People in the houses along the way looked out of their windows and shook their fists at the marchers.

"Damned Huns!" they shouted. The prisoners lowered their heads and marched glumly on. After traveling a day and a night by train and boat, they found themselves being marched up a hill on the Isle of Man. Word filtered down to them, whispered from one to the other, that they were heading for a new, still uncompleted camp called Knockaloe.

As they came over the brow of the hill, they could see it plainly, spread out below them in all its immensity. Though the smell in the air was clean and fresh and the view of the hills beyond quite lovely, the sight of the camp itself destroyed Dov's hopes of freedom. The long, low buildings said prison on every inch of their slatted walls, and the huge fences of thick barbed wire surrounding them gave the last vestiges of hope a final blow. This camp was not designed for temporary detention. There was something about it, despite its ramshackle appearance, that indicated permanence. Dov knew with a devastating certainty that he was stuck for the war's duration.

His one remaining glimmering of optimism depended on a theory commonly espoused by everyone who had any expertise in politics: that the duration would be short. The war would not last past Christmas. This conviction was shared not only by the knowledgeable prisoners but by the guards. One could even read that prediction in all the newspapers. The war couldn't last long. Not possibly.

Part Four

DVORA
1914-1919

1

Dvora was to say later, in tones of bitter irony, that the only thing she learned in the years of the war that had any effect on her later life was how to smoke. But of course this was far from the truth. She learned a great deal: how to speak like the Viennese, for example, and how to carry herself like an aristocrat.

. . . If you'd press her, Sam, she'd admit that the war years had changed her, but she'd say that what she'd learned was all so much nonsense. What good did it do for her later to have learned how to order wine in a fine restaurant or when to wear white gloves? But it seems to me that she learned something of much greater importance: she learned how to suffer . . . in silence, and alone. . . .

By the time she was twenty, at the war's end, Dvora Weisenberg was no longer a naïve, provincial Jewish girl. She'd been completely transformed.

The city in which the transformation took place was Vienna. It was there that Leutnant Franz Gebhardt had taken her after he'd completed his cavalry maneuvers at the Czernowitz military reservation. With passes for ten days' leave in their pockets, he and his companion at arms, Leutnant Berthold Heintz, had smuggled Dvora into their compartment on the Athens-Belgrade-Vienna express. The two soldiers had pretended they were abducting her, and the deed was done with such boyish high spirits that their hilarity was contagious. Dvora was kept laughing throughout the entire journey, and she had neither the time nor the inclination to consider the enormity of what she'd done.

Before the bedazzled girl could catch her breath, she found herself installed in a suite of rooms in a hotel on the Näglerstrasse with her Franz, his friend Bertie, and Bertie's blond sweetheart, who called herself Bibi. "And you must call yourself Dori," Bibi instructed her at once. "Your name must end with *i* if you wish to sound *wienerisch.*"

The terrible feeling of oh-God-what-have-I-done struck her the first moment she found herself alone. A day and a half had gone by since she'd stolen from her bed in Czernowitz. How could she have done it? she asked herself. How could she have left her home and family on such a whim?

But it wasn't a whim. From the first moment she'd met Franz she'd known that something special had happened to her. During that first meeting of their eyes, when he'd gazed down at her from atop his enormous horse, his eyes gleaming with the shock of attraction, she'd known that their futures would be bound up with each other. She'd *had* to leave home. It was as if she'd had no other choice. It was not her will that had done it—it was fate.

But the city, the hotel, and the people with whom she was now living were strange to her, and in this first moment of reflection she was assailed with doubts. What sort of girl was it who would run away with a soldier? Her mother would have a ready answer—*corve.* Her mother had long ago decided that Dvora was whorish. Now she'd be convinced of the truth of her assessment. Even if Dvora had the desire—and the money—to go back home, she wouldn't do it. She'd ruined her chances to return home unscathed. Her reputation was destroyed, and she had no wish to face her mother's vituperation.

Besides, she told herself, her mother was wrong about her. She'd come away with Franz because she loved him, not because she was a *corve.* Love was beautiful . . . true . . . almost holy. It ennobled any act, even the act of running away with a soldier. Let her mother think what she liked—Dvora didn't care. She would stay here in Vienna with her love, and put Czernowitz and her past life out of her mind. She would live a new life now.

That new life began at once. It required a major mental adjustment. In the first place, Dvora had not expected to find herself part of a group. When she realized that all four would be living together in the suite, something inside her curdled in disappointment. In Czernowitz, Franz had been so fervent and passionate that she believed he thought of nothing and no one but her. Now it seemed he wanted the constant companionship of Bertie and Bibi as well. The only time she saw him alone was in their bedroom in the wee hours of the morning.

It wasn't that she disliked Bertie and Bibi. Bertie was a good-natured, jolly sort whom it was impossible to dislike. He had ruddy cheeks, an infectious laugh, and an endearing habit of finding something witty in everything that was said to him. The only quality Dvora didn't admire was his doglike adoration of his sweetheart. Everything that Bibi said or did pleased him; the girl twisted him about her little finger with complacent ease.

From the moment Dvora met Bibi she'd felt uncomfortable. Bibi was taller than she, a large-boned but well-proportioned young woman of spectacular good looks. The only part of Bibi's body that was not in proportion was her neck, which was too broad. But instead of spoiling her appearance, the wide neck gave her a look of intense sensuality. Everything she wore she opened at the neck to reveal the enticing swell of her throat, where a pulse seemed to throb with promise. The curve of her throat was accented by a large, ornate gold cross that hung around her neck on a heavy chain. Dvora wondered if it was that flagrantly displayed cross that caused her feelings of discomfort in Bibi's presence.

But it was more than that. Bibi, four years older than Dvora in real time, was decades older in experience. She seemed to know all sorts of things of which Dvora had no knowledge. The hotel, for instance. To Dvora, the Hotel Nägler was as magnificent as a palace. Their suite, consisting of two bedrooms and a huge drawing room, had high ceilings, crystal chandeliers, tall double casements, cornices painted in gold, plush upholstery on all the chairs, and thick Orientals on the floor. But it was one small detail of the decor that really convinced Dvora of the hotel's elegance. At home in Czernowitz, they had also had double casements. Mama used to put strips of turf between the outer and inner casement to sop up condensation and to keep out drafts. Here at the Nägler, however, instead of strips of turf there were long cushions of real velvet! What could be more palatial than that?

But Bibi told her, in the casual, drawling, amused tone that was her usual way of speaking, that the hotel was really second rate. She explained that it was the sort of place which—because of its secluded location—was appealing to army officers indulging in secret liaisons. "But don't concern yourself, *Liebchen,*" she added, lighting a cigarette. "Everyone on the staff is well rehearsed in discretion."

Dvora didn't quite understand what Bibi meant, but she had no time to dwell on it. Franz and Bertie were determined to embark on a round of gaiety so intense that not a moment of their ten days' leave would be wasted, and Dvora was swept up in a whirlwind of activity.

Her three companions expected her to gape, openmouthed, at the sights and sounds of Vienna. Surely the little country mouse from the hinterlands of the Bukovina would be overwhelmed by the "Paris of the East." But Czernowitz was not a village—it was the capital of the province. Dvora was less provincial and more widely read than they supposed. She knew what to expect from her first glimpses of the city. Nevertheless, it was thrilling to see the things she'd so often read about: the huge, magnificent palaces, the parks, the elegant thoroughfares, the grand statues and sparkling fountains, the church spires and domes, the sounds of different languages spoken on the streets, the music from the cafés, the clang of the trams, and the rumble of the hurrying crowds. She didn't mind being laughed at when she gaped at all that.

But she didn't always play the role of the overwhelmed provincial. Sometimes she surprised them, like the afternoon they took her on a tour of the Inner City. Noting the great number of heraldic emblems on the public buildings—the double-headed eagle with its wildly splayed wings, which had been the symbol of the Habsburgs since the twelfth century —she asked why there were so many of them. Franz answered somewhat pompously that "they are there to remind the populace that the Emperor gazes out on his people both east and west."

"Yes," Bertie agreed, putting a fond arm over her shoulder and pointing up toward an enormous, gilded stone *Doppeladler* atop the Bürgerliche Zeughaus, "see how the eagle's heads are looking out in opposite directions? That's to show how vast are the regions of the empire."

"Hummmph!" Dvora said, quite unimpressed. "No wonder the poor bird looks so frantic."

Despite her occasional remarks of disparagement, Dvora was really awed by the city and by the miracle of finding herself living there in such luxury. She would have been content merely to walk the streets and watch the life of the city unfold itself before her, but her companions had grander ideas about how they wished to spend their time. First they took the girl to the elegant shops of the Kohlmarkt, where Franz bought her a number of gowns for day and evening, three pairs of shoes, a couple of silly little hats, and, most thrilling of all, a stole of real fur from Russia. When she emerged in her new finery, she hardly knew herself.

As soon as she was properly bedecked, the four embarked on a ten-day round of gaiety that left them exhausted when they fell into bed not much before dawn. They strolled along the Ringstrasse and the Corso so that they might laugh at "Dori" as she gaped with disbelief at the magnificent palaces with their rococo decoration; they romped through the amusement park at the Prater, riding Riesenrad, the famous wheel, shooting arrows at colorful targets, and nibbling on roasted chestnuts purchased from street vendors; they sipped *Mokka* or *mélange* at Franzi's special table at the Café Sperl, and the two girls watched while Bertie and Franzi played billiards at the café's famous billiard tables; they went to the racecourse at Freudenau and screamed with excitement when Bertie's horse came in first; they went three times to the theater: once to see a glittering operetta called *The Beggar Student,* once to a drama by Schnitzler called *Professor Bernhardi,* and finally to a comedy in English called *Pygmalion* (during which Dvora won Bibi's respect because of her ability to follow the main thread of the plot with her meager understanding of the language), all three of which Dvora found so thrilling that she floated from the theaters almost speechless with joy; they dined in undreamed-of luxury at Sacher's or Demel's; and they indulged in as many as they could squeeze in of the hundreds of other delights that Vienna offered to its citizens who could afford them.

And Franzi (as Bibi insisted they call him) seemed quite able to afford them. He appeared to have an unlimited supply of money. He was not yet a baron, but his father, the present Baron Gebhardt, supplied his son and heir with a very generous allowance, which, when added to several months of accumulated army pay, made all this good life possible. Bertie was almost equally plump in the pocket, so nothing was stinted to make their ten days' leave a period of continuous pleasure.

Only one incident occurred during the frenzied round of pleasure that caused Dvora discomfort. It was during the evening at the Volksoper, where they'd seen the operetta. When they'd first taken their seats, Dvora had become aware of a gentleman's eyes on her. He was sitting in a box with a spectacularly beautiful woman in a satin gown that revealed a shocking display of bosom. The gentleman himself seemed to Dvora to be elderly—forty at least—with graying hair and a thick gray moustache. He was the essence of magnificence in his red-and-gold staff officer's uniform. But when he raised his monocle and stared at her through it, she felt herself redden. During the intermission, the spectacular couple passed close by where she and her friends were standing and sipping champagne. Again she felt the man's eyes on her and blushed hotly. As he went by, he gave Franz a very distinct wink.

"Do you know that gentleman?" she asked Franz when he'd passed.

"It's my uncle, the Count Otto Gebhardt," Franz answered with a casual lack of interest and turned to talk to Bertie.

Later, in the ladies' lounge, she asked Bibi about the Count. Bibi was well informed and said that the Count was a bachelor noted for having had a succession of beautiful mistresses. The one on his arm this evening had been a singer and had once performed a minor role at the Vienna State Opera.

"But why didn't he and Franzi speak to each other?" Dvora asked.

Bibi's eyes searched her face for a moment, but then she only shrugged. It was to be many months before Dvora learned the answer to her question.

Dvora couldn't believe, when the ten days passed, that they'd gone so quickly. She hadn't found a moment during all that time to have a serious conversation with Franz about their future. Before she knew it, Franz was kissing her a fond farewell and promising a quick return. The suite in the Hotel Nägler was paid for through the next three months, he assured her, and he handed her what seemed a small fortune for "pocket money" to see her through his absence. In a fog of bewilderment, Dvora watched as Bertie said the same words to Bibi. Then she was swept into a fervent embrace, and they were gone.

Suddenly there was time for her to evaluate what had happened to her. The whirlwind that had swept her up and out of her past life now seemed to have deposited her into this new life with a thud. She didn't know whether to feel elated or depressed. While she had to admit that she was living in luxury undreamed of in her old life, she was also aware that her present situation might be nothing but a gilded facade with tragedy lurking underneath. Franzi's absence was painful, and she could foresee that his military life would leave him little time for her in the future. And Franzi had shown definite reluctance to speak of that future. She'd tried to tell him that they couldn't live in a hotel forever, but whenever she'd attempted to speak of the future he'd tweaked her nose and talked of other things. Now she had time to wonder what was to happen next. Did Franzi expect her to live here with Bibi indefinitely?

For the immediate future, Bibi's presence was her greatest concern. But as the days passed and she grew to know the young woman better, her concern completely faded. Bibi's self-assurance, her way of smoking with a long cigarette holder, her constant wearing of the large gold cross, her air of easygoing unconcern, had all been intimidating to Dvora. The younger girl had believed that Bibi felt nothing but scorn for her and her obvious, provincial Jewishness. But she soon learned that that was not at all the case.

Bibi was blasé and unexcitable. She seemed to slough off any deep feelings about anything. Even her Catholicism seemed to go no deeper than an urge to wear her cross. She felt no animosity toward Jews at all, and she remarked to Dvora with a shrug that the anti-Semitism that had marked Viennese politics for decades was "the socialism of the morons." Dvora learned that Bibi was fundamentally good-natured. So long as she herself was comfortable, Bibi didn't begrudge comfort to anyone else.

Bibi liked her new friend Dori. Bibi had been the last child born to an aging mother and had been the abused youngest of a large family, so she enjoyed playing the role of big sister to the younger girl. Dori's admiration of her sophistication pleased Bibi, and she was quite willing to instruct her new friend in the various tricks of making one's way in Vienna.

After the initial period of adjusting to each other's ways, the two young women got on very well. Dvora was content to let Bibi take the lead in planning their days. They slept late every morning and breakfasted in their drawing room (in order, Bibi explained, to put the cost of the meal on the hotel bill rather than deduct it from their cache of "pocket money"). Then, if the weather was fine, they strolled out on the Kärntnerstrasse to look at the shop windows, sat in the Café Sperl for an hour or two in the afternoons, and then chose a place for leisurely dining. In the evening they returned to the hotel and amused themselves by taking various steps toward self-improvement. Bibi was eager to learn English, and in return for Dori's help in selecting books and reading with her, Bibi gave Dori instruction in all sorts of important matters. She taught the girl how to improve her German accent so that she might sound less *jüdisch* and more *wienerisch*. She taught her how to use mascara and the secrets of rouging her cheeks with proper subtlety. She spent hours devising a way for Dori to wear her hair and even took her to a stylish hairdressing salon where Dori's hair was trimmed, waved, and, with Bibi standing by and directing the proceedings, bound into a knot at the nape of her neck. And, lastly, she taught Dori how to smoke.

Dvora, now Dori even in her own mind, found the days more pleasant than she'd expected. Nevertheless, both Dori and Bibi yearned for the return of their lovers. Life was, at bottom, quite empty without them.

Twice more during the next few months, Franz and Bertie were given leave. During each of those periods, the mad, headlong quest for pleasure that had filled their days during the first leave was resumed. Dori, more familiar with the ways of Viennese life than before, permitted herself to enjoy everything to the full. She would be like Bibi, she decided, and take life as it came. If a feeling of concern assailed her about her future, if a trick of memory brought the faces of the loved ones she'd left behind to her mind, if she experienced the warning twinges of oncoming guilt feelings, she pushed them away. All thoughts of past or future were summarily banished. She trained herself to live only for the here and now.

Sometimes, after a long night of carousing and lovemaking, her sleep would be very deep. Her mind would come slowly to consciousness in the morning with a sense of complete confusion. For a moment before she opened her eyes, she wouldn't remember where she was. It would seem to her that her Viennese experience had all been a dream and that when she opened her eyes she'd find herself in the tiny room in Czernowitz lying beside her little sister on the simple wooden bedstead she'd always slept on. It was only when she forced herself to open her eyes, and she saw the ornate, gilded cornice over the hotel's window, that she knew the truth—she was truly in Vienna, sharing a bed with the man she loved.

At such times she would turn on her side and gaze fondly at Franzi's face as he lay deep in sleep beside her. It was a gentle, boyish face, especially when it was relaxed in sleep. The moustache, which when he was awake gave him a look of mature authority, looked in the early mornings like a schoolboy's disguise—a ruse to fool the observer about his identity. She would smile and brush it with her fingers. His *goyishe* nose was small and straight, his forehead high, and his light-brown hair straight and silky. But it was his mouth she loved best, for it was mobile, expressive, and sensuous. On many a morning she would lean over and press her mouth to his just to feel the reality of it.

Nevertheless, despite his presence at her side, she couldn't completely shake off the conviction that this existence was precarious. Such easy days, such unceasing pursuit of pleasure, such daily indulgence in nothing but frivolity—it was all sinful. She couldn't help wondering when and how this wicked life would end, and what price she would be required to pay for having lived it.

But when, less than eight months after she arrived in Vienna, on a calm, warm, ordinary Sunday in June, the Archduke Franz Ferdinand was shot at Sarajevo, it didn't occur to Dori (who was growing more sure of herself and more Viennese with each passing hour) that the day of reckoning was at hand.

2

On the streets, in the cafés, in the drawing rooms and bedrooms, everyone talked of the assassination. All Vienna was incensed at the intransigence of the Serbs in general and the fanaticism of the eighteen-year-old, tubercular student who'd fired the shot in particular. But it was not so grave an incident that it should cause a war, they all agreed. It was even rumored in the coffeehouses that the Emperor Franz Josef was relieved to be rid of the heir apparent. The succession would now pass to the young Archduke Karl, whom everyone suspected the Emperor preferred to the murdered Franz Ferdinand.

Bibi and Dori discussed the event at length. Bibi, true to her nature, refused to be concerned. "Even Franzi says in his letter that nothing will come of it. Why are you so serious about everything?"

Franzi had also written that they would be back in Vienna in late July. But when they came, they broke the news that their leave was to be for the weekend only. Dori grew uneasy. Was war coming after all? Was that why the leave had been shortened? What would happen to them if war came?

Franz assured his frightened sweetheart that war was quite unlikely. To calm her fears and distract her mind from morbid thoughts, he declared his intention to buy her a piece of jewelry. Leaving Bertie and Bibi behind, he took her to the Albertinaplatz in a *fiacre* drawn by two horses, and they spent an entire afternoon wandering from one fashionable shop to another, looking at a bewildering array of costly baubles. Franzi finally chose a gold and diamond circlet that, he suggested, "you can wear on the lapel of that new brown walking suit of yours."

Dori was overwhelmed. At least a dozen diamonds were scattered around the circle of gold. But she shook her head. "It's too expensive," she murmured, pulling at his arm to urge him from the shop.

"Don't you like it, *Liebchen*?"

"I've never seen anything so beautiful. But it's too extravagant. Besides, what if it worked itself loose and fell off? I'd never forgive myself if I lost it."

The clerk smiled at her superciliously and explained that the pin had a safety catch. "See? Nothing at all to worry about," Franzi declared and told the clerk to wrap it at once.

While they waited for the clerk's return, the bell over the door of the shop jangled. Dori paid no attention, for her mind was preoccupied with her magnificent present. She felt like royalty. She couldn't believe that she, Dvora Weisenberg, would be wearing a diamond pin on her walking suit! She was choked with gratitude. She struggled to find proper words with which to express to her lover her heartfelt thanks. Smiling shyly, she peeped up at his face.

But he was not looking down at her with his indulgent smile as he'd been a moment ago. He was staring over her shoulder toward the door of the shop, his face set, his mouth stiff, and his eyes oddly wary.

Dori turned. Two ladies had just entered, both middle-aged and richly dressed. One was so busily chattering to the other that the feathers on her hat were quivering. The other was listening with a small smile on her lips. As Dori watched, however, the silent lady's eye fell on Franzi. Her brows rose, her eyes lit, and she opened her mouth as if she were about to utter his name. But before she made a sound, her eyes took note of Dori. They flicked quickly from the girl's face down the entire length of her body and up again. By the time they returned to Dori's face, the woman's mouth had clamped shut and her expression had become icy.

With barely a break in her stride, the woman tightened her hold on her friend's arm and moved her quickly and smoothly past where Franz and Dori stood. She gave Franz a barely perceptible nod as she went by, Franz stiffly clicking his heels and inclining his head in return.

Some instinct told Dori to say nothing until they were out of the shop, but once on the street she couldn't restrain herself. "Who was that lady, Franzi?" she asked curiously.

Franz threw a quick glance at her face and then looked away. "That was my mother," he said with a brusque finality.

Dori felt her insides lurch in astonishment and dismay. "Your *mother*? But why didn't you—?"

"Do you want to take some tea at Sacher's?" he cut in blandly. "It's just around the corner. And here, take your present, please. Tuck it into your handbag, so we won't leave it behind somewhere."

He obviously wished to avoid the subject of his mother and their strange encounter, and Dori was uncertain about pursuing it. She took the gaily wrapped little box from his hand and did as he bid. They walked to Sacher's in silence. As soon as they were seated, Franzi returned to his former, charming self. He smiled and chatted pleasantly about inconsequential things all through tea. Dori tried to respond in kind but found herself too angry to speak. She had been slighted, both by the mother and by the son, and she didn't know what to make of it. Uncertain of the significance of the incident, she didn't wish to provoke a quarrel. And after all, Franzi had just purchased that magnificent gift for her. So she sat at the little table across from him with her head lowered, crumbling the luscious pastry with her fork and barely uttering a word. The joy had gone out of the afternoon.

Franz and Bertie returned to their regiment on Sunday night. The next morning over breakfast, Dori confided to Bibi the details of the encounter. "Why didn't his mother speak to him?" she asked the older girl. "And why didn't he try to make me known to her?"

Bibi shook her head, leaned back in her chair, and looked at Dori pityingly. "You really are an innocent, aren't you?" She lit a cigarette and handed it to Dori. "Don't you remember when we met Franzi's uncle, the Count, at the Volksoper? They didn't speak to each other because 'Uncle Otto' was with his mistress. It's understood that one is never recognized when accompanied by one's light-o'-love."

"I don't see the connection," Dori said, confused. "This was his *mother* . . . and she was with a friend."

Bibi sneered. "Do you really think that a gentleman of Franzi's sort would ever introduce his mistress to his mother?"

Mistress! Dori's hand, about to bring the cigarette to her lips, froze in midair. She stared at her friend for a moment in a kind of shock. Why hadn't she thought of it before? She was Franzi's mistress! The meaning of the words seeped into her consciousness in the same way that the icy rain used to seep into her shawl on December mornings long ago when she walked to school—slowly, relentlessly, and bringing with it the same chill depression. In the excitement of her new life, and because of the intense love she felt for her Franz, she had kept herself from facing the truth squarely. But now it was before her, starkly clear in Bibi's blunt word. What else was she? When one stripped away the trappings, when one discounted the intensity of the emotions, when one faced the essentials, she was nothing but a wanton. Just as her mother had predicted.

She drew deeply on the cigarette and felt the smoke's welcome haze rise up into her brain. It was soothing, a little dizzying, and it somehow made her feelings less alarming. She thought of Franz, and a ray of optimism crept in through the gloom in her head. Franz loved her. She was certain of that. He had said it too many times with too choked a voice for her to doubt it. Therefore, he would surely marry her one day . . . wouldn't he? At least she'd always assumed . . .

She looked across the table at Bibi. The older girl was eating a croissant with hearty appetite, but her eyes were fixed on Dori's face with an expression of both amusement and sympathy. Dori lowered her eyes and took another puff on her cigarette. "Don't you mind it, Bibi? Being someone's mistress, I mean?"

Bibi shrugged. "Why should I mind? It's better than being a drudge of a wife for a certain pharmacist in Salmannsdorf who once asked me."

"Is it?"

"Of course it is, though my mother wouldn't say so. Silly *Nichtswisser,* my mother. She bore eight children and died of overwork to obey the dictates of the church."

"But Bibi, Bertie adores you! Don't you think he will marry you one day?"

"Ha!" It was a snort of utmost contempt. She reached for the cigarette and blew a cloud of smoke in Dori's face. "Try not to be such a dunderhead, *Liebchen.* The sons of the upper crust don't marry our sort."

Dori winced. "Our sort?"

"Yes. Face facts, Dori. I'm nothing but a *Flitscherl,* and so are you."

Dori was by this time *wienerisch* enough to know what the word meant: prostitute. She shook her head in vehement denial. "How can you say that? You love Bertie, don't you?"

"I don't know, Dori. You know me. I don't feel anything very strongly."

"I don't believe you. You love him all right. You love each other, just as Franzi and I do."

"So?"

"So love makes a difference. It must! They'll marry us. They *will.* If love means anything at all—"

Bibi sneered. "What has love to do with marriage in the world of the upper classes?" She poured some coffee into a cup and handed it to Dori. "Here, do something sensible. Drink your coffee."

"Are you telling me that it could never happen?"

"Not even in a Strauss operetta."

The coffee cup rattled in Dori's hand. "I don't . . . I won't believe that!"

"All right. Believe what you wish." Bibi rose from her chair with her lazy, sensuous grace. "But if you have an ounce of sense, you'll put marriage out of your mind. I don't dream of it, and I, at least, am born in the true church. For a Jew, that sort of marriage is out of the question. Don't waste your time on fools' dreams. Better get up and dress. We may as well have fun while we can." And with that blunt admonition, she sauntered to her room.

Dori cried herself to sleep that night. But the next day, Tuesday, July 28, the Emperor declared war on Serbia. And before the war was six months old, that conversation with Bibi had ceased to be important.

3

*F*rom the first the war had not gone well for Austria, and by January of 1916 defeat had become a habit. It was cold in Vienna that winter. There was no coal and little wood. Hundreds of Viennese, who in better times had waltzed to the strains of "Tales from the Vienna Woods," now stole out at night to cut down the trees of their beloved Wienerwald for firewood. The snow accumulated on the streets in little piles, for there was no one—no workmen, not even one of the Italian *lavoratutti*—to shovel it and cart it away. It grew hard, black with soot, and difficult to walk upon. It was depressing to leave one's house, so different had the streets become from the Vienna of two years before. The buildings had darkened from smoke and neglect. The crowds on the streets were shabbily dressed and hunched with misery. Many wore the black of mourning, and a number of crippled soldiers had begun to appear on the street corners, begging. There were queues everywhere to buy anything, even a tiny amount of milk, a loaf of the tasteless "war bread," or the *ersatz Kaffee* made from burned barley and chicory, and the few butchers who still remained in business shut their doors by ten in the morning. The people on the queues were grim and silent. There were no exchanges of greetings with neighbors, no war news, no quarrels about who had come first. Hunger had made people listless, and the ceaseless grind of war had etched their faces with hopelessness.

Dori, wrapped in a shabby shawl, her head covered with a raw-edged kerchief, emerged from the bakery (after an almost two-hour wait for her bread ration) and clutched at her shawl. The wind was so strong and icy that it took her breath away. She tucked the loaf of bread into her basket with the two turnips and the precious pack of cigarettes she'd managed to coax from the old man at the *Tabaktrafik* by giving him the silver buttons from her last good blouse, and she started to pick her way carefully over the packed-down mounds of snow.

At a distance down the street ahead of her, at the far corner, she noticed a group of three black-coated, black-hatted men huddled against the wind and talking to each other with hand gestures and head shakings that reminded her of the way men talked in Czernowitz. The men were plainly Jews, the sort of Jews whom the Viennese had named Polish Jews, not because they were actually from Poland but because they were Jews of the *shtetl.* Thousands of refugee Jews had been pouring into Vienna from the towns and villages of Galicia and Bukovina, where most of the fighting on the eastern front had occurred. The Viennese didn't welcome them; their arrival meant only more mouths to feed.

The sight of these shabby, alien men smote Dori's breast. She felt a sudden, sharp yearning for her family. It was strange, for she rarely thought of them these days. She wondered what had become of them. She'd heard that Czernowitz had changed hands more than half a dozen times since the war started. The Russians alternated regularly with the Austrians in using the city as staff headquarters, she'd heard, although she hadn't heard that any actual fighting had taken place there. Probably everything at home was the same as it always had been.

She wondered idly where the men down the street had come from. From her district, perhaps? Wouldn't it be wonderful if perhaps one of them was from Czernowitz and could tell her something?

Just as she made up her mind to stop and talk to them as soon as she could catch up to them, the men dispersed. One went off down the Siebensterngasse, and another turned left toward Ulrichsplatz. The third paused to stuff some newspaper into his boot, and then he, too, walked away. His posture and his manner of walking were comical and reminded her of someone. That funny walk that was half a shuffle and half a run . . . it was so familiar!

"Papa!" she shouted like a person possessed, her heart pounding in eagerness. "Papa, *wait*! It's *me, Dvora*!" But the wind whipped the words out of her mouth and sent the sound up in the air where it dissipated unheard. The black-clad man ahead didn't break his awkward stride or look around.

Desperately, she began to run. She'd closed the gap between them by half before she slipped on the ice and tumbled down heavily. The basket was crushed under her, its contents rolling out into the street. "Papa!" she gasped, stumbling to her feet and snatching up the cigarettes. "Papa!"

Her basket and the bread were crushed beyond repair, one turnip seemed to have disappeared, she'd bruised an elbow and torn a stocking, and her hip ached painfully, but she ran on. "Papa!" she cried again as she caught up with him and tapped his shoulder.

The man, a complete stranger, turned around. His eyes were frightened. He stepped backward, away from her, as if she meant him harm.

"Oh, I'm . . . I'm sorry," she mumbled in Yiddish, her disappointment terrible. "I've made a mistake."

He backed away further, turned, and hurried away from her down the street. She watched after him until he disappeared from sight, tears of blighted expectation filling her eyes and spilling down her cheeks.

After a while, she turned back toward her flat, limping from the pain in her hip and weeping. The incident had brought back to her mind the dreams she'd had when she'd first left home. Such foolish, childish dreams. She'd imagined then that she would promptly be wed and that, soon afterward, she would put on her finest clothes, climb into a magnificent carriage bearing the Gebhardt family crest on its side, and drive to Czernowitz. After dazzling her family with her magnificence, she would bundle them all—yes, even Mama—into the carriage and take them away with her to a new life of ease and luxury. How ridiculously naïve she'd been. She'd thought life was going to be a fairy tale.

Turning into the archway that led to her flat, she brushed the wetness from her cheeks and nodded grimly to Frau Pauli, the caretaker, who was peering out at her suspiciously from behind the glass door where she sat most of the day watching the tenents come and go. The sight of Frau Pauli, the *Hausbesorger,* frowning at her with distaste, was a bitter reminder of just how far from a fairy tale her life had become.

The flat she and Bibi now occupied was located on the second floor of the farthest wing of this large apartment building on the Lindengasse. One had to pass the caretaker's door and then go through three dark archways and three inner courtyards to reach the door to the stairway that led to the flat. She and Bibi had moved in a few months after the war had begun. The mail from the front had become infrequent by that time, and even though the letters they received contained a number of banknotes, their arrival was too irregular to permit the pair to remain at the hotel. The flat they'd found seemed to them perfectly adequate. There were two square bedrooms and a little sitting room (which, being the location of the stove, was also used as kitchen and dining room), and since they were able to purchase furnishings from the vacating family for a reasonable sum, they felt quite comfortable. They'd been concerned that the hotel staff would be careless about forwarding their mail, but the desk clerk had, in fact, been punctilious in his duties, even directing Bertie to their new abode when he'd wangled a leave in the late fall of 1915.

Bertie's leave had been a strange few days. The Fourth Army, to which his and Franzi's division was attached, had been through two major campaigns in the Carpathians. Despite the circumlocutions and the persistent optimism of the reports in the *Neue Freie Presse,* it was hard to disguise the fact that both campaigns had been disastrous. Even if Bibi and Dori had been able to fool themselves into believing that the fighting was going well for the Austrians, one look at Bertie's face would have told them the truth. His once ruddy cheeks were pale and sunken, and the laughter had died from his eyes. Bibi made an agonized, choked sound in her throat at her first sight of him. He made a great show of heartiness, of course, insisting that they dress up for dinner and taking them to Meissel and Schadn's Hotel for a wonderful meal. But during the course of the dinner they often found him unresponsive to their quips. Instead of laughing, he'd be staring off into space.

But the worst moment of his leave occurred on his last day. With a ghostly echo of his once tireless pursuit of pleasure, he roused them early, helped them to pack a picnic basket with whatever cold meats, cheese, and bread they had on hand, and ushered them into a *fiacre* for a trip to the suburbs to spend the day at his favorite *Heurigen.* These rustic inns, where the local vintners could sell their recent vintages by the glass at outdoor tables to the sound of music and merry voices, had always been beloved by the Viennese. The day he'd chosen for the excursion was beautiful—autumnally gold and pleasantly warm—and Bertie talked compulsively during the ride about all the good times they'd shared together in the past.

They were among the first arrivals, but by midafternoon the tables were crowded with patrons from the city: elderly couples in their Sunday best, groups of young women looking for a way to forget their absent husbands or sweethearts, a boyish-looking young man in the uniform of an infantryman having a last outing with his parents before going off to the front, and an impressively uniformed Hungarian officer with a large, noisy party. Music for the occasion was provided by a woman with white hair and long, slim, wrinkled fingers who sat on a bench playing folk tunes on a zither. The wine flowed, the smell of roast chicken and good cheese filled the air, and one could almost have forgotten there was a war.

197

Then a woman in a printed silk dress rose to her feet, raised her glass in Bertie's direction, and made a loud toast to "our victorious soldiers." The Hungarian officer, whose resplendent uniform and complacent expression suggested that he'd secured for himself a safe berth at army staff headquarters in the city, jumped to his feet and seconded the sentiments, adding, ". . . and may our victories lead to the swift and final annihilation of our enemies!"

One by one the people at the tables rose and, with broad smiles, raised their glasses. Only Bertie was left seated. He stared at all of them as if they were creatures who'd materialized from some nightmarish inner vision . . . as if he'd found himself in a world distorted beyond all reality. He put his right hand to his forehead and with his left made a thrusting movement outward, as if to push away the entire scene. The gesture sent three glasses crashing to the ground. He rose slowly, seeming to hold the crowd mesmerized by his gaze of disbelief. "You fools!" he said in a hissing whisper. "You *damned fools*!"

Then he turned and stumbled away, repeating those words over and over under his breath. As soon as his back was turned, a murmur broke out among the crowd. "Shell-shocked," someone said.

Bibi and Dori exchanged frightened glances, but Bibi immediately turned in the direction of the voice. "He's no more shell-shocked than you are," she said contemptuously.

They rode back to Vienna in silence, and none of them ever referred to the incident again. But Dori couldn't help wondering what Bertie had seen and what he'd suffered to cause him to undergo so drastic a change.

They'd seen Bertie once more since that day. In the early spring of this year, he and Franzi appeared without warning at their door. Franzi was a captain now. Dori was beside herself with joy; it had been almost two years since she'd set eyes on her beloved. But, though the first night of their reunion was a miracle of passion, the gaiety of their earlier holidays was impossible to recapture. Nothing was the same. The city had lost its sparkle. The restaurants, even the best of them, served meals that were barely edible. The theaters still offered nightly performances of the concerts and plays that had made Vienna a theatrical and musical center of the world, but now the liveliness was forced. Worse still, neither Bertie nor Franzi had the energy or the urge for pleasure seeking that they once had had. They seemed lethargic, stayed in their beds for half a day, and when they did go out soon lost interest in the type of easy banter that had marked their conversational style before. Now they would sit at Franzi's table at the Café Sperl, ignoring the girls, the pastry, and the billiard tables, and spend hours mumbling to each other about the formidable talents of the Russian General Brusilov, whispering about their alarm at the actions of their own General, Conrad von Hötzendorf, and debating about the value of his retreat from Warsaw. Bibi tried to distract them. "Must we hear about nothing but war?" she would ask periodically. At those times, they would look at her guiltily and make an attempt to change the subject. But they couldn't stay away from the subject for very long. The war had become their only reality.

The summer and fall that had followed that leave were the worst months of the war for the young women. The funds that their lovers had left for them were rapidly depleted by escalating inflation. Food was becoming harder and harder to find. Only by trading on the black market could one get hold of decent edibles. On Sundays, they took to riding on the train with thousands of other city dwellers out to the country, where they could barter with the farmers for produce, eggs, cheese, and sausage by trading away their beautiful clothes. After a while, the farmers refused everything but jewelry, furs, and solid valuables. Some of Vienna's *haute bourgeoisie* (and even representatives of the nobility) were bringing their paintings, their musical instruments, and their treasured antiques to barter for food. As for Bibi and Dori, they had nothing of the sort to barter. But they were not supposed to complain; there were signs posted all over the city bearing the word DURCHZUHALTEN—stick it out.

By the time the cold weather had set in, Bibi and Dori had nothing left. No letters came from the front, and no money. They had little food and less heat. Dori began to go out daily to look for work, but she didn't know what sort of work she was capable of doing. To make matters worse, the good-natured caretaker of their building, Herr Hausbesorger Pauli, had been conscripted in September when they'd called up the over forty-fives. His place in the little *Hausbesorge* office with its glass door was taken by his sour-faced, suspicious, difficult wife. She had narrow, beady eyes and a mole on the lower part of her cheek from which a patch of wiry hairs sprouted. She nagged at them constantly about the rent, cut off their water at the slightest provocation, watched their comings and goings with such suspicion that one would have thought they were black marketeers, and locked the building so early that they didn't dare leave the house for an evening stroll lest they find themselves locked out. Dori hated the woman; she was the final straw on their haystack of misery.

And now, in addition to all their other troubles, Dori had foolishly lost a turnip and made a *Schlamperei* of their two-day supply of bread.

She nodded again to the ever watchful Frau Pauli and limped past the glass door as quickly as the pain allowed. Frau Pauli opened the door of her little office. "What happened to you?" she shouted after Dori. "Why are you limping?"

Dori gritted her teeth in annoyance. There was no limit to the woman's interference in her affairs. Dori would have liked to ignore the question and walk on, but it didn't seem wise to antagonize the woman over so small a matter. After all, they owed two months' rent. "I slipped on the ice," she explained, looking over her shoulder.

"You should be more careful," Frau Pauli said with obvious disgust. "You young people are always in such a hurry. If you'd slow down a bit—"

"Yes, Frau Pauli," Dori muttered through tight lips, walking away through the archway.

"You'd better hurry now, though," Frau Pauli called after her. "I think you have a visitor."

But Dori had already passed through the tunnellike archway and had reached the second courtyard. She was not sure the sour old *Hausbesorger* had really said what she thought she'd said. After all, who could be visiting them?

Nevertheless, when she reached the stairway, she took off her ragged kerchief and stuffed it into her basket. If there was indeed a visitor, she didn't want to look more shabby than necessary.

She pushed open the door without knocking. "Bibi," she announced, offering the good news first, "he gave me the ciga—*Franzi!*" The basket fell from her arm as she flew into his embrace.

Bibi picked up the basket and retrieved its contents. "Is this the sort of bread they're selling nowadays?" she remarked drily.

But Dori didn't even hear. "You're *here*!" she marveled, putting a hand to her lover's face to assure herself she wasn't dreaming. "When Frau Pauli said we had a visitor, I didn't let myself even *imagine*—!"

"Dori, *Liebchen,*" Franz muttered convulsively, burying his face in her hair.

Dori felt a twinge of fear. "Franzi? What is it? Why did they give you leave just now? Is something wrong?"

She could feel him stiffen as he lifted his head and glanced at Bibi. Bibi, putting a cigarette in her holder, froze.

Franz withdrew Dori's arms from about his neck. "Why don't you sit down, both of you? I have something to tell—"

A shudder passed through Bibi's body. "Oh, my God!" The words were barely a breath. "It's Bertie."

Franz took a step toward her, his arms out to support her, but she held up a hand to ward him off. "Not . . . *dead?*"

Franz nodded.

There was a cry, but it came from Dori. Bibi merely stared at him. Franz's shoulders seemed to sag. "I'm sorry. I hated to have to . . . but I knew no one would inform you, so I prevailed upon the Major to let me come."

"I see. Thank you, Franzi. That was very kind." She continued to stand there staring at him. It was like a moment of suspended time caught in a photograph.

Franz couldn't bear the silence. "It was so unnecessary, you know," he muttered miserably, sinking into a chair. "He didn't have to go. It was Radler, you see, who was supposed to take the message to Trentino. But he had the dysentery, and Bertie volunteered to go in his place. He should never have been there. None of us should have been there. Those damned Italians, they'll never get across the Isonzo anyway. It's such a damned waste!"

Dori, shaken, trembling, her throat burning with unshed tears, took a step toward her friend. "Bibi, dearest, don't you want to sit down? Or shall I help you to bed?"

Bibi's eyes slowly focused on Dori's face. "No, no, don't bother."

Franzi, recovering himself, got to his feet. "Perhaps a drink—?"

"No, nothing. You said before you have only a few hours. Well, don't waste them standing about staring at me. I'm all right." As if to prove it, she put the cigarette holder in her mouth and lit up.

But Dori noticed that her fingers shook. "Bibi, please. Let me—"

"I'm all right, I tell you." She went to the door of her bedroom, turned around and gave them a strained smile. "You know me, Dori. I don't feel anything very strongly." She went in and shut the door.

Dori started to run after her, but Franz caught her arm. "Don't," he ordered. "Let her be. She's all right."

"Don't be a fool. She's not all right. I have to go to her."

"Leave her alone. If it had been the other way, and it was you who'd gotten such news, you'd have wished to be alone, wouldn't you?"

Dori stared at him in horror and covered her mouth to stifle a cry. Then she nodded slowly.

He took her arm and drew her toward her bedroom. "Bibi's right, you know. I've such a short time left. It would be a shame to waste it."

They made love with a desperate urgency, as if by the act they could generate a life-force to counteract the atmosphere of death surrounding them. After he left, Dori kept watch on Bibi's closed door for a long while. When she could stand it no longer, she tapped at it gently and whispered Bibi's name. There was no sound from within.

She pushed open the door. Bibi lay sprawled on the floor at the foot of the bed in a faint. Dori knelt at her side, slapping her cheeks and calling her name until Bibi opened her eyes. Dori watched as the blank look was replaced with the agonized realization of where she was and what had happened.

There on the floor, Dori took the girl, now sobbing hysterically, into a tight embrace. Yes, my poor Bibi, she thought bitterly, rocking her friend gently to and fro, I know, I know. You don't feel anything very strongly.

4

*W*inter set in with a vengeance. No letters came from the front. For weeks, Bibi moved about in a daze, lying in bed for most of the day staring at the ceiling. Dori was terrified of everything—of the war news, of the face of Frau Pauli at the entrance of their building, of their dwindling supply of cash, and of the increased difficulty of getting food. But in the middle of February she found a job. It was in a small dress shop in the Kärntnerstrasse, where once she'd purchased a walking suit. Now, of course, there was so little to sell that Herr Sperling, the elderly owner, would have had to board up his door had he not had an idea for a way to keep himself afloat. He'd put up a sign in his window reading OLD GOWNS TURNED AND REFASHIONED. Suddenly he found himself swamped with business. The only new fabrics now available for civilian clothing were the *ersatz* stuff made from such things as the fibers of nettles and willows. Many of his old customers could see the advantage of reusing the fabric of their old clothes to make new ones. Herr Sperling employed his wife and two other seamstresses to restitch old garments on the reverse side to give the dresses new life. To Dori he gave the tedious task of ripping out the old seams. The work had to be done with great care in order to keep from tearing the fabric. It was much more painstaking than sewing, and much more tedious, but it paid the rent.

The salary was not even large enough to keep the two women adequately fed, and certainly not enough to permit them to buy cigarettes. It was Bibi's hunger for tobacco that finally pushed her from her lethargy. She left her bed and went out to look for work. But she could find nothing, and she came home from the search each day feeling more and more hopeless.

Dori came home from the dress shop one evening to find Bibi packing. "What's this?" she asked. "What are you doing?"

Bibi sat down on her bed and motioned her friend to do the same. Before she answered, she took from her pocket a brand-new packet of cigarettes. "I traded my cross for four packs," she grinned sheepishly.

"Your *cross*?" Dori gaped at her. "But you *always* wear it!"

"I know. But it wouldn't look right to wear it where I'm going." She offered a cigarette to Dori and lit one for herself.

Dori was appalled. "You can't be going . . . leaving me alone! Where can you go?"

"I'm moving to the Rotenturmstrasse. You can come, too, if you wish. There's plenty of work there, if you want it."

"The Rotenturmstrasse? But isn't that the . . . the . . ."

"Yes, the sin district." She laughed at Dori's expression of shock. "Right in the shadow of the cathedral, too."

"But, Bibi, you *can't*—!"

"No? Why not? It's not so different from what I did before. I'll just have more . . . variety."

"Come now, Bibi, don't act this way with me. I know you better."

Bibi's eyes fell. "Maybe you do. But that doesn't change anything. I don't know what else to do. Do you know that I tried to get a post as a maid? To do cleaning in a townhouse in the Mariahilf district. Even if I had got the job, I don't know how I would've gotten there every morning with the trams so irregular. But I didn't get it. The lady of the house said flatly that I was too pretty to be a hard worker. Can you imagine that? Too pretty to clean her damn floors!"

Dori sat down beside her and put an arm around her shoulders. "Don't be discouraged, Bibi. The war can't last forever. Just obey the posters . . . *durchzuhalten*. Stick it out a while longer. When the men come home—"

"And what can we do in the meantime? Starve and pay the rent, or eat and let Frau Pauli put us out in the snow? I've thought and thought about it, Dori, and my mind's made up. I've even got a license, see?"

She waved an official-looking paper under Dori's nose. Dori took it and let her eyes skim over the fine print. "My God, they give licenses for prostitution?"

"Yes, and they take a nice tax from the proceeds. So you see, my dear, what I'm doing is quite legal . . . officially sanctioned by the government."

Dori pleaded and argued all night, but Bibi was adamant. She proved to Dori with the actual numbers how dire were their present straits. It was impractical, she pointed out, to expect Dori's tiny salary to support them both and equally impractical to expect help from Franz while he was engaged in a life-and-death struggle at the front. "If you take a smaller flat, you may be able to survive. And don't worry about me, *Liebchen*. The girls on the Rotenturmstrasse make good money, I hear."

By dawn all Dori's arguments had been answered a dozen times. Bibi had folded all her belongings into one small suitcase and was ready to leave. There was nothing more to say or do.

The friends embraced tearfully, making solemn promises never to forget each other. At the door, Bibi took a last look at the sitting room. "I've been wondering, Dori," she said, her lips curling in a bitter smile, "if my whole life isn't a mistake. Maybe I should have married that pharmacist in Salmannsdorf when I had the chance."

It took great effort for Dori to return the smile. "Yes, maybe you should have."

Bibi laughed at herself and shook her head. "*Ach,* no. Don't encourage me in such foolish speculations. I would've had seven babies by this time, like my poor mother. Who needs that?" She picked up her bag, gave Dori an ironic little salute, and was gone.

Thus Dori found herself completely alone for the first time in her life. It was a frightening experience. Every worry grew enormous when there was no one to confide in. She felt strange and displaced, as if her life was in limbo while she waited for something to happen. Where was that life headed? She needed some sign, some clue to give her a sense of direction. But no sign came.

One of her problems—the need to move to a smaller flat—was solved more easily than she'd expected. Frau Pauli went into action as soon as Dori explained that she was now alone. The caretaker knew just which tenants in the building were waiting for a chance to enlarge their living space. In addition to making the arrangements for the switch, Frau Pauli was surprisingly helpful in executing the move. She found a young lad to carry the furniture and dishes, she and the boy moved the heaviest pieces into place, and she even helped Dori pack and unpack her clothes. Dori didn't know how to account for this unexpected assistance until she realized that the sour old *Hausbesorger* must have received a large gratuity from the tenant who was taking over Dori's old flat; it was to Frau Pauli's advantage, she realized, to expedite the move.

The new flat was similar to the old one except that it had one room less, but it was in the first court—very much closer to the *Hausbesorger*'s glass door. Dori felt more spied upon than before. And the feeling of being watched became even worse in the spring, when Dori became aware that she was pregnant.

She tried not to believe it, but by spring she couldn't avoid facing the truth. Pregnant. Just like the thousands of other unmarried women all over Europe made pregnant by soldiers they would never see again. Her mother wouldn't have been a bit surprised that Dvora's life had come to this.

Pregnant. One more terror piled upon her mountain of misery. What would become of her now? Would Herr Sperling keep her on at the shop when her condition became apparent? Where was she to get the money to pay for a doctor and a hospital bed for the lying-in? And didn't pregnant women need special foods, like milk? How was she to get milk these days? She could line up on the food queues only in the evenings after work, and by that time the milk was usually gone.

She hadn't had a word from Franzi since his visit in January. She clung to the conviction that he was still alive; if he had died she would have felt it in her bones. She wrote to him regularly, of course, but she didn't know if any of her letters had reached him. Never in any of her letters, no matter how desperate her mood when she wrote them, did she give a hint of her condition. She would not tell him about the life growing inside her. If he was ever to marry her, it would be because he loved her and for no other reason. Her pride demanded it. She would have it no other way.

But her future was uncertain and fraught with dire forebodings. She was so very alone. Even if Franzi was alive and well, there was no assurance that he would return to her before the baby's birth. The war had dragged on for three years already, and there was no end in sight. The government had no word for those who waited except *durchzuhalten*.

She often thought about going home to Czernowitz, but that was now no more than a dream. She could never go back like this—poor, ragged, and pregnant. She couldn't bear the thought of seeing herself so debased in her mother's eyes. She'd brought this fate upon herself, and she would cope with it by herself or die in the attempt.

It was a gloomy spring, the despair of the endless war almost palpable in the air. Only the chestnut blossoms on the Ringstrasse showed signs of gaiety. By the middle of June the war news was so discouraging that the fine weather gave no solace. Rumors were rife that the Russians under General Brusilov had begun another offensive in Galicia. If the rumors were true, there would be hundreds of thousands more Austrians dead, no matter how the campaign went.

In another few weeks it was more than a rumor. The Russians had broken through the Austrian lines, and the Fourth and Seventh armies had collapsed. Wounded soldiers from the front, filtering into the city by train, horse, and wagon and on foot, gave heartbreaking evidence of the truth of the reports. The campaign had been a disaster.

Whenever Dori could beg some time from Herr Sperling, she ran to the Westbahnhof to speak to the soldiers coming off the trains. "Are you Fourth Army? Do you know Captain Gebhardt?" No one did.

Her mind was in a turmoil of fear and dread. There had been no word of him for five months. Where was he? Was he still alive? Something dreadful must have happened; how else could she account for the prolonged silence? Her increasing alarm made the tension in her chest unbearable. Sometimes she felt she was going mad.

And the business with the milk only added to her sense of disorientation. For the past month someone had been entering her flat and leaving a small pitcher of milk on her table. How this intruder managed to get into her flat was a mystery, for she never forgot to lock her door. She'd questioned Frau Pauli at length on the subject, asking if she'd seen anyone near her door, but Frau Pauli had declared quite firmly that if anyone had been loitering about she would have noticed. Dori wondered if the tenant with whom she'd exchanged flats had kept the key and was letting herself in when Dori was at work. But why? Nothing was ever touched. The old tenant was someone Dori didn't know, but she'd heard from Frau Pauli that the woman had two children. Certainly she would need any milk she could get for her own family. Dori drank the milk hungrily every time she found it, washed the pitcher, and left it on the table. She supposed she should be grateful to whoever was supplying it, but she felt more fear than gratitude. She couldn't understand what was going on.

The sense of going mad was heightened one day at the shop when she began to shake from head to toe for no reason at all. She couldn't hold her scissors in her trembling fingers, nor could she catch her breath. She began to gasp in terror as the scissors clattered to the floor. The little seamstress who sat opposite her began to scream that Fräulein Weisenberg was having an epileptic fit, but Frau Sperling, who sat at the table near the workroom's only window, knew better. She sent the seamstress for her smelling salts and chafed Dori's hands until the girl's trembling gradually ceased.

"It's the war," Frau Sperling said when they'd all settled down again to their needlework. "They're starving us to death. Look at you, all skin and bones. No wonder you had a seizure. Before the war, I used to drink a glass of hot water with lemon juice every morning of my life, and I was never sick a day. Now I have headaches and this dreadful lethargy. Nowadays, if one can find a lemon once a month, one can call oneself lucky. But take it from me, *Fräulein,* the juice of a lemon in a glass of hot water is what you need. Try as hard as you can to procure for yourself some lemons. I will see what I can find for you, too. They will do you more good than those cigarettes you like so much."

Dori thanked her, obediently agreed with everything she'd said, and resumed her work. But she knew she'd not be able to buy any lemons. And as for being only skin and bones, she was glad of it. It was an advantage to be so thin. She was late in the fifth month of pregnancy, but no one yet had guessed that she was *schwanger.* Her thin frame and loose clothing masked her condition.

Except for the shaking seizure, Dori felt well enough physically. The morning nausea that had troubled her in the first few months of the pregnancy had now passed. And the baby inside her was apparently healthy enough; it had begun to kick her vigorously in the past few weeks. She had the mysterious intruder to thank for that, she supposed. The milk was keeping the baby healthy.

That afternoon, Frau Sperling ordered her husband to send Fräulein Weisenberg home early, to rest. Dori thanked them both with sincere gratitude and hurried home. There was nothing she wanted so much as the chance to take a nap. But when she let herself into the flat, she found Frau Pauli standing at the table, the pitcher of milk in her hand. *"You?"* Dori gasped in horror.

Frau Pauli flushed hotly and bit her underlip. "You're early," she muttered in embarrassment.

"How dare you enter my flat without permission?" Dori demanded, her lips white with fury.

"I . . . I'm the *Hausbesorger,*" the old woman stammered. "I have a right to—"

"No, you haven't! This is an intrusion on my privacy. How dare you?"

Frau Pauli's eyes fell. "Well, you see, you haven't the time to wait on queues for milk, so I . . . I thought . . . I'd do it for you."

"Do it for me?" Dori's anger thickened her mind, clouding her ability to understand the generosity of the woman's act. She'd felt the *Hausbesorger's* eyes on her for so long that she couldn't believe Frau Pauli's intentions could be anything but nasty. "Who asked you to do it for me?"

"I only thought . . . you need some milk in your condition."

"What?" Dori's hands flew to her belly. "What do you mean? How did you find out—?"

The older woman shrugged. "I have good eyes."

Good eyes! Something in Dori seemed to explode in rage. Was nothing in her life to be secret from those prying eyes? "Your eyes are too good, Frau Pauli," she said furiously. "My condition is none of your business. Or is it the province of a *Hausbesorger* to be caretaker even of *that*?"

"I'm s-sorry." The woman's gnarled hands began to shake. "I didn't mean . . . I only wanted to help—"

"You only wanted to *pry*!" Dori snapped.

To Dori's amazement, Frau Pauli's eyes filled with tears. "No, no, I never looked at anything . . . or touched—"

The woman looked so pathetic, standing there in miserable discomfort with the pitcher in her hand, that Dori's feelings became confused. Frau Pauli had always seemed to her to be an ugly creature with her hairy mole, her wrinkled skin, her close-set eyes, and her sour expression, but suddenly Dori noticed the knobby fingers reddened by years of scrubbing and the swollen feet stuffed into a pair of shabby, misshapen slippers, and she was overwhelmed with a wave of pity. Not knowing what to make of this sudden shift in her feelings, she wanted only to be rid of the woman. "All right, all right," she cut in coldly. "Just go away. Just get out and leave me alone."

"Yes, I'll go. I'm sorry." Frau Pauli brushed at her eyes with the back of her hand and shuffled to the door. But before leaving, she turned and held out the milk-filled pitcher. "Please, won't you . . . this once—?"

Dori stared at her. Why was the woman being so humble? Frau Pauli had really done nothing wrong. In fact, she'd been a benefactor. All that milk . . . she must have spent *hours* waiting in lines. And the cost of it! She hadn't asked for a penny. Why had she done it? Dori put a hand to her forehead and sank slowly into a chair. "I *must* be going mad," she muttered.

Frau Pauli took a step toward her, her brow wrinkled worriedly. "*Fräulein,* are you ill?"

Dori studied the old woman's face. There was nothing threatening or curious in her expression. There was only concern. Had Dori made a terrible mistake in judgment about the character of this woman all this time? "Frau Pauli," she asked, bemused, "*why?*"

"Why?"

"You must have spent hours getting that milk for me, when you should have been keeping watch at your door."

Frau Pauli shrugged, relieved to see that Dori was no longer angry. "So I watched at my door a few hours less. Who cares?"

"But why did you do it?"

"You need milk. How else could you get it?"

Dori shook her head to try to clear away the cobwebs that seemed to be clogging her brain. She'd disliked the old woman for so long that this overwhelming act of kindness made no sense. "But I don't understand. I've never done anything for you."

Frau Pauli's eyes widened. "Why should you do anything for me?"

"Why should you do anything for me?" Dori countered. "You don't even like me."

Frau Pauli gave a little snort of laughter. "Your eyes aren't nearly so good as mine." Her face didn't show a sign of the humor in her voice.

Dori had never guessed the woman could laugh. And the thought that Frau Pauli felt some affection for her was utterly amazing. "Are you saying you *do* like me? Knowing what you must know about . . . about the way I've lived? Even now that you know I'm going to have a baby and have no husband?"

"I don't judge. It's the Lord's task to make judgments, not mine. And there's nothing so terrible about the way you live. You work hard; you don't whine; you bear your burdens all alone. I know what it is to be alone."

Dori felt a wave of shame. She'd been so cruel to this lonely old woman who'd only done what she'd done out of simple generosity—secretly, without any desire for reward. "It was . . . very good of you, Frau Pauli, to get the milk for me," she muttered in apology.

Frau Pauli padded over to the table and put the pitcher down. "You'll drink this, then?"

"Yes. Thank you. I don't know how to . . . to reciprocate."

"No need. So long as you're not angry at me for my intrusion."

"I'm sorry for my outburst. It was just so . . . so unexpected."

Frau Pauli went to the door, her slippers making shuffling sounds along the bare floor. "And is it all right if I bring you some more?" she asked. "After all, you really need—"

Dori got up and followed her to the door. "I'd be most grateful if you would . . . when you can. I'll pay you, of course. For what you've already bought and for whatever you buy from now on."

The *Hausbesorger* nodded, her expression seeming, as always, to be sour and disapproving. "When you can," she said brusquely and left.

It was only after she'd gone that Dori realized that the sour expression was caused more by Frau Pauli's facial lineaments than by her inner feelings. The old woman's eyes, small and closely set though they were, were filled with kindness and the special sort of sadness that comes from being too much alone. Why hadn't she noticed that before?

5

She tugged at the waistband of the skirt desperately, but it would not close. "It's no use. I can't wear this either. And I can't go to the Gebhardt house in the smock I wear to work. Let's forget the whole idea."

"Tie the ends together with a shoelace. Your yellow blouse will cover it," Frau Pauli suggested placidly from her place at Dori's table, where she sat shelling the peas she'd bought from a *Schleichhändler* at an exorbitant price.

"I'll look pregnant. I can't let them see I'm pregnant. It's no use. I can't go."

"Put on the blouse and let's see," Frau Pauli insisted. But when Dori did so, she had to agree that the swelling middle was a bit obvious. "Wait, I have an idea. Finish shelling these peas. I'll be right back."

Dori looked after the old woman with an affectionate but negative shake of her head. It had been Frau Pauli's idea in the first place that Dori pay a visit to Franzi's mother. "You'll go out of your mind if you don't find out what's happened to him," she'd said one evening when she'd found Dori in another of her trembling seizures. "There's no harm in just asking."

The mere anticipation of calling on the Baroness Gebhardt had set Dori in a quake, but Frau Pauli was right to tell her to go. Her nerves couldn't stand any more of this agonizing suspense. The wounded of the Fourth and Seventh armies were pouring in every day, and Dori found herself imagining her beloved in the direst of straits. She would see him lying dead in the forest or hideously wounded and unattended while shells burst all around him. She would wake up screaming from a nightmare in which she saw him run over by a caisson. Any truth would have been easier to face, she thought, than the horrors her mind was creating. She had to know if he was still alive.

If it hadn't been for Frau Pauli, she might really have lost her mind. Everything terrified her these days. With her pregnancy becoming more obvious daily, she was afraid that Herr Sperling would give her notice. With every discouraging rumor she heard from the front, she agonized about the fate of the man she loved. But her terrors were eased by the new relationship with the old caretaker. It was soothing to come home from work to find a bowl of soup waiting for her on the table. It was pleasant to sit with Frau Pauli on a rainy night and exchange stories about their families. In the mornings, when she left for work, it was cheering to have someone to whom to wave goodbye. The woman who sat behind the glass door still didn't smile at her, but Dori felt the affection that hid behind Frau Pauli's sour facade. Frau Pauli had become like a mother to her. Her own mother had never shown her such uncritical affection.

Frau Pauli returned with a garment of black silk over her arm. "It's called a sack coat. My husband bought it for me years ago, to wear to the opera. It was a ridiculous extravagance—we went to the opera only twice in our lives. It will be big on you, of course, but that's what we want."

She helped Dori put it on. The silk swirled around her in loose folds, and the wide sleeves felt light and cool on her arms. Its lines were graceful, and the sheen of the silk was elegant. From what Dori could see in the small mirror, the coat covered her swelling belly quite adequately.

"It's really an evening jacket," Frau Pauli murmured worriedly, "but with the gray skirt below and the collar of your blouse showing on top, maybe it will pass."

Dori looked herself over critically. "As long as it hides my belly, it will be fine." She kissed Frau Pauli's cheek gratefully. "I don't know what I'd do without you."

The flush in her cheeks was the only outward sign that Frau Pauli glowed with pleasure. She'd never had children, and now God had sent to her this girl who so desperately needed mothering. It was the closest thing to happiness the old woman had felt since her husband was conscripted.

By the time Frau Pauli had helped her complete her dressing, Dori felt pleased with her appearance. Her hair was pinned into a ladylike bun at the nape of her neck, her best shoes were polished to a mirrorlike glow, her only pair of silk stockings looked like new (for the mended places were completely hidden by the skirt), and Frau Pauli's silk jacket billowed around her gracefully as she walked. There was a mild summer breeze cooling the air, and the long walk down the Mariahilferstrasse to the Inner City was not the least tiring. Her spirits rose with her hopes. She would learn that Franzi was alive and well.

But by the time she knocked at the door of the magnificent house on the Singerstrasse, her spirits fell again. What sort of greeting could she—a strangely dressed, ignorant Jewish country girl—expect behind this heavy, ornate door? They were nobility. She remembered the cool, disparaging look the Baroness had given her when they came face to face on the Albertinaplatz so long ago.

Suddenly it seemed to her that her belly had swollen perceptibly since she'd started out this afternoon, that her face was dewed with the sweat of a peasant, that her silk jacket was cheap and tawdry for daytime wear, and that her tongue had thickened in her mouth so much that she wouldn't be able to utter a word. Nevertheless, she was here, and she would not turn back. Franz loved her. That gave her the right to ask about him. She knocked firmly at the door.

Her knock was answered by a neatly dressed housemaid in white apron and cap. Dori had prepared a speech. "My name is Dori Weisenberg," she announced more loudly than she'd intended, "and I've come to inquire of the Baroness the whereabouts of her son."

"Yes, *Fräulein*. If you will wait here, please." The maid left her standing in the huge entryway while she stepped through an arched, curtained doorway to what Dori could see was a circular area surrounding a double stairway, the two branches of which curved in opposite directions up from a marble floor and met again at the floor above.

"Madam, there's a Fräulein Weisenberg waiting to—"

"Weisenberg?"

"Yes. She's come to inquire about Captain Franz."

"Tell the person I am not at home."

Dori couldn't bear it. She ran to the archway. The woman she remembered from the jeweler's shop was reaching the top of the stairway. "Please, Baroness, I only want to know how he is!" she cried urgently.

The Baroness paused at the top of the stairs where the two curved staircases met and looked down impassively. Her eyes swept over Dori with utter disdain. Then she turned away and disappeared into a hallway above. "Show that person out, Betta," came the voice from the shadows above. "The Baroness is not at home."

Dori had to put a hand to her mouth to keep from crying out. She shook with rage. Why had the Baroness been so cruel? She'd intended to ask for nothing but information. The woman had treated her as if she were a creature beneath contempt. She was Franzi's mistress, true, but she was a human being! Hadn't she a right to know if Franz was alive?

A light hand touched her arm. "Will you follow me, please?" the maid, Betta, asked timidly.

Dori, in a daze, did as she was asked. Her head was pounding with fury, and her blood was pulsing through her veins with alarming thumps. But her mind stumbled on one encouraging fact—the Baroness had not worn black. Her skirt had been a light lavender. Dori was sure of that. There was no mourning in this house.

The maid opened the door, and Dori stumbled over the threshold into the bright summer sunshine. She paused on the doorstep, blinded.

"*Fräulein?*" the maid whispered timidly.

Dori blinked at her. "Yes?"

"He's all right." The maid glanced nervously over her shoulder into the house to make sure no one was about. "He's been taken prisoner."

"Prisoner?" Dori echoed stupidly.

"Yes. The Russians have him. But he's all right."

She grabbed the maid's hand gratefully. "Alive? You're sure?"

The maid smiled and patted her hand. "Certain. They've had letters."

Dori nodded her thanks and went dazedly down the steps. Letters. They had had letters. Where were hers?

6

The baby was born in October, 1916, in the tiny flat on the Lindengasse, brought into the world with the assistance of a midwife and Frau Pauli. It was a girl, a dark-eyed, light-haired girl whom Dori named Frieda. "For Franz?" Frau Pauli asked, wrapping the baby in three blankets and rocking her delightedly.

"For no one," Dori said from the bed, turning her face to the wall. She would have liked to name the child for her father, but Jews didn't name their children for the living, and as far as she knew, her father was still alive.

In the style of true Viennese, they began to call the baby Fredi. She was a good baby, healthy and contented. Even though Dori had to ween her early, so that she could go back to work, the child thrived. Food was scarcer than ever, and the streets were thronged with starving, begging children, but little Fredi didn't want. Frau Pauli diligently followed every lead for food supplies, and the Sperlings, who had come to visit Dori after the baby's birth, fell in love with the child and gave Dori little gifts of foodstuffs whenever they could. Even Bibi (who had turned up one day to tell Dori the news gleaned from one of her "clients" that Franzi had been captured by the Russians, and who was shocked to discover that her friend had had a child) became a regular visitor and could always be counted on to bring a treasure of fruits or sweets.

The war ground on, despite talk of peace and signs of discontent and rebellion among the populace. But Dori seemed to take little interest in the war news now. She moved through her days in a kind of haze, as if part of her mind was numb. She would lose the thread of a conversation, she would smile at the baby's antics with an air of abstracted sadness, and her friends would catch her from time to time sitting absolutely still and staring at nothing. If her brother or sister had been there to see it, they would have told her she was acting like Mama.

By the time the baby was six months old, the world around them was changing drastically. Everything seemed to be falling apart. The workers in Russia had revolted and the Czar had abdicated, and the shock waves were felt all over Europe. The upheaval in Russia affected even the workers in Vienna; there had been strikes and demonstrations, and, in January, Herr Sperling and other merchants had closed their stores in fear of radical activities. But nothing seemed to jar Dori from her abstraction until word came that the Russian armies were disintegrating and that their prisoners were simply walking out of their compounds and heading for home. They began to flood into Vienna in droves, filling the hospitals, the taverns, and the streets. Dori returned again and again to the Westbahnhof asking for word of Captain Franz Gebhardt. One day in late April of 1917, she was rewarded. A battered, bearded officer on crutches told her he'd seen him—that he might have been taken to the Allgemeines Krankenhaus, Vienna's largest hospital.

She took a succession of trams, bursting with impatience. But when she arrived at the Spitalgasse, breathless and eager, she realized that he would not be easy to find. The hospital was enormous, and inside all was noise and confusion. The corridors, the stairs, the alcoves, the passageways, were all thronged with wounded. Nursing sisters, orderlies, doctors and aides picked their way in and out among the bodies with expressions of harried concentration. No one seemed to be in charge. No one had time to talk to her. No one was available to give her information or assistance. Slowly she walked through the halls of the first floor of what she thought was the main building, peering into each crowded room, studying the face of each man stretched out in the hallways. The corridors seemed to go on for miles. Once a bony hand stretched out and grasped her skirt. "Water?" the man begged, his voice a mere croak. She sought out a nurse. "Where can I find some water for that poor man?"

"There's water in the alcove near my station, there. And while you're at it, will you pick up the box of antiseptic powder and sprinkle this fellow's arm? And get yourself an apron, too. How can we tell you're an aide if you're dressed like that?"

Dori didn't bother to explain. She fetched the water and the antiseptic powder, and then went on her way again. After hours of searching, the sights and smells making her feel like retching, she made her way to the second floor. Things there were the same as below, but after a short while she found him.

He was in a tiny cubicle that had evidently been meant for a single patient. Three cots had been pushed into it, all occupied. Franz, unshaven, dirty, and worn, was sitting upright upon the cot farthest from the door, his back against the wall and his arms crossed over his chest. His right arm was in a sling, heavily bandaged and awkwardly positioned. It was clear that something was very wrong with it. Worse, the right side of his head was bandaged from above his right eye down to his neck. His right cheek, the part not covered by the bandage, was hideously disfigured with raw-looking scars. Dori was stricken with pain at the sight of those ragged, badly healed wounds.

At the left of Franzi's cot someone had squeezed in a chair. The Baroness was sedately perched upon it, calmly reading aloud from a leatherbound book. Franzi didn't seem to be listening. He was staring out ahead of him at nothing, as if his mind was a thousand miles away.

Dori backed away from the door. She didn't want her moment of greeting marred by the presence of Franzi's mother. She walked a little way down the corridor, where another hallway joined it at right angles. She could hide herself at this corner and watch the door of Franzi's room unseen. She would wait here until the Baroness left.

"My dear young woman," said an irritated voice behind her, "you can't stand here like this. You're decidedly in the way." It was a doctor in a bloody white coat. He brushed by her and went on his way. A nurse, who'd been following closely behind him, gave her a look of disapproval. "What are you doing here?" she demanded suspiciously.

"I . . . er . . . they told me to get a clean apron," Dori said quickly.

"In the closet behind you," the nurse said in disgust and ran after the doctor.

Dori opened the closet, took off her coat and covered herself with an apron. Then she busied herself with tending the men lying in the corridors. She fetched water, wiped dripping brows, bandaged superficial wounds, and tried to give words of comfort to the suffering. Every once in a while she went down the hall and peeped into the cubicle where Franzi sat, but the Baroness was still there.

Once, after she'd bandaged the feet of a soldier who'd evidently walked for miles without shoes, the nurse who'd scowled at her came along and examined her work. "This is the sloppiest bandage I've ever seen," she said. "You're not really an aide, are you?"

"I . . . I just thought I'd help," Dori stammered.

The nurse nodded. "We can use all the help we can get. Keep on doing what you've been doing."

Dori walked along the corridor with her. "That man in the room at the end of the hall. The one with his head bandaged. Can you tell me what's wrong with him?"

"You mean Gebhardt? A shell burst near him just before the Russians got him. Lost an ear, part of his face, and the use of his arm. It was terrible neglect. There weren't proper facilities for medical care in the prison camps, you know."

She walked away, and Dori went to the nearest window. She had to lean her forehead on the cold glass for a long time before she could go back to her work.

It was turning dark when the Baroness finally took her leave. Dori crept into the little room on tiptoe. Franzi was still sitting with his back against the wall, his expression unchanged. She lowered herself onto the cot and gently caressed his scarred cheek with her fingers. "Franzi, my dearest," she whispered.

He stared at her blankly for a long, long moment. Then his face seemed to crumble, his eyes filled with tears, and he collapsed upon her shoulder, his good arm around her and his whole body wracked with sobs.

She held him in her arms for hours. The nurse came in from time to time, looked at them, hesitated, and walked out again. But when everyone had settled down to sleep, she came in again and gently told Dori she had to go.

"I'll be back tomorrow, my love," Dori whispered to Franzi, giving him a last embrace. "Tomorrow, as soon as they let me in."

But when she came back the next morning, the bed was empty. The nurse looked at her with sympathy. "His mother took him home," she explained, not letting that sympathy tinge the crisp efficiency of her tone. "He'll have private doctors and the very best of care. He's a very fortunate young man."

Dori left the hospital and walked along the Berggasse, distraught. His mother had taken him home. He'd meekly gone with her, leaving not a word for Dori. What did it mean? He'd clung to her last night as if he'd caught a grip on life itself. Didn't that mean he loved her still? Didn't he realize that his mother would never permit them to be together? Was he going to allow his mother to come between them?

She had to know. She presented herself at the Gebhardt house and instructed the maid, Betta, to tell the Captain that she was here and had to see him at once.

Betta looked troubled, but she bobbed and disappeared into a room to the right of the stairs. She returned shortly to say that Captain Gebhardt would be with her in a moment.

Dori could hear voices issuing from behind the closed doors. The masculine voice was low and nervous. The feminine one was high and shrill. "I want that Jewish whore out of my house," Dori heard the Baroness say quite plainly.

A little while later, Franz emerged and strode across the marble floor to her. He was still bandaged, but he'd been washed and shaved, and his ragged uniform had been replaced with a dressing gown of luxurious silk. "You shouldn't have come here," he muttered.

Her chest contracted in pain and disappointment. "But, Franzi, I *had* to. How else could I speak to you? There's so much to—"

A knock sounded at the outer door. Franz moved her into the shadow of the curtained archway and watched uneasily as Betta came up from somewhere down below and went to the door. Count Otto Gebhardt, looking as aristocratic as Dori remembered him (even though he was dressed in subdued, civilian clothes), entered and handed the maid his hat and gloves. Betta led him across the marble floor toward the door to the right of the stairs. She was about to open the door for him when he noticed Franzi and Dori. His eyebrows rose; he put his monocle to his eye and stared at them. Then, with the slightest motion of his fingers, he waved the maid away and stood still, as if waiting for Franzi to finish with Dori and join him.

Franzi looked from his uncle to Dori in acute discomfort. "I'm sorry," he said in an undertone, "you'll have to go."

Dori felt a stab of revulsion. Where was the strong, cheerful, self-confident man she loved? Why didn't he take her in his arms and carry her from this dreadful house with its cold, snobbish inhabitants? But before her revulsion could take hold, her eye fell on his scarred cheek, the bandage over what had been his ear, the arm that lay tied against his chest in awkward uselessness, and her heart softened. He'd been battered and mutilated and had suffered God knew what dreadful experiences in the past months. He needed her, no matter how he might deny it to his mother or himself. He needed her, and she would wait until he realized it. "When will I see you, Franzi?" she asked, her voice quivering with desperation.

"I'll come to you. Soon."

No, Dori thought suddenly, her heart clenching in her chest, he can't come to me. He mustn't know about Fredi, not yet. Not like this. "But there's no place you can come, my dear," she said, her eyes falling. "I . . . I've had to give up the flat."

He sighed. "I see. Well, then, wait here a moment. I'll get some money for you, and you can go to the hotel. I'll come to you there." He walked quickly over to his uncle, and the two stood together speaking in low voices, the Count glancing over at Dori several times. After a while Franzi came back to her. "Here. Uncle Otto gave me this key. It's for a flat in Bäckerstrasse Number 19. Take it—and this money—and wait for me there."

Dori looked over at the Count, who remained standing on the other side of the stairway watching them with an arrogant directness. She met his eye, put up her chin for a moment, and then turned her back on him. "I'll take the key," she said to Franz coldly, "but I don't need the money." And without another look at either of them, she went quickly from the house.

7

She waited in the Count's suite of rooms—it was much too magnificent to be called a flat—for three long days, desperately hoping each moment that she would hear Franzi's knock at the door. But the hours dragged by, and no one came. She became more and more distraught. If the situation had been reversed, she could never have stayed away from him as long as this.

She didn't dare leave the apartment for fear of missing him. She went out only once, in the very early morning, to buy a small supply of edibles. She felt imprisoned in the large, high-ceilinged, plushly upholstered rooms and was tempted more than once to forget about Franz and go home. She yearned to see her baby, although she knew that Fredi was being well looked after. Frau Pauli was completely devoted to the child and wouldn't take her watchful eyes from little Fredi even for a moment. Her caretaking duties might suffer from neglect, but the child never.

Dori suspected that the old woman guessed that she'd gone away to meet her lover, but if Frau Pauli had felt any disapproval she hadn't let it show by so much as the blink of an eye. She'd declared often enough that she left judgment to God, and she seemed to act on that belief. She'd helped Dori pack a few belongings, she'd assured her that she would take the tenderest care of the child, and she'd embraced her at parting. Dori's own mother would not have been so indulgent.

But knowing that Fredi was in good hands did not keep her from missing the baby. Time passed too slowly to bear. She wandered through the rooms aimlessly, examining the suggestive paintings on the walls, the erotic books on the shelves, the luxurious nightclothes in the drawers. As she fingered the soft silk of the nightdresses, waiting for the Count's next mistress, a wave of deep resentment filled her breast. Vienna's upper classes were living very much as they always did, as if the war did not deeply affect them. They still had their silks and their wines and many of their other luxuries, while the poor starved and died. No wonder there were uprisings and rebellions. It was only the sacrifice of such men as Franzi who ennobled the so-called nobility. For the rest, they were self-indulgent and corrupt and would deserve the same fate the Russian nobles were now suffering.

She looked around at the rococo decor and the lush decadence of the suite. Even Bibi would have been appalled, she thought, at the lack of subtlety in the decoration of the rooms. The very draperies on the windows, with their red velour and gold fringe, seemed to announce that this was a den of Eros. Dori hated it. When Franzi came, she would make him leave at once. She didn't want to spend one night with him under this roof. As soon as they came to an understanding about the future— as soon as he learned about Fredi and agreed to make them all a family —she would take him to her own place. It was tiny and very shabby, but she could make it cozy for him. She and Franz and the baby could be very happy there.

By evening of the third day her patience was almost exhausted. She swore to herself that she would give him only one more day. She couldn't wait here for him forever. Why, her child might already have forgotten her by this time!

That evening she was shaken out of her lethargy by the sounds of a disturbance in the street. She opened the sitting-room window casements and peered out into the dimly lit roadway. A small group of people were gathering at a street corner a couple of streets down from her, but she could hear their shouts very clearly. "Peace and bread!" they were chanting. "Peace and bread!" She tried to make out who the people were, but from this distance it was hard to tell. Factory workers, she supposed, and women who were having trouble feeding their families. She wondered if the crowd would grow, and if there would be a riot. *Peace and bread*—they weren't too much to ask for after all these years of deprivation. She was tempted to go down, to join the crowd and shout with them.

Just as the thought took hold, she heard a knock at the door. Completely forgetting the scene below, she pulled herself from the window, flew across the sitting room, dashed through the vestibule, and flung open the door. "Franzi! At *last*!"

But it was not Franzi. It was the Count.

He was dressed in evening clothes, with a white silk scarf thrown carelessly around his neck and a coat hanging in equal negligence from his shoulders. He was looking at her with a slight smile on his lips. "May I come in?" he asked. But he walked by her without waiting for an answer.

She followed him into the sitting room. "Where's Franzi?" she asked, her mouth tight.

"At home, of course. With his mother."

"But . . . isn't he coming?"

The Count tossed his hat and gloves on the chair with his coat. "No, my dear, I'm afraid he isn't."

She felt a sickening lurch in her stomach. "You mean, not to-night—?"

"I mean he isn't coming at all."

"That's ridiculous. Why did he tell me to wait here if he didn't intend to come? I've been waiting three days!"

The Count strolled over to the sofa. "I hope you don't mind if I sit." He seated himself, crossed one leg over the other, and threw an arm across the back. Every movement expressed utter self-assurance. "If you'll take my advice, you'll put my nephew completely out of your mind."

"Why?" She strode to the sofa and faced him angrily. "Why should I take your advice? I don't mean to sound ungrateful to you, Count Gebhardt. You were kind to permit me to stay here in your . . . your establishment, and I do thank you for it. But I don't see what you have to do with Franzi and me."

"I have a great deal to do with you both, as you shall soon see. It was my nephew, you know, who asked me to come."

"Did he?" Her inner turmoil became worse. "Franzi himself?"

"Franzi himself. He asked me to tender his goodbyes for him."

Her knees felt as if they would give way, so she sank down on the nearest chair. "No, it can't be true. He wouldn't do such a thing . . . send you instead of coming himself. He *couldn't*—!"

"I'm afraid he did, though. Try to understand, my dear. His injuries are severe. He needs care and the most expert medical attention. His mind isn't on anything else."

Outside, the sounds of the gathering crowd were becoming louder. "Peace and bread!" The shouts from the street were meaningless to her now. "I know he needs medical attention. I know that. But he couldn't be so wrapped up in himself that he wouldn't even take time to . . . to *talk* to me."

"But he's not here, is he?" The Count crossed to the window as he spoke and shut the casements with a thump. "That fact seems to speak for itself, does it not? Franzi's final statement."

"No!" She put both hands to her ears. She didn't want to hear another word from the Count. "You're lying to me. I know you're lying. He *must* be coming."

The Count's lips twisted into a dry smile. "Try not to speak stupidly, child." He went from the window to her chair. "Use your head and the evidence of your eyes and ears." He lifted her chin, making her meet his eyes. "Forget him. His mother has him now."

"I won't believe it," she muttered, thrusting the Count's hand from her face. "He must have had *some* thought for me."

"Yes, of course he had. My nephew doesn't lack a sense of responsibility. That's why he asked me to tell you to put yourself in my hands."

The words didn't make sense. "Your hands?"

The Count strolled back to the sofa. "Yes. He was very grateful— and quite relieved—when I offered to take the burden from him."

She still couldn't follow. "Do you mean the burden of . . . of *me*?"

"Exactly. I told him that I was quite willing to replace him in your life."

Dori felt the blood drain from her face. "You're . . . joking!"

He leaned back against the sofa cushions, his smile broadening. "Not at all," he said with a complacency that amazed her. "You may not be quite in the style of my usual choices, but you have something . . . something *très provoquant*. A quality that excites me." He was amused at her expression of shock. "You needn't look so surprised, *Liebchen*. I didn't make the offer out of kindness, I assure you. Fond as I am of Franz, I wouldn't have taken you off his hands if you were beneath my standard."

"Did Franzi ask you to . . . to take me off his hands?" Her heart seemed to have turned to ice within her chest. "The matter was discussed between you?"

"Of course, my dear. At length. It was a fortunate accident that I took a fancy to you. Fortunate for you, fortunate for Franz. Since he's in no condition to continue the liaison, he's happy to see that you've been placed in better hands."

"How very generous of him."

The Count's eyebrows rose. He lifted his monocle to his eye and studied her with interest. "Ah, I see. You're still committed to him in your emotions. I must say that I find such loyalty charming in a demimondaine. It adds to your value. But don't indulge in it too long, or you'll become a bore."

Dori turned away from him in revulsion. "No, it wouldn't do for a demimondaine to turn boring; I can see that."

"You can also make yourself boring by continuing too long to be moody." He rose again from his seat, came up behind her, and turned her to face him. "I like to be greeted with a cheerful face and eager arms. I shall overlook tonight, of course, but—"

"That's good of you."

He ignored the irony in her voice and pulled her close. "But next time be ready for me—bodily and in spirit." He tightened his hold and kissed her with practiced urgency. She didn't respond at all. He lifted his head and gave her another of his amused, reproving smiles. "I think I'll have to teach you a great deal."

"Assuming, of course, that I want to learn from you."

"You'll want to." He took her by the shoulders and held her away from him just enough that only the tips of her breasts touched him. Slowly he rotated her shoulders so that her nipples drew two faint circles on his chest. "I'm an excellent teacher," he said softly. "You'll enjoy every lesson, I promise."

Her body reacted with a surprising, immediate flush of warmth and weakness, but her mind was appalled. How easy it was to slip into decadence, she thought. Dim lights on plush, rose-colored walls; soft, suggestive words in the ear; light touch of body on body; and everything else can so easily fade away . . . love, morals, heartbreak, war, and even the cries of anguish from the streets. She could hardly hear the chanting any more.

He recognized the weakness of her body, and his smile broadened. He pulled her close to kiss her again, but she broke away from him. She was not yet so decadent as he supposed. With what she hoped was the appearance of icy calm, she crossed the room to the vestibule and took her coat from the large wardrobe near the door. She pulled from the pocket the key to the flat and returned to the sitting room doorway.

He was standing where she'd left him, watching her with raised eyebrows.

She lifted the key and dangled it in the air. "I regret to have to disappoint Your Excellency," she said, dropping the key down on the chair with his coat, "but I prefer to select my own 'teachers.' " Without a further word or a moment's hesitation, she turned and went to the door.

Downstairs, she saw the crowd of demonstrators not too far down the street. She ran and caught up with them. She walked along with them for several hours, shouting "Peace and bread!" until she was hoarse. It was cleansing for her.

In her own bed that night, she succumbed to a kind of hysteria. She beat her pillow, choking with suppressed rage. The perception that she'd never been more to Franz Gebhardt than a piece of merchandise was so painful that it felt like a physical wound in her chest. She wanted a surgeon to come and cut it out of her with a knife. She'd left her family, she'd disregarded all the values of her past, she'd lived for years on the fringes of life for what she'd thought was a love that ennobled everything. But it had been nothing but a tawdry affair dressed up in a silly girl's dreams. In reality, she'd been exactly what her mother had always believed her to be—a camp follower, a soldier's plaything. The humiliation of that self-image was as devastating as her lover's rejection. She didn't know what pained her most—the end of love or the beginning of self-disgust.

It was many days before she was able to pull herself together. But when she began to feel sanity return, she found herself looking at the world with new eyes. Vienna was suddenly an ugly place, full of deprivation, defeat, and the hypocrisy that comes from the disparity of the classes. Count Otto Gebhardt was not the only one whose way of life had not been greatly affected by the war. Most of the members of the nobility and the *haute bourgeoisie* were still eating meat, keeping servants, dressing for dinner, and attending the opera. She became more aware of the bitterness of the returning soldiers and felt a new sympathy for them. She could sense the undercurrent of hostility that pervaded the city. This was not the place in which she wanted to bring up her child. There had to be a better place.

Her mother had been right. America was the goal, the last refuge for people who could still dream. Slowly, with icy logic, she made a plan. But to execute that plan, she needed money, a great deal more money than she'd ever had in her life. And there was a way she could get it . . . a quick and almost certain way.

She took a fortnight's leave from Herr Sperling's shop, and she went to visit Bibi. "If I'm going to be a demimondaine," she told her friend, "I want to do it right. Teach me what I need to know."

Bibi tried to dissuade her. "You're not the type," she insisted.

"Why not? Am I so different from you?"

"You're too intense. You suffer everything so deeply."

"So do you, Bibi. Don't try to deny it. You just hide it better."

"No, *Liebchen.* I have feelings, but I'm not a bleeder. It's no good to be a bleeder in this profession."

"I *was* a bleeder," Dori answered, fitting a cigarette into a holder and puffing it with a swagger like Bibi. "Not anymore."

Eventually Bibi was convinced. And she taught the younger woman what she knew was expected of a rich man's mistress. She told her the things she must never say and the places she must never go. She taught her when to offer her favors and when to withhold them, what to give and what to hold back. And Dori absorbed it all.

Just as they'd done when Dori first arrived in Vienna, they remade her. They cut her hair—quite short, this time—giving her bangs in the front and long, straight strands at the back. The sides were trained to make a single curl at each side of her face. It was simple and smart, and Dori could go to sleep at night and wake in the morning looking presentable. They spent their meager reserves of funds on a coat for her, which Herr Sperling, not knowing what it was to be used for, let her have at cost. It was of black velvet and lined with silk—of the finest prewar fabric, which Dori herself had helped to remake—and felt and looked sinful. Then, as a *pièce de résistance,* Bibi polished Dori's fingernails a bright, bright red.

When they decided she was ready, she kissed Bibi a thankful goodbye and went home. She stripped off all her clothes, put on a new pair of stockings that Bibi had managed to obtain for her and her best shoes. Then she buttoned her new coat over her naked body, pinned her diamond and gold brooch to the lapel, and set out on her new path.

The Count lived on the Franziskplatz, in a house that had belonged to his family for generations. When the aged butler opened the door for her, his expression grew aloof and he refused to let her in. "The Count is engaged right now," he said. "Dining with friends."

Dori brushed by him with the assurance of a member of the family. She went directly to the staircase, moving with the authority of an actress who'd rehearsed her role well. "Tell the Count that Fräulein Weisenberg wants to see him in his bedroom. At once."

The butler tottered after her. "Please, *Fräulein,* this is quite impossible. The Count never permits any interruption of his Tuesday evening dinners. A bachelor affair, you see. A gathering of intimates. I'm not permitted to interrupt once the brandy's been brought in. And I couldn't allow you to wait for him in his bedroom. Perhaps you could come back later, when his guests have gone—"

"Give him my message, please, exactly as I gave it to you," Dori ordered, throwing off the old man's hold and proceeding up the stairs with calm deliberation, her coat sweeping the carpet grandly behind her.

The butler was shaken. He knew he should go after her and drag her out bodily, but he was bewildered and unnerved.

Dori, meanwhile, opened the doors on the second floor until she found a room that was obviously the Count's bedroom. She went inside, closed the door behind her, leaned on the bedstead, which faced the door, and waited.

She didn't have to wait long. Not two minutes after she'd taken her pose, the door banged open and the Count, fuming, stood glaring at her from the threshold. "What's going on here?" he demanded icily. "This house is out of bounds for my . . . for persons like you! How dare you barge in here and order my butler to deliver that arrogant message?"

Dori smiled calmly. "Shouldn't you at least have said good evening first?"

"Good *evening*? Are you mad? I don't like scenes, my girl, I don't like to suffer embarrassment before my friends, and I don't care to have my household disturbed. Now, I suggest you take your leave at once, before I—"

"I think you'd better close the door," Dori said, sweetly but firmly.

Her calm voice and unperturbed expression confused him. "What?"

"Close the door. Your butler is standing in the hall behind you, observing everything. I'm sure you don't want him to witness all this."

Nonplussed, the Count closed the door, all the while eyeing Dori with wary eyes. "Now, you madwoman, what's this all ab—?"

The rest of the word died on his lips, for Dori had begun to unbutton her coat. "I've come to tell you that I want to . . . to take lessons, after all."

The Count gaped as the coat slid slowly to the floor.

Meanwhile, the butler was tapping nervously at the door. "Your Excellency? Your Excellency? Is everything all right?"

"Good God!" the Count gasped, and then he threw back his head and guffawed loudly.

"Your Excellency?" came the butler's voice through the door.

"Go away, Ulrich, go away."

"But, sir . . . your guests!"

"Tell them to go on with the dinner without me." He shook his head in amused appreciation of the girl before him. "I'm afraid I'll be . . . otherwise occupied for the rest of the evening. Giving lessons."

8

*F*or the Viennese, the war didn't end on a particular hour of a particular day. It simply seemed to disintegrate, to fall apart at the seams. It happened slowly at first, with a little rend here and a tear there: the disclosure of the facts of the Sixtus letter, a series of workers' strikes, small incidents of plunder. Then came the hunger riots in July, rumors of mass desertions in the army, the frenzied revolt of a hoard of women in the suburbs who demanded food, the assassination of the Prime Minister in a hotel dining room, a frightening antimonarchy demonstration in the Ballhausplatz. By the end of October of 1918, it was clear—from the numbers of deserters clogging the streets, from the mass demonstrations, from the political upheaval discussed openly in the press, from the agitations of the Bolshevik sympathizers waving their red banners everywhere, from the almost daily instances of rioting and pillaging—that the very fabric of the society they'd known was in the process of complete disintegration.

Dori observed the chaos with a strange detachment. She'd never felt herself to be truly *wienerisch,* and now she no longer accepted Austria as her country. She'd set her sights on a new land, and she would not let herself be drawn into concern for Austria's fate. They might become a republic or join with the Bolsheviks. She didn't care. She'd planned her future with a single-minded determination; if she let herself become sidetracked, she might not make it.

The night she'd witnessed the minor cockade-and-star commotion was a case in point. She'd left the Count's bed and was returning by *fiacre* to her flat on the Lindengasse when she saw a group of eight or nine armed, rough deserters accost a pair of uniformed officers on the street. She'd watched from the carriage as the ruffians pulled the imperial cockades from the officers' hats and the stars indicating their rank from their collars. She knew that such incidents were happening all over the city; embittered ex-soldiers were tearing away all symbols of military authority. The cockade-and-star gangs were becoming notorious.

Dori had felt a momentary sense of panic. The plight of the outnumbered officers was pathetic, and this example of the anarchy existing on the streets of the city was appalling. But her feelings as she watched the scene were mixed. Though she understood the resentment of the soldiers toward the officers (the cockades and the stars represented the authority of command and of the monarchy that they felt had so badly betrayed them), she was revolted by their bullying lawlessness. Yet she felt no sympathy for the officers either. One of them looked a little like Franzi as he'd been before his disfigurement, and she couldn't help wondering how many innocent girls *he'd* betrayed. The officers represented a class of men like Franzi and the Count, whom she'd come to despise.

While she watched the commotion, she debated about whether or not to seek help (from the police or a contingent of the newly formed *Volkswehr* that had been organized to try to "keep the peace"), for she didn't know which side to support. Fortunately, however, before she was forced to decide, the assailants tired of the uneven struggle. Having achieved what they'd set out to do—the removal of the cockades and stars —they stumbled off noisily down the street, leaving the officers, chagrined but unhurt, to pick themselves up. Dori went on her way without having to commit herself to one side or the other.

By the time of this upheaval in Vienna, Dori had been the Count's mistress for more than a year. It had been a relationship that she subtly but firmly controlled. The Count had found her favors so to his liking that he'd agreed to her peculiar conditions. She would make an appearance at his special flat only twice a week and only for a few hours. She'd made it clear to him that the rest of her life was her own, and that he would be as unwelcome in her Lindengasse home as she would be in his house in the Franziskplatz. In addition, she'd indicated to him at the outset that she wanted payment for her "services" not in Austria's rapidly devaluating currency but in regular gifts of jewelry. This procedure had been advised by her friend Bibi, and the Count had made no objection. In fact he'd been quite generous with those gifts. She'd accumulated, in the months of their "association," a hoard of gems substantial enough to provide for herself and her daughter a very sound foothold in America. She waited only for peace to become reestablished in the world. As soon as passenger ships were again sailing across the Atlantic, she and little Fredi would be aboard one of them.

Despite the chaos of defeat that was visible all around her, Dori's life had not drastically changed in the months since she'd taken up with the Count. She still went to work at Herr Sperling's shop and supported herself and her daughter with her wages. Only Frau Pauli and Bibi knew of her liaison with Count Gebhardt. If any of the neighbors gossiped about the *fiacre* that deposited her at the front of the house on the Lindengasse very late at night two times a week, she could count on Frau Pauli to squelch it.

She couldn't have managed without Bibi and Frau Pauli. Bibi was a frequent visitor. And Frau Pauli helped in all sorts of ways, especially in caring for the child during the many hours Dori was away from home. Even though her husband had returned from the army, the elderly woman maintained her attachment to Dori and Fredi. Herr Pauli took over again as *Hausbesorger,* leaving Frau Pauli with more time for the baby she adored. Fredi seemed to thrive on the arrangement. She never cried when Dori went away; she looked on Frau Pauli as a second mother. The only thing that troubled Dori was that Fredi did not yet speak. But Frau Pauli always reassured her. "Don't worry about Fredi. She's so clever, you know. She understands everything, and she's not yet two. She'll be babbling away soon enough."

So Dori went about her life, making plans for her future and waiting for the world to be at peace again.

Among all the signs of deterioration of the monarchy that surrounded the Viennese in the autumn of 1918, one of the least noticeable to the general population was the defection of the noble families from the royal court. Many of the mansions in the Inner City were suddenly closed up, and if anyone inquired, he was told by the retainers who'd been left behind that the nobleman in question had "retired to his country estate," or "gone abroad." Dori learned (not from the Count but from Bibi, who missed nothing that was gossiped about in Vienna) that Franzi and his mother had moved to Switzerland in mid-October. The news had little effect on her, she told Bibi. She had other matters, much closer to her heart, to think about. She hardly acknowledged even to herself the pain she felt at the news. The bad feeling told her that a little part of her dreams of him had still survived, and she had to endure this last bit of mourning.

It touched the hearts of many royalist Viennese that their Emperor, whom they thought of as Poor Karl, did not defect. He and his family remained in the Schönbrunn Palace in Vienna, protected only by a company of cadets from a military academy who had volunteered to defend the palace—boys of fifteen and sixteen. With the memory of the execution of Czar Nicholas and his family in July still fresh in everyone's minds, even those who fervently wished for the end of the monarchy felt a grudging sympathy for Poor Karl. But when word came that Kaiser Wilhelm had abdicated, it was clear that Karl's days as Emperor were numbered.

When word leaked out, on November 12, that the Emperor had been forced to sign a document withdrawing his power and had removed himself and his family to his hunting lodge at Eckartsau, Dori's instincts told her that the time had come for her, too, to proceed with her plans for withdrawal.

She took all her jewels from their hiding place behind the wardrobe in her bedroom, packed them in a shoebox, and took them to a Jewish-owned *Pfandhaus* that Bibi had recommended because the pawnbroker was reputed to be honest. She found the pawnshop locked and its windows boarded, as were all the shops in the street, but she knocked at the door nevertheless. The door was unlocked and opened a crack. An eye observed her for a moment, and then the door swung wide to permit her to enter. The pawnbroker gave her an apologetic shrug. "Looters, you know," he muttered in explanation. "We have to be careful."

The pawnbroker, a bearded man whose thin face and watery eyes reminded her a little of her father, looked at her jewels through a jeweler's glass. Then he glanced up at her warily. "Paste," he said after examining each piece carefully, "except for the garnet necklace and the topaz ring. Pretty stuff, the rest, and not completely worthless. I can let you have a thousand or so for it, and a couple of thousand for the garnets and topaz."

She blanched. Her knees began to shake so badly that she had to clutch at the counter to keep from falling. A thousand paper florins would scarcely buy a decent dinner these days, much less passage on an ocean liner! "Are you telling me the truth?" she asked hoarsely. "They're all . . . paste?"

The bearded man shrugged. "Sorry."

"But he . . . they were supposed to be heirlooms . . . family jewelry handed down from one generation to the next! How—?"

"It happens. Especially in times like these. The owners want to protect their riches from wartime marauders, so they bury the real stuff in vaults and wear paste. The best families do it."

With hands that shook, she swept the imitations back into the box.

No wonder the wily Count Otto Gebhardt had been so willing to accede to her terms! She'd been made a fool of *again*.

"If it's big money you need," the pawnbroker said, "the diamond pin you're wearing seems to be the real stuff. I can give you a good price for that, if it's truly genuine. Take it off and let me take a closer look."

She shook her head. "I'll be back."

Fighting back a feeling of murderous fury, she went immediately to the Count's abode on the Franziskplatz. Even if it did no good, a confrontation with him was the only way in which she could soothe the turmoil in her chest.

Ulrich answered the door. She could see behind him that dust covers had been placed on the furniture. He can't be gone! she told herself. She'd seen him only the night before last!

But he *was* gone. "His Excellency," Ulrich informed her with a slight tinge of pity in his voice, "left just last night to join the other Gebhardts in Switzerland."

With the family gems safely packed in his suitcase, no doubt, Dori added to herself in despair. Without a word, she turned and walked away, her head high despite her feelings of frustration and humiliation. The country lay in ruins, but the Gebhardts would survive—with their riches intact. It was a bitter pill to swallow, but when she'd swallowed it, her step quickened and her resolve hardened. She fingered the diamond-and-gold circle pin she'd worn over her heart for four years. I will not be defeated, she told herself. If the Gebhardts could survive, so could she.

9

*F*our months later, in March of 1919, Dori and her two-year-old daughter stood on the tiny rear deck of the *Noordam* with the other steerage passengers, trying to get a whiff of air. She'd managed to get the passage money by selling everything she had. Her remaining funds would not keep her in America for a month. This was not how she'd originally planned it, and she was not even certain that, with her meager resources, the American authorities would admit her, but she was on her way. Somehow she would make a new life for herself and her child. But it would not be the way she'd done it before. She'd signed the ship's register with the names Dvora and Frieda Weisenberg. No more Dori. The *wienerisch* life was over.

Clutching her little girl's hand, she found a place for them at the railing. While Frieda sucked greedily on a hard candy given her by a kindly gentleman from second class who'd taken a fancy to the child, Dvora took a cigarette from her pocket, fitted it into a holder, and smoked. She ignored the stares of the people around her. If they found the cigarette holder an affectation, it didn't trouble her. She was used to their stares. They, with their beards or their *babushkas* and their *shtetl* rags, had already found her short hair and Viennese smartness out of place. She didn't care what they thought. She blew out a cloud of smoke and stared down into the gray Atlantic waters.

As the wake foamed up endlessly in two widening lines behind the ship, she relived in her mind the scene at the Westbahnhof when she'd said her goodbyes. She didn't even have to close her eyes to see Frau Pauli, holding Frieda in her arms for the last time, trying to coax her darling into saying, "Ta-ta." Though the child couldn't say it, she'd been well aware that this was goodbye. "*Auf Wiedersehen,* my little sweetheart, my baby, my *Liebling,*" the old woman had moaned as she and Frieda clung to each other and wept, while Herr Pauli stood mournfully in the background, hat in hand and tears in his eyes. Meanwhile, Dvora and Bibi had walked aside, fighting back their tears. But they hadn't been able to find words to say to each other. All Dvora could do was to take Bibi's hand in hers and squeeze it tightly.

Bibi had lifted Dvora's hand to her cheek, and Dvora had felt a tear. But Bibi'd quickly brushed it away. "What? No more nail polish?" she'd asked, trying to laugh.

Dvora'd lowered her head. "No nail polish, Bibi. Not anymore."

Bibi had nodded with understanding, and then they'd embraced. "Good luck!" Bibi had muttered hoarsely in her ear.

Dvora had stroked the other girl's silky blond hair. "You, too."

Then she'd taken Frieda in her arms, kissed Frau Pauli's cheek one last time, and climbed up into the train that would take her to Rotterdam and the ship. She'd found a window seat, raised up the sash, and, with Frieda still in her arms, hung out the window for a last look back. Somewhere in that desolated land she was leaving behind was all she'd ever been or ever known. Back there were a sister, a brother, a father . . . yes, and a mother. A childhood and youth that would never be hers again. A lifetime of pain and rifts. Twenty years of memories. And they'd all come down to this—to the tears of the two friends waving forlornly up at her, a pocketful of worthless paper currency, and the little girl she held in her arms.

A large wave that struck the side of the ship with a crash shook her from her daydream. Why was she dwelling on that scene at the train? She'd made up her mind that this voyage would be a bright new beginning. Yet all her thoughts seemed to hover on endings. She had to snap out—

"Frau Weisenberg?"

The deep voice at her shoulder startled her. She looked around to find herself addressed by the portly gentleman from second class who'd given Frieda the candy. He was a neatly dressed Jew in a velvet-collared coat who stood out in this company of ragtags and paupers. He'd already become an object of speculation among the steerage passengers because he was the only passenger from above who'd come down to mingle with them. Dvora wondered how he'd learned her name. She looked him over curiously. He was short and paunchy, and he had a thick, ugly pair of lips, but his eyes behind his steel-rimmed glasses were kind. She'd learned at last to see the kindness in people's faces. "It's *Fräulein* Weisenberg," she corrected with pointed frankness.

"*Fräulein?*" His eyes blinked. "But . . . this child is your daughter, *nicht wahr?*"

"Yes, she's mine."

He was surprised, but not revolted. "She's a most beautiful little girl."

"Thank you."

"My name is Leo Glassman. I . . . noticed that you and your daughter are . . . unescorted. I'm an optician from Salzburg. I am also alone, you see, so I was wondering if you and your little girl would care to dine with me upstairs this evening."

Dvora hesitated. It would be pleasant to get away from the stench of steerage for an evening, but she didn't wish to become involved with any man just yet, especially one who was twice her age. But he seemed a decent type. An optician. They probably had place for skilled men of that sort in America. *He* wouldn't be turned away by the authorities, even if he had a family to support.

She dropped her eyes and gave a small smile. "That would be very nice," she said quietly.

"Good." Mr. Glassman bent down and picked Frieda up in his arms. "Ah, my little one, finished your candy already? Would you like another? A red one this time?" He looked over at Dvora. "Is it all right for her to have another?"

"Yes, I think so. It's three hours to dinner time."

He chucked little Frieda under the chin with a laugh. "See, *bubeleh,*" he said, switching from his perfect German to Yiddish, "your mama says it will be all right. So shall it be a red candy, eh? What do you say?"

"Pa-pa," Frieda said distinctly.

10

They lived in the Bronx in a two-bedroom apartment over the store where Leo made and sold eyeglasses. And they prospered. Dvora kept house, cooked the meals, took care of her husband and daughter, and spent her spare time reading novels in German about prewar Vienna. She gradually expanded her reading to include the financial pages of the newspapers and a number of business journals, but she still found time to read German novels and to smoke cigarettes in a long holder. Her daughter often discovered her sitting at the bedroom window, smoking and staring out at nothing.

. . . Frieda told me about how her mother sits and broods about the past, Sam. Doesn't that sound just like Mama? But when I pointed out to Dvora that she takes after Mama remarkably, she denied seeing any resemblance at all. . . .

By the time Frieda was thirteen, she was already quite pretty, very rebellious, and as American as the movies. One day when she came home from school and found her mother sitting at the window again, smoking her ever-present cigarette, she couldn't hide her disgust. She made a sneering sound.

Her mother looked up. "What's the matter with you?" she asked.

"It's you, Mama. I hate the way you always smoke with that stupid holder. Who do you think you are, a countess or something?"

Dvora laughed. "Well, I was once the mistress of a count."

"Oh, sure." Frieda made a face at her mother and walked out. No matter how many times she heard her mother make that claim, she never believed a word of it.

Part Five

DOV
1919-1928

1

*I hope you're not thinking me a creature of superstition, Sam.
I swear I don't believe in fate or destiny, or that there are three sisters sitting
somewhere spinning the threads of our lives. I agree with you when you say
there's no such thing as predestination. I'm not saying that my family is in some
way doomed to repeat the past. Yet . . .*

*And then there was Dov. He rebelled against Mama with more vehemence
even than Dvora had. It amazes me to see so many subtle similarities in the
patterns of their lives. Do you realize, for example, that six months to the day
after Dvora arrived in America, while we all thought that Dov was long since
settled in Palestine, he was standing on the deck of the* Royal George *heading
in the same direction she had taken? . . .*

The *Royal George* sailed from Liverpool to New York in September
of 1919 with Dov aboard. He himself found it difficult to account for
it. After more than four years of enforced inaction in the confines of
Knockaloe prison, the whirlwind of the last couple of months was
bewildering.

He stood leaning on the polished railing of the upper deck of the
Cunard liner, watching the prow cut through the water. The sight glazed
his eyes, freeing his mind to wander through another sea—an ocean of
memories—probing and prodding for an answer to the question of how
fate had brought him so far from his original destination. Once, when
he'd been about twelve or thirteen, he'd believed that he had a firm
control of his future. But everything that had happened to him since only
proved that he'd had no control at all. He'd left home after Papa died,

expecting to make it to Palestine within a year. Now, more than five years later, he was heading in a completely different direction. He was almost twenty-three—a full-grown man!—yet not at all sure how he'd got to this point in his life.

He stared out at the immensity of ocean feeling lost. After the confines of Knockaloe (where each prisoner was allotted a space only six feet by four feet—twice the width of a coffin), even his modest, second-class cabin seemed enormous. In Knockaloe it would have held two and a half prisoners.

Thinking of Knockaloe made him shiver. Those endless, hopeless years, without news, without any contact with the outside, without a moment of real privacy. For four years the only reality had been the association with the men in his barracks. Everything else he'd experienced had been inside his head. For four years the world had been a dream, unfriendly and unknowable.

By the time he was released, he could barely remember his previous life. Oh, he remembered his childhood well enough—Mama, Papa, and his sisters; his yearning for them had been a constant ache during his incarceration. It was the time in Warsaw that was difficult to remember —Mendel Goldblum and the girl Chava, whom he was supposed to wed. He could hardly bring their faces to his mind. That was why the packet that had been delivered to him on the day of his release was such a surprise.

It had been the strangest day of his life. He'd just learned that Conrad Klahr (the young architect who'd been arrested because he'd made sketches of the great houses of England), who'd been his best friend at the camp and who'd been removed to hospital six months before the end of the war, had died of tuberculosis. Equally painful, he'd only minutes before said goodbye to Steigmuller, the wild-haired leftist who'd lived for four years in the bed next to him, who'd been like a father to him, and who'd spent hours every day teaching him economic theory and trying to convert him to Marxism. He'd also had to bid adieu to Fuchs, the cultivated German Baron who'd been with him since the first day in the police station and who'd tried ever since to convert him to Christianity. These two—so completely opposite in character and upbringing— had decided on repatriation to Germany and were leaving together. They'd begged Dov to join them, but Dov had been too confused by his sudden freedom to make a decision. It was then that one of the guards found him and handed him the packet.

It was larger than a letter, and it was wrapped with brown paper that bore a Warsaw postmark. Inside was a small box with a letter on top. He opened the envelope with hands that shook; it was the first letter he'd received since he'd been imprisoned.

The letter was in Yiddish and signed by Taube Goldblum:

Dear Dov,

I hope this finds you well. It was like a miracle when we finally learned that you are alive. Mendel, till the day he died, loved you like a son. He never forgave himself for telling you to stay in England when war was so close. But maybe it was all for the best. Warsaw has been a hell during these years. The business died right away, and Mendel took ill shortly after. I regret to tell you that he passed away in December of 1917.

I hope it won't hurt you too much to learn that our daughter, Chava, married Pinhas Pinofsky. We thought you were dead, you see, and Pinhas, being conscripted into the Russian army, needed the security of a wife. We thank the good Lord that he has returned to us unharmed. We hope that with God's help he'll be able to start up the business again, now that peace has come.

Mendel never forgot you, Dov. The best day he had since the war began was when he heard from the landlord of your lodging house that you were safely interned. Before he died, he handed me the note that I've put in the enclosed box and a sum of money that he hoarded especially for you. He made me swear to make the arrangements he wanted as soon as the war ended and it was possible to make them. I followed his instructions to the letter, and you'll find his legacy in the enclosed box. Mendel prayed that it might be the beginning of a happy future for you, and so do I. With very best wishes, I remain,

Taube Goldblum

Inside the box was a second-class ticket for passage to America on the *Royal George* and fifteen English pounds. There was also a little note written in a very shaky hand. "Forgive me, Dov," Mendel Goldblum had written, "for causing you to waste away your youth in prison. I can never make it up to you, but I pray that a new start in America will. I know I was wrong about England, but I think I'm right about America. God be with you. Mendel."

After reading Mendel's note, Dov had had a difficult time making a decision about what to do. He returned to London and took a room in a quiet lodging house, trying to get some sort of grip on himself. For four years he'd yearned for privacy, and now that he had it, he was overwhelmed with loneliness and misery. After four years of isolation from world events, the sight of war-devastated London was shocking. The city that had so excited him was now grim and unswept, its buildings dirty, its flowered borders neglected, its squares and odd spaces filled with little sheds and large barnlike structures hastily constructed for wartime purposes, its people worn and dressed without color in dark grays, blacks, or khakis, and its attitude subdued now that the frenzy of victory had abated. Dov walked the streets, looking about him in depressed astonishment. It was horrible to have to learn in a short time what had happened to the world.

He couldn't help thinking about his family in Solitava and wondering what had happened to them. He had no idea of what the war had done to them. He read old newspapers and asked questions in pubs, and he learned that Czernowitz had changed hands numerous times during the course of the war, but it seemed not to have been a battleground. His mother and Yudi had probably survived. If they had, his dear little Yudi would be almost grown up by this time. And Dvora. He wondered if they'd ever heard from her. He would have given anything to know they were all alive and well. Perhaps, he thought, he should trade in the ticket to America and go home to Solitava.

But before he took action, a wave of memories swept over him. He remembered Papa and the way his mother had treated him, and the old bitterness returned. Beset with the conflicting emotions of homesickness and resentment, he weighed them both, one against the other. It seemed to him that the bitterness that still lay deep within his mind was an emotion of justifiable validity while the homesickness was a symptom of a tendency to sentimental weakness. In the end he decided against returning home.

What he really should do, he thought, was follow his original plan. Palestine. With the money he could get from the return of the *Royal George* ticket—probably as much as twenty pounds—and the fifteen pounds that Mendel had left him, he would have a good start. But now he wasn't sure that Palestine was where he wanted to go. The Zionism that had been so important during his idealistic youth seemed strange to him now. His Jewishness had not been a significant part of his life during the years of the war. There had been no services to attend at Knockaloe and no religious tomes to study. Now, while one part of him wished to find his faith again, another part wanted to enter the secular world of the twentieth century.

244

Maybe America *was* the place to go. Throughout his childhood, the call of the Goldeneh Medina had twanged in every boy's ears. The only reason he'd rejected it had been because Avrum Gentz had gone there. Now that reason seemed foolish to him. In such an enormous country as America, how would Avrum Gentz's life touch his, even if they lived in the same city? Even if they passed each other in the street, what difference would it make? They wouldn't know each other.

And then, too, there was Mendel to think about. Would it be right to accept his legacy and then not use it as Mendel wished?

In the end the lure of America won. He sailed on the *Royal George* just as Mendel had arranged. And now he was standing on an upper deck watching the waves and thinking about the future with feelings too confused to be called eager.

For the moment, however, he was enjoying the voyage enormously. Mendel had been very generous in arranging for the passage in second class. Dov had never lived so luxuriously. Besides the spacious cabin, there was a steward who was always available to bring him towels, to serve him drinks, or to turn down his bed, and there were meals too sumptuous for words. He felt as if he were living a masquerade—small-town Jewish boy pretending to be British royalty.

The trouble was that he wasn't prepared for such a masquerade. He was living in too much luxury for his resources or his nature. The rich meals were not what he was accustomed to, and the sweets and creams (which he couldn't resist eating), combined with the rocking of the ship, made him ill every day. And the few items of clothing that he had with him (not enough to fill half his gleaming new suitcase—the other half was filled with books he'd kept with him since Knockaloe) were not adequate to see him through the social rituals of a day on shipboard. Even his wonderful new suit was not adequate.

He'd bought the suit in London shortly before leaving. It was the finest suit he'd ever seen, and he'd spent a great deal of money to acquire it. It was made of soft English tweed, tailored to perfection with a set-in belt at the back and double-stitched pocket flaps in front. The pants were called knickers, and when he tried them on he was enchanted with them. The tailor assured him that he couldn't have chosen a better style for daytime wear. "Like a regular English country gentleman," the tailor had said.

What the tailor had *not* said was that an English country gentleman also had evening clothes, town clothes, morning coats, and a full assortment of trousers, vests, sport coats, and sundries to see him through the day. Dov had only his one beautiful suit, a couple of extra shirts, two sets of underwear, and a woolen cap that the tailor had said was absolutely necessary to wear with the suit. While the suit was perfectly adequate for strolling on deck in the morning and sitting down in the second-class dining room at lunchtime, it was not at all the sort of outfit worn during the evening. When he'd come into the dining room during the first evening on board, he'd received a number of shocked stares from the other diners, and the two waiters who'd served him were careful to avoid his eyes. He thought it was his beard, and the next morning he offered the steward a generous tip to shave it off.

"I wouldn't do that, sir," the steward ventured. "It's quite a good growth you've got there. Very impressive, if you was t'ask me."

"But it makes me too conspicuous. I'd better take it off."

The steward remained reluctant. "All of it, sir? I could give it a nice trim—"

"All of it."

When the barbering was finished, Dov looked at himself in the mirror in some surprise. It had been many years since he'd seen his naked face. The sight was not displeasing. His face was a little too long and thin, but the chin was strong, the mouth full, and his light-colored eyes made, he thought, an interesting contrast with his dark hair. The steward seemed to approve, too. "I 'ave to admit, sir, that you were right arfter all," he said, smiling at Dov's reflection in the mirror. "No point 'idin' a face as good-lookin' as that, I'd say."

"That's a relief," Dov admitted. "Now maybe I can go to the dining room without being stared at."

The steward coughed suggestively. "Are y' referrin' to last night, sir?"

"Yes." Dov turned from the mirror and peered at the steward in surprise. "Why do you ask?"

"Well, y'see, I saw you goin' in last night. If y' don't mind my sayin' so, it wasn't yer beard."

"No?"

"It was yer suit, sir. It just ain't right fer evenin'. I'm surprised that a gentleman like yerself ain't brought along a few changes of costume."

Once Dov realized what had been wrong, he stopped going in to the dining room for dinner. The steward served him his evening meals in the cabin, and since the meals were just as sumptuous eaten alone, he found he didn't mind at all. He enjoyed every morsel, sat back and waited for the sick feeling to overwhelm him, then ran upstairs to the railing, disgorged the meal, and went down to bed.

Nine days at sea is a long time, especially if one keeps to oneself, and Dov had plenty of time to gaze down into the water and think about life. What bothered him most was the awareness that a man couldn't really control his destiny. Destiny, it appeared, controlled the man. A man, like the leaf on the surface of the river, was the helpless victim of whatever chaotic events churned around him. It seemed a pathetic prospect to contemplate.

Too pathetic, he thought. He could not accept such a view of life. Perhaps his analogy was weak. Man, after all, was not a leaf. He had a mind and a will. And if one's destiny was like a river, then a man's mind and will could be used to make a rudder, as this ship had a rudder, to cut into the water and carve out a direction. One couldn't prevent the storms that tried to drag one under, but one could fight to maneuver one's way through them. A man didn't have to let himself drift.

In America he would start again. A new beginning. America was the place for the young and strong. If he had any character at all, this would be the place where his grip on the future could be regained. He no longer expected full control, but his drifting days were over.

2

As the ship neared land, the excitement of the passengers was almost tangible in the atmosphere. Dov, standing near the rail of an upper deck, looked over at the shabby steerage passengers crowding the rear decks to get a glimpse of the city looming up on the horizon. The excitement and awe on their faces moved him, but he, himself, didn't expect to be stirred by his first glimpse of New York City. After all, he'd lived in large cities before. A city was a city, wasn't it?

He knew that he was not very far removed in assets from those shabby peasants on the rear decks, but in his expectations he was quite separate from them. Their faces shone with hope as they stared out through the morning fog at the outlines of the city they were slowly nearing. He, however, had no expectations at all. A city was a city; people were people; there were thieves, cutthroats, and villains everywhere. He knew better, by this time, than to expect a Goldeneh Medina. He wasn't sure there was a heaven in heaven, so how could he believe in a heaven on earth?

But when the fog cleared and the New York skyline showed itself plain, its million windows glinting in the morning sun, he gasped with the same awe as the peasants behind him. There was something about New York that was unlike any place he'd ever seen, something enormous and vital and—there was no use denying it—full of hope. One could feel it in the air.

During disembarkation, his English country-gentleman suit stood him in good stead. Unlike the throng of humanity in steerage who'd been taken off the ship at Ellis Island, the first- and second-class passengers disembarked right on the pier in Manhattan. He felt like a criminal imposter when he walked down the gangway, realizing that he was no better off than the hoard on Ellis Island. In his suitcase were his two shirts and two sets of underwear and a couple of dozen books that wouldn't bring him a half-dollar in a second-hand bookstore. In his pocket were five American dollars. And that was all. After he'd tipped the headwaiter, the two table waiters, their four helpers, the wine steward, the cabin steward, and the porter, those five one-dollar bills were all he had left of Mendel's bequest. Most of the steerage passengers were probably better off than that.

But they didn't have the suit. When the officer at the customs gate looked Dov over, he didn't hesitate to admit him. The officer barely looked at the Turkish passport and didn't bother to match the name on the passport with the name on the passenger list, even though Dov had been very careful to sign on as Dov Gentz. (He would be Dov Gentz until he was safely admitted into the country; then he would become Dov Weisenberg again.) The customs man smiled politely, nodded, said, "Welcome to New York," and let him through. The suit had done it; he was certain of that.

He walked with the other upper-class passengers out to the New York street, eyeing them with envy. They all seemed to know exactly where they were going. Once off the pier, he found the city less magical and more frightening than it had seemed from the deck. It was noisy . . . dirty . . . teeming with people. He stood clutching his suitcase, looking about him in bewilderment. A couple he recognized from the ship hailed one of the taxicabs (just like the motorized hackney cabs he'd seen and admired in London) lined up along the curb. The driver drove up, helped a porter load their luggage on the little platform beside his seat, and assisted the pair into the back. As soon as they drove off, Dov waved his arm with bravado to the next cab in line. He thrust his suitcase on the platform, let the driver open the back door for him, and climbed in. Pulling a dollar from his pocket, he said, "Let's go as far as this will take me."

The driver turned and looked at him curiously. "Anywhere?"

"Anywhere."

He leaned back and tried to appear nonchalant, but he couldn't keep it up. Before two minutes had passed he was hanging out the window gaping at the huge buildings and the crowded streets with fascination. They drove through a bewildering number of streets, all of them crammed with tall buildings. Construction seemed to be going on everywhere, and men, women, and even children were moving about with hurried purposefulness, on foot and in every sort of conveyance. There were electrified trams, London-like omnibuses with double tiers, horse-drawn carts and carriages, bicycles, and an alarming number of motorcars, their engines noisy and their horns deafening. The driver was amazingly undisturbed by all the confusion. A dozen times Dov tensed in fear of a collision, but the driver merely continued to sing a lively tune under his breath. He only tooted his horn twice to clear the path before him, but each time he tooted, Dov jumped. He was sure he'd never become accustomed to the raucous sound of American auto horns.

Every few moments the driver stopped his singing long enough to point out something of interest: a wide street called Broadway "where all the theaters are"; the El, a train that rattled over their heads terrifyingly just as they passed under the track; the Woolworth tower, which was higher than anything Dov had ever seen; and Fifth Avenue, "where we have the best shops in the world."

As they waited to cross this impressive avenue the driver looked over his shoulder. "Well, what'll it be next? Uptown or down?"

"What's the difference?" Dov asked, confused.

"Money's the difference," the driver responded promptly. "Uptown's where the money is, and downtown's where it ain't."

Dov, with four dollars in his pocket, laughed. "Better take me downtown, then."

They passed through Union Square and then a smaller square called Washington that reminded him of London, and then the driver turned east. The streets became narrower, dirtier, and more crowded. Dov began to notice Jews in old-world dress, and Hebrew lettering on some of the store fronts. He was in the Jewish section. He leaned out the window and peered at everything—at the pushcarts loaded with wares, at the shouting boys playing ball in the streets, at the washing that hung from the lines strung between tenement windows, at the baby carriages and the wheelbarrows, at the young boys hurrying along carrying dry goods on their shoulders and the women in cotton housedresses looking out of their windows. Everywhere he could hear the sound of Yiddish being spoken, shouted, shrieked. Good God, it was wonderful. Despite the noise, the grime, the confusion of colors, the refuse in the gutters, the many signs of poverty and overcrowding, it was wonderful. The people were purposeful, lively, *loud*. They were not like the Jews of eastern Europe, huddled under their dark hats, whispering and scurrying about and avoiding public notice. Here in the bright American sunshine, nobody seemed ashamed of his Jewishness. He'd always been told that in America a man was free to be anything, but maybe the truth was that a man was free to be himself.

His eyes drank in the sights as if they'd been thirsting for them for years. Dov loved it all . . . every dirty, noisy, teeming inch. How thrilled Mendel would have been to see this. Mendel had been right all along. This was the place to be.

The taxi turned a corner. The street sign said Vesey Street. "You'd better decide where you wanna go, Mac," the driver said. "I can't be drivin' you all day for one lousy buck."

"You can let me out right here," Dov said.

The driver pulled up. Dov got out and dragged out his suitcase. He was standing before a rotting old brownstone with a flight of stone steps leading up to a pair of half-glassed doors, in one of which was a sign in both Yiddish and English reading ROOMS FOR RENT. A few children sat on the bottom step playing marbles, and on the top sat a young woman with a baby in her arms. She had brown hair messily piled up on the top of her head like a knit hat that had come unraveled, and her eyes were dark and shaped like almonds. But what instantly caught Dov's eye was the sight of one smooth breast almost completely revealed because the baby's chubby little hand was pulling down the neckline of her cotton blouse. The young woman met his eye, stared at him with a slight smile, and coolly loosened the infant's hold on her blouse.

The noise of the departing taxi drew the children's attention to the stranger standing at the curb. "Hey, lookit," said a red-haired boy to the others. "Lookit the Dook."

The young woman at the top of the steps laughed throatily. "Anything we can do for you, Duke?" she asked.

"I would like to rent a room," Dov said, unaware that the British tinge in his accent only added to the impression already made by his country-gentleman suit.

"Oh, you would, wouldja?" Without taking her eyes from him, the young woman reached out behind her, opened the door and shouted to someone inside in Yiddish, "There's a duke here who wants a room."

From inside came a loud guffaw, and a woman's voice, also speaking in Yiddish, responded. "Tell him we have no rooms here to please a duke."

The young woman got up, shifted her baby to her shoulder, and came down the steps, her hips swinging enticingly beneath her loose skirt. "The super says," she translated in English, smiling provocatively, "that we ain't got rooms to suit a duke."

"That's all right," Dov answered in Yiddish. "This duke is easy to please."

The woman laughed. "What's this? A Jewish duke?"

Dov smiled back at her. "Well, in America everything is possible, isn't that so?"

"Only if you got money. You got money for a room, Duke?"

"Not much."

She looked at him with suspicion. "With a suit like that, you probably got plenty. Enough for a room here, anyway."

"It depends. How much is the room?"

The young woman shrugged. "The prices vary. Just watch out for the super."

"The super? I don't know that word."

"The superintendent. Like a janitor, you know? The owner of the building lives uptown, see, and the Farbers are the caretakers. Mr. Farber, he takes care of the water and the furnace and things like that. And Mrs. Farber, she has the head for business. So, like I say, watch out for her. She's a shark. She'll take you for as much as she can get."

"Oh, she'll be fair with me, I promise you," Dov said, tipping his cap to her and starting up the steps.

"Oh, yeah? How can you be so sure?"

"Because, you see, I'm family."

The young woman followed him up the stairs. "Family? Whatdya mean?"

Dov merely threw open the door. "Mrs. Farber?" he called into the dim interior. "It's Dov, your cousin from Cracow."

3

*T*he almond-eyed young woman with the baby was named Jennie Shapiro. She told him this while leaning in the doorway of his new lodging (room, they called it in America), watching him unpack. She was surprised by the scantiness of his belongings and impressed by the number of his books. He suspected that she was weaving a romantic story about him in her head. She couldn't believe that he, with his English accent and his gentleman's suit, could be the poor Jewish immigrant boy he said he was.

"Sorry the room is so small, Duke," she remarked, trying to see the shabby room through the eyes of royalty. The room was actually rather large, but with a double bed, a bureau, a table and chair, and even a small kitchen in one corner, it looked terribly crowded.

"If you feel hungry later on, Duke, you can come over to my place and share my supper with me," she said from the doorway. "I live just across the hall."

"Thank you, but . . ."

"But what?"

"Won't your husband mind?"

She gave him an enigmatic look. "We don't have to worry about that. He won't be home."

Her rooms were larger than his, and the curtains at the windows and the feminine touches, like cushions on the chairs, made her quarters seem much more pleasant. Over supper, he asked her advice about looking for work. He confided to her that he wanted to get a job as a bookkeeper and to save enough to go to school.

"School?" she asked, surprised. "You mean *college*?"

"Yes, I think so. Why not?"

"Gee, I don't know. I never knew anyone who went to college. But I guess all you dukes have to be ejicated."

"Why do you keep calling me Duke, Mrs. Shapiro? Is it my suit? What's wrong with it?"

"Nothing's wrong with it. It just ain't right for Vesey Street, that's all. It's too . . . dukish."

"But can I wear it to look for a job? Is it too dukish for that?"

"Wear it to look for a job? Are you nuts? With those knickers, they'll laugh you out of the office."

Dov looked down at the offending knickers and frowned. "Then the first thing I'll have to do is earn enough money somewhere to buy a suit. Is there somewhere you can suggest where I can work looking like this?"

Jennie, feeding her baby in the American style, from a bottle with a rubber nipple, shook her head. "How would I know? The only place I can think of is the garter factory, and that wouldn't suit the likes of you."

"Anything would suit me right now, Mrs. Shapiro. Where is the garter factory?"

"It ain't really a factory. We just call it that. It's Mr. Epstein in the basement apartment. Mr. Okay Epstein. He makes men's garters. He can always use help. And, Duke, stop calling me Mrs. Shapiro, will you?"

The next morning, Dov went down to the basement and rang the bell on the door, on which was pasted a yellowing, hand-lettered sign that read GENTLEMEN'S GARTERS MFG. CO.—I. EPSTEIN. In response to a grunted "Come in," he opened the door. The Gentlemen's Garters factory was set up in the larger of the two rooms of the apartment. The only light came from a row of small windows set high on the rear wall on the level of the ground of the backyard. Through the dirty glass he could see some scrubby grass, discarded newspapers, and assorted kitchen debris. The room Dov now stood in was devoted solely to Mr. Epstein's work. The other, part of which Dov could see from his place near the door, seemed to contain whatever Mr. Epstein needed to keep himself alive.

The workroom was unlike anything Dov had ever seen. It had no decoration of any kind to make it cheerful. There were boxes and cartons piled against all the walls, all seeming to contain garter parts. Several were open, and he could see that they were filled with elastic bands, brass buttons, hooks, and other supplies. Mr. Epstein himself (for who else could it have been?) sat at a long table that took up most of the room.

The table was made of a number of planks placed across two rows of trestles, and it was almost completely covered with piles of loose garter parts. On the side of the table to Mr. Epstein's right was a young boy of fourteen or fifteen. Both Mr. Epstein and the boy were busily working away. Mr. Epstein was small, stooped, and sharp-featured, with gray hair and a grizzled beard. On his head he wore an embroidered *yarmulke,* as did the young boy. They both seemed absorbed in what they were doing.

Neither one had looked up at Dov's entrance. "I was told you could use help here," he said after a moment of silence.

Mr. Epstein threw him a glance. "A dollar ninety a day," he said in a heavy mid-European accent. "Ten hours. Half-hour lunch, piss time twice a day. No work on Shabbes. Okay?"

"Okay," Dov said. "Do I start now?"

"Okay. Sit down. Here's what you do. You pick up a piece elastic, like this, okay? It got holes on each end, see? You press a button in on one end, fasten the back, press the hook in the hole on the other end, fasten the back, clip the garter in the middle, pull down firm, hook it together, and then drop in a box on the floor near you. Press, fasten, press, fasten, clip, pull, hook. Like that, see? Rhythm. You gotta keep a rhythm if you're gonna fill three boxes per day and be worth your pay. Okay?"

"Okay," Dov said.

Press, fasten, press, fasten, clip, pull, hook. Dov said it so many times that day that he couldn't seem to stop when quitting time came. He fell into bed that night in exhaustion, the words "press," "fasten," "clip," "pull," "hook," repeating themselves endlessly in his dreams.

It was a strange place in which to work. The young boy who'd worked with them the first day came on some peculiar schedule of his own, three or four days a week. Sometimes other young men came in to work. They were paid at the end of the day. Sometimes they came back, and sometimes they disappeared forever. There seemed to be no long-term agreements involved in Epstein's enterprise. Dov, however, worked every day. He wanted to save enough for a suit as quickly as possible.

After a few days it wasn't so bad. The work had become so automatic that his mind was free to think of other things. And then one day, Epstein began to talk to him. Dov found him interesting to listen to. The old man had come to America ten years before and had found a job in the place that manufactured the elastic. They'd set him to work assembling the garters—a small and not very remunerative part of their large operation. Eventually, he'd convinced them that it would be cheaper for them to farm out the whole assembly operation. He took it over in his home, and they picked up the assembled garters once a week. "I'm the only one in the whole city, practically, doing it now. For three other companies, too," he chuckled. "Practically a monopoly."

"Then they pay you well for this work?" Dov asked.

"Why else would I do it? Believe me, I'm putting away a nice few bucks."

"I don't understand you, Epstein," Dov said bluntly. "Have you a wife hidden away somewhere who's making you slave away like this?"

Epstein chuckled again. "Not me. I lost one wife, such a nag there never was. No more. I ain't the marrying kind."

"Then why do you keep doing this? Why do you have to put away so much money?"

"For my old age, you *narr*, my old age. In a few more years, I'll be able to stop. I'll find myself a little place somewhere where it's warm, and I'll live out my years in ease and contentment. Believe me, it'll be worth it. Take my word, okay?"

"Okay," Dov said.

Epstein talked about the people in the building, too. Dov couldn't figure out how he learned so much about them when he spent every waking hour pressing, fastening, clipping, pulling, and hooking. But Epstein knew about everyone. He told Dov how long the Farbers were married and how their grown children had moved uptown and never came to visit because they were ashamed of where they'd come from. He told him that the screaming he heard at odd hours came from the throats of the two sisters who lived together on the top floor, who hated each other passionately but would never dream of living apart.

"How do you know all this, Epstein? All you ever do is work and sleep," Dov would ask.

"I have my ways, okay?"

"Okay, okay! So if you know so much, tell me about Mrs. Shapiro."

Epstein actually paused long enough to throw Dov a leer. "Interested in our little Jennie, eh? And her a married lady yet."

"Where's her husband? I've never seen him."

"And you won't. He left six months ago already—to work for Henry Ford, to make cars in Detroit. They're saying that Ford pays six, seven bucks a day. A day, you hear? If the *shmendrik* had bothered to ask me, I could've saved him the trip. Big plants so far from New York, they never hire Yids."

"You mean he didn't get the job?"

"Of course not. Last I heard, he was working for *bubkes* in a tannery, trying to save enough to come home like a big shot. He won't make it."

"You can't be sure of that, can you?" Dov objected.

"Take my word for it. I know the type, okay?"

"Okay," Dov said.

Epstein liked him. Every day he became more friendly. After two weeks of press, fasten, clip, he told Dov to get out. "Go find something more worthy of you, okay?" he ordered.

Dov's hands didn't stop assembling garters. "I can't, Epstein. Not till I've saved enough to buy a suit. With what you pay, I've only managed to save six dollars and eighty cents so far. What kind of suit can I get for six dollars and eighty cents?"

"So why didn't you tell me before? I'll lend you a few bucks, okay?"

Now Dov's hands stopped. "You'll *what*? Epstein, why—?"

"Because I like you, that's why. You'll pay me back. So put away those damn garters and get out of here." He pulled a ten from his pocket. "Here. Buy yourself a good suit. And not with knickers, okay?"

4

*J*ennie left the baby with Mrs. Farber and went with Dov to buy the suit. She dragged him to every haberdashery on Orchard Street. They finally chose a dark blue serge with a light pinstripe. And he had enough left over of the sixteen dollars and eighty cents to purchase a black fedora.

But finding a job was not so easy. After spending four full days answering want ads in *The New York Times* with no luck, he was thoroughly discouraged. He stuck his head in Epstein's door. "They all want experience," he said miserably. "I may never be able to pay you back."

"Don't worry, you will. You'll find something, just keep at it. Take my word for it, okay?"

Jenny was even more encouraging. "I know how to cheer you up," she said, ruffling his hair. "Something guaranteed to soothe the blues. Just wait till the baby's asleep."

It was after nine when she slipped back into his room. She was dressed in something soft and filmy, and she smelled of perfume. "I been waiting to do this for a long time," she whispered, winding her arms around his neck.

He kissed her hungrily. "Me, too," he murmured, his fingers edging toward her silky-smooth breasts. He hadn't held a woman since before the war. He was so eager that he barely noticed when she reached a hand out behind him and switched off the room's overhead light.

But before they fell upon the bed, he stopped himself. "We'd better not," he said hoarsely, breaking away from her with an enormous effort of will.

She brushed a strand of hair from her eyes, trying to peer at him through the darkness. A narrow streak of light shone in under the window shade from the street lamp outside. It shone right across her bare breast, making her seem to him almost inhumanly delectable. She took a step toward him. "Why not?" she asked.

"Well, you see, Epstein and I . . . we have something in common—"

"You and Epstein?" She laughed her throaty laugh. "You ain't trying to tell me that *your* dingle is dried out, too!"

When he realized what she meant, he snorted. "Hardly that. No, I mean that Epstein and I are not the marrying kind."

There was a silence. He couldn't see her face, but he could feel her anger. "So who asked you?" she said tightly. "I'm married already."

He knew it was a mistake to go on—he wanted her so badly he was tempted to promise her anything—but he had to make her understand. He didn't want to make another mistake, as he'd done with Chava Goldblum. "I know you're married, Jennie. But suppose your husband doesn't come back?"

She was sizzling in fury. "I don't have to suppose anything, Mr. Fancy Duke. I was doing *you* a favor, not the other way around."

He could barely see her, but he could hear the angry click of her heels as she stormed to the door. He caught her arm. "Wait, Jennie. I didn't want—"

"I don't care what you wanted! You can go to hell!" She pulled her arm from his hold and slammed out of the room.

He had a hard time falling asleep. And the next day, the heavy rain that poured down from the low, dark sky seemed to him to be the very last straw. After answering two ads, he was drenched. He just gave up and went home.

Jennie must have heard him unlock his door, for she came to the door just as he was removing his sodden jacket. Her eyes were red from a night of weeping. "Dov, I'm sorry. I never shoulda . . . Hey! Whatsa matter with your shirt?"

"What?" He looked down at himself. His shirt was stained all over with dark blue splotches.

"It's from the *suit*," she cried, horrified. "The dye musta run." She ran up to him and grabbed at his sleeves. "Just *look* at you! The shirt's *ruined*. What kind rotten, cheap material is that suit made of anyway?"

But he couldn't think about the suit now. Not when she was standing so close to him, and the frustration of the night before was still causing an ache inside him. He pulled her into his arms. "Never mind the suit, Jennie," he murmured, kissing her hair. "Never mind anything, now."

"Oh, Dov," she sighed, turning her face up to his. "I'm so sorry that I—"

"Never mind." He backed her to the bed and began to strip off her clothes. She was crying. "I wouldn't trap you, Dov," she wept, clutching him to her. "I would never hang on to you if you didn't want me."

"I know," he soothed her. "I know. I was a bastard last night—"

She put her mouth to his and stopped all speech. Her skin was as smooth as silk to his touch. And, yes, she was soothing.

Afterward they lay still, listening to the rain against the window. He felt lethargic with contentment. She was lovely and pliant and ripe with desire, and the prospect of many such encounters stretched before him like the view of an orchard bursting with the fruits of an endless summer. They understood each other. They'd cleared the air beforehand of any possible misunderstanding. There would be no ties, no bonds, no demands that he'd be reluctant to fulfill. He smiled to himself. If it weren't for that deuced serge suit, this would be a perfect day.

Then she stirred in his arms and turned her face to him. "Dov, do you love me?" she whispered, nibbling sweetly at his ear. "Tell me that you love me."

He froze for a moment. Except for the accent, the voice could have been Chava's. He leaped from the bed.

"Dov? Whatsa matter?"

"I'm going to take back that damned suit," he said, rummaging in his closet for the English suit.

"Now?" She sat up and gaped at him. "This minute?"

He hastily buttoned up the knickers. "Why not?" He did up his collar, knotted his tie, and pulled on the tweed jacket. "You'd better get dressed, too. I think I hear your baby crying." And he picked up the wet suit and ran out.

As he strode through the rain to the store where the suit had been bought, he got angrier and angrier. Why didn't anything ever go smoothly for him? Why was everything so unfair? Didn't promises mean anything? How could anyone make plans, live in an orderly way, keep control of the future if people didn't do as they promised, if agreements weren't respected? Was there no honor in the world? Was life always going to be so damned messy?

Well, he couldn't do very much about women, or about his plans for work, or about his dreams of going to college, or any of those things. But, damn it, he could do something about this damned suit, even if he had to punch someone in the nose to get satisfaction. At this moment there was nothing he would have liked better to do than punch someone in the nose.

The clerk at the clothing store was not intimidated by Dov's angry accusations. He remained adamant. "No refunds," he said firmly. "Whatdya think this is, R. H. Macy? You want refunds, go uptown."

Dov reached over the counter, grabbed the clerk by the lapels, and lifted him off the floor. "Listen you little *vantz,* either you give me my money back or you're going to feel my fist on your face! Do you think I'm going to pay thirteen dollars and ninety-nine cents for a suit that leaks ink every time it rains?"

"Hey, why blame me?" the clerk muttered fearfully. "Did I make the suit? Did I know it was gonna run? Go punch the manufacturer, not me."

Dov's arm stopped in midswing. "The manufacturer?"

"Sure. W and W, isn't it? Lemme look inside, on the label."

Dov set him down, and the clerk hastily backed away. He took the soggy jacket and showed Dov the label, keeping well out of reach. "There, see? It's W and W, like I said."

The label was impressive. The two *W*s were embroidered in ornate script on the little bit of fabric. Beneath the large initials were the words "Men's Clothiers" in small letters, and below, even smaller, the legend *Designed for the Discriminating.* "Huh!" Dov snorted. "Where can I find this manufacturer?"

The relieved salesclerk shrugged. "How do I know?" But a threatening look from Dov reminded him of his manners. "I mean, I can't keep all those addresses in my head. Can'tcha find the address in the phone book?"

Dov blinked. "Phone book?" he echoed stupidly.

"What're you, some kinda greenhorn? Ain't you never heard of the New York phone book?" He went into a little room at the back and came out with a thick pamphlet. "Look in here. It gives addresses and phone numbers."

Dov stared at the book the man had placed before him. "Of . . . of everyone?" he asked, amazed.

"Everyone with a phone, which ain't too many. Who can afford a phone, eh? But manufacturers, they're all listed here. They all got phones, right?"

Dov opened the book with fascination. The pages were filled with column after column of names, listed alphabetically. To his own complete surprise, he turned immediately to the names beginning with *G,* his pulse suddenly racing. Genton, Leonard . . . Gentry, Clifford . . . Gentry, John Albert . . . Gentry, William . . . Gentzler, Frank. No Gentz, Avrum. No Gentz at all. Avrum wasn't one of those who could afford a telephone. The hero of Ilinghovka was not such a big shot in New York. If he *was* in New York.

Dov was amazed at the sharpness of his disappointment at not finding the name. He didn't know what had made him look for it in the first place. And why should he be feeling this disappointment? Who was Avrum Gentz to him anyway?

"Whatsa matter with you, looking in the *G*s?" the salesclerk asked in disdainful superiority. "Look in the *W*s, fa Chrissake!"

W&W Fine Clothiers was located in a shabby building on Twelfth Street. Dov took the elevator up to their floor. He had ridden on elevators several times while looking for work, but they still fascinated him. Sometimes he had the urge to spend the day riding up and down, like a child. Not today, however. He'd walked all the way to Twelfth Street in the rain, and he was soaked and very cold. But at least he could show Mr. W&W that the English suit did not run.

The elevator opened on a small anteroom that was separated from a large loft by wood-and-glass partitions. Boxes and bolts of cloth were stacked haphazardly in the corners and on the area's one piece of furniture —a scarred, torn, rickety old imitation-leather sofa. Beyond the partitions, Dov could see a number of men and a few women working away at assorted machines and tables, perhaps twenty workers in all. No one seemed to be in charge. Dov walked through the anteroom into the loft. The noise of the sewing machines and a large, sawlike cutting machine was deafening. "Hello?" he shouted over the din.

A stooped little man hunched over a sewing machine closest to him glanced up at him and then back down to his work.

"Is there somebody I can see about a complaint?" Dov asked the man, bending over him to make sure he could hear.

"Kenisht reddn Yinglish," the man muttered, not looking up from his stitching.

Dov repeated his request in Yiddish. The man lifted one hand, pointed quickly to a paper-covered glass door in the corner, and resumed his work.

Dov walked to the door and tapped. "Come in," someone inside yelled.

DOV, 1919–1928

Dov entered a tiny room not much larger than a closet. It contained a desk with a chair behind it, a second chair squeezed in beside the desk, and more boxes and bolts of cloth. There was a fat, heavily moustached man sitting behind the desk, smoking a cigar, and talking on a tall, black telephone. His desk was a shambles, littered with ledgers, papers, fabric samples, patterns, and the remains of a lunch from a brown paper bag. "No can do," he was saying into the phone. "Not by the tenth. Listen, Sol, if you think this is bad, just wait. Don't you read the papers? The Labor Conference in Washington just endorsed an eight-hour workday. Can you beat that? Everyone'll be living like bankers!"

The fat man flicked a glance at his visitor and made a motion with his cigar for Dov to sit down. Dov looked down at the chair. It was covered, like the desk, with papers and debris. He decided to remain standing. It would give him an advantage, he reasoned, to tower over his opponent.

"Sit down," the fat man said, glancing up at Dov again. "Just shove the stuff on the floor." Then his attention returned to the phone. "What? No, not you, Sol."

Dov remained standing. Something about the fat man had caught his attention. At first Mr. W&W had seemed to be about thirty years old, but now Dov realized he was younger. Perhaps not even much older than Dov himself. It was the girth and the slightly receding hairline that had made him seem older—those physical qualities and the air of authority with which he was speaking into the telephone. But there was something else about him—something that Dov found vaguely familiar. It was ridiculous—Dov could never have met him before. The number of people he'd met in New York could be counted on the fingers of one hand.

The fat man hung up the phone and began to rummage about on his desk. "Where's my damn ashtray?" he muttered and added, without looking up, "What can I do for you?"

"You can give me my money back for this miserable excuse for a suit," Dov said, thrusting the still damp jacket under his nose. "It leaks ink."

The fat man brushed Dov's arm aside and reached for his half-buried ashtray. "We don't give refunds here. Take it to where you bought it."

"I've already done that. If you're the one who made it, you should—"

The phone rang shrilly. The fat man stubbed out his cigar into the ashtray and reached for the phone. "Sit down, I'll be right with you. Yeah, hello?"

Dov glared at the fellow as he launched into another telephone conversation. It was not pleasant being ignored. Maybe he ought to use the threat of his fists again. But somehow he couldn't work up the required anger . . . not until he got over the feeling that he'd seen this man somewhere before.

The fat man was laughing at something being said at the other end of the wire. Even the way he laughed seemed familiar to Dov. Then the fellow reached into the brown paper bag and removed a sugar-covered doughnut. He flattened the bag, placed the doughnut on it, and licked the sugar from his fingers.

"Oh, my *God!*" Dov gasped, his eyes widening.

"Whatsa matter?" the fat man asked, glancing at his visitor in surprise.

"Hang up the telephone," Dov ordered, barely able to contain himself.

"What?"

"I said, hang up that telephone. Right now."

Gaping in confusion, the fat man did as he was told. "Are you out of your head?" he asked nervously. "Is this a holdup, or what?"

Dov grinned at him. "What's the matter with you, Hersh? Is this the way you greet old friends?"

Hersh Waksman from Czernowitz stared at his visitor's face for one long moment before the light dawned in his eyes. Then his mouth dropped open. "Dov? *Vay iz mir! Dov!*"

The last was shouted so loudly that the cry was heard outside in the loft. Chortling like a demented hyena, Hersh jumped up and enveloped Dov in a tight embrace, pounding him on the back in joyous frenzy. Neither one could speak coherently, but Hersh kept making hysterical shouts of elation. "Dov!" he kept yelling. "I can't believe it! You *came!*"

Some of the men in the loft were pounding on the door. "Waksman, what's going on? Are you all right in there?"

Hersh threw open the door and drew Dov out, his arm about his shoulders. "Look at this," he announced to the curious workers, "my best friend in all the world comes in to complain about a suit! Just like that! Did you ever hear such a tale? My best friend in the *world!* Say hello, everybody, to my friend Dov Gentz from Czernowitz."

"Dov Weisenberg," Dov corrected, shaking hands with everyone he could reach.

Hersh threw him a shrewd glance. "Oh? How did that happen?"

"It's a long story."

"Damn, we got a lot to catch up on. Come on, let's get outta here. There's a coffee shop on the corner where we can talk. God, I can't believe this is happening. I would've sworn you'd be in Palestine by now."

They chose a back booth and talked for hours, stopping in the middle of a sentence to grin at one another in delight. Dov learned that Hersh was doing well in New York. He'd gone to work at W&W as soon as he'd arrived in New York and was now managing the place. The W&W stood for Morris and Benny Waksman, the uncles his father had sent him to. Both of the uncles preferred to be out selling the suits; they were happy to leave the management of the factory to Hersh. Hersh was now married, had a little two-year-old daughter, and lived in a "nice, new four-room walk-through" across the bridge in Brooklyn Heights. "Wait till my wife gets a load of you! I talked about you so much, she doesn't even believe you're real. When she sees you, she'll die!"

But the pinnacle of Hersh's excitement came when he learned that Dov was looking for a job as a bookkeeper. "If it's one thing that W and W absolutely needs, it's a bookkeeper," he declared.

"Please, Hersh," Dov said in remonstrance, "this isn't Czernowitz. You don't have to buy me pastries any more. Stop being the kind-hearted rich boy of the town. I'll get a job on my own. What I really need from you is a suit that won't run."

Hersh chuckled. "It's the lining. A cheap rayon we got stuck with once. Don't worry. For you I've got the best suit in the line. And I really *do* need a bookkeeper. I swear it on my daughter's life!"

Hersh was looking at him with so eager, so sincere, so good-natured an expression that Dov decided then and there to accept the offer. He didn't believe that W&W really needed a bookkeeper, but he'd find a way to make himself worth his salary. And working with Hersh every day would be like old times. How could he refuse?

5

Dov watched the painter carefully fill in the black outlines of the letters of his name with gold leaf on the opaque glass door
of Suite 604 in the Boyd Building on Twenty-second Street. DAVID
WEISENBERG, B.A., the painter had lettered in beautiful capitals. And centered impressively below, the single word ACCOUNTANT.

It had taken him seven years of night school at City College to earn
the right to see those words on the door. Seven years of hard days at
W&W and long nights over the books. It was June of 1926. He was
almost thirty and only now starting on a proper career. Hersh was already
an established entrepreneur with a partnership in a large business, a stock
portfolio, three children, and a summer place in the Catskills, while Dov
had a small bank account (which would be eaten up by renting and
furnishing this office), a two-room apartment facing Gramercy Park, and
three good suits. But he had no complaints. Seeing these letters on the
door of his new office made him feel proud. Who would have dreamed,
back in Czernowitz, that he would ever have a college degree?

The seven years had flown; working at W&W had been that absorb-
ing. The business had grown so quickly that he'd had to use all his
ingenuity to set up a bookkeeping system to handle it. And keeping the
system going without assistance had taken long hours. His college course
work had to be done in the wee hours of the morning. While he still
lived on Vesey Street, Jennie Shapiro had complained constantly that he
never seemed to have time for her.

From the first Jennie resented his new job with W&W, his schooling, his friendship with Hersh, and the fact that he liked spending every Friday evening and Sunday afternoon in Brooklyn with Hersh's family. Dov felt guilty every time he went out, especially when he knew that Harriet, Hersh's wife, had found a new girl for him to meet.

Arguments with Jennie became more and more frequent. When he confided the details of the situation to Hersh, his friend offered a simple solution: "Why don't you find yourself a decent apartment, *nudnik,* and just get out of there?"

Dov thought about it for months after that and secretly looked around for another place. The day he found the Gramercy Park rooms was a day he'd never forget. It was on the very day he was granted his American citizenship. That was a really special day—the first time he admitted to himself that he loved America . . . that his father and Hersh and Mendel and everyone else who'd said it was the Goldeneh Medina had been right. This was where he wanted to spend his life. When the certificate of citizenship was placed in his hands, he felt like crying. And that afternoon, when he looked at the neat, clean rooms overlooking the park, he knew he had to take them. It was time to live like a permanent member of this society, not like a temporary boarder. He signed the lease at once.

That evening he tried to break the news to Jennie as gently as he could. "We'll still see each other," he assured her. "My new place isn't far from here."

But Jennie stomped out of the room as she'd done so many times before. The next day she told him she was going to Michigan to be reunited with her husband. "You don't really want me, Dov," she said, trying to keep the heartbreak from showing in her voice. "I don't think you'll every let yourself really feel love for a woman. There's something in you that's closed and . . . and cold."

Her words infuriated him. "Maybe it's not me," he countered angrily. "Maybe it's something in you women. You're always setting your hearts on men you can't have."

She gave a hopeless shake of her head. "Who are you talking about?" she asked. "Me, or someone else? Who made you like this—some girl in the old country? Your mother? Who?"

But he hadn't bothered to answer. Two days later, she was gone, without giving him a chance to say goodbye to her little girl, whom he'd grown very fond of. He himself moved away a few days later. Since then, whenever he dropped in to say hello to Epstein he asked about Jennie, but no one in the building had ever heard from her again.

He didn't mourn. There had been other women. Harriet's girlfriends, girls he met at work, even women he picked up on the street. He'd been too busy to allow himself to become seriously entangled with any one particular female after Jennie had left. The bachelor life had suited him very well all these years.

But now he was beginning to feel differently, and it was because of the Girl Downstairs. He'd seen her on the elevator two months before, in the spring, on the very first day he'd come to the Boyd Building to look for office space. The lobby was wide and clean, with a checkerboard marble floor and an iron-grated elevator rising in the middle of it. It was the kind of elevator you could look right into and watch as it rose in creaking dignity from one floor to the next. That first day, the Girl had passed him as he'd stood with the agent in the lobby, and she'd stepped into the elevator. He'd stared at her through the grillwork in fascination as the elevator rose. First her hat had risen to his eye level, its deep crown and turned-down brim almost completely covering her dark-gold hair; then her eyes—a sort of ocean gray—had met his and instantly dropped away. Then up had come a slender neck half covered by a small squirrel collar; then a low-belted blue wool coat that fitted over her form too loosely to indicate more than a suggestion of slimness and modest curves. Finally, up had come a pair of shapely, silk-clad calves followed by slim ankles bound by the narrow T-strap of her shoes. His eyes had followed those charming ankles until the elevator had disappeared above the lobby's ceiling.

The sight of that girl rising up before his eyes should not have been anything out of the ordinary. He saw lovely women on the street every day. But seeing this one had left him stunned—as if he'd been given too brief a glimpse of a breathtaking work of art.

The agent had been watching the elevator's ascent, too. "She works here," he'd grinned. "Right under the suite you're going to look at. Number 504." He consulted the directory. "George B. Simpson, Philately." (Dov had looked up the word in his dictionary that night. Stamp collecting. What sort of business was that?)

The suite the agent had shown him was on the top floor. It had two rooms. The reception area was small and neat, but since he couldn't yet afford to hire a secretary or an assistant, he didn't much care about it. He could put in a couple of chairs and a table, and it would do. The inner room, which would be his office, had a rounded bow window that he liked. He'd saved enough money to furnish the office, and he'd stood in the middle of the newly painted, empty room and envisioned how it would look with a large, roomy desk in the center, a leather swivel chair behind it, file cabinets near the inner door, and some large bookshelves flanking the window. "I'll take it," he'd told the agent.

It had been an impulsive decision. He'd told himself that the decision had been made because of the bow window, but now, as he watched the painter fill in the last bit of gold, he wondered if he'd really made the decision because of the Girl Downstairs.

Now that he was actually moving in, however, he was glad he'd chosen this place. He already liked being there. The Boyd Building had four suites on each of its six floors, two of them, like his, facing the front and two the back. Every one of the suites was occupied by an interesting tenant, all of whom could be potential clients. There were several lawyers in the building, a dentist, a couple of printers, a bookbinder, a dealer in antique clocks, a man who repaired violins, a photographer, an importer of Oriental artifacts, George Simpson the philatelist, and several others. Not that Dov's goal was handling clients of that caliber—he hoped someday to have a good number of the city's largest clothing manufacturers as clients—but at this stage of his career any small clients would be gratefully accepted. He only had three so far—W&W (whose yearly retainer would at least pay the rent) and two smaller garment manufacturers who had retained him on Hersh's recommendation. But if he was to make ends meet this first year, he needed to find three or four more.

Nonetheless he was full of hope. There was a pile of engraved cards on his new desk, his name in gold on the door, his very own telephone about to be installed, and a new, bushy moustache on his face to make him look distinguished. He was on his way.

He came to his new office every morning at eight-thirty. He chose that time because that was when the Girl Downstairs arrived. In order not to miss her, he would read the paper in the lobby until he saw her waiting at the elevator door. Just riding up with her made his pulse race. They were rarely alone in the elevator at that hour, and they never spoke, but the chance to feast his eyes on her gave a good start to his day. He rarely saw her in the evenings. He usually worked at his clients' offices in the afternoons, and on most days he didn't get back to his office until late. The lights behind the glass of George B. Simpson's door were always dark by then.

Dov wondered how he could meet her. Sometimes his mind would wander from his work, and he would daydream about her, making up little wishful dramas in which he would endear himself to her by performing some knightly feat—saving her from a pickpocket, reviving her from a faint, pulling her from the path of a speeding taxi. He imagined her catching her heel on the threshold of the elevator and spraining her slim little ankle. He'd pick her up in his arms, carry her to her office, take off her pretty shoe, and massage away her pain. "Oh, sir," she'd breathe, "how can I ever thank you?"

"Don't worry," he'd grin, "I'm sure I can think of something."

It was adolescent, he knew. Here he was, almost thirty years old and dreaming like a schoolboy. But he couldn't seem to help himself. He kept inventing silly little dialogues that he might use in specific situations that might possibly arise—if he met her outside the building in the rain, for example. "Pardon me, miss," he'd say, "may I offer you the shelter of my umbrella?"

"Oh, sir, I wouldn't wish to inconvenience you."

"It's no inconvenience, I assure you. My pleasure, really."

Or perhaps he could *make* a situation arise. He could buy a pretty lace handkerchief, for example, douse it with her perfume, and then hold it out to her the next time he saw her. "Pardon me, miss, but did you drop this handkerchief?"

"No, sir, I did not."

"But it has your scent, hasn't it?"

"Why, yes, so it has. What an amazing coincidence!"

But he didn't know what perfume she used (though a whiff of her scent on the elevator could make him dizzy), and he didn't know how to find out. Besides, the dialogue was so stilted and silly it belonged to another century.

He tried to figure out a strategy for meeting her, the way he might figure out the moves in a game of chess. He considered various opening gambits, from "Did anyone ever tell you that you ought to be in movies?" to "Excuse me, miss, do you have the time?" None of them rose above the idiotic:

"Excuse me, but there's a ladybug on your shoulder."

"May I carry your parcel, miss? It looks much too heavy for you."

"Good morning. I hope you won't think me presumptuous if I tell you that your hat is (depending on the circumstances) (a) lovely, (b) breathtaking, (c) wet, (d) dripping on my shoes, (e) crooked, (f) hitting me in the eye."

"Tell me, pretty maiden, are there any more at home like . . . ?"

"Help! Get a doctor! I'm having (a) a stroke, (b) a heart attack, (c) a seizure (air of mystery in that one), (d) a baby."

"Excuse me, but I must tell you that you look just like (a) my sister,

(b) a painting by Degas, (c) Theda Bara, (d) my cousin from Cracow."

"Excuse me, please, but it just occurred to me that I might be your cousin Dov from Cracow."

"Excuse me, please, but it just occurred to me that I love you. This condition could be fatal. Don't you think there's something you should do about it?"

Of course he rejected them all. And the more situations he concocted in his head, the more impossible it became for him to speak to her in reality.

After several months, however, Dov began to know the people in the building. The clock dealer and the photographer became clients. Dov said good morning to them when he met them at the elevator. Soon he was saying good morning to everyone, including the Girl. But she never said anything in return. She always responded with an infinitesimal smile and an incline of her head. Nothing more.

This went on for a month or two longer, until Dov ruined everything. It happened on a Friday evening in October. He was going to Brooklyn to have Shabbes dinner with Hersh's family. He'd finished his work early so that he could leave the office before sundown. He was riding down the elevator when, to his amazement, he saw the Girl Downstairs waiting on five. She was wearing her deep-crowned hat and blue coat, just as she had when he'd first set eyes on her, and she carried a thick folder under her arm with her handbag. Dov was so startled that, when she got on, he stammered out a barely audible good evening. She gave him her little nod and turned to face the door. He could hardly breathe. She was just as lovely at the end of the day as she was in the morning.

He pulled the gate closed for her, and the elevator creaked down past four ... then three. Dov prayed that it would get stuck, but it lumbered down past two. Dov couldn't believe how quickly the creaky old mechanism was moving. Before he knew it, they'd come to a stop in the lobby, and the Girl—evidently in a hurry to pull open the gate before Dov could reach over and do it for her—dropped her folder. A number of cards, with colorful stamps pasted on them in neat groups, spilled out. The Girl gave an embarrassed cry and knelt down to pick them up. Dov bent down beside her to help. She threw a quick look over her shoulder. "Thanks," she murmured, breathless and awkward, "but I can manage."

Her face was only inches from his own. A flush of color tinged her cheeks, and her mouth was slightly open. It seemed to him that he'd never seen anyone so beautiful. "It's okay," he mumbled, shoving cards into the folder without looking. Damn, he thought, wincing, what did I say? *"It's okay"?* That was his scintillating response? He wanted to kill himself. Fate had smiled down and given him this once-in-a-lifetime opportunity, and he'd said, "It's okay"? He'd answered like a real klutz! He must have sounded like . . . like, for God's sake, *Epstein!*

She was reaching for the folder. In another minute she would be gone, with the distinct impression that she'd just met a nincompoop. He couldn't let her go like this. For God's sake, he told himself, *say something!* One of those lines you're always making up! Anything!

He held out the folder to her, feeling dazed, tongue-tied, and thick-headed. She was so lovely that he was overcome with awe. "Oh, God," he sighed, "I don't think I've ever seen such a kissable mouth."

Her eyebrows flew up and her cheeks paled. With a gasp, she pulled the folder out of his hands and backed out of the elevator, keeping her eyes on him with the same sort of wary fright with which she'd watch a rabid dog. Then she turned on her heel and ran for the door.

He realized he was still kneeling. Desperately, he got up and lunged after her. "Wait," he yelled, "don't be afraid! I won't—"

But the heavy door banged behind her. She was gone.

All weekend long he stewed about it. What had he done? How could he have done it? Where were his brains? How could he ever face her again? And, most important, was there any way to change the situation from a disaster to a triumph?

Here was a test of his ingenuity. Here was a situation he didn't have to concoct. All he had to do was to think of a way to turn it around. At last he found an answer. On Monday morning, he went to the flower shop down the street from the office and ordered a dozen roses. The florist laid them lovingly in a long white box, on the cover of which the florist's name was stamped in gold. Under the name were the words FLOWERS ARE THE LANGUAGE OF LOVE.

Dov tucked a note in among the blooms: "Dear Girl Downstairs," he wrote, "I'm very sorry I frightened you the other night. I must have sounded brash. I'm not so brash, however, that I would actually have kissed you, no matter how much I may have wanted to. Very penitently yours, David Weisenberg from upstairs."

He took the box with him and laid it at the door of Suite 504. All day he pictured her opening the box, smelling the roses, arranging them in a vase, smiling at them on her desk. A disaster could sometimes turn into a triumph, he thought, if one tried hard enough.

That evening, when he returned to the office, he saw, as the elevator passed the fifth floor, that Suite 504 was dark. But lying in front of his own office door was the box from the florist. There was no note inside, but it was full of flowers. He counted them. Twelve. She hadn't even taken one. If flowers were the language of love, she'd spoken out loud and clear: she didn't want anything to do with him.

6

Dov thought he smelled smoke, but he was so engrossed in trying to untangle the mess that Finestein of Finest Fabrics (his latest client) had made of his books that, though the smell of smoke irritated his nose, it didn't penetrate his brain. It wasn't until Hanson, the lawyer from across the hall, hammered on the glass of his door that he realized there was trouble. "Weisenberg, are you in there?" Hanson yelled. "Better get out—there's a fire!"

Dov was not very alarmed as he got up from his desk to see what was going on. New Yorkers, he'd discovered, had an obsessive fear of fire, probably caused by the terrible Triangle fire that had occurred fifteen years before. He'd endured false alarms both at the rooming house and at W&W several times. One time at W&W, he'd even smelled smoke, but it had been a minor blaze in the wiring and had been quickly handled. So he was shocked when he opened his door and found the hallway hazy with a thin cloud of smoke. It seemed to be coming from the elevator shaft. Hanson, following his secretary and his nervous young law clerk, was already at the fire escape door. "Don't bother with the elevator," he shouted over his shoulder as he ran. "It's not working. And the stairwell's full of smoke."

Dov hesitated in the doorway. If this was truly a fire, wasn't there something he should save? There were Finestein's books on the desk—six heavy ledgers—and the W&W records . . . and the files . . .

He realized that there was no way he could save them all. Besides, the smoke was getting thicker and becoming very unpleasant. He could hear shouting and screaming from the floors below, and the two typists from the Eastern Imports office next door came screaming past him, followed by their bewildered employer, whose Oriental eyes were already tearing but who mumbled, "Calm, ladies, calm. Please to go calm."

Dov, now convinced that this was a true emergency, decided not to be foolhardy. Time might be of the essence, and his life was more valuable —at least to him—than a pile of accounts receivable. So he shut his door behind him and ran after the Oriental importer.

The fire escape, which Dov had not bothered to look at before, was located in a sort of air shaft. It was rapidly filling with smoke, though breathing was decidedly easier here than inside. The clatter of feet on the iron stairs, and the noise and screams of the tenants below, echoed deafeningly against the surrounding brick walls. There was no doubt that, down below, the tenants were in a state of hysteria. His own pulse began to race. What was happening down there? Were people trapped? He looked over the railing, but the smoke down below was so thick he couldn't see anything.

Hard on the heels of the still-screaming typists and their now silent employer, Dov rounded the turn of the stairs to the fifth floor. There in the doorway was the Girl Downstairs, her hair disheveled and one arm held out pleadingly to everyone who passed. "Please, someone . . . help me! My uncle . . ."

The typists went shrieking past her. The Oriental gentleman tugged at her outstretched arm. "No good to stay, lady. Come down."

"You don't understand!" the Girl cried. "My uncle's still—"

The importer shook his head and hurried on. Dov stopped. "What is it? What's the matter?"

She clenched her hands in terror. "My uncle! He's still in there. He's been taken ill!"

It flashed through Dov's mind that this "uncle" was the philatelist, George Simpson. "All right, I'll get him," he said quickly, opening the door behind her. "You go on down."

"No," she said, "I'll come with—"

"Do as I say!" Dov ordered and pulled the door shut behind him.

The smoke struck his face in a cloud. He could barely breathe. It was pouring from the elevator shaft in thick, black puffs. He pulled out his handkerchief, covered his nose and mouth, lowered his head, and ran for Suite 504. It was a relief to open the door, for the smoke was not nearly so thick inside.

Mr. Simpson was not in the outer office. Dov couldn't help noticing how expensively the place was decorated. It was hard to believe that these rooms were identical to his own. There were rugs on the floor, gilt-framed paintings on the walls, plush sofas flanking the door to the inner office, with tables alongside holding a pair of tall lamps. But he heard coughing from the inner office and ran for the door. He found Simpson on the floor, trying to reach up along the wall as if he wanted to pull down the picture that hung there several feet beyond his reach. Dov bent over the fallen man and tried to raise him up. The man turned to him, his face deathly pale, his lips ashen. "No! The safe! Must . . . open the safe," he gasped.

"No time," Dov said shortly. "Can you stand?"

The gray-haired man shook his head. "The *safe*! Urgent. Must open—"

"Don't be a fool, man! In another few minutes we won't be able to breathe out there. Can you get your arm around my neck and help me get you to your feet?"

Simpson shook his head again, a lock of gray hair falling over his forehead. He grabbed at Dov's lapels. "Please! Only a moment. Three right . . . twelve left . . . fifty-nine right . . ."

Dov wanted to throttle him. "I don't even *see* a safe. Come on, put your arm—"

"Behind the painting. Three . . . twelve . . ."

With a shrug of disgust, Dov stood up and tried to lift the painting. But he found that it was hinged and could easily be swung aside like a cabinet door. Behind was a small safe. In his nervous haste, he had to dial the numbers twice. When the safe opened, he saw inside only a pile of folders, very like the one the girl had dropped that evening on the elevator floor. "*All* of this?" he asked the stricken man, who was still on the floor with his back against the wall, holding his hands against his chest. "You can't take all of it."

"No, just . . . black leather case . . . like a billfold . . . in back."

Dov sighed and rummaged about till he found it. Only when he'd placed the case in Simpson's hand did the man put his arm about Dov's neck.

Haltingly, Dov led him to the door. When he opened the door to the hallway, Simpson gasped. The smoke was so dense that there was almost no visibility. It was impossible to take a breath. The poor old fellow began to choke at once. "I can't . . . make it," he wheezed between coughs. "Here. Take this and . . . save yourself."

Dov ignored the proffered billfold. "Come on!" he said, tying his handkerchief like a mask over Simpson's nose and mouth. But Simpson slumped down, and Dov had all he could do to keep him from falling over. Dov bent his knees under Simpson's legs as a brace and, with all his strength, heaved the man over his shoulder in a carry he'd learned in the fire-fighting class at Knockaloe. Coughing, he tottered as quickly as he could through the smoke cloud to the fire escape door.

His eyes were tearing when he opened the door, and he could barely see, but out on the fire escape the breathing was a little easier. "Thank God!" he heard the Girl gasp.

"Damn it, why didn't you go?" Dov asked her furiously, wiping his streaming eyes with the sleeve of his free arm.

She was looking at her uncle's head, behind Dov. "Is he all right? I don't think he's conscious."

"I don't know. Come on, we'd better get down."

He became aware, as they started clumsily down the iron stairs, that the sounds of screaming from below had ceased. Everyone else must have gotten out. They, too, even if they were the last ones, could probably save themselves if only they could make their way through the choking smoke. He held tightly to the limp Simpson with one arm and grabbed the Girl's hand with the other. "Hang on," he ordered. "Don't stop moving, but if you have anything to cover your nose with, do it."

She nodded, coughing, and pulled the ruffle of her blouse over her nose.

On the fourth floor the smoke was thicker, and by the time they came to the third, breathing was again impossible. Besides, a wave of heat seemed to envelop them, and Dov could see flickering reddish gleams through the clouds of smoke. Were they heading down into the flames?

He realized now, with his lungs seeming to be on fire and his eyes burning, that they might well be trapped. They were coughing incessantly, and with the smoke thick around them and the flames below, he wasn't sure they should continue in this direction. But strangely, he felt completely free of fear or panic. His mind was clicking away like a machine. A window. They had to get to a front window. "Here," he said, choking out the words, "come . . . this way."

Heaving Simpson a little higher on his shoulder, he pulled the Girl behind him into the hellish blackness of the third-floor hall. He could see through the smoke that flames were flickering in the rear suites. To take a breath was painful. "Keep . . . head down . . . low . . ." he managed. He felt with his free hand along the wall until they came to the first door. Suite 302, he knew. The door had been left wide open, and the suite was as full of smoke as the hallway. Praying that the door to 304 had been closed, he continued to feel along the wall. But when they got to the door of 304, he groaned aloud. It was not only closed, but locked. Not even aware that he was uttering a stream of Jewish curses under his breath, he laid his burden down, propping Simpson up against the wall, and pulled off his jacket. The Girl, coughing pathetically, watched him over the ruffle of her blouse with helpless, confused admiration as he wrapped his jacket twice around his fist and pounded it in desperation right through the glass of the door.

With Dov taking Simpson under one arm and the Girl taking the other, they dragged the elderly man through the anteroom of Suite 304, now rapidly filling with smoke, and into the inner office. Dov quickly shut the inner door. They paused, gasping and choking, their lungs gulping in the cleaner air. As soon as his chest stopped heaving, Dov went to the window and threw it open.

Then he turned and looked down at the stricken man. Simpson's face looked blue. Dov straddled him and motioned the still-gasping Girl to watch as he slowly performed on Simpson's chest the movements of artificial respiration he'd learned in Knockaloe's first-aid class. "Can you do this?" he asked her.

"I think so," she answered, her voice hoarse.

"In my rhythm," he instructed and began to count. As soon as she'd taken over, he returned to the window and looked out. The street below seemed miles down. It was crowded with screaming people, fire engines, and ambulances. He tried to shout at them, but only a croak came from his throat. Nevertheless, a fireman—one of several holding a hose to a second-story window—looked up and spotted him. "Jesus!" he yelled in alarm as others began to look up. "Are you alone up there?"

Dov shook his head and held up three fingers. "Jesus!" the fireman shouted again, and people in the crowd began to point and shout. The fireman held a quick conference with the others, and with amazing speed a large canvas net was spread out. Dov turned to the Girl. "Is he breathing?"

"Yes, I . . . think so. . . ."

"Then come here."

The Girl came fearfully to the window and looked out. "Oh, my God!" she whimpered.

"Don't be afraid," he said, his voice a croak. "It'll be all right. It's only a jump."

She nodded fearfully. Her face was black with smoke, and her eyes seemed enormous pools of light in the dark face. He squeezed her hand for encouragement and lifted her to the sill. A loud cry came up to them from the crowd below at the sight of her in the window. The sound sent a shiver right through her. She glanced down at Dov, waiting for him to give her her cue.

"Tell them we'll have to have a ladder," he told her. "We can't throw an unconscious man out of the window."

She nodded again, gave him a quick, brave little smile, and leaped.

He hung out of the window, watching and barely breathing. The canvas seemed to billow around her as she dropped into it, and for an agonizing moment he couldn't tell what was happening below. But a cheer from the crowd and a signal of triumph from the first fireman told him she was safe. Already the ladder on the fire truck was being turned around and extended toward him, and a fireman, impressive in his over-sized hat, boots, and gloves, was climbing with unbelievable agility up the still-expanding ladder. In another moment, the fireman was over the sill.

"I don't think I was ever so glad to see anyone," Dov said, his knees only now beginning to shake.

The fireman grinned at him. "Wanna jump," he asked, lifting the still-unconscious Simpson over his back, "or wouldja rather follow me down the ladder?"

"I'll follow you," Dov answered promptly. Now that he had a choice, he was only too happy to avoid taking that terrifying leap.

The fireman, with Simpson slung across his back like a rucksack, was already backing off the sill onto the ladder. "Okay, now, just follow me down, in the same way that I'm doing," he said to Dov. "And don't look down."

His head disappeared below the sill, and Dov climbed up. Turning to face the window, as he'd seen the fireman do, he saw on the floor of the suite, under the cloud of smoke that was quickly becoming dense, the leather case he'd taken from the safe. He hesitated. Mr. Simpson had been willing to die for the contents of that case. He climbed back into the room.

"Hey!" yelled the fireman from below. "Whatdya think you're *doin'*?"

"I'm coming," he yelled as he picked up the case and stuffed it into his pants pocket. Then he clambered up on the sill again and started down.

Two stretcher-bearers were waiting for Simpson at the bottom of the ladder. By the time Dov got off the ladder (for he'd been much slower than the fireman), Simpson had been covered up and given some medication. His eyes were open, and he was looking up at the Girl in confusion. "The case . . ." he mumbled. "Where—?"

Dov came up to him and drew back his blanket just far enough to reach his hand. He pressed the case into it. "Here," he said, looking down at the sick man, "I hope it was worth the risk you took."

The police were trying to keep the crowd back, but the three of them, so dramatically rescued from the building that still was pouring black smoke into the atmosphere, were the center of everyone's attention. People were cheering and shouting behind the barricades, policemen and firemen were moving about trying to do their work, and the ambulance orderlies were trying to load a few victims of smoke inhalation and minor injuries into the ambulances. Simpson, apparently suffering from a heart attack, was surrounded by medical attendants. As if the scene were not chaotic enough, two newspaper reporters and a photographer jumped over the police barriers and ran up to them. "What happened?" one asked.

"Why didn't you get out with the others?" the second demanded, notebook and pencil poised.

"What was in that case you gave the old man?" the first reporter asked Dov.

They began to move Simpson's stretcher toward the ambulance, and the Girl, holding her uncle's hand, walked alongside. The photographer, knowing his business, followed the Girl, who, despite her begrimed condition, was a splendid subject for a picture. "Turn this way, will you, miss?" he asked, his large camera aimed and ready.

"Don't bother with me," she said, looking at Dov. "He's the one you should be taking pictures of. That man saved our lives."

"Yeah? Really?" The photographer turned his lens toward Dov at once and snapped.

"He did?" the reporters asked, brightening eagerly. "What'd he do?"

"What's his name?"

"Give us the whole story."

A white-clad orderly held them off while two others lifted Simpson's stretcher onto the ambulance. One of the reporters tugged at Dov, but Dov pushed him aside.

"Come on, miss," the other reporter persisted. "At least tell us his name."

"It's Weisenberg," she said to the reporter distinctly. "His name is David Weisenberg." Then she threw Dov a smile so wide it gleamed like sunshine from her dirty face. "David Weisenberg, from upstairs."

"You goin' on the ambulance with him?" an orderly asked her.

She nodded, and the orderly helped her up. Dov pushed through the throng to get closer to her. "That's not fair," he yelled to her. "I don't know *your* name."

The orderlies were trying to clear the crowd away so that they could close the ambulance doors, but the Girl beamed over their heads at him. "It's Simpson," she said, reaching out a hand to him. "Margaret Simpson."

There were two orderlies, the reporters, the photographer, and a few policemen between them. He stretched his arm over one of the orderly's shoulders but couldn't reach her hand.

She made a little gesture of helplessness. "I'll never forget what you did, David Weisenberg," she said, ignoring the tumult around her. "Never, as long as I live. How can I ever thank you?"

Dov couldn't believe he'd really heard her say those words. "What did you say?"

"I said, how can I ever thank you?"

He gave a choked laugh. "Don't worry," he yelled over the din as the ambulance doors began to close, "I'm sure I can think of something."

He saw her laugh and wave just before the doors closed on her. While the reporters vied for his attention and the photographer snapped away, he watched the ambulance disappear down the street, his face wreathed in what everyone thought, considering the circumstances, was a completely inappropriate grin.

7

*T*he morning after the fire, Dov turned off his ringing alarm clock. Since he had no office to go to, he turned the clock to the wall and decided to let himself sleep as long as nature permitted. Till noon maybe.

As it turned out, he managed to sleep only till a little past nine. He was dreaming that he was back at the house in Czernowitz, where a black cloud of smoke was pouring out from under his mother's bedroom door. He was pounding on it, trying to awaken her, when he became aware that the sound of pounding was coming from his own door. He sat up, blinking himself back to reality.

"Dov, are you in there? Wake up!" Hersh was yelling from the hallway.

Surprised, he crossed the apartment in his bare feet and opened the door. "What's wrong?" he asked, yawning. "You woke me."

Hersh was grinning at him idiotically. "What're you doing *sleeping*, today of all days?" He pranced past Dov in a state of high excitement, holding a pile of newspapers over his head. "How can you stay in bed when, overnight, you've all at once become *famous*?"

Dov scratched his head sleepily as he followed Hersh into the kitchen. "What're you carrying on about?"

"Will you wake up? *Look! Your picture!* Right on the front page of the *Daily News*!" He dropped the pile of papers on the table and picked one up to wave under Dov's nose. "Take a look, Mr. Hero."

Dov took the paper and gaped at it incredulously. A bold headline declared ACCOUNTANT TURNS HERO IN 22ND-STREET BLAZE. Underneath was his picture, the one taken as he'd watched the ambulance pull away. His face was black, his hair matted, his shirt torn and filthy; and, worst of all, his smile—the stupidest smile he'd ever seen—stretched from ear to ear. "Oh, my God," he muttered in disgust, "how can they do that? I never gave permission—"

"What's wrong with you?" Hersh surveyed his friend with the affectionate indulgence of a father toward a slow-witted son. "You're a *hero,* for Chrissake!"

Hero! If there was one thing in the world Dov didn't want to be, it was a hero. Like the hero of Ilinghovka, Avrum Gentz. Was he doomed to follow his father's footsteps in *everything* whether he wanted to or not?

He turned his back on Hersh and tossed the paper on the pile. "That's the most idiotic picture I've ever seen. I ought to sue!"

"Don't be an ass. You look great! Like you really went through something. Here, read what they said. *Read!*"

Dov took the tabloid Hersh was so eagerly foisting on him. The report of the fire started right under his picture and continued on the next page.

Dov could only shake his head in amazement. The facts, he supposed, were accurate enough, but the report seemed to have no relationship to his experience of the event. The people in the account were strangers who existed in that other, rarified world of the famous—people like President Coolidge, Babe Ruth, or the murderer Judd Gray, people who didn't exist in the reality of his daily life. Even his own name, right there in black print, seemed to belong to someone else. The fact that his name and his picture were being looked at all over the city—by riders in the subway, by people in their kitchens as they sipped their morning coffee, by workers in their shops when they took their morning breaks—gave him no pleasure. He felt uncomfortable, as if he were somehow involved in a fraud. "Ugh!" he muttered, tossing the paper aside.

"Ugh? That's what you have to say? Ugh?" Hersh laughed and pounded him on the back in excited pride. "You're a hero, damn it! Isn't it marvelous? A hero, like . . . like Daniel, like the Maccabees, like Gene Tunney!"

Dov snorted. "Don't be a jackass."

"Okay, but don't throw the paper away just yet, Mr. Hero. There's more. Read the back page. Here."

Hersh was pointing to another picture. It filled almost the whole back page. It showed Mr. Simpson in his hospital bed, with Margaret Simpson at his side. Simpson was holding up for the camera the open leather case, with three stamps in plain view. Across the top, the headline blared $30,000 IN RARE STAMPS SAVED FROM FIRE. Underneath, the story was just as sensational:

> The Philatelic Society of New York was spared a devastating loss yesterday by the daring rescue from fire of three highly prized stamps, displayed above by stamp dealer George B. Simpson. The stamps, insured by the society for $30,000, are identified as a two-cent Hawaiian Missionary, a Swedish three-skilling Banco Orange, and a Mauritius one-penny Orange. "It would have been an irreplaceable loss," Mr. Simpson told the News. "Stamp collectors around the world are grateful for Mr. Weisenberg's daring rescue."

"You'd think I went through flames to save those things," Dov said in disgust. "Actually, I didn't even want to bother with them. It was just that Simpson wouldn't go without them."

Hersh beamed at him. "So modest. Just like a hero."

"Cut it out, Hersh," Dov said, rolling up the paper and swatting his friend's legs with it. "I'm some hero."

Hersh chortled as he hopped around the kitchen, trying to avoid Dov's attack. In self-defense, he picked up a frying pan to use as a shield. "You *are* a hero. It says so in the paper. Would the *Daily News* lie?"

"Wouldn't it?" Dov got under his defenses and landed a good swat on his rear. "What if I tell you that all the W and W ledgers were left behind, eh? Will you still say I'm a hero? Will you still say the *News* doesn't lie? Come on, old boy, what do you say now?"

After he'd sent the still-exhilarated Hersh on his way, Dov looked at the paper again, shaking his head over it in wonder. It was all so much bunkum. All he'd done was save himself. It hadn't been much harder to take the other two along. Some hero. How many other heroes had been created like this, he wondered, out of exaggeration and thin air? Was it possible that his father, the hero of Ilinghovka, too, was more fabrication than real?

Later that afternoon, unable to bring himself to concentrate on the books at Finestein's office, he wandered over to Twenty-second Street to see if he could get into his office to examine what remained of his ledgers and files. But he found a police barricade blocking the entrance. "The elevator's shot," a policeman told him, "and the stairs on the first two floors ain't safe."

"Hey, there's Weisenberg," someone yelled, and Dov found himself surrounded by a group of the building's tenants, each of them taking a turn to shake his hand or clap him on the back.

Pepillo, the antique-clock dealer, and Welker, the photographer, remained with Dov and the lawyer Hanson, gazing up glumly at the smoke-blackened building. "I wonder what becomes-a my stock," Pepillo sighed. "If on'y I could get up-a stairs, maybe I find something for *salvare.*"

"Oh, we'll be able to salvage our things," Hanson assured him. "They'll let us in once they make the stairway safe."

"Hey, Weisenberg," the photographer said, clapping him on the shoulder, "Miss Simpson came looking for you. You lucky dog, you probably made her a slave for life."

Dov grinned at him. "That's what comes from clean living, Welker. Clean living, sterling character, and the talent to seize opportunity when it knocks."

"Oh, yeah?" Welker gave a rueful laugh. "Clean living and sterling character never helped me. Grabbing your opportunity is the whole story, fella, the whole story. You rescued the fair maiden in distress, while I rescued my Speed Graphic. Some people have luck, and some—"

"—are doomed to take pictures of the event," Dov finished for him.

"I didn't even do that! Can you believe this, Weisenberg? I dash downstairs with my camera, and I'm so intent on saving my ass that I don't even take a shot!"

"That's too bad," Dov sympathized. "If you'd have gotten a good shot, they might've used it in the *News* instead of my picture with that stupid grin."

"Yeah. The front page of the *News.*" Welker sighed dreamily. "That would have been something."

Pepillo tapped Dov's shoulder. "Weisaberg," he whispered, "there's a lady 'cross the street, *lì,* watchin' you."

"Me?" He turned around curiously. A woman standing on the sidewalk opposite did indeed seem to be looking at him. She was dressed in a soft wool suit with a fur scarf draped over her shoulders. Something about her stance and her smart cloche hat (from under which two dark locks of hair escaped and curled against her cheeks) made her seem continental. He was willing to wager that the woman was a Parisienne, but why she was studying him so intently was a mystery. While he stood taking surreptitious looks at her, she removed a page of newspaper from her handbag, studied it, and looked at him again. He recognized the page. It was the front page of the *Daily News.*

"Do you know her?" Hanson asked.

Dov shook his head. "How would I know someone like that? She's definitely an uptown type."

"Never mind that one," Welker interrupted. "Here comes La Simpson again. There, down the street. She's after you, Weisenberg, mark my words. Some people have all the luck!"

Margaret Simpson came up to them, smiling in delight. "There you are, Mr. Weisenberg," she said, trying very hard to sound businesslike but unable to hide the high color of her cheeks. "I'm so glad you came. When I was here earlier looking for you, no one could tell me where you lived. I was afraid I'd never find you."

The blood began to dance in Dov's veins. "No reason to be afraid," he grinned. "Sooner or later I'd have found *you.*"

Welker choked and Hanson chortled. Miss Simpson tried not to notice, but her color deepened. "Sooner or later wouldn't do, Mr. Weisenberg. My uncle is very impatient for you to have this." She withdrew a large white envelope from her handbag. "I don't think he'll rest easy till I tell him it's in your hands."

Dov eyed the envelope with a feeling of disappointment. She hadn't wanted to see him for his own sake but for her uncle's. What good was being a hero if it didn't help to win the fair maid? "What is it?" he asked, deflated.

"It's a reward. For the stamps. We could never find a suitable reward for our lives, of course, but Uncle George says that ten percent of the value of the stamps is the very least you deserve. He said to tell you that he can't afford to give you the whole three thousand at once, but that he hopes you will accept three hundred now and three hundred for the next nine years on the anniversary of the fire."

Now it was Dov who flushed. "It's not necessary, Miss Simpson. I don't want any reward."

"No be *imbecille,*" Pepillo whispered in his ear.

"Take it, Mr. Weisenberg," Miss Simpson urged. "Uncle George says you saved the stamps not once but twice!" She pressed the envelope into his hand and smiled pleadingly up at him. "Please—?"

The smile turned his knees to jelly. "All right," he said, thrusting the envelope into his jacket pocket. "Tell your uncle I thank him."

She nodded, smiled her good-day smile at the others, and started back the way she'd come. Dov's heart sank. Had his great opportunity just passed him by? Welker had said that grabbing opportunity was the whole story.

Abruptly, decisively, he loped down the street after her. "Miss Simpson—?"

She paused and turned. "Yes?"

He came up to her, breathless. "May I see you home?"

"Oh, thanks, but . . . it's not necessary. I'm going back to the hospital. I can catch a bus right on the corner."

"I'll walk to the bus with you, then, if I may. I have an admission to make to you."

They fell into step and started toward the corner. "An admission?"

"I know I shouldn't look a gift horse in the mouth," he said, boldly taking her arm, "but I must admit that the check wasn't the reward I wanted."

Her lips quivered, shaping themselves into a tiny smile. "No?"

"No. What I had in mind was dinner."

"Dinner?" Her eyes glimmered with amusement. "With Uncle George?"

Down Lexington Avenue he could see the bus approaching. "Hang Uncle George!" he muttered hastily, grabbing both her hands. "Will you have dinner with me, Miss Simpson?"

"After all we've been through together, Mr. Weisenberg, I think you can safely call me Maggie."

"Maggie? Is that what they call you?" He shook his head in disapproval. "It doesn't suit you. Margaret is better, I think." But the bus was bearing down on them, and there was no more time. "Well, damn it, Margaret, will you have dinner with me or not?"

The bus door opened, and she removed her hands from his grasp. "Yes, of course I will. How can I refuse? You did save my life."

"Tonight?" he pressed as she stepped up on the bus.

She looked back over her shoulder and threw him a nod and a small smile. "Seven-thirty?"

A great hulking beast of a man elbowed Dov aside and stepped up on the bus behind her. "Yes, seven-thirty!" Dov shouted, trying to get another glimpse of her before the door shut. "But *where*—?"

"On the envelope," she said, standing up on tiptoe to look over the shoulder of the gargantuan creature between them. "Look on the envelope!"

But the bus door closed. Dov chased it for half a block, waving farewell to her. "Okay!" he shouted, waving wildly. "Seven-thirty! *Okay!*"

He walked back to the office building on air. He didn't want to go back home yet. He had to tell Welker or Hanson or *somebody* about his date with La Simpson. He'd done it! The Girl Downstairs was going to dinner with him! He could hardly wait to brag about his triumph to the others.

While Welker and Hanson slapped his back and made rude remarks about the impossibility of a successful seduction with such as La Simpson, Pepillo kept his eyes fixed on the lady who still lingered across the street. "Look-a that, now," he whispered suddenly. "That lady . . . she's-a comin' over."

"Who *is* she?" Hanson wanted to know.

"I dunno. But she's-a had an eye on Weisaberg, and she was lookin' at his photo inna paper."

"Maybe she admires you, Weisenberg," Welker suggested. "After all, you're a hero."

"Maybe she wants your autograph," Hanson said.

"Shuddup da mout'," Pepillo warned. "She's-a come." The clock dealer turned to the approaching woman, tipped his hat, and gave her a courtly bow. "*Buon giórno,* missus. Need-a some help?"

"Yes, please," the lady replied. "I was wondering if that gentleman there is the same man as in this picture."

"Oh, *sì.* Yes, yes, the same."

The woman fixed her eyes on Dov's face. "I thought so," she murmured.

Dov felt a peculiar sensation in his stomach. The woman—good-looking, with an air of sophistication and aloofness—was a stranger to him. She had a voice made distinctive by a throaty richness and a marked German accent, neither quality at all familiar to him. But *something* . . .

She came over to him. "You are this David Weisenberg?" she asked, her manner tense with controlled excitement.

"Yes."

"Is it possible that your name is really Gentz? Dov Gentz?"

He felt the blood drain from his face. "How did you—?"

"Who should know better than I?" The woman's hands began to shake and a tremulous smile lit up her face. "I'm Dvora."

8

Dov kept back his tears while he and his sister sat together in a corner of the Garden Cafeteria and tried to bridge thirteen years of separation, but as soon as he returned alone to his apartment, he sat down on his bed and cried. He'd found a sister. It seemed miraculous. Both of them had sat smiling at each other in fond, foolish disbelief for a long while without saying a word, just drinking in the sight of the other. They'd both felt so proud—each delighted by the other's good looks and prosperity, each touched by the joy of reunion so easily read in the other's face.

But once they'd begun to talk, some sadness was inevitable. Dov had had to tell her about Papa's death, a thirteen-year-old tragedy she only now could mourn. And both had been depressed at learning that the other had no news of Mama and Yudi. Both of them had been too angry and stubborn to write home in the early years, and each one admitted that, later on, it had seemed too late.

But at least, Dov consoled himself, they'd found each other. He learned that he had a niece—a real, live, ten-year-old niece—and a brother-in-law named Leo Glassman who, though quite ill, was eagerly waiting to make his acquaintance. It was a *family*. He would have a family again.

He wiped the tears from his face with the back of his hand. He didn't know where those tears had come from. He hadn't suspected how deep his loneliness for his family was. Yet every time he'd had an urge to contact them, something had held him back. The old bitterness. The new guilts. Ambivalence.

Well, he sighed, getting to his feet, things would be different now. Better. He'd found one of his sisters, and he was soon to meet the girl of his dreams for dinner. If all went well, he might one day soon be starting a family of his own. Instead of dwelling on the ambivalent past, he should start planning a happier future.

Margaret Simpson lived uptown, on Riverside Drive. She had a small apartment on the top floor of her uncle's townhouse. When Dov rang the bell, she came right down, her coat over her arm. She was wearing a mauve silk dinner dress with a high-necked bodice and long sleeves, and Dov, when he helped her on with her coat, was almost stricken speechless by her loveliness.

They had dinner at Luchow's (which Hersh told him was the very best restaurant in town), but the atmosphere was so formal and the clientele so showily wealthy that Dov felt out of place. Margaret ordered the venison, and Dov did the same, because it was the house specialty, but when he tasted it he almost gagged. His attempts to make conversation over dinner were abortive, for Margaret answered in stilted monosyllables. Dov was soon convinced that the girl was bored to death. She was merely enduring the evening out of gratitude. Her basic feeling toward him—the lack of interest that had once made her return his roses without a word—still remained.

He'd given a lot of thought to what they might do after dinner. He wanted to take her someplace where they might sit and listen to music. (He'd intended to admit to her that he couldn't take her dancing, for he'd never learned to dance.) But now he wanted nothing more than to see the evening end. It had been a fiasco, and like a good accountant, he wanted to cut his losses.

When they left the restaurant, he raised his arm to hail a passing taxi. He waved vigorously, eager to thrust her inside and send her on her way, but the taxi went speeding by. However, in the energetic frenzy of his waving, he wrenched his shoulder. It was all he could do to keep from groaning aloud.

"If you're in a hurry," Margaret suggested softly, "we can probably find a taxi at the next corner."

He nodded curtly, averting his head so that she wouldn't see him wincing in pain, and they began to walk up the street.

"This hasn't worked out very well, has it?" she asked after a strained silence.

"Oh, you've noticed that, have you?" He couldn't keep himself from sounding rude; the pain in his shoulder was the last straw.

She nodded. "Trying too hard, I'm afraid," she murmured, half to herself.

Dov stopped in his tracks. "You flatter yourself, Miss Simpson," he said, inner fury making his voice icy.

Her eyes flew to his face, startled. "Oh, I didn't mean . . . not *you. Me.*"

"What?" Her expression and her words were bewildering to him, but he was in no mood to show patience or understanding. "I don't know what you're talking about."

"I meant that *I* was trying too hard, not you. I always get sort of . . . bottled up . . . when I'm . . ."

"When you're what?"

Her eyelids fluttered down, hiding a sudden look of embarrassment. "When I'm afraid someone doesn't . . . like me."

This uncharacteristic shyness seemed artificial to him. "What nonsense is this? Would I have asked you to dinner if I didn't—?"

"I just thought . . . with dinner so awkward . . . you might have changed your mind."

He couldn't make himself believe in the sincerity of this unexpected humility of hers. Was she playing with him in some way? Trying to make a fool of him? He glared down at her suspiciously. "Look here, Margaret, or Maggie, or whatever your favorite name is," he growled, rubbing his aching shoulder, "I have no experience with upper-class flirtation, so I don't know what sort of game you're playing. I don't know the rules, and I have neither the time nor the inclination to learn them. So let's skip the games, shall we? You've endured this obligatory evening in exemplary fashion. You've done your duty. But it's over now. So you don't have to say these coy little things; you don't have to throw me any shy little looks; you don't even have to be polite. I'm no hero, and I don't want your damned gratitude."

She was staring at him with eyes widened by confusion. "But it was *you* who suggested this dinner as a reward, wasn't it? Why are you suddenly so angry at *me?*"

"Because you accepted it out of gratitude, that's why."

"Are you very sure of that?"

"Are you playing games again? Yes, I'm sure. You said so yourself when you hopped on the bus this afternoon. 'You *did* save my life.' Weren't those your words of acceptance?"

"Were they?" A hesitant little gleam appeared deep in her eyes. "I guess I did say that. And very true, too. You *did* save my life."

She was right, of course. He had no right to be angry at her. It *had* been he who'd demanded her gratitude. "Well, that's what's been wrong with this evening. Gratitude is a lousy basis for . . . for this sort of thing."

"Upper-class flirtation, you mean?" she asked, the smile appearing now at the corners of her lips.

He wouldn't let himself respond to her teasing. "Whatever you want to call it. The fact remains that you wouldn't have come out with me if you hadn't felt obligated."

"Oh, I don't know about that. You never asked me before."

He glared at her. "What are you talking about now? You didn't even take my flowers."

"Oh, that." She took his arm and began to stroll slowly down the street again. "That was my uncle's fault. He made me return them. He didn't approve of you."

"What has he to do with it?"

"If you'll only stop glowering, I'll tell you." She'd taken his sore arm, but suddenly he didn't mind the pain. "Uncle George considers himself my guardian, now that my parents are gone. Not that I need a guardian at my age, but since I work for him and rent my rooms from him, I generally take his advice and abide by his rules. He saw you looking at me on the elevator once or twice and told me to watch out for you. He thought you were a lecher."

"Oh, he did, did he?"

"Yes. Actually, so did I, especially that night when I dropped my folder."

Dov felt himself redden. "Can't say I blame you. I acted like an idiot that night."

She giggled. "I thought you were a loony. An utterly mad, certifiable loony."

"I see. And it was only when you saw that I could keep my head in an emergency that you changed your mind?"

"No."

"No?"

"I didn't have to change my mind. Even when I thought you a loony, I . . ." She cast him a quick, timid look. "I thought you very appealing. And I loved your note, you know. The note you put in with the roses. It was charming."

"If it was so damned charming, why did you return the roses without a word?"

Her smile dwindled. "Uncle George was . . . was very firm about it.

We almost had a scene. He was afraid of what the . . . the consequences might be."

"Because he was still convinced I was a lecher?"

She hesitated, and her eyelids veiled her eyes again. "Yes, I suppose . . . that, too."

Dov gave her a long, hard look. "Oh, yes. Now I see. Stupid of me not to have thought of it before. David Weisenberg, Jew. Not at all appropriate company for Miss Margaret Simpson."

She gave his arm a squeeze that, he supposed, was meant to be comforting. "Don't take offense, David. You have to understand Uncle George. His brother, my uncle Lester, is an Episcopalian minister, and the whole family is very High Church, you see."

Dov gritted his teeth. "No, I don't see. I only see that I'm not supposed to take offense. I'm supposed to be grateful that your uncle let you have dinner with me at all, right? He might've refused his permission even for this 'reward' dinner. He probably wanted to tell you that the three hundred dollars was enough of a reward for me, isn't that so?"

"No, of course not. He isn't as bad as that, David. Truly he isn't. He's really very grateful for what you did. And he means well. But, to tell the truth, my uncle had nothing to do with my having dinner with you. It was my own idea."

"Was it? Good of you. Your gratitude must be overwhelming."

"I told you I didn't do it out of gratitude." She looked up at him, her brow furrowing in little, worried lines. "You're not going to associate my uncle's way of thinking with mine, are you? I have a mind of my own."

"Have you?" His tone was unmistakably cold.

"Yes, I have." She lifted her chin in offense. "I don't care if you're a Jew or not."

"Now, that *is* good of you," he muttered drily.

"Really, David, are you going to be touchy about this?" She stopped walking, pulled her arm away, and put both hands angrily on her hips. "You're being ridiculous. I'm not my uncle, and I won't have you believing that your Jewishness matters a jot to me! I'd heard you Jews are touchy, but—"

"*Touchy?*" He burst into a laugh. She was so adorably ludicrous, standing there declaring herself on a subject that had caused centuries of bloodshed in terms she could as easily have used about his moustache or the color of his tie. Touchy! The blatant inadequacy of the term revealed her appealing innocence. "All right," he said, shaking his head and drawing her arm into his again, the wrenched shoulder forgotten, "I won't be touchy. And to prove to me that you really don't care about my Jewishness, you can call me Dov. It's my Jewish name, and it suits me best."

They walked in silence for a while before Dov finally hailed a cab. He wondered what he'd gotten himself into, and he sensed that the girl on his arm was wondering the same thing. He knew they'd each experienced those impressions of the other that make the beginnings of a love affair so intense. Each had tried to grasp at a sense of the true quality of the other, but there was too much to learn in one encounter. Dov wasn't even sure that he *liked* her, while he could sense that she was both drawn to and frightened of him. It was that damned ambivalence again. Attraction and revulsion both at once. But something of significance had begun to happen between them, and he knew that he'd feel impelled to see it through.

The silence enveloped them even in the back of the taxi. They sat side by side stiffly, afraid of saying the wrong thing—words that would crack the fragile beginnings of the intimacy they both hoped would develop between them. "Dov?" she ventured at last, her voice low and shy, "do you remember what you said that night in the elevator?"

"Sure."

"Well, then," she whispered, turning sideways on the seat and putting a hand lightly on his lapel, "if you'd still like to kiss my kissable mouth—"

"Okay," he grinned and pulled her close, "if you promise you won't think I'm a certifiable loony."

He came home that night as much confused as exhilarated. He was falling in love, really in love, for the first time in his life. But the girl was as different from him as wine from blood, and he sensed that he was heading for difficulties.

He wondered what his mother would have said if he'd announced to her that he was thinking of marrying a girl whose family was High Church. Would there have been a scene? Screaming and crying? A session of psychological flagellation from Great-uncle Nathan? Not necessarily, he realized. He remembered that his mother had been far from commonplace. You couldn't always guess how she would react. She might very well have been more broad-minded than other Jewish mothers in such circumstances.

It was seeing Dvora again that had set his mind to such imaginings. For the first time in many years he felt a painful hunger for contact with his mother and his past. But the estrangement was of too long standing. It was inconceivable to do anything about it now. In a way, he didn't want to know what had happened to his mother and Yudi. He wasn't sure he could bear to learn the truth if tragedy had befallen them. The guilt would be insupportable.

He pulled off his tie and unbuttoned his jacket. His hand brushed something in his pocket. Of course—it was the envelope Margaret had given him earlier that day, on which she'd written her address. Was it only this afternoon it had happened? It seemed eons ago. The world had become a different place for him since then. He'd rediscovered a sister and embarked on a love affair. It had been quite a day.

He tore open the envelope and stared at the check, suddenly mesmerized. An idea, a really brilliant idea, struck him with the force of a blow. He knew with startling and absolute certainty just what he wanted to do with the money. He'd send it to Solitava, to Yudi and Mama! He'd send it every year, without letting them know who it was who sent it. He could make arrangements for it tomorrow morning at his bank. Surely they could figure out a way to send it anonymously. It was really a marvelous plan! Though three hundred dollars a year was far from a fortune, it might be enough to make a difference in their lives.

He smiled contentedly as he lay on his bed and gazed up at the ceiling. He'd found a way to make contact with his past at last. And he didn't feel ambivalent about it in the least.

9

By the end of 1928, Dov had six big clients, more than a dozen small ones, an assistant, a large new office uptown, and an "understanding" with Miss Margaret Simpson. Dvora, who had taken an instant liking to Margaret the first time Dov had taken her to the Bronx to meet his family, once asked him what an "understanding" really meant. Dov shrugged. "It means we're thinking about starting to think about thinking about getting married," he'd explained.

"What's to think about so much? Just do it," his sister had said.

He'd merely shaken his head. "I don't want to rush into anything. I'm not sure I'm the marrying kind."

But that wasn't strictly true. He desperately wanted a family. He was wild about all of Hersh's noisy children, and when he'd met Dvora's enchanting little Frieda, it had been a case of instant and mutual adoration. When Leo Glassman—as good and kind a man as Papa—had died, only a month ago, no one had been able to console Frieda but Dov. Deep inside, he yearned to have children of his own, but something seemed to keep him from committing himself to a wife. He didn't know why.

He'd never told Dvora about the checks to Mama. So far, two checks had been cashed in Solitava and had come back endorsed with the name Mindel Gentz Weisenberg in a firm hand. The bank had once received an inquiry about the identity of the donor, but he'd instructed them to reply that the information was not available. Even if he *had* been tempted to reveal himself to his mother, the sight of that signature would have hardened his resolve to keep silent. That she, after all these years, still kept the Gentz so proudly in her name was unforgivable to him. It filled him with disgust.

He and Dvora didn't talk much about Mama and the old days any more. There were too many matters in their present lives to discuss. There had been the months of Leo's illness, when Dov's and Margaret's presence in the Bronx apartment had been soothing to the worried Glassman family. The three Glassmans all leaned on Dov's reliable good sense to help them through those difficult days. His presence had not only been helpful to Dvora and her daughter but Leo, too, had clung to Dov for reassurance. It eased his mind, during those last months when he felt the approach of death, to know that his wife and daughter would not be left entirely alone.

After Leo's passing, Dov and Dvora found another shared interest—the stock market. Much of their time together was spent talking about Dvora's investments and poring over brokers' reports and Wall Street news. Then there was Frieda to talk about. She was proving to be intellectually gifted, and Dvora wanted to give the child the very best education she could afford. They talked about schools and private lessons and special savings accounts for the child's future. If they had any time left after discussing all this, Dvora nagged him to get married. "You'll never find a finer girl than your Margaret," she said repeatedly. "Why don't you marry her already?"

It was hard for Dov to find an answer. He couldn't blame Margaret for his delaying tactics, for Margaret was very willing to change their "understanding" to a definite engagement. In fact, she was eager for marriage. She'd admitted it very soon after they first began to see each other. She loved him. She loved him so much she'd even convinced her Uncle George that marriage to him would be a good thing for the family. She'd actually made Simpson believe that bringing a Jew into the family would shake them out of their starchy Episcopalian complacency.

But Margaret's sort of love was strange to Dov. The other women he'd known had been quick to take him to their beds, but not Margaret. Her High Church upbringing made her cling to her virginity with a desperate tenacity. It was as if she spent her passion fighting her passion. Every evening they spent together became an exercise in rectitude. Sometimes, in anger and disgust, he stayed away for as long as a week, but then the separation became unendurable, and he came back. After two years of this enforced chastity, they were afraid even to kiss with more fervor than a mere peck, for fear of igniting their tethered desires. Dov felt like a monk who'd taken a vow to live on bread and water but who had to sit every day at a table covered with juicy, aromatic samples of all his favorite foods, looking but never tasting.

It might not have been so painful if he'd permitted himself to seek release in other arms, but part of his understanding with Margaret was an implicit pledge of mutual fidelity. When, at times, his frustration with the entire situation threatened to become overwhelming, and he railed long and nastily on the ridiculousness of their continuing chastity, she quietly pointed out that he could make an end of his torture whenever he wished, simply by marrying her. Her obvious logic took the sting from his attack. How could he answer that?

One rainy night, after they'd been "keeping company" for two years, she permitted him to come upstairs to her rooms. It was the first time. It was not the proper way to behave, and the only reason she'd permitted it this time was because he'd seemed particularly moody that evening, and she was afraid he would indulge in one of his periodic fits of the sulks and stay away for a week. If it hadn't been pouring, she would have offered him her usual soothing murmurs on a park bench or in the back of a taxi.

She unlocked her door with the tense excitement of a naughty child stealing into a forbidden room. "Take off your shoes," she whispered as she let him in. "I don't want Uncle George to hear us."

Dov felt like a fool. He came in on his toes and sat down on her sofa to take the shoes off. She, meanwhile, hung up their wet coats and went into the kitchen to make them coffee. He looked around with interest. The apartment was very like her—neat and tastefully restrained. The sofa he sat on was upholstered with striped satin that Finestein of Finest Fabrics would no doubt call top of the line. There was a dark red rug on the floor, a row of bookcases on the wall opposite him, a round, old table with an embroidered runner and a feminine lamp on it, and two good still lifes on the walls. It was a feminine room, but not cloyingly so. There weren't the little porcelain figurines and china cigarette boxes and fussy little *tsatskes* that so many women—like Hersh's Harriet—seemed to like to scatter about. Here, there were only books and lamps and a few family photographs in silver frames.

He got up to take a closer look at her books. Best sellers, mostly. Galsworthy and Willa Cather, *Sorrell and Son* and *Elmer Gantry*. Not really his type of books, but not bad choices. And she had several volumes of poetry, too—Housman and Emily Dickinson and *The Oxford Book of English Verse*. He wondered what she would have made of his books— Aldous Huxley, Lawrence, Kafka, Stefan Zweig, John Dos Passos' *Manhattan Transfer*, and the memorable, moving English novel he'd just finished, *A Passage to India*. They should have talked more about books during their evenings together, he thought, rather than the endless bickering about their frustrating situation.

He found himself peering interestedly at the family pictures she'd so lovingly framed. One photo was obviously of her parents. They were posed before the porch of a white frame house, squinting a little in the sunlight. They were standing close together, but not even their shoulders touched. Their smiles were prim and subdued and their expressions guarded, as if they weren't certain about what sort of faces to leave to posterity. He wasn't sure he would have liked them. But then, Margaret might not have liked Mama's looks either, if he had a picture to show her. Mama, with her mannish chin and piercing eyes.

Next to the picture of her parents was a picture of a minister with the black shirt and turned-about white collar, surrounded by a large family. Uncle Lester and his brood, no doubt. And then there was a portrait of a young man of about twenty-five, casually elegant in an open-necked shirt and college sweater. He was blond, smiling an all-American smile, and handsome enough to pose for ads in the Sears, Roebuck catalog. His self-assured smile annoyed Dov.

He heard Margaret come in, not by her footsteps (for she'd also taken off her shoes) but by the rattle of the cups on the tray she carried. "Who's this?" he asked.

There was a moment of hesitation as Margaret set down the tray. "Oh, that's Ward," she said.

Dov thought her voice sounded funny. "Ward? Who's Ward?"

"Ward Fowler. I told you about him."

"No, you didn't. I've never heard the name before."

"I must have told you. We were engaged once."

Something in his chest froze instantly. "Were you really?" He turned to face her, the picture in his hand. "Engaged, you say? To be married?"

She sat down and began to pour the coffee. "Of course to be married. What other kind of engagement is there?"

"There are other kinds," Dov said absently, his eyes fixed intently on the picture in his hand. "An engagement for a tennis match, or for lunch. But this engagement was for wedlock, eh?" He put the picture down and strolled over to her. "Funny that I can't remember hearing about this before. Can it be that a little thing like a previous engagement slipped your mind?"

"Oh, come on, Dov, sit down and have your coffee. There's no reason for you to take on about this."

"I love your little *goyishe* expressions like 'take on.' I suppose if I never happened to come up here and see that photo, you'd never have said a word about him."

She stirred her coffee, her expression tense and defensive. "I don't know. Maybe not."

"That's great. Just great." He returned to the picture and picked it up again. He loathed the fellow. That wide, all-American smile seemed more patronizing than ever. "Well, what happened?" he demanded, his jaw tight. "Why didn't you marry this paragon, this bully boy, this Pepsodent Adonis, this tennis court *shaygetz*—?"

"*Stop* it, Dov! You don't know what . . . He's . . . he's dead."

He looked up from the photo, eyes narrowed. "Dead? How?"

She busied herself with the coffee cups, but her hands were shaking. "He had a boat . . . a small yacht. There was a storm, and he . . . drowned."

He put down the picture. "So he died, did he? On the eve of the nuptials, no doubt. Is that how it was? Look at me, Margaret! I'm asking you a question. Did he die on the eve of your nuptials?"

She met his eyes. "What difference does that make?"

"Not much. I was just curious. It probably made a deep enough mark on you *whenever* it happened." He put on his shoes, went to her hall closet, and rummaged around for his coat.

She jumped up. "What are you doing?"

"I'm getting my coat."

"You're not *going*? You haven't even had your coffee—"

"You're wonderful, you know? You women are really wonderful. You expect a man to accept whatever crumbs you hand him . . . and with gratitude, yet. I should sit down and have my coffee, right? And then, you'll give me my nightly peck on the cheek, and I'll thank you for letting me visit this sanctum sanctorum, and everything will go on just like before."

She stared at him in sincere amazement. "But why shouldn't it go on as before? Why should Ward make any difference between us? I really don't understand you, Dov. He's *dead.*"

"Yeah, I know. But not in there." He pointed to her breast. "I know how you women can keep the memory of a first love alive. Oh, how well I know! You clutch the memory to you like . . . like a live kitten, to stroke when you're feeling down, to pick up and fondle in the dark night, when the poor slob you've married—the one who's alive and devoted and slaving away his days for you—is innocently asleep. Every once in a while, you get that faraway look in your eyes, and the second fiddle—the *living* one, the one who's *there*—thinks, How beautiful she is, how *deep*! And he has no idea you're secretly making love to someone else's memory."

"Dov, you're *crazy*. I never—! I love *you*."

"Yeah, I know. That's why you never told me about him."

"It's true! I never think about him when I'm with you. Never."

"Sure. What else would you women say in a situation like this?" He put on his coat and went to the door. "Don't look like that, Maggie, my love. You'll find someone else to play second fiddle for you. The woods are full of fools ready and willing to believe you when you assure them they're first with you."

It was still pouring when he left the building, and he stood unmoving in the drenching rain until the bottled-up rage that had filled his chest subsided. Then he walked the streets until he found a cab and went home. He took off his wet clothes, threw them carelessly into the bathroom, got into his pajamas, and climbed into bed. He knew he wouldn't be able to sleep, so he picked up the copy of Thomas Mann's *Der Zauberberg* that he'd just yesterday got hold of and tried to read. But he couldn't concentrate on it, and he tossed it aside. He put his arms up under his head and glared at the ceiling. It was laughable. He was thirty-two years old, and the one woman he'd ever really loved turned out to have an Avrum Gentz in her past. A blond, smiling, Episcopalian Avrum Gentz.

An hour went by. The rain beat incessantly on the windows. Wide awake, he stared up at the ceiling, unable to wipe away the recollection of a white-toothed smile on the face of a now dead yachtsman. How many nights must Margaret have done the very same thing? Women! They disgusted him, all of them. Never again would he let himself become vulnerable like this.

Then he heard the doorbell. He sat up, shuddering in alarm. It must be after two, he thought. Whoever it was really leaned on the bell, for it rang without stopping. He walked warily to the door. "Who—?"

"Let me in, damn you!" came Margaret's voice.

He unlocked the door, and she brushed by him. She was drenched. He'd never seen her look like this. She wore no hat, and her hair was flattened against her head, a few strands falling over her forehead and dripping down her face. Her face was wet, pale, and devoid of any makeup. The little squirrel collar of her old blue coat was pathetically sodden, and her shoes squelched as she stormed down his little hallway and across his living room. He ran after her. "Margaret, what's the matter with you?"

She wheeled around. "Get into bed!"

"What?"

"I said, get into bed. Is that the bedroom?"

"Yes, but . . . Let me get you a towel. You're soaked."

"I know I'm soaked. I'll find a towel myself. Get into bed."

Bewildered, he followed her into the bedroom. She went to the bathroom door, flicked on a light, and picked up a towel. Mopping her hair, she turned back to him. "I told you to *get into bed*!" she hissed at him through clenched teeth.

"Okay, okay!" He climbed under the blanket, propped himself up on his elbow and gaped at her in the light from the bathroom. "I think you've gone off your trolley."

"Just shut up, okay?" She'd thrown aside her coat and was now pulling her dress over her head.

"Margaret!" He was aghast. "What're you *doing*?"

"What does it look like I'm doing?" Her slip followed her dress to the floor.

He started out of bed. "Stop this, you idiot! I don't want—"

"Oh, yes, you do! *Stay where you are!*" She sat down on the room's one chair in her bra and underpants and began to pull off her stockings, all the while mumbling to herself in a frenzied undertone. "Making a scene over a guy who's been dead for four years! As if I don't know why! It's this *celibacy* that's making you so crazy jealous over nothing!"

Her rage had made her completely brazen. This was the very first time she'd ever undressed herself before anyone, yet there was not a sign of shyness or embarrassment as she ripped off the last of her underthings. He was afraid that when she came to her senses she would suffer agonies of remorse. He couldn't let her. "Margaret?" he ventured, moving slowly toward her. "Don't do this. You don't have to—"

"I do have to. I *do*! You won't believe me otherwise. Stay where you are, I say! I'm going to prove it to you."

"This isn't going to prove anything—"

"Yes, it will. I never did anything like this with Ward." She stood up before him, straight and proud in her nakedness. "I didn't even know what love was, then."

Her beauty dazzled him, but he turned himself away. He wasn't going to be weakened by sexual desire. "You became engaged to him because he was nothing to you, is that it?" he asked in the ironic tone she hated.

"I became engaged because it was expected, that's all. Both families expected it."

"Yeah? Is that why his picture is still prominently displayed in a place of honor? Because he meant so little to you?"

"You're impossible, do you know that? A completely impossible person. His picture is prominently displayed only because he *died*. When someone dies like that, young and tragically, you have to honor him, don't you?"

"No."

"You bastard! Move over!"

" 'Bastard'? What a word from those ladylike lips. What would Uncle George say?"

She sat on the edge of the bed. The light from the bathroom made the sight of her breasts and her belly dizzying. "Move over," she ordered again.

"Damn it, woman," he muttered, his will failing, "this isn't going to make any difference—"

"Oh, no? Move *over*!" She slipped under the cover, threw her arms around his neck, and pulled his head down. "Now you'll believe me," she muttered in his ear. "You'll have to."

"Oh, God!" he moaned, conquered. He embraced her hungrily. How could he refuse a gift like this? "Damn it all, you win. Come here to me. We'll worry later about what we'll have to pay for this."

They made love all night long. In the morning, flushed, spent, and peaceful, she lay sleeping in his arms. But his eyes were open. He was wide awake, bombarded with a mixture of feelings that had nothing to do with contentment or satiety. There was gratitude, yes, for the sacrifice she'd made of her ideals. How could he help but love her for it? But there was the anger, too. He knew he wouldn't marry her. Not even for her would he accept the role of second love, no matter what she said to try to change his mind. Knowing what he knew of life and of women, he could never do it.

Margaret didn't understand at first how much she'd lost. It had seemed, that night, that she'd won. But when she finally realized that he was adamant, she did what so many women had done before and would do after—she surrendered and became his mistress. Having once given her body, she let him take her soul as well.

. . . So am I not right, Sam, that destiny was marking each of us with the stain of Avrum's legacy? It's not hard to see why Dov didn't marry his dearest love. He couldn't play Leib to her Mindel. . . .

Part Six

YUDI
1926-1933

1

Meanwhile, Mama and I, back in Solitava, knew nothing of what was happening. The lives of the missing members of our family became the subject only of wild speculation and wilder dreams. Dov and Dvora were remembered as they'd been as youngsters, yearned after but no longer real. Mama and I expected to go to our graves without ever seeing them again. As for Avrum, he remained alive and young in Mama's mind, but everyone else hardly remembered him at all. Then the first check came from America. . . .

It was late autumn of 1926 when the check arrived, and every gossip in the town whispered about it, puzzling over the mystery of who had sent it and why it had been sent to someone so undeserving as the sour, taciturn, crippled Mindel Rossner Gentz Weisenberg. But Mindel knew who'd sent it. There wasn't a doubt in her mind.

She didn't say anything at first. She just sat at the kitchen table staring at the little slip of greenish paper with a twisted expression on her face—an expression that only her daughter, her mother, and her sister could recognize as a smile. The stroke that Mindel had suffered two years before had left her with a lame leg, an almost useless left arm, and a slight upward twist to the left corner of her mouth. It gave her face a permanent sneer, which the gossips decided perfectly fit her sour nature.

Her sister Raizel was seated at the table opposite her, also staring at the check. The years had been kinder to Raizel than they'd been to the unfortunate Mindel. Only two years younger than her sister, Raizel now looked ten years or more her junior. She had run over from her house down the street to see for herself the check that everyone was talking about.

Behind them, rinsing dishes in a basin under the window, stood Etel Fruma, still strong and hearty at seventy years of age. And standing beside her, drying the dishes absently, was Yudi.

Etel Fruma glanced over at her granddaughter with a little sigh. It did her heart good just to look at Yudi. Now that her family was dwindling (with Ephraim and Nathan dead and Raizel's children dispersed, one to Bialystok and one to America), Yudi was her last remaining joy. It didn't surprise her a bit that everyone in Solitava loved this girl. Her nature wasn't like her mother's. Yudi was always cheerful and giving and, now that she was a young woman, pretty as a wildflower. She had a full mouth that smiled even in repose, a pair of large, laughing eyes, and a high forehead framed by a mass of auburn, crinkly hair. Etel Fruma had to admit that Yudi's hair was disastrous. But it was in keeping with the rest of the girl's appearance. It made you want to smile.

Etel Fruma only hoped that this check, for the enormous sum of three hundred American dollars, would bring Yudi some good. The girl was throwing away her life because of her innate goodness. First she'd gotten herself engaged to Eliezer Reiss, not because he was a worthy suitor (God knew that Yudi had had offers from men that were cleverer, wealthier, and handsomer than Eli) but because she was sorry for him. Eli had never gotten over losing Dvora and had transferred his emotions to Yudi because she was Dvora's sister. For years he'd pursued her, traveling every week all the way from Czernowitz to see her, but Yudi had held him off. She'd given him the warmth of her friendship but nothing more, until the awful explosion in the glassworks where Eli worked. The poor fellow had lost an eye, and Yudi took it on herself to make it up to him by giving the fellow her hand. That was how Yudi was made.

And then Mindel had been felled by a stroke. It had been dreadful. They'd found her lying on the floor of the barn, her face horribly twisted, beyond mere pain, unable to move or speak. It was Yudi who brought her back. Yudi, with her ceaseless encouragement, her devotion, her patient assistance in exercising her mother's paralyzed muscles. The girl was a *gute,* a giver. There was no other way to describe her. This money from America, this unexpected windfall, should be used to do something special for Yudi. If Mindel would only ask her, that was certainly what Etel Fruma would advise. But Mindel wouldn't ask. Mindel never asked.

"Three hundred dollars!" Raizel was sighing for the tenth time. "A *fortune!*"

"Yes," her mother muttered, swishing away at the dishes with her dishrag, "but the question is, who sent it?"

"The name on the check says Vincent G. Armstrong, Special Accounts," Raizel said, peering closely at the check.

Yudi put down the dish she was drying and picked up the slip of paper. "He must be someone at the American bank," she explained, looking it over front and back. "Not the sender. The sender is this account number—92018."

Etel Fruma stared at it over Yudi's shoulder. "Do you think it could be Yossele . . . ?" she suggested, reaching for straws.

"*My* Yossele?" Raizel looked at her mother as if the woman had suddenly become demented.

Mindel threw her mother a look of disgust. "Why would Yossele send *me* money? He never sends money even to his mother. Does he, Raizel?"

"He has enough trouble taking care of his wife and himself. And he wrote me they're expecting. Didn't I tell you?"

"You told me, you told me." Etel Fruma opened the window and tossed the dishwater out. "Then who—?"

"Why are we pretending?" Mindel asked. "We all know who it's from."

"I don't," Yudi said, her eyebrows lifting in bewilderment. "Who do you think—?"

Etel Fruma began to stack the dried dishes with a clatter of disgust. "You can guess who she thinks. Her *Avrum.*"

Yudi blinked at her mother. "Avrum? Avrum *Gentz*? Why on earth do you think *he*—?"

Mindel took the check from Yudi and stared at it. "Who else could it be?"

"It could be anyone. Maybe Dov."

Mindel shook her head. "How could it be Dov? He went to Palestine."

"Dvora, then."

"Dvora's soldier was an Austrian. She's probably living in Vienna with a brood of children, struggling to make ends meet, not in America with money to throw around."

"You can't be sure, Mama."

"Sure I'm sure. If it was Dvora, she'd sign her name. She'd write a letter, crowing about her success. Dvora wouldn't give such a gift without wanting credit for it. I know Dvora."

Etel Fruma nodded in reluctant agreement. "Not a shy, retiring flower, our Dvora. Never was, never will be. Your mother's probably right about that. Dvora didn't send it."

"And it would be *like* Avrum to do such a thing," Mindel said, her eyes still fixed on the check as if the intensity of her gaze would reveal some hidden clues in the paper. "He's the kind to do something like this . . . to let me know that he's well and successful and . . . and remembering."

Etel Fruma slammed down the pile of plates. "Well, he didn't have to make such a mystery of it. He could have signed his name. Damned adulterer! He waited long enough to send you a little support—!"

"*Enough,* Mama! I won't have him maligned in my presence," Mindel said with quiet firmness.

Etel Fruma stalked to the door. "All right, I won't say anything more. I'm going to bed. But why the Almighty should have arranged circumstances in such a way that Avrum Gentz's name is again uttered in this house is beyond me! I would rather the three hundred dollars had stayed far away in America, with Avrum and his cursed memory, than that we should be talking about him again."

Raizel sighed and got up from her chair. "I'd better get along, too. Itzik will be back from the tavern by this time." She kissed her sister's cheek with gentle affection. "At least you're remembered," she murmured. "It's better than nothing."

Yudi stared after her departing aunt, startled at her immediate acceptance of Mindel's identification of the unknown benefactor. Could the sender of the check *really* have been the mysterious, transcendent, almost mythic Avrum Gentz? Had the ghostly phantom from her mother's past really sent this prosaic, mundane, very tangible sign of his existence? Yudi, her eyes wide with awe, turned back to her mother.

Mindel was gazing at the check as if it were a holy thing, while a single tear spilled down her cheek. "Oh, Avrum," she whispered, suddenly clutching the check to her breast, *"thank you!"*

"Mama!" Yudi exclaimed, startled by the depth of her mother's emotion.

Mindel, embarrassed at being caught in such a nakedly revealing moment, put down the check and wiped her cheek with the back of her good hand. "You see, it's . . . just knowing he's alive. That alone makes my cup run over. But more than that . . ." She lowered her eyes from her daughter's face. ". . . that he hasn't forgotten me, even after all these years . . . as I haven't forgotten. . . ."

YUDI, 1926–1933

Yudi reached over and squeezed her mother's hand. It was deeply moving to realize that someone from her mother's tragic past had tried to bridge the years with this tentative, impersonal, unobtrusive attempt at contact. From everything she'd heard about the fabulous Avrum, this act seemed in keeping with the legend. Like her grandmother, she, too, accepted her mother's interpretation without further questioning. The identity of the sender was no more in doubt. Avrum Gentz had entered their lives again.

2

*M*ore than anything else, Sam, you have to understand about Mama and me. So far I've painted her as I think Dov and Dvora saw her. But to me she was someone very different. I'd always, even as a child, liked her better than they had. And after they left, she became my rock, my security, the buoy to which I clung when the seas of life turned rough. You see, since I was ten, I had only Mama. All of a sudden, in the space of a few weeks, there was left only Mama in what had been a family of five. It's hard to describe how shattered I was the night they buried Papa, and Dov ran off. That night was the worst in my life. I was terrified to see the sun rise, afraid that a new day would bring a new loss. I drew into myself. I couldn't cry. I couldn't talk. I sat in a corner and shivered.

No one understood but Mama. "I'm here," she kept assuring me. "I'll always be here."

"No. It's a l-lie," I stammered, finally admitting what was eating away at me. "You'll die, too. Or go away."

"No, I won't. Not ever. I promise you," she said.

"You can't promise that," I said. "I'm not a fool. If God sends for you, like he did for Papa, you'll have to go."

"Not me," she said, so firmly that I had to believe her. "I'm a fighter. Ask anyone. Ask Grandma. Ask Uncle Shmuel. Ask Great-uncle Nathan, even."

"You can't fight with God," I argued.

"Who says? For the sake of my Yudi I can fight even with God. If he sends for me, I'll tell him I can't go. 'Almighty,' I'll say, 'you have to wait. I can't come to you until Yudi is all grown up with children of her own.'"

312

You know, Sam, I believed her. I was old enough to know that people can't choose the time of their dying, but I believed that she could fight off death if she had to. She was that remarkable to me.

And she was remarkable. She took a loan from Uncle Shmuel after we moved out of the Czernowitz house and bought another cow. She built a shed for the pair of them in Grandma's backyard, doing most of the labor herself. All during those years she supported us by selling milk and butter. I helped, of course, but she was amazing. Whatever time I got up in the morning to do the milking she was there before me. Whatever the work—the washing, the churning, the raking, the cleaning—she was tireless. She filled me with confidence. I began to feel that she was like the daylight. No matter how dark the night, the next day would come and she would be there.

Even when she had her stroke she didn't fail me. I remember her lying on the bed, right after we carried her in from the barn, unable to move a muscle —not even her tongue or her eyes. I took her hand. "Can you hear me, Mama?" I asked her. I think she tried to blink. "Good," I said. "Then I want to remind you of your promise to me. You mustn't lie here and wait to die. You have to fight Almighty God for the use of your body. You promised me, remember? I haven't any children yet." I thought I saw her smile. And she did it, Sam. It took every ounce of courage that she had, but in spite of the incredible pain, she got herself to her feet again. No one knows but me how much courage it took.

The people of Solitava, the ones who never liked my mother, think that my so-called good nature comes from taking after my sweet Aunt Raizel, but I think that if I have it at all, it comes from knowing that I have a stiff-necked mother who would fight Almighty God for my sake. . . .

"So, Mindel," the gossips would ask when they passed her on the road, "what will you do with three hundred American dollars?"

"I have plans," she would answer. "I have my plans."

No one knew what those plans were. They only knew that she gave the check to her brother Shmuel to bank for her. Even Yudi had no idea what her mother was saving it for.

A year later, a second check arrived. Mindel glowed. But all she would say was that her plans would soon be put into execution. When the third check came, in the autumn of 1928, she thought the time had come. But before she could put the plan into action, Shmuel came to her for a loan. He'd been employed by the glassworks all these years, but lately the plant boss (a large Berlin firm had bought the factory after the death of old Mr. Waksman) had grown angry with him for daring to propose a scheme of accident compensation for the workers. After a stormy meeting between management and workers, Shmuel found himself unemployed. He asked Mindel for temporary use of her savings so that he could reopen and expand his old bookstore. She couldn't refuse him. After all, he'd always been generous to her when the children were small and she'd been so greatly in need.

It was a chill December day when the fourth check came. Yudi found her mother crying over it, as she probably had every year before. Yudi was about to put her arms around her mother's shoulders in sympathy, but something stopped her. Some echo of her brother's resentment of his mother suddenly overwhelmed her. She could almost hear Dov's angry words ringing in her ears: "Was Papa such a nothing that you can't even mourn for him?" What was so wonderful, she asked herself, about Avrum Gentz sending a sum of money every year? What was three hundred dollars a year to compare to the lifetime of devotion that Papa had shown? Yudi loved her mother, but something about Mindel's obsessive attachment to the memory of Avrum Gentz made her feel troubled and uncomfortable. She sat down at the table and looked her mother in the eye. "Do you still care for your Avrum so much?" she asked.

Mindel lifted herself to her feet, leaning heavily on her cane. She hobbled to the window and stared out to where a few early snowflakes were swirling about in the late afternoon light and edging the fields with white lace. "When one's love is torn away, as mine was, I don't think it's possible to get over it," she said quietly, the little sibilance of her impaired speech making the words even sadder than her tone of voice. "It's like a wound in the soul. Beyond healing."

Yudi felt for her, just as she'd felt in childhood when she, Dvora and Dov used to hear her crying in the night. But this sort of grief was obsessive, and obsession shouldn't be indulged. "But Mama," she heard herself saying, "that means that Dov was right."

Mindel's head turned. "What do you mean?"

"You never *did* love Papa, did you?"

Mindel slowly turned from the window to meet the challenge in Yudi's words. The expression in her eyes was puzzled, confused, and oddly at variance with the little sneer with which her stroke had disfigured her mouth. She put her almost useless hand to her forehead. "Why can't anyone understand? I was a good wife to your father. I took care of him, cooked his meals, washed his clothes, suffered with him in his disappointments, bore his children, tended him in sickness." She hobbled over to Yudi's chair and lifted the girl's chin. "Wasn't that enough?"

Yudi found herself trembling with feelings she'd suppressed for years. She wrenched her face away, unable to stop herself. "No, I don't think it was." Even her voice shook. "Papa deserved more."

Mindel, remembering that she'd lost Dov in just such a discussion, winced in agony. "Please, Yudi, not you, too! Surely *you* understand. Can't anybody see? *I had no more to give!*" The words seemed to come from the depths of her soul.

Yudi, her head lowered and her hands clenched in her lap, shivered. What did those words mean? Was the supply of love a woman had in her heart a finite thing? Had Avrum Gentz taken so much from her mother that there wasn't enough left to go around? But that made no sense. Everyone said that a woman who bore a dozen babies could stretch her love to surround them all. Why couldn't Mama have stretched her heart to include Leib? "*Why* did you have no more to give?" she asked, feeling desperate to understand.

Mindel was taken aback. "Why?" she echoed.

"Yes, why?" Yudi glanced up at her, frightened at her own departure from her usual steadfast loyalty and at this unprecedented incursion into her mother's secret heart. She'd never spoken to anyone this way. But she'd never experienced the sort of love her mother had felt with Avrum (although Dvora had once tried to explain it to her, and Eli constantly pressured her to declare that she loved him). Now she felt an urgent need to find out. *What had there been in Mama's feeling for her first husband that had been strong enough to destroy so many lives and to tear the family apart?* She had to know. "There are women, right here in Solitava," she persisted, keeping her voice as soft and gentle as she could, "who've taken second husbands after the death of a beloved first one, and they've loved the second just as warmly. Like Gussie Mimeniss after Berg died. And Mrs. Hurvitz. Why couldn't you?"

Mindel, her knuckles showing white on her cane, took a backward step. "It was different for me."

"In what way different?"

"Just different. You should know in what way. They tore him from me—"

"Yes, but death tears a loved one away, too. Yacob Berg died so suddenly that poor Gussie wouldn't believe the news for two days, remember?"

Mindel drew herself up in fury. "Are you comparing my loss of Avrum Gentz to Gussie *Berg's*?"

"Yes. Why not?"

"Why *not*?" Mindel began to tremble in rage. "How dare you speak to me like this?"

Yudi gaped at her. "How dare I? What do you mean? I haven't said anything offensive, have I?"

"The very *thought* you expressed was offensive."

"That Gussie Berg suffered too? That's offensive?"

"Berg was a *schneider*! A homely, awkward *bulvan*! How can you possibly compare—?"

"But Gussie loved him, didn't she? The same way you loved your Avrum?"

"Don't be a fool!" Mindel snapped, her voice like ice. "It wasn't at all the same."

"But, Mama, that's what I'm trying to understand. *Why* wasn't it the same?"

"Because it wasn't! What I had with Avrum . . . it was *special*! *Unique!* You *degrade* me with your nonsensical comparisons, and you degrade *him*. I refuse even to discuss the matter anymore."

"Mama, I—"

"Enough! If you're too insensitive to see that what happened to Berg and what happened to my Avrum are on such different planes that they cannot even be *spoken* of together, then there's no point in continuing this conversation."

Yudi, shaken, couldn't press the matter further. Everything she'd heard repelled her. What she'd heard from her mother's lips didn't sound like love at all. It sounded like *pride*. "All right, Mama. I'm sorry if I offended you," she muttered, wishing she hadn't stirred up these tensions.

"Yes, you've offended me. God knows, Yudi, that you're all I have in my life of any value, and if my answers to your questions drove you away from me as they did Dov, it would kill me. But I can't allow you to belittle what was most important in my life, even if it means I've alienated you forever."

Yudi recognized the fear behind her mother's proud words. She lowered her head and let out a small, silent sigh. "It's all right, Mama. You haven't alienated me. I'm not going to leave you because of . . . of feelings you can't help."

Mindel nodded, hobbled over to the table and picked up the check. "I suppose you think I should thank you for that. But I won't. This conversation has accomplished nothing but the destruction of some of the great joy I felt today at receiving this message."

Yudi kept her eyes fixed on her hands. "It wasn't a message, Mama. It was only a check."

"To you it's only a check. To me it's a message." Even hobbling across the room with her cane, Mindel made her progress to the door seem a proud rebuke. "Good night, Yudi."

Yudi got up and went to the window, looking out at the blowing snow without really seeing it. She was appalled at what her mother had revealed. Mindel's love had not been able to expand to include her second husband, and even to an extent her children, because she hadn't *permitted herself* to love them. In a kind of desperate need to believe that her first love was special, Mindel Gentz had held herself back from repeating the love experience. She'd convinced herself that her first love was something superior—higher, stronger, *better* than that experienced by other people. Yudi couldn't even blame her for it. It was quite understandable. Her mother had *had* to believe that her love for her Avrum, which her family had so cruelly cut short, had injured her beyond repair. If she could have recovered from the wound, the experience would have been belittled, not only in the eyes of the world but in her own. The memory of Avrum's love was so precious to her that she'd been afraid to dissipate it by giving her heart completely to anyone else, even her children. If she could have gone on to a second love, *what would have been the sense of all that pain?*

Yudi understood at last, and in the generosity and largeness of her spirit, she forgave. She loved her mother still. But love itself had shown a new and terrifying face. Her mother, in some primitive part of her mind, had built a shrine to the memory of her love, and like the primitive shrines of ancient days it existed on human sacrifice. Papa's blood had been shed on that altar, and Dov's and Dvora's, too. As she stared out at the whirling snowflakes, Yudi wondered how much of her own had been shed . . . and what other sacrifices were still to come.

3

*W*hen the seventh check arrived, at the end of 1932, Mindel decided that, if her plans were to be realized at all, the time would have to be now. She'd managed to hold on to most of the last check, and now, with this one, she might just have enough. It wasn't as much money as she'd hoped to have, but prices had fallen during the Depression, and she might just be able to manage it.

That evening, she sat down with Yudi at the kitchen table and revealed what had been on her mind ever since the first check had arrived. "I'm going to send you on a trip to America," she announced, her eyes glowing with excitement. "We'll start making arrangements tomorrow."

To Yudi, who'd heard nothing of this before, the idea seemed demented. "What nonsense is this, Mama? Why should I go to America?"

"Because I want you to. It's my *dream,* Yudi. The one dream I have left that has a chance for fulfillment."

"What are you talking about? You want me to leave you? That's your dream?"

"No, of course not. It'll be for a few months only. A trip, that's all. You'll be back. Wouldn't you enjoy taking such a trip? You've never had such an opportunity in all your life."

"Naturally I'd like to take a trip. If we were rich. But we haven't the money to throw away on meaningless luxuries."

"I have the money. More than five hundred American dollars."

"I can think of a hundred ways to use that money, instead of wasting it on a trip. We can hire someone to help with the dairy work, so life

318

will be a little easier for you. We can buy another cow—after all, Tzickerl is getting too old to give milk. We can buy some new clothes for the holidays next year. And shoes. We all need shoes."

"Never mind all that. We'll manage as we always have."

"Besides, if I were going to take a trip, I'd take it to Palestine, not America."

"That's *your* dream, Yudi, not mine."

"Mama, none of this makes sense. If this is your dream, *you* take the trip to America."

"I can't, sweetheart. I'm not able. Look at me. My face is so twisted it frightens little children, my arm is almost useless, and my walking is so labored that it's torture for me to wander more than a few yards from home."

Yudi, with a twinge in her tender heart, reached across the table and squeezed her mother's hand. "Then we'll stay here together. We'll stay put and make the best of things as they are. My taking a trip to America wouldn't change anything for the better, but buying a new cow—"

"Listen to me, Yudi, my sweet. There are things more important than new cows and new shoes. Dreams are important, too. My two other children are lost to me—whatever dreams I had that I would see them again have been dissipated by the years. My dream to live in America . . . well, it's too late for that, too. But this one thing—"

"What one thing, Mama? What is it you want me to do in America?"

Mindel looked at her daughter's face with a burning intensity in her eyes. "I want you to find him. Avrum. I wrote to the bank, you know, when the first check arrived, but they wouldn't tell me anything. You'll go to the bank in person and make them tell you where he is. Then go to see him. When you come back, I want you to be able to tell me how he looks, that he's well, that he has a new life. That's all, Yudi. That's all I want."

"Then *you* do it, Mama. Go and see him for yourself."

"No, I can't. I told you. I've thought it over very carefully. We can't pick up our lives again, Avrum and I. I'm too old to bear such stirrings up. How could we look at each other after all this time? The changes . . . the scars . . . the marks that years of trouble have left on us . . . they would be too hard to look at. If you live with someone through the years, you can accept the changes, because you see them gradually happen, step by step and day by day. But to see them all at once . . . on a face you've loved . . . the pain would be beyond my imagining. I haven't such courage anymore."

Yudi got up from the table, confused by the contradictory feelings flooding through her. A trip to America—it could be the greatest adventure of her life! For a young woman who'd never had a real adventure, the temptation was overwhelming. But she couldn't agree to this proposal. The whole idea was . . . well, crazy. "This is nonsense, Mama. How could I go? You need me here. Grandma is too old now to be of help in the dairy. And Eli. What could I say to Eli?"

"I'll manage in the dairy. And as for Eli, if you've put him off for all these years, you can put him off a few months more."

Yudi began to pace about the room. She had to, to keep herself sane. If she let herself go, she would be carried away on the tide of her mother's romantic insanity. But she had to say something to give her mother a sense of proportion. "Mama, for God's sake, let's talk sensibly. Is it so important to you to have me go so far, and at such great expense, only in order for me to come back and tell you I've seen him?"

Mindel turned in her chair and caught Yudi's arm in a clawlike grip. "Look at me, girl. You think I'm crazy, don't you?"

Yudi forced herself to face those glittering eyes. "I think the *idea* is crazy, yes."

"But *is* it so crazy? Put yourself in my place, and in his. Avrum has sent a message to me, every year for seven years now. Every year a message that I can't answer. I only want to send a message back. The same kind of message—one that wouldn't interfere with his life or disturb anything. Remembrance is all we have left to give each other now. I only want to tell him that I, too, remember. Is that so wrong of me?"

Yudi looked down at her mother's eager, twisted face and let herself be swept away. Why not? she asked herself. What was so wrong? Mama wasn't asking her to shed her blood; she was urging her to have a grand adventure. Well, why shouldn't she take that chance, just this once?

She knelt down beside her mother's chair and put her arms about her. "All right, Mama," she said, rubbing her cheek against her mother's shoulder, "I'll go. I'll find your Avrum for you and deliver your message. And when the whole world says we're both as crazy as loons, we'll just tell them they're absolutely right."

4

Yudi arrived in New York in the spring of 1933. She was met at customs by her cousin, Aunt Raizel's son Yossele. He was a large man, swarthy and perspiring, who picked up her suitcase, grabbed her arm, and hurried her out of the pier impatiently. "Don't call me Yossele," he said to her after they'd embraced. "It makes me sound like a greenie. In America, I'm Joe. Joe Kramer from the Bronx."

Cousin Joe, whom Yudi hadn't seen since childhood, was a very nervous man. He owned a small grocery store, he told her, on a street called Stebbins Avenue (which sounded entrancingly American to Yudi) and he, his wife, and their two little children lived in the three rooms at the back. He'd left his wife in charge of the store so that he could come to fetch Yudi, but his wife would, he was certain, "mess up the whole works." He was so impatient to get back to the Bronx from "downtown" that he didn't give Yudi a moment to look around her. He hustled her from the pier into a taxi for a brief ride through the most crowded, forbidding streets she'd ever seen, then down into a tunnel to catch a subway to the Bronx. "The I.R.T.," he said.

The subway, she discovered, was a nightmarish train that howled through black underground passageways at chilling speed, screeching around turns and rumbling along the tracks with such a terrifying racket that she wanted to scream in fright. But everyone else on the train wore an expression of complete unconcern, so she told herself that there was probably nothing to be afraid of. Nevertheless her heart pounded fearfully in her breast throughout the ride.

"Do we go to another city?" she whispered to Cousin Joe when they'd ridden for what seemed like ages. It was the first full sentence she'd spoken in English since her arrival. The words, which would have sounded fine if she'd been reading them aloud from one of her English books in Solitava, sounded awkward and alien now.

"You mean, are we leaving New York?" Cousin Joe laughed. "We didn't even come to the Bronx yet. Wait, we'll soon be coming up on the elevated tracks, and then you'll be able to see something."

What she saw when the train came up into the light was an overcast, heavy sky hanging over a seemingly endless row of apartment buildings. The train tracks were high above the street, and the train raced past the upper windows of the buildings so closely that she could see into many of them. Here and there a face peered back at her from one of the windows with calm unconcern. She wondered how those people could bear to live so close to the tracks and to listen to these fiendishly noisy trains go roaring by. Solitava seemed Eden-like in comparison with this.

"Is all this New York?" she asked, awestruck. Never had she seen so many large buildings in one place. There seemed to be no room even for a tree. Every bit of terrain was covered with structures of brick and cement. Everything was man-made as far as her eye could see. There was not a sign of nature anywhere.

Cousin Joe chuckled at her innocence. "This is only one part of New York. This is the Bronx. New York is so big, you wouldn't be able to get to know all of it in a year."

Oh, God, Yudi thought, how would anyone *find* anyone in such a place? How would she find Avrum? The task would be impossible.

Stebbins Avenue turned out to be a drab street, crowded on both sides with flat-fronted, five-storied tenements, each one pressed against the next. The only low building on the street was a one-storied structure that Cousin Joe called a taxpayer. It had three shops in front—the grocery, a candy store, and something called a dry cleaners. Each shop, Joe told her, had a three-room apartment at the rear. Joe had to take Yudi through the store to get to the apartment.

As soon as he'd deposited her suitcase in the large, square room just beyond the store, he took off his hat and suit jacket and put on a white apron. "Sit down," he said, motioning to a shabby sofa against the far wall. "I'll send Hannah right in."

She looked around her uneasily while she waited. The room was unlike anything she'd ever seen before. In one corner was a stove, a sink, and some storage cabinets that made a kitchen area. Strung cater-cornered across the kitchen was a line hung with at least a dozen drying diapers. In the center of the room was a round table covered in oilcloth and surrounded by four rickety chairs. Behind her a half-windowed door looked out on a tiny, ragged backyard.

Near where she stood was the sofa that her cousin had indicated, flanked by a high, clumsy piece of furniture that she realized (because of the metal handle protruding from its side) was a Victrola—an American contraption she'd read about but had never seen. And overhead, providing the room with most of its light, was a dirty but glowing skylight. The room was a kitchen, dining room, and sitting room all in one.

Hannah came in, a baby in her arms and a little boy clinging to her skirt. She introduced herself awkwardly. She was a small woman, now big with child. Her enlarged belly seemed to throw her off balance and made all her movements precarious and clumsy. Her eyes were a watery blue and looked warily at the stranger who'd been foisted on her. "I can't give you a bedroom," she said apologetically, her manner as nervous and harried as her husband's. "Joe and me, we sleep in that room there, and the kids are in the other. There's only room for the crib and a small bed in there. When the baby comes, I'll have to put Irving in here." She bit her underlip and pushed the boy forward. "Say hello to your second cousin, Irving. Her name's Yahudis."

Yudi had to struggle to decipher Hannah's rapid, nervous speech, but she managed to understand most of it. She smiled down at the little boy. "Call me Yudi," she said, surprised again at how alien the English words felt on her tongue. Slipping into Yiddish, she told Hannah how grateful she was for the hospitality and that she was sure the sofa would be fine.

"We don't talk Yiddish in this house," Hannah said, biting her lip again. It seemed to be a nervous gesture, increasing in frequency when she was under a strain. "We don't want the children to get into the habit. Joe says if we're going to make a success in America, we have to be one hundred percent American. You talk English, don't you?"

"Don't the lady know how to talk?" the little boy asked his mother with a smirk.

Yudi blushed. "I . . . understand a little. My speaking is not so well."

"It sounds fine to me," Hannah said without conviction. "Irving, you don't be so fresh!"

Yudi was then introduced to the baby (named Shirley), and she and Hannah spent what was left of the afternoon feeding, playing with, and picking up after the two children. When it became dark, Hannah excused herself to put the children to bed. While she was gone, Yudi took down the diapers and folded them, smiling to herself at the very unexpected way she was spending her first day in America.

The patch of sky that she could see through the skylight grew very dark. Judging by the growling of her stomach, Yudi surmised that the hour was very late. She hadn't eaten a morsel of food since early morning on the boat, and she began to wonder if people did without supper in America. But after a while, Cousin Joe closed the store and came into the back room, and Hannah invited her to sit down at the table. She explained, in the same apologetic tone in which she'd described the sleeping arrangements, that she'd not had time to cook today, so they were having only "dairy from the store." The fare consisted of bread too stale to sell, some slices of a bland, orange-colored cheese, two large, rotting tomatoes, reheated coffee, and a plate of cookies shaped like little animals—cookies that were far more suitable for teething babies than the palates of adults. "Listen," Cousin Joe said, shrugging off his wife's apologies, "that's what happens when you're in business. Instead of eating up the profits, you eat the losses, see? Better than throwing this stuff out. Besides, as our great-uncle the Tzaddik used to say, 'The rich eat what they want, the poor what they can.'"

After supper, Cousin Joe treated his guest to an hour of music. He took out several black discs, opened the top of his Victrola, cranked the handle at the side, and put one after another of the discs onto a revolving wheel. Out came the voices of Enrico Caruso and Madame Galli-Curci. During each solo, Joe closed his eyes, his face transfixed with beatific joy, and swayed back and forth on the balls of his feet, transported. Only when the thin, distant-sounding voices would suddenly deepen and go flat did he open his eyes and hastily crank up his machine again. Yudi, standing with him at the Victrola and watching, fascinated, as the needle bobbed on the spinning discs, begged to be permitted to crank for him, but he would not agree. No one in the household, he told her, could touch his precious Victrola but himself. Then, as if to soften his refusal, he confided that he'd once seen the great Caruso in person. "It was when I first came to America. I saved up every cent I could spare to buy a ticket to the Metropolitan. Oh, God, such a voice he had, Caruso! Never again will there be such a magnificent voice."

But Hannah, sitting alone on the sofa, biting her lips and moving her hands nervously over her belly, soon had had enough. "Opera! That's all he cares about. I don't know what it is he loves so much. To me it's just a lot of whining. Come, Mr. Music Lover, get the bedding for Yudi's bed. It's time to go to sleep."

Later, huddled under a dank-smelling blanket on the lumpy sofa, Yudi struggled against admitting to herself that she felt miserable. What had she expected from her first day in America anyway—a brass band? Flowers? A suite of rooms in a palace? Her cousin and his wife didn't have very much, but what little they had they were willing to share with her. It would be worse than ungrateful to permit herself to feel unhappy about her surroundings.

The pattering sound of rain drew her eyes to the skylight. At least the rain in America was the same as at home. Everything else was so strange, so frightening, so alien. It was like being in another world—a world that was *manufactured*. Fabricated by the hand of man instead of being allowed to evolve by the hand of nature. She supposed there was much that was admirable in a world in which mankind imposed on nature his own design and built with his ingenuity and his toil an environment uniquely his own, but, so far, what she'd seen of that environment was devoid of grace and beauty. It had no softness. She found it fearful.

But these are ridiculous thoughts, she told herself, her optimistic character reasserting itself. She'd been here only *one day*! How could she make judgments based on the glimpses of the Bronx that she'd caught from the window of the I.R.T. train and a look at one little flat behind a store? There was a whole world out there she hadn't yet seen, a world that was undoubtedly as varied and surprising as the individuals who peopled it. Tomorrow was another day . . . and life would be offering her all sorts of surprises in the next few months. Many of them, she was certain, would be good ones. After all, she'd heard of the law of probability. When you tossed a coin, half the time it came up heads.

With this promising expectation, she consoled herself. She wiggled her backside more deeply into the hollows of the sofa and looked up at the raindrops spattering on the window glass of the skylight over her head. There was light coming from somewhere—a streetlamp, she supposed—which lit the drops and gave them a crystallike luminosity. It was fun to be sleeping under a skylight. It reminded her of a fairy story she'd read in her childhood about a princess who was forced by a cruel stepfather to live in an underground house with a roof of glass through which she could see the sky. She giggled at the recollection. Princess Yudi from Solitava. All she needed now was a prince to come riding to the rescue, who would free her with a kiss.

Did princesses have to go to the bathroom? she wondered, her smile fading. She'd forgotten to relieve herself earlier, and now the need was suddenly urgent. And the bathroom was on the other side of Cousin Joe's bedroom. She'd have to walk right through their room. Blushing with embarrassment, she threw off her blanket and padded across the room. She was about to tap on their door when she heard their voices. "Enough, already!" she heard Cousin Joe say. "It's only for a few months."

"But the baby will be here in a few *weeks*," Hannah said, her voice a plaintive whine.

"So what? So we'll be a little crowded for a while."

Yudi's hand froze in midair. They were arguing about *her*! Her whole body stiffened. She'd realized from the first that Hannah was made uncomfortable by her presence in the house, but she hadn't realized the woman was as unhappy as this.

"Sssh!" Hannah whispered. "Do you want her to hear you?"

"She won't hear," Joe said, "Besides, she hardly talks English."

"She understands plenty. I tell you, Joey, I can't have her here when the baby comes. It's hard enough as it is, but with three little ones in these tiny rooms . . . with the diapers and the bottles and—"

"Shut up the mouth, Hannah! She's my *cousin*. It's for six months at most. You can stand it for a few months, can't you? Now turn off your tongue and let me sleep. I have to open up at six."

Yudi's whole body seemed turned to stone. The optimism she'd managed to revive a few moments earlier died again. She couldn't deny, now, that she felt lonelier and more miserable than ever before in her life. And she still had to go to the bathroom. But she could not, under any circumstances, knock on her cousins' door now.

She looked around her in desperation. In the light from the skylight, she could see the door to the backyard. That was the solution. It wouldn't be the first time in her life she went out on such business on a rainy night; in Solitava, everyone had outhouses.

After she'd made her silent exit and equally silent return and had locked the door again, she crept back into bed, shivering from the dampness of her nightgown and the misery of her situation. Loneliness welled up in her chest like a malignant chill. She gazed up at the skylight, which a moment ago had seemed like the roof of a crystal palace, and, startlingly, felt a laugh bubble up inside of her. "Hello, Yudi," she whispered, grimacing ruefully at the unheeding raindrops, "welcome to America!"

5

She thought she hadn't slept at all that night, but the bright morning light shining down on her from the skylight woke her with a start. She was up and dressed before Cousin Joe emerged from his bedroom to open the store. Hannah soon followed, rushing about to ready Irving for school. He went to kindergarten, he told Yudi proudly. Yudi offered timidly to change and dress the baby, but Hannah rejected the suggestion in spite of being more harried and nervous than she was the day before.

In order to get out of her way, Yudi wandered into the store. She was curious to see what an American grocery store was like. The store was surprisingly busy. Customers—mostly women—were lined up at the long counter. They came in with their own quart-sized tins in their hands, and they ladled out the milk themselves from the large cans Joe had lined up in front. Meanwhile, Joe presided over everything else from his post behind the counter. He cut pieces of butter quickly from a wooden tub much larger than those Yudi's mother had in Solitava, and he wrapped the chunks with professional neatness in sheets of waxed paper. He assembled eggs in special cartons from large crates stacked behind him. He sliced cheese, counted out rolls, weighed vegetables, took cans from the high shelves with a special long-handled claw, stacked up the orders, listed the charges on the brown bags with a stubby pencil, and added them all up like lightning. Yudi was impressed with his speedy efficiency.

After watching for a while, she walked around the counter and asked if there was anything she could do to help. "G'wan," he said (the word completely strange to her) and patted her on the shoulder. "You didn't come to America to help me in the store. Go take a walk. Look around. Go see something."

She returned to the back room and asked Hannah if she could take the baby for a walk. Hannah hesitated. Yudi could see that she was afraid to trust her little Shirley to the care of a—what had Joe called it yesterday?—a greenie. "Wait," Hannah said, "I'll put on a sweater, and we'll both take her."

With little Shirley sitting up in a baby carriage that looked to Yudi like a miniature royal coach, they squeezed their way past the people at the counter and went out to the street. Yudi looked about her in pleased surprise. The sunshine seemed to have transformed everything. It lit up the millions of motes that floated in the air, giving the atmosphere a sparkle that made Yudi tingle. American air. It *was* different. It was exciting.

She could hear the rumble of the I.R.T. in the distance, but it sounded less forbidding now. Her spirits rose again. She took a deep breath, looked over at Hannah, and launched into the speech she'd prepared in the night. "Hannah," she said, "I think I must look for a room of my own. You see, I—"

Hannah gasped. She immediately stiffened and stopped walking. "You *heard* us last night!" she cried in real distress. "I was afraid that . . . I *knew* we shouldn't have—"

"No, no," Yudi said quickly, putting a hand on her arm. "Please don't make upset yourself. Is only that the Bronx is . . . how shall I say? . . . so far. To do my business, I must ride the I.R.T. subway, which makes in me much . . . much fear. Please not to be angry with me. I think will be much better if I live . . . how does Cousin Joe tell me? . . . downtown."

Instead of the expression of delight that Yudi expected to see on Hannah's face, there came a look of anguish. Hannah's eyes filled with tears. "I didn't mean what I said, Yudi," she whimpered. "You're so *nice*. I don't want you to move out, really I don't. It's just that yesterday was such a lousy day. I hate watching the store, y'know, and that upset me right off. Then Shirley got cranky, and I had a terrible time. I'll do better today. I'll make you a real nice dinner, really I will, and I'll give you some drawers in the cupboard for your things—"

"No, Hannah, please! Is not any reason to cry. My aunt Raizel did not write to ask you to make for me a home, only to *meet* me, so that when I arrive I will not be alone. That you have done. You are very kind . . . very *haimish*. But now is time for me to do what I must do."

Hannah pulled a handkerchief from the sleeve of her sweater and blew her nose into it. "Do you mean it, Yudi? You really *want* to go? To be all alone?"

Yudi smiled at her and bent over to kiss her cheek. "Yes, really. Only tell me how to find the downtown, and where to seek for a room."

Hannah wiped her teary eyes and smiled. For the first time Yudi could see that she was pretty. "Boy, that's the least I can do," she said (the use of the word "boy" giving Yudi another twinge of linguistic confusion), "but you have to promise to come back for visits. At least for Shabbes dinners."

"If I can stand to ride in your I.R.T. subway," Yudi laughed. "But, Hannah, do you know to tell me where to find a room?"

"Sure I do. I got a relative who has a rooming house on Essex Street. A cousin."

A week later, Yudi was feeling almost at home in America. The room in Hannah's cousin's rooming house was clean and adequate for her needs, the neighborhood was filled with Jews to whom she could speak Yiddish if her English failed her, and she'd become accustomed to the crowded, noisy streets. She could even go down to the subway if she had to, though she still found her heart beating rapidly every time she tried it. She preferred to ride the buses, and she spent several afternoons just transferring from one bus to another, riding all around Manhattan for a nickel. It helped her to learn her way around.

During the second week of her stay, she decided it was time to visit the bank. She'd already ridden past it twice on the bus. On the day she'd chosen to go, she put on her good suit and the new blouse she'd brought from home, tucked the slip of paper with the bank man's name on it into her purse, and set out. The Merchants' Security Bank of New York was located on a busy corner of Lexington Avenue, and the bus stopped right at its door. The door of the Merchants' Security Bank was a wide, double one, made of brass and glass and flanked with two intimidating marble pillars. Yudi was tempted to remain on the bus and ride past as she'd done before. But sooner or later, she reasoned, she'd have to enter, so why delay? She stepped down from the bus, hurried across the sidewalk, walked up two flat steps, and pushed open the brass door.

The inside of the bank was even more intimidating than the outside. It was huge, with the highest ceilings she'd ever seen. There were potted palms everywhere, and right across the center of the room was a row of elegant mahogany desks with brass fittings and brass inkstands at which a few well-dressed clients were filling out checks. Even the tellers behind their brass cages were intimidating, dressed as they were in dark suits, stiff-collared white shirts, and striped ties, like a row of diplomats from a wealthy foreign government.

Bravely, she pulled the slip of paper from her purse and approached one of the cages. "I wish to see Mr. Vincent G. Armstrong, please," she said.

The teller raised his brows. "Mr. Armstrong? Well, I hardly . . . that is, may I inquire what you wish to see him about, madam? Perhaps I can help you."

"I think . . . not. I wish information about a . . ." She looked down at her paper. ". . . a special account."

"You wish to open one?"

"No. I wish information about account number 92018."

"I see. Is it your account?"

"Mine? No, not mine."

"Then, madam, I'm afraid we can't help you. We're not permitted to give out information about our accounts."

Yudi felt herself grow tense. "Yes, I understand so. But, you see, I've come from a very long way. From Europe, especially for this information. Please to let me speak to Mr. Armstrong."

The teller hesitated. The girl was so sweet and innocent looking that he weakened. He turned and picked up a telephone. Covering the mouthpiece, he asked her, "What name shall I say?"

Yudi paused before answering. Some instinct told her that her request was going to be refused. Why should this big, important bank break its rules for Yahudis Weisenberg, a nobody without so much as a nickel deposited in its vaults? She was a stranger to this Mr. Armstrong. Her name would mean nothing to him. He would be quite justified in refusing to see her, and even if he did, why should he give out information to any person who walked in from the street? But if her name was the same as that of the man who was account number 92018, there might be a chance. "My name is Gentz," she said firmly. "Miss Yahudis Gentz."

The teller turned away and spoke softly into the telephone. Then he listened, nodded, and listened again. After more headshakings he hung up and turned back to her. "I'm sorry, Miss Gentz. Mr. Armstrong says there's absolutely nothing he can do to help you. The information about our accounts is completely confidential."

"But he doesn't *understand*. I've come all this way—!"

"I'm sorry." The teller shrugged and turned his attention to a gentleman who had come up behind her.

Yudi tried to argue, but the proper English words didn't come. The teller ignored her continued presence, so, with cheeks burning in humiliation, she turned away. She started to move slowly toward the door, wondering desperately what to do next, when her eye fell on an area of desks and doorways at the rear. One of the doors had the words VINCENT G. ARMSTRONG—SPECIAL ACCOUNTS printed on it in gold letters. She squared her shoulders, took a quick look around to see if anyone was watching her, and started toward it. She would get into that office by —what was that funny English expression?—hook or crook.

But before she reached it, someone grasped her arm. With a little cry, she looked up into the face of a uniformed guard. He was looking down at her with frowning disapproval. "The exit is this way, ma'am," he said firmly.

"Please," she begged, her eyes filling with embarrassed tears. "I only wish to speak a moment to Mr. Armstrong."

"Sorry, lady, but it ain't allowed. This way, please."

She looked around desperately as he began to lead her across the marble floor to the doorway. The teller was watching her with troubled sympathy, but when their eyes met, he looked away. All sorts of words and feelings welled up in her. She wanted to cry out to the teller and the guard that she was not a thief. That their rules were mechanical, not human. That *hearts* were involved in this matter, not regulations. That people's futures were at stake here. That this refusal to grant her request had significant ramifications. But her English was inadequate, and the embarrassment of being led across the room like a common thief had made everything a jumble in her brain. The tenses of verbs, the declensions of pronouns that in Europe she'd thought she knew so well, now seemed terribly confusing. "Please try to understand," she mumbled to the guard. "I mean no trouble. . . ."

"No, of course you don't," the guard said, not ceasing his remorseless march to the door.

"Then you needn't hold me." Yudi forced herself to address him with calm dignity. "I shall leave on my own."

"Yes, ma'am," the guard said, dropping his hold and touching his cap. "Good morning."

She cast the teller a glance of reproach before sweeping past the guard, her shoulders back and her mouth set in an angry line. She pushed open the brass doors, wishing she could slam them. But they were the kind that swung on two-way hinges and couldn't be slammed.

Back in her room, she paced about in perturbation. It was ludicrous to have come so far without achieving the purpose for which she'd been sent. How could she face her mother and say she'd failed at the very first step? She would have to try again. But next time she would have to handle herself better. She would have to prepare better arguments. She'd have to express herself clearly and convincingly.

There was no question about it—she had to study English. But she didn't know where or how, and she didn't know what it would cost. At the end of the week, when she went to the Bronx to have Shabbes dinner with her cousins, she asked Joe for advice. He told her about night school. In America, he said, night school was *free*.

Yudi was overjoyed. She would start night school as soon as possible. She still had more than five months to accomplish her mission. The Merchants' Security Bank of New York hadn't seen the last of her.

6

By the time they'd finished testing her down in the school office, the class was half over. She stood in the corridor outside Room 307, too shy to go in. It was embarrassing to have to make an entrance after the class had already begun. Through the little glass window in the classroom door, she could see the teacher standing at the blackboard, engaged in an animated exchange with an elderly lady in the front row. The whole class was laughing. The teacher, too. He looked very nice. Kind, she thought.

The people downstairs in the office had not seemed so kind. They'd been bored and perfunctory. They'd asked her some questions and given her a printed test. After they'd marked it, they'd told her without comment that she was being admitted to Level 3. She'd had to ask what that meant. "Third level out of four," the clerk had told her. "There's Beginners, Secondaries, Advanced, and Senior Advanced. You're Advanced."

She'd found her way to Room 307 with considerable difficulty. The corridors were long, empty, and dimly lit, and the rooms weren't always numbered in logical sequence. By the time she'd found the place, she'd begun to wish she hadn't come. But now that she'd had this glimpse of the teacher, her eagerness reawakened. She looked down at the slip they'd given her downstairs: "English for the Foreign Born, Level 3, Section B. Instructor: Mr. Samuel Goldenson."

She was surprised that Mr. Goldenson was so young. She hadn't expected him to look like this. When she'd first read his name on the slip, she'd imagined a much older man, someone scholarly and gray and a little forbidding. But the teacher standing there at the blackboard was no more than thirty-five, and very good-looking. So American, with his bow tie and sweater-vest under a tweed jacket. Even though his light hair was slightly receding from a high forehead, even though the humorous twinkle of his eyes was slightly obscured by a pair of eyeglasses with thin wire rims, even though his face was slightly rounded—too cherubic to be considered handsome in a classic sense—Mr. Goldenson's face was one you had to like. He looked not only intelligent but, well, sweet.

The elderly lady in the front row suddenly pointed at her. Yudi felt herself flush, and she backed away from the door in mortification. But Mr. Goldenson immediately came to the door and pulled it open. "Come in," he said with a warm smile. "There's nothing to be afraid of. We only eat new students on Wednesday nights. This is Thursday."

Yudi paused on the threshold, blinking at him in confusion. "But . . . today is Tuesday, no?"

The class broke into a laugh, and they all began to clap. "She passed," a man yelled.

"She talks good," a woman sitting nearby said.

Mr. Goldenson grinned down at her. "It *is* Tuesday, isn't it? I never can remember. But please come in. We don't eat new students on Tuesdays either."

Yudi crossed over the threshold, flushed and timid but pleased at having "passed" Mr. Goldenson's little test. She handed him her slip and glanced about her. The room was full of people of assorted ages and types, sitting in rows at desks too small for them. There were only a few vacant desks in the room. It was evidently a children's classroom in the daytime. There were childish drawings on the bulletin boards flanking the clothes closet; charts of the alphabet with small letters and capitals hung over the blackboard, along with a picture of George Washington; and a list of names was tacked up behind the door with rows of gold stars after each name. America children were certainly fortunate—this was a cheerful place for children to study in.

The elderly lady was smiling benignly at her, and there were several others who were watching her with equally encouraging expressions. This was a very friendly group, Yudi realized, and some of her trepidation evaporated.

"Miss Weisenberg?" Mr. Goldenson was studying her with cordial interest. "Where would you like to sit?"

"Let her sit here, near me," the elderly lady offered.

"What are you *talkink*?" came an offended voice from the doorway. "Dat's *mine* seat!"

"Oh, good evening, Mrs. Nissenbaum," Mr. Goldenson said cheerfully to a plump, white-haired matron in a flowered dress who stood in the doorway in an attitude of haughty indignation. "We thought you were going to be absent again today."

"Well, I ain't," Mrs. Nissenbaum said sourly. "And I vant mine seat!"

Mr. Goldenson, without losing a bit of his good humor, pointed an accusing finger at her. "*What* is it you want?" he prodded gently.

Mrs. Nissenbaum stared at him a moment and then clapped a hand to her mouth. "*Oy vay,* I mean *my* seat." Having corrected herself, she marched purposefully across the front of the room (giving Yudi a triumphant look as she passed) and crammed herself into the little front seat in question.

"Don' mind, lady," said a young man in the rear of the first row. "Dere's a good seat right here."

The elderly lady in front chortled. "Sure. Susko wants the pretty girl should sit nexta *him.*"

"Will that seat do, Miss Weisenberg?" Mr. Goldenson asked. "If you agree, it will make Mr. Susko very happy."

"Yes, all right," Yudi mumbled, her blush deepening to a fiery red. The whole class watched as she hurried down the aisle and slipped into the rear seat of the second row.

Mr. Goldenson, having entered her name in his roll book, tapped his pencil for attention. "Let's give our new member a few minutes to get used to us, shall we, before we ask her to introduce herself? Meanwhile, let's get back to what we were doing." He pointed to the blackboard, on which he'd written:

Last year I was _____.
This year I am _____.
Next year I will be _____.

"Who's thought of a story that will use all three sentences? You, Mrs. Bodjarski? Good. Read it to us."

Mrs. Bodjarski held her notebook with hands reddened from years of scrubbing. Her face was very serious. "Last year I was Polish. This year I am in America. Next year I will be citizen. *A* citizen."

"Very *good,* Mrs. Bodjarski," Mr. Goldenson said with enthusiasm. "That's the idea. Who else has a story for us? Mrs. Poliakoff? Already?"

"It don't take *me* long to think," the elderly lady in front chirped, making a sprightly leap to her feet.

"*Doesn't* take me long," Mr. Goldenson put in.

"Right. It doesn't." Mrs. Poliakoff looked around the class, making certain that everyone noticed she was speaking without referring to her notebook. "Last year I was sixty-four years old. This year I am sixty-five. Next year I will be sixty-six," she declaimed proudly.

"So vat's so vonderful?" a heavy man near the window muttered.

"That *was* wonderful, Mr. Mandel," the teacher said. "Do you think you can do as well?"

Mr. Mandel pushed himself to his feet. "Lest year I was sixty-*eight*. Dis year I am sixty-*nine*. And next year I em . . . vill be . . . *sevendy*!"

"Good!" Mr. Goldenson said, giving Mrs. Poliakoff a wink to indicate he still gave her credit for initiating the idea.

"See? I *told* you," Mr. Mandel said, sitting down.

Mrs. Nissenbaum's hand shot up. She squeezed herself out of her seat. "So what's so great, I ask you? Listen to mine. Last year I was seventy-two. This year I am seventy-three. Next year I'll be seventy-four. There!"

"Oh, shaddup," said Mrs. Poliakoff in irritation. "You ain't a day over fifty-nine."

Yudi could see that Mr. Goldenson was having difficulty holding back his laughter. "I didn't mean this to become a competition in seniority," he remarked. "But why not? Why don't you get into this, Mr. Henriksen?"

A grizzled, darkly tanned, and wrinkled little man jumped to his feet. "Las' year I vass seventy-nine," he said with a Nordic intonation. "Diss year I am eighty. Next year . . ." He paused for dramatic effect, looking around the room proudly. "Next year . . . *eighty-one*!"

The class broke into applause, and Mr. Henriksen took a dignified bow, the undisputed winner.

"So how about you, Mr. Goldenson?" the irrepressible Mrs. Poliakoff asked. "Last year how old was you?"

"Last year, Mrs. Poliakoff," he answered, a grin breaking through, "I was one hundred and twelve. And since you asked, you may go to the board and write down my answers for me, starting with . . ." He turned to the board, erased the "I was," and substituted "you were." "Starting with this."

"Aw, Mr. Goldenson," she objected, "you know I don't like to write."

"You can do it," he said, handing her the chalk. "I have complete confidence in you. And meanwhile, let's introduce ourselves to our new classmate. Mrs. Cervenka, show Miss Weisenberg how we introduce ourselves."

Mrs. Cervenka, tall and beautiful, with thick dark hair pulled back into a bun at the nape of her neck, rose gracefully. "My name is Irena Cervenka," she said, pronouncing each syllable with precision. "I am a dressmaker and a housewife. I do alterations and take care by my two children."

"*Of* my two children. But that was excellent, Mrs. Cervenka."

Mr. Henriksen, still flushed with victory, volunteered next. "I am Henry Henriksen. I am gardener with New York park department. I take care of plantings in the park."

"I am *a* gardener," Mr. Susko corrected, "with *the* park department."

"That's right, but he remembered *the* park," Mr. Goldenson pointed out. "Now, then, Mr. Susko, do you want to be next? Here's your big chance. Go ahead, introduce yourself to Miss Weisenberg."

Mr. Susko, swarthily handsome and endowed with a pair of broad, muscular shoulders, got to his feet with sublime confidence. He looked right at Yudi as he spoke, making her blush again. "My name is Immanuel Susko," he said with formality. Then he leaned over and added with a wink, "In America, Manny." Resuming his formal stance, he continued, "I am a plumber's helper. I fix pipes."

"Good, Mr. Susko. Well, Miss Weisenberg, do you think you've heard enough to be able to introduce yourself as the others have?"

Yudi nodded and got slowly to her feet. Her heart was pounding and her pulse racing. So many people to listen to her speak in English—it was terrifying. But if she was to learn, she had to try. "My name is Yahudis Weisenberg," she said in a small voice. "In old country is Yudi. In America, I . . . I don't know yet my American name."

"I can tell you that," Mr. Goldenson offered, looking at her again with that smile of warm interest. "In America your name is Judith. It's a lovely name. Here, I'll write it on the board for you."

After he had done it, he asked her to go on.

"I don't know what more to say."

"Can you tell us what you do?"

"What I *do*? Here in America, you mean?"

"Yes. Here in America."

"In America I . . . I . . ." Yudi struggled to phrase an answer. The eyes of the whole class were fixed on her. Even Mrs. Poliakoff, at the blackboard, had stayed her hand, her chalk poised in the air. No one even seemed to take a breath. It was as if they were all tensely pulling for her, helping her with their will, struggling with her to find the words. They were a brotherhood—the brotherhood of the foreign born—who knew what it was to be locked in and held down by their difficulty with an alien tongue.

She sensed their support. It was almost tangible in the silence of the room. She suddenly felt surrounded by friends. This was a place where she could say whatever was on her mind. There was nothing to be afraid of here. She could tell the truth.

She took a long breath. "In America," she said quietly, "I search."

7

Mr. Goldenson required that each student hand in a short piece of writing every Tuesday (even three or four sentences made a "composition" of acceptable length if the writer had no more to say), which he read, marked, and returned on Thursday. In her first composition, Yudi had to describe how to get from her room to the nearest library. She wrote and rewrote her five sentences four times before she was satisfied with them and was rewarded for her efforts by seeing a large A scrawled at the top of her paper. Underneath Mr. Goldenson had written, "Excellent job, Miss Weisenberg," with his red pencil.

The next composition was to be on the subject of "A Memory of Childhood." She wrote about how Tzickerl, the cow, came into the family. She was so carried away by her eagerness to tell the story that she wrote two and a half pages, and after she'd finished, she wrote it over twice more to make sure her sentences were clear. This time Mr. Goldenson wrote across the top, "Miss Weisenberg, your story is charming— a delight to read. May I have your permission to read it to the class?" She gave her permission, and when he read it, the class applauded so loudly and long that she had to hide her face in her hands so that they wouldn't see how red her cheeks had become. But afterward Mrs. Nissenbaum asked her how she'd managed to write so many pages. "Don' make trouble fa us, Veisenboig," the white-haired lady scolded only half-humorously. "Us plain folks, ve ain't got time to write a whole *megillah* every week."

Yudi withered under Mrs. Nissenbaum's chastisement. She didn't want her classmates (for whom she had a real affection) to think she was trying to show them up. Nor did she wish to give the impression that she had nothing else to do but prepare her work for English class. She promised herself that, next time, she'd write only a brief half page.

But the truth was that there was nothing she would rather do than go to English class. It had become more than a strategy for accomplishing her purpose here in America—it was her favorite activity. She liked the people in the class better than the boarders at her rooming house, and she enjoyed her studies more than wandering aimlessly around Manhattan. If Mr. Goldenson had told her he wanted her to come to class every day of the week, she would have happily agreed.

She could hardly wait for Tuesdays to roll around. There was only one day between the Tuesday and the Thursday session, but the four days between Thursday and the following Tuesday seemed interminable.

For her third writing assignment, Yudi had to write about her first impressions of America. Somehow this assignment gave her difficulty. She couldn't seem to do it. Her first impressions of America had been so bleak that she was ashamed to admit the truth in writing. She didn't want Mr. Goldenson to think she disliked his native land, but when she wrote about meeting Cousin Joe at the pier, the feelings she described sounded so pathetic that she threw the paper away. Then she tried to write about the grocery store, but her words seemed too mundane to represent first impressions of America. She even wrote a few lines about seeing the American sunshine through the skylight in Hannah's back parlor, but that attempt seemed too affected. She threw it away, too. She carried her notebook around with her wherever she went that weekend, hoping she would be struck with an inspiration.

On Sunday evening, in spite of a persistent and depressing April drizzle, she decided to eat out. She didn't enjoy dining every night with the other boarders at the rooming house. For a change, she took a short bus ride uptown to the Garden Cafeteria, where, after placing a piece of chicken, a salad, and a slice of melon on her tray, she found herself a table near the corner and settled down to enjoy a quiet dinner all by herself. But the sounds of an argument from a table somewhere behind her disturbed her peace. She looked over her shoulder to see where the noise was coming from. A group of seven or eight men were crowded around a table meant for four in the opposite corner. The men were arguing about politics at the top of their voices. Even from across the room, Yudi could make out something of what they were saying. They were talking about Germany. From what she could make out, they were in disagreement about the importance of the new German Chancellor, Adolf Hitler. Yudi's interest was piqued. This Hitler had been appointed by the German President, Hindenburg, a month before Yudi had left Europe, and she had spent many hours listening to Eli curse the appointment.

One of the men at the noisy table, shouting louder than the rest, was evidently as upset about Germany's new Chancellor as Eli was. Yudi was amazed that Americans could become so emotional over European politics. "A little nobody?" the man was shouting. "You think Hitler's only a nobody? Then ask Sam to tell you about this new Enabling Law, if that's what you think. Go ahead, Sam, tell him!"

The man named Sam leaned forward to speak. Yudi gasped. The new speaker (who addressed his friends in a voice too low for her to hear) was none other than her teacher, Mr. Goldenson. His appearance differed markedly from the way he usually looked in class. Today, instead of his neat tweed jacket and carefully pressed trousers, he was wearing a dark, high-necked, shabby sweater and baggy pants. His hair was tousled, and he'd removed his glasses and was gesturing with them as he spoke. ". . . control of the press . . ." he was saying, and ". . . arrest and seizure without due process . . ." His expression was serious and earnest. He looked younger and even more handsome than in class, and a lot less formidable. In fact, he looked like a young revolutionary. Yudi liked this new view of him. It charmed her.

As if he felt her eyes on him, he suddenly looked up over his shoulder and caught her eye. His words died on his lips, and he quickly put on his glasses and stared at her. She felt herself grow hot with humiliation, and she dropped her eyes to her plate, wishing she were dead.

A moment later he was standing before her. "Miss Weisenberg!" he exclaimed in obvious delight. "Good evening. What a nice surprise to see you here. Do you eat here often?"

She pressed her knees together to keep them from shaking. "Only once in a while."

"Are you alone? I'm just having coffee with some of my friends. Would you like to join us?"

"Oh, n-no, thank you, Mr. Goldenson." She shook her head vigorously and got to her feet. "I was just going."

His face fell. "Were you? But you haven't finished your melon. I disturbed you—"

"No, not at all. It wasn't very good."

"But . . . are you sure you can't join us for coffee?" He gave her a quick grin. "I'd like my friends to meet my best student."

The compliment made her color up again, but she managed to smile back at him. "Shame on you, Mr. Goldenson. Mrs. Poliakoff, if she heard you, would take large offense."

"Ah, but Mrs. Poliakoff would hardly make the impression on my friends that you would, Miss Weisenberg. Please come."

"No, no, thank you." She struggled into her coat, aware of his gentlemanly attempt to help, aware of the racing of her pulse and aware of the implication of what he'd said. He thought she was pretty!

"Are you sure you have to go?" he was asking. "Just come over for a little while."

"No, I must not. Such an exciting discussion you were having. I must not keep you from it."

"It wasn't so exciting. We always argue like that."

"Then you must take in it much pleasure. Please, they are looking at us. You must go back to them."

He glanced back at his friends. They were watching his unsuccessful attempt at flirtation with fascination, a couple of them grinning lewdly. He threw them a gesture of contempt and turned back to her. "If you won't come and meet them—and I can't say I blame you; they're a bunch of animals—then will you at least let me see you home?"

"See me home? Certainly not. From your friends I wouldn't dream of taking you. Thank you, Mr. Goldenson, for making such politeness, but you must go back to your friends." She was filled with an unfamiliar, very girlish confusion, but she was determined not to spoil his evening. "Good night, Mr. Goldenson."

He appeared to be sincerely crestfallen. "Good night, Miss Weisenberg."

She turned and hurried to the door. Just before leaving, she glanced back at him. She didn't want to do it, but she couldn't help herself. He was standing where she'd left him, looking positively woebegone. But his face brightened when he saw her turn. "See you in class. Tuesday," he mouthed, waving.

She smiled, nodded and waved back. Then she strode purposefully out of his line of vision.

She walked through the drizzle to the bus stop, wishing she could skip down the street. Her heart was doing a dance in her breast. He likes me, something sang inside her. I really think he likes me.

That evening she sat at the enameled table in her room with her dictionary and her pad of paper, and she wrote her composition. "My first impressions of America was on the I.R.T. subway. I was much frightened of it. Such a roaring and rumbling there was, with nothing but blackness around it. It seemed to me to be a monster which had swallowed me up and was carrying me to hell. I am more accustomed to the subway now and not anymore frightened. I do not any more believe it takes me to hell. Sometimes I believe the exact opposite, especially on Tuesdays and Thursdays when I ride on it to school."

She read it over and decided to tear it up. It was too revealing. He would know from those few sentences how much his English class meant to her. It wouldn't be seemly for her to admit in a school composition such intimate feelings. But as she was about to tear up the sheet, she remembered the look on his face when she left the cafeteria. He seemed truly regretful that she was leaving. Since he'd revealed that he liked *her*, would it be so terrible to give him this hint that she liked *him*?

A dozen times between Sunday night and Tuesday evening, she vacillated between the urge to destroy the composition and the urge to let him see it. She didn't make a final decision until the last second, when Mrs. Poliakoff, who was collecting the homework, stopped at her desk to pick up hers. "No homework, Weisenboig?" the old lady asked. "Whatsa matter, you been sick?"

She didn't want to be unprepared. She pulled the folded sheet from her notebook. "No, here it is," she mumbled and handed over the incriminating document.

The moment it was out of her hands she regretted her decision. He would think her a silly woman. Why had she revealed so much? For the next two days she suffered excruciating humiliation. How could she bear to face him again? She almost decided to skip school on Thursday. But she didn't.

Mr. Goldenson returned the papers on Thursday in his usual manner, giving each person a smile or a quick comment as he handed over the paper. When he came to Yudi, however, he lowered his eyes and handed her the paper without a word. Yudi wanted to die.

There was an envelope clipped to her sheet. It had her name written across the front in his red-penciled scrawl. She tore it open with trembling hands. Inside was a note, written in red on a sheet of paper torn from a notebook.

Dear Miss Weisenberg. Judith. Yudi, my dear,

When I don't have you in front of me to drive me crazy, I have your compositions. This can't go on. The board of education frowns on fraternization between teachers and students, you know. I've been aware almost from the first that I'd have to tell you this, but I've been holding back for my own selfish reasons. Well, the time has come, so here goes. Miss Weisenberg, your English is too good for Level 3. You really ought to be upstairs in the Senior Advanced group, Level 4, with Mr. Atellino. I didn't tell you before because I didn't want to lose you. However, I have to be fair. It's your choice. If you wish to move up to Senior Advanced, please see me after class tonight and I'll arrange it. I'll be crushed, but I'll arrange it.

In all honesty I must tell you that Mr. Atellino is a very good teacher. He will love you. Please, Yudi, if you do go to him, don't love him back. He has a nice, fat wife and at least four children and doesn't deserve the extra blessing of having you to look at every Tuesday and Thursday night.

Sincerely,
Sam Goldenson

Yudi didn't let herself dare to believe what she was reading. She'd never received a love letter in her life, and she wasn't sure she'd received one now, but it certainly sounded like one. It was in English, of course, and there were phrases she wasn't sure she fully understood, but it really seemed to be a love letter.

Her heart bounced around in her chest like a balloon gone berserk. Could this beautiful, sweet, brilliant, wonderful man really care for her? After giving the letter a dozen readings, it still sounded like a love letter, and she still couldn't believe it. And there was Mr. Goldenson himself, standing up in front of the class, going on about the difference in pronunciation between "ship" and "sheep," and "slip" and "sleep," as if nothing unusual was happening. However, he didn't glance in her direction at all during the class. And he didn't call on her once. She was glad. She couldn't concentrate on the lesson for a moment. All she could do was read her beautiful letter over and over again.

After class had ended (and after she'd refused once again Mr. Susko's familiar invitation to go out with him for coffee), she picked up her books and her letter and went to Mr. Goldenson's desk. He was trying to appear unconcerned as he busily packed away his papers into his battered briefcase. But as he saw her approach, his movements ceased and his face fell. "Are you going to transfer to Mr. Atellino, then?" he asked, not even trying to disguise his disappointment.

She shrugged. "I don't know. What means 'frater . . . frater . . .'?"

"'Fraternization'?" He peered at her intently, one corner of his mouth curling up in amusement. "It means taking a student out to dinner."

She was puzzled. "Teachers are not permitted to eat with pupils in

344

America? But the other night in the cafeteria . . . you asked me—?"

"That would have been all right. That wasn't a premeditated invitation." He had to grin at her obvious confusion. " 'Fraternization' means that it's against the rules for a teacher to take a student out to dinner if the intentions of the teacher go beyond the eating."

Yudi's eyes widened. "Beyond the eating?"

"Yes, Miss Weisenberg." He sat down on the edge of the desk and took her hand, playing with it absently as he spoke. "If I took you to dinner, I would want to do more than eat, you see. After a while, I might even want to kiss you."

"You might?"

"I'm absolutely sure of it."

"Oh." Yudi was standing so close to him that she hoped he couldn'ı hear her heart beating. "And naturally, such things are not permitted by your board of education."

"No, they're not."

"I see." She lowered her eyes to the hand holding hers. It was such a large, strong hand, covered with blond hairs and bound at the wrist with an American watch with a leather band. She loved the manly look of it. "Is that why you say in the letter that I drive you crazy?" she asked in a small voice. "Because is not permitted to kiss me?"

"That's one of the reasons."

There was a long pause, during which Yudi kept her eyes on the masculine hand holding hers. Then she peeped up at his face. "If I go to this . . . this other class, would then this . . . fraternization . . . be permitted?"

His eyes lit up, and the grasp on her hand tightened. "Is that why you're considering the transfer to Mr. Atellino's class? So that we can fraternize?"

She smiled and nodded shyly. "I wouldn't wish otherwise to leave your class . . . ever."

"Yudi!" His voice was choked, and he lifted her hand to his face and rubbed his cheek against it. "I don't think I can bear to let you leave. To hell with Mr. Atellino and to hell with the board of education. Let's fraternize all we want. Come here!"

Before she knew it, he had her in his arms. "But Mr. Goldenson—!" she breathed, awed at his sudden daring.

"Sam," he said, beaming down at her. "I'll only be Mr. Goldenson to you on Tuesday and Thursday in class. It's Sam from now on." And he lowered his head to hers and, right there in the classroom, with the door to the corridor wide open, he began the fraternization.

8

*E*verything changed for Yudi after that. New York became a magical place with Sam as her consort and guide. He showed her
a world of wonders: museums, theaters, concert halls, parks, galleries,
libraries, restaurants, shops, playgrounds, and beaches. He taught English
in Boys' High in Brooklyn during the day, but on weekends they
explored the city together. And every weekday evening, too. On Tuesday
and Thursday there was class (where they carefully kept up the appearance of a distant formality) but on the other evenings they rode the
open-topped buses, walked hand in hand through the streets, sat shoulder
to shoulder in Carnegie Hall listening to Brahms, rode the subway to
Luna Park to gape at the lights, and kissed on a bench on Riverside Drive
until they were dizzy. Yudi found every day to be a marvelous adventure.
Life had taken a turning that was so wonderful it made up for all past
disappointments.

One Friday night she brought Sam to dinner at Cousin Joe's, on
Hannah's specific invitation. Hannah outdid herself and served a real flank
steak. A few days later, Sam returned the compliment and took them all
out to the opera. Hannah glowed in her best pink blouse, and Cousin Joe
was overjoyed at being given this opportunity to hear the tenor Edward
Johnson (who some critics said was the best tenor the Met had had since
Caruso) sing his most famous role, Pelléas, in Debussy's *Pelléas et Mélisande*. They sat in the second tier, all of them transported by the uncanny
beauty of the music. Joe wept unashamedly, and during the fourth act,
when the lovers sang their famous duet, with Pelléas's simple, stark

declaration *"Je t'aime,"* and Mélisande's equally stark *"Je t'aime aussi,"* Yudi felt Sam press her hand with a heart-stopping intensity. Later, when Sam took her home, they couldn't seem to shake off the emotions stirred up by the haunting, brooding atmosphere of the opera. He took her in his arms in a trembling embrace. *"Je t'aime,"* he muttered hoarsely, the words seeming to come from the depths of his being.

"Oh, Sam," she whispered into his shoulder, dissolving into tears, *"Je t'aime aussi."* For the first time she knew the feeling of love—the sort of love Dvora had tried to describe to her so many years before.

They talked so much together, Sam and she, that English was becoming comfortable on her tongue. But she didn't tell him very much about her past. She was so interested in everything about him that she always turned the conversation away from herself. There was so much he could tell her that she didn't know. He knew poetry and music and science and history. She could almost feel how her mind was expanding with all the new concepts he introduced to her awareness. He explained the theory behind Cubist art; he took her to see the most astounding films; he taught her about vitamins, automobile engines, democratic government, figurative language, and the best way to eat hot dogs. He introduced her to his friends and encouraged her to express her ideas to them—what she thought about Zionism, socialism, and European politics. She became more self-confident than she'd believed possible. She sometimes felt that she'd been transformed into someone very different from the ignorant girl she'd been when she'd arrived. Never had she felt so fully alive, so happy.

But there is no happiness that's completely pure. She could never forget that this joy was only temporary. In the back of her mind, behind every joyous moment, she could hear the ticking of the clock. It was like the poem Sam had read to her one day when they were spending a Sunday afternoon sitting on the sand at Coney Island: "But at my back I always hear/Time's winged chariot hurrying near." She had only a few months. The days were flying by with whirlwind speed. May and June, gone. Soon she would have to think about going home. And she'd done nothing to accomplish the task for which she'd been sent here.

She'd tried to tell Sam from the first that her time was limited. That her mother and Eli were waiting for her. That she'd given her word, and that her return passage on the *Mauritania* was already booked. She would sail on the second of September. She wanted him to be prepared. There wasn't much time left for them.

But Sam refused to accept the facts. "I'll never let you go back," he'd mutter angrily whenever she brought the subject up.

"I must, Sam. My visa runs out in two months."

"Hogwash! If you marry me, you'll become a citizen automatically. The visa means nothing."

"I can't marry you, Sam. I already am pledged. I *told* you—"

"I don't care what you told me. Pledges have been broken before. You don't love him, and I'm not going to let you sacrifice yourself just because he lost an eye. You're staying in America with me."

She couldn't let him say these things without an argument. She didn't want him to delude himself. He had to prepare himself, just as she had to prepare herself, for the end. "I cannot stay here, Sam. You must accept that. My mother has much need of me . . . and Eli, too. I couldn't hurt them to—how shall I say?—to snatch happiness for myself. I couldn't."

Eventually they learned to avoid the subject. They put aside thoughts of the future so they could enjoy the present.

But Yudi still had to find Avrum Gentz. She'd told Sam enough about her purpose in coming to New York so that he could help in the search. She told him, too, about the failure of her visit to the Merchants' Security Bank. He suggested that they might locate Avrum in another way. He took her to city hall so that they could consult lists—union lists, property owners' lists, immigration lists. They spent hours poring over dusty ledgers. But they found nothing.

The Merchants' Security Bank seemed the only answer. Sam made Yudi tell him exactly, in explicit detail, what had happened on her first visit. He listened closely to her account and then said he was afraid they would run into the same difficulties again. But after much discussion they concocted a scheme. It was tricky and a little dangerous, but it was the only way they could think of to get the necessary information. They reviewed the details of their plan several times before the day chosen for the actual enactment, and the night before, they rehearsed it as carefully as a play.

The next day, Sam took off the afternoon from school. With Yudi clinging to one arm and a businesslike leather briefcase under the other, Sam strode into the bank and approached one of the tellers. "I'm Sam Goldenson, attorney-at-law," he announced. "I'm here on a legal matter in connection with special account number 92018. I'd like to see Mr. Armstrong, please. Tell him it's a matter of some urgency."

To Yudi's delight, they were ushered into Mr. Armstrong's office after only a brief wait. Mr. Armstrong was taking a folder from his secretary's hand as they entered. He dismissed the secretary, put the folder on his desk, stood up, and shook Sam's hand. "Good afternoon, Mr. Goldenson. What may I do for you?"

"This is my client, Miss Gentz. She's retained me to locate her father. We have reason to believe that he has a special account here." He opened his leather case and pulled out a legal pad. "Account number 92018," he read with official importance.

Mr. Armstrong shook Yudi's hand and held a chair for her. Then he returned to his seat behind the desk. "That may be, Mr. Goldenson, but I don't see what I can do for you." He opened the folder his secretary had given him, glanced at it quickly, closed it again, and placed his hands on it. "These accounts are confidential, as I'm sure you're aware."

"Yes, but my client is not seeking privileged information. She doesn't wish to learn anything about the size of the account or any other matter of finance. She wants only an address where the man may be found."

"Surely you realize, Mr. Goldenson, that even *that* information is privileged."

Yudi sighed. She'd known from her first glance at Mr. Vincent G. Armstrong that he wouldn't cooperate. He was a man who lived by rules. She could see it in the way he placed his hands on the folder with such cold steadiness. She could see it in his detached manner and the precise way he tied his bow tie. Even the watch on his wrist, the clock on his desk, and the larger clock on the wall behind him gave him away: a man who needed three timepieces was not the sort who would be flexible.

"Yes, but there have been cases," Sam was saying, improvising wildly, "where family relationships have been established—"

Mr. Armstrong looked dubious. "I have no way of determining family relationships."

"No way? Of course you have. The similarity of names alone—"

Mr. Armstrong's eyebrows rose. "There *is* no similarity of names."

Yudi caught her breath. "No similarity?" She threw Sam a look of real confusion. "But there *must*—"

"But even if there were," Mr. Armstrong went on, "I couldn't reveal anything to her. There is no stipulation in our rules that relatives, even close ones, can be given information."

"I see," Sam murmured, giving Yudi an almost imperceptible nod. "Then there's nothing at all you can do for us?"

"I'm afraid not."

Yudi rose from her chair, her hand fluttering to her forehead. "Oh," she cried in a quavering voice, "I can't bear it! The disappointment . . . the shock . . . !" She wavered on her feet a moment, gave a long, low sigh, and slipped to the ground.

"Miss *Gentz*!" Sam gasped in very convincing alarm. "What's wrong?" He knelt beside her and picked up a limp hand. "Miss Gentz, *speak* to me!"

Mr. Armstrong came hurriedly around his desk. "Good God, what is it? What's the matter with her?"

"She's fainted," Sam said worriedly, not looking up from Yudi's face. "Water, I think. Can you get me some water?"

"Yes, right here."

Sam clenched his fist in frustration. He'd hoped the fellow would have to go out for the drink, but a pitcher of water and a glass were right there on the desk. He'd never even noticed!

Mr. Armstrong, agitated by this unaccustomed deviation from the way business was usually conducted in his office, poured some water into the glass with hands that were a bit unsteady. Then he came up to the still-kneeling Sam. "Here, try this."

"Will you try to force it between her lips, please?" Sam asked. "I'll look to see if she has some smelling salts with her." He reached for Yudi's handbag, which was lying on the floor beside her, got up, and began rummaging through it.

The banker hesitated for a moment, eyeing Sam dubiously, but a moan from Yudi drew his attention to her. He knelt down and raised her head to try to get her to drink.

As soon as he bent down, Sam turned to the desk. He whipped the folder around to face him, flipped open the cover, and ran his eyes over the top sheet. Then he closed it, turned it back to its original position, and leaned over the supine Yudi. "No, she has no smelling salts," he told the banker and began to chafe her wrists.

Yudi blinked and moaned. "Where—? What—?" she mumbled, opening her eyes.

"You fainted, Miss Gentz," Sam said. "Don't try to speak. Do you think you can stand? Here, let me help you up. We'll find a taxi and get you home."

"Yes, please. Take me h-home."

With Sam holding her under one arm and Mr. Armstrong under the other, she got to her feet. They led her to the door, which the banker sprang ahead to open. Relieved that the incident had passed without more inconvenience for him, Mr. Armstrong was eager to see them go. "I'm sorry to have had to upset you so, Miss Gentz," he said unctiously as Yudi passed him by. "But regulations must be—"

"We understand," Sam said, nodding at him. "Rules are rules, after all."

"Yes, that's my philosophy of life. We must live by rules if civilization is to exist at all. Good afternoon, Mr. Goldenson. I hope Miss Gentz will soon be feeling better."

Out on the street, Yudi looked up at Sam eagerly. "Did you see it?"

"Yes, I saw it," Sam said, his brow wrinkled in perplexity. "I saw it, but I don't understand it."

"What do you mean?" She stopped in her tracks and gave a gasp. "The name wasn't Gentz? Is that why Mr. Armstrong said there was no similarity?"

"Yes, that's why." Sam took her hand and peered down into her face. "Yudi, why did you and your mother think the person who sent the money was Avrum Gentz? The name on the account is completely different. In fact, it's *your* name. Weisenberg."

"Weisenberg? *Who* Weisenberg?"

"David Weisenberg. There was a home address in Gramercy Park and an office address on Thirty-eighth Street."

Yudi gaped at him blankly. "How can it be? I don't know any David Weisenberg."

"But you must. Isn't there a David Weisenberg in your family? An uncle? A cousin?"

"No, of course not. If Papa had ever spoken of a relation named David, wouldn't I remember? After all, my own brother's name was . . . Oh, my God! *Dov!*"

Sam stared at her. Her lips had turned white and her eyes had grown enormous. "Dov?" he echoed, uncomprehending.

"My brother! It *must* be!"

"You think this David Weisenberg is your brother? But his name is Gentz, too, isn't it?"

"Yes. Dov Gentz."

"And you said he went to Palestine."

"That's what we've all these years believed."

"Then, Yudi, sweetheart, don't jump to conclusions. The name is different; the country is different. It's foolish to imagine that this David Weisenberg is your brother."

"I know. It's . . . crazy." But she began to tremble as the idea took hold of her. If this David Weisenberg really was her brother, it would be a dream come true. To find Avrum Gentz was her mother's dream, but to find Dov was hers. Avrum Gentz was a shadow to her, but Dov was her dear brother. The empty space his departure had left in her heart had never been filled. But she was afraid to let herself believe it. To have found Sam was a miracle enough—to also find Dov would be too much to hope for.

She looked up at Sam, uncertainty written in her eyes. "It's foolish, I know. But also possible. Dov loved Papa so much, you see. He might have taken Papa's name when he came to a new land to begin a new life. Maybe he never went to Palestine after all. Maybe . . ." She pressed her hands to her breast to try to quiet her pounding heart. "Maybe, Sam, he's right here."

Sam didn't like to see her build up hopes that might so easily be dashed. He took her arm and began to walk again. "Look here, my sweet, you mustn't do this to yourself. You and your mother were so sure you knew the identity of the check sender that you had no doubts at all."

"Yes, that's so. Mama was so certain that she . . . persuaded me, too."

"Well, you were both wrong. Now you may be wrong again. Don't build up new hopes on the same weak foundation as the old. Hold on to yourself until we see the fellow. I have his address. We can pay him a visit at his home tonight."

Yudi stopped him again. "Oh, Sam, no. Till tonight is so long to wait!"

His face was troubled as he frowned down at her. "Yudi, wouldn't it be better to wait till you're calmer?"

"I'll never be calm till I know. Sam, my dearest, please! Let's go and find him . . . right now!"

9

The offices of David Weisenberg, C.P.A., took up half the ninth floor of a new office building on East Thirty-eighth Street. There was a list of five accountants who worked for him lettered on the door under his name. Sam didn't know what to think. This Weisenberg was evidently a successful professional man. It seemed unlikely that he could be the same person who'd run away from Solitava twenty years ago without a penny in his pocket. Nevertheless, it was this man who'd sent an anonymous check to Yudi's mother every year for seven years now, so he must have some connection with the family. Sam could only hope that his true identity would not be too great a disappointment to Yudi.

They opened the door and found themselves in a small reception area. Beyond was a long hallway with many doors, filled with the sounds of adding machines and typewriters. The reception area was lushly carpeted and contained two leather sofas and a low table to their right, and a large desk to their left. At the desk, busy on the phone, was a lovely blond woman who seemed to Yudi not much older than she herself. If this is really Dov's office, she thought, he's picked himself a beautiful secretary.

When the secretary hung up the phone, she smiled up at them. "May I help you?"

Sam took the initiative. "We'd like to see Mr. Weisenberg, please."

"Have you an appointment?"

"No, I'm afraid not. But it's urgent."

"I'm sorry, but he's not in right now. Is this in connection with one of our accounts?"

"No, it's . . ." He looked at Yudi as if asking for permission. "It's a personal matter."

The woman's eyebrows rose, and she glanced from Sam to Yudi and back again. Yudi got the distinct impression that there were few of Mr. Weisenberg's personal matters that she didn't know about. "May I have your names, please?"

Sam threw Yudi another questioning look. Yudi gave a tiny, negative shake of her head. "Goldenson," Sam told the secretary. "Samuel Goldenson."

The secretary smiled at him. "I'm Miss Simpson, Mr. Weisenberg's office manager. I expect him back within the hour. Do you care to wait, or shall I make an appointment for you?"

"We'll wait," Yudi said quickly. "Is that all right, Sam?"

"Yes, if . . . if you're sure you want to," he said, feeling very uneasy.

"Please sit down and make yourselves comfortable," Miss Simpson said.

Sam took hold of Yudi's elbow to lead her across the room, but Yudi didn't move. Her eyes were fixed on a framed photograph on Miss Simpson's desk. "Is that . . . Mr. Weisenberg?"

"Yes, it is," Miss Simpson said, looking at her curiously.

"May I take a closer look?"

Miss Simpson handed her the picture. Yudi took it to a lamp near one of the sofas and peered at it in the light. Sam followed her. "Well?" he asked.

"It's him! Sam, my knees are shaking."

"Yudi, take it easy. It's been twenty years. This man has a moustache. You can't be *sure*—"

"I'm sure. Here, give this back to her. I must sit down."

They settled down to wait. Miss Simpson returned her attention to the work on her desk, though she glanced up at them speculatively every few moments. The sounds from the hallway clattered and clicked. The clock on the cabinet behind Miss Simpson's desk ticked away. The phone rang somewhere in one of the offices down the hall.

Suddenly the door opened, and a man with a briefcase came in. Yudi's heart sank. It was not Dov. The man glanced absently at the two visitors, nodded to Miss Simpson, and walked down the hallway to a faraway door. Yudi couldn't bring herself to ask, but Sam looked up at Miss Simpson with the question plain on his face. Miss Simpson smiled and shook her head. "That was our Mr. Burka. All our accountants come and go like that. Mr. Weisenberg will be here soon, I promise."

Yudi was sitting on the edge of her seat, rigid with tension. Sam leaned back but kept a worried eye on her. The machines continued to clack away and the clock to tick.

When the door burst open, even a stranger could tell it was Weisenberg. There was an authority in his step and an expression in his face that told an observer that this was the man in charge. He was wearing a dark blue business suit, but his shirt collar was unbuttoned, his tie loose, and his hair untidy. "Maggie, damn it," he said peremptorily before he looked around, "what were the Finestein returns doing in the—?"

Yudi, with a gasp of recognition, had risen to her feet. Mr. Weisenberg froze, his eyes locked on her face and wide with shock. Sam and Miss Simpson watched in fascination, not knowing what to make of what they were seeing. No one moved for a long moment.

Miss Simpson broke the spell. "Dov, this is Mr. Goldenson, who says—"

"Yudi?" The name came from Dov's throat in a croak.

Yudi pressed her fingers against her trembling lips, but that didn't keep the tears from spilling out of her eyes. She couldn't say a word.

Dov's briefcase fell from his hand. *"Yudi!"* he shouted, so loudly that all the clicking and the clacking in the back rooms stopped. He grabbed her in his arms, lifted her from the ground and swung her around. "My little Yudi! Oh, my God, I'd know you *anywhere*!"

10

*T*here is no such thing as too much happiness, Yudi told herself. When one gets too much of anything, it results in pain of some kind, and that would be, in one of Sam's favorite phrases, a contradiction in terms. If there were such a thing as too much happiness, the surfeit would cause distress, like a too full stomach or a too rapid pulse. It would then be a disease, and the American doctors would have already identified the symptoms and come up with a name for it, like Overjoy or Hyperdelightsia. (They wouldn't have to worry about discovering a cure; the cure would be built into the symptoms: surfeit causes pain, pain cuts down happiness, end of problem.) But after feeling such an overflow of joy at finding her brother—and then learning from him that Dvora was also in New York!—the feelings within her were too overwhelming to bear. Those feelings were not unrelated to pain. She knew that large doses of happiness could not cause illness, but for a moment it seemed to her that if happiness *were* a disease, she would die of it.

But no, there was no such thing as too much happiness. Even Dov, whose joy at seeing his sister again was as great as hers, had had his happiness tempered by pain. Real pain. When Yudi told him about Mama—her stroke and her enormous courage in fighting it and in facing the debilitating and disfiguring consequences—he'd turned his face away and sobbed, great, dry, body-wrenching sobs that told Yudi clearly the extent of his love and his guilt. And then later, when she confessed the reason why Mama had sent her, his scorn and anger were also quite revealing. After all these years, Dov's feelings for Mama were such a mixture of love and resentment that they bordered on the abnormal. So, Yudi realized, even at happy times, pain is much too close.

That very night, Dov arranged for a chauffeured car to pick up Dvora and bring her to his Gramercy Park apartment, and the three of them had an emotion-filled reunion, all by themselves. They studied each other's faces, each remarking on how much time had changed them . . . and yet how little! There was enough of the familiar and the recognizable left in each of them to make them feel not in the least like strangers. Yet there was enough that was new and different to keep them talking for hours. Even at dawn they could not bring themselves to part.

After that night they saw each other frequently. Sam and Yudi went the next evening to Dvora's apartment in the Bronx and met Frieda. Seventeen-year-old Frieda charmed Yudi beyond words. To have a niece, blood of her blood, so bright, so beautiful, so American. She loved the girl at once.

Dov and Margaret met Sam and Yudi many evenings for dinner or a concert. Dov and Sam had much in common and took a real liking to one another. They both loved music, they both read the same sorts of books, they both enjoyed arguing about politics, and they both laughed at the same sorts of jokes. Yudi and Margaret got on well, also. Yudi admired Margaret's American loveliness and independent manner, while Margaret felt sisterly and protective toward the wide-eyed, innocent Yudi.

One evening less than two weeks after the reunion, Dov threw a wonderful party for the whole family. Margaret acted as hostess for him. Yudi came with Sam, Dvora came with Frieda, Cousin Joe and Hannah were invited, and even Hersh and his wife were present. When they had all gathered around the table in Dov's dining room, Yudi gazed with amazement at all the faces glowing in the candlelight, and a silent little prayer welled up in her: Oh, God, I thank you from the core of my soul for making us a *family* again!

Yudi and Dvora met frequently for lunch. They sat across the table from each other, looking at one another and beaming. They were so delighted to be in each other's company that sometimes they forgot to talk. When they did talk, it was more about present-day situations in New York than old times in Solitava. Yudi wanted to know everything about her brother and sister as they were now. "Why isn't Dov married?" was one of the questions she asked.

Dvora couldn't answer it. "Margaret is the sweetest creature in the world," she explained, "and she's been devoted to Dov for years. I don't understand our brother at all."

"Is it because she's a *shiksa*?"

"Yudi, don't be such a little *provincial*. This is New York, not Solitava. There's no Tzaddik here to tell Dov whom to marry. I don't think he cares whether she's Jewish or not."

"Then what is it?"

Dvora looked into her wineglass as if seeking an answer in the dregs. "I think it's Mama. Mama made him distrust women. I don't think he'll ever get married."

Yudi sighed. What Dvora said was probably true. Even Sam had remarked about Dov's "ambivalent" feelings toward his mother. Yudi, not knowing what to do about it, didn't like to dwell on the matter. "What about you, Dvora?" she asked, changing the subject. "Will you ever marry again?"

Dvora shrugged and lit a cigarette. "Who knows?" she murmured, brushing aside a lock of hair that persisted in falling loose from her short, stylish coiffure. "I'm thirty-four, but I've lived enough to be fifty. Sometimes I feel like fifty. I've had enough of love and its agonies. And I don't really need a man, you know. I have an income. I lost a great deal after the crash, but I'm still financially independent. So who needs to worry about love again?" She blew out a cloud of smoke and smiled wickedly at her sister. "Of course one can't make rules about such things. If I should meet someone like your so-appealing Sam, I might begin to feel very young again."

Yudi lowered her head and began to fold her napkin into pleats. "Yes, my Sam is appealing, isn't he?" She glanced up at her sister with troubled eyes. "Dvora, promise me you'll look after him when I'm gone. At least until he gets over the pain."

Dvora made a face of disgust. "Are you still insisting that you're going to leave him and go back home? Yudi, you're a fool." She stubbed out her cigarette impatiently. "Who says you have to make such a sacrifice of yourself?"

"Please, Dvora, don't start. I have enough of this argument with Sam."

"All right, I'll stop. But if it was me, I'd be damned if I'd give up my happiness for someone else's. Well, it's getting late. Come, Yudi, I'm taking you to my hairdresser to cut off all that awful hair of yours. If you insist on going back home, at least you're going back looking as if *some* sophistication has rubbed off on you."

So the minutes of July slipped away and August came. The time of her departure was looming up close, and its shadow was clouding the pleasure of her days. One day, when Sam came up to her room to call for her, he saw that she'd begun to pack her books. They had a dreadful quarrel about it, and he went storming off into the street. She flew down after him, and they had a tearful reconciliation. But the same disagreement cropped up again and again. Sam could not find it in him to understand her need to return to her homeland. He used every argument he could think of to dissuade her. A terrible time was coming for the Jews in Europe, he warned. He begged her to send for her mother. But Yudi knew her mother would never come. There was no argument he could give her, she told him, that would make wrong right.

In the end they had to part. She had more than two weeks before her departure, but she told him that they had to stop seeing each other. Their time together had become too painful, too quarrelsome. She wanted to remember only her happiness with him. The memories would soon be all she had, and she didn't want them spoiled. So, in hurt and anger, he went away.

She tried to cover her misery by keeping herself very busy. She shopped for wonderful American presents for all the family and friends in Solitava. She spent as much time with her American family as she could. She made a last-ditch effort to find Avrum Gentz (hating to have to face her mother with no word of him) by returning to city hall and going through more lists, but without success.

A week before the *Mauritania* was due to sail, Dov brought the family together again for a dinner in Yudi's honor. The spirit was not the same as it had been before. Everyone missed Sam, and everyone was dejected at the thought of losing Yudi again, perhaps forever. They all tried to smile and make optimistic predictions, but underneath was an undercurrent of sadness and loss.

The doorbell rang while they were at the table. Dov went to answer it. It was Sam. "It came to me while I was doing lesson plans for next term's English for the Foreign Born," he explained to Dov quietly. "I was making up a pronunciation drill. The sort of thing where you show the difference between vowel sounds: 'hat-hot,' 'bit-beat.' "

"What are you talking about, Sam?" Dov asked, completely puzzled.

"Listen, it's so simple. I was writing 'dance-dense,' see?"

"No, I don't see."

"Foreigners don't hear the difference right away. When they mean 'dance,' they say 'dense.' "

"So?"

"So people who deal with foreigners learn that after a while. We learn to understand them when they say, 'I'm going to a dense.' "

"Sam, are you drunk?" Dov asked affectionately. "You're not making any sense."

"Yes, I am. You see, it suddenly occurred to me that an immigration officer would learn the same thing."

"Okay, so he would. So what?"

"So what if a man got off a boat and said to the immigration officer, 'My name is Gentz'?"

Dov drew in a breath of comprehension. "Gentz-Gantz!" he exclaimed. "The officer might interpret it as *Gantz*! Is that what you're saying?"

"Exactly!"

"Sam!" Dov peered at him in astonishment. "You're not telling me that you've—?"

Sam gave him a pathetic smile. "Yeah. I had to. As a gift for her. It's the only thing she'd let me do for her."

Dov clapped him on the shoulder. "Well, come on in! She's at the table."

They walked into the dining room together, Dov's arm still around Sam's shoulders. Yudi gasped when she saw him. *"Sam—?"*

Dov shoved him over to her. Sam withdrew a slip of paper from his pocket. "Here," he said hoarsely, unable to give her a greeting or even a smile because his throat had tightened at the sight of her. "I've brought you a present. Avrum Gentz's address. I found him for you."

Part Seven
AVRUM
1933

1

Avrum Gentz's address! Such a gift to give me, Sam. All my life I'll be grateful that you did this thing for me. It was more than a gift, it was a marvel. Only you, with your inspired cleverness, were able to find him. And you handed your gift to me with so large a generosity—knowing that I could never give you such a gift. Yes, I know what you want to say—that there is only one gift you want from me. Oh, my dear Sam, it breaks my heart that I cannot give it. . . .

The address on the paper Sam gave Yudi was on Avenue C. Abraham Gantz, as Avrum was called in America, lived so close to Yudi's rooming house that she could have walked there. She might have passed him on the street or taken a seat beside him on the bus! The idea of such proximity made her shiver. It was strange how even the *idea* of her mother's first husband was awe-inspiring.

Dov and Dvora denied feeling that way. As they lingered at the table in Dov's dining room after everyone but Margaret, Frieda, and the three of them had gone, Dov and Dvora agreed that all they felt for the ghost named Avrum Gentz was a strong dislike.

"I don't know why you say that," Frieda said to her mother, her eyes shining with a speculative gleam in the light of the candles Margaret had set in the center of Dov's table. "If you ask me, I'd be wild with curiosity to meet someone like that—someone I'd heard about for years and never seen. Even if I disliked him."

"Well, nobody's asking you, *Plauderle,*" her mother said dismissively.

Frieda, spirited and independent for her seventeen years, would not be so summarily dismissed. "Listen to my mother, will you? That's her Viennese mode. She has three modes, you know—Yiddish when she's down-to-earth mad, American when she's acting the businesswoman, and Viennese when she plays the Countess."

"Hush, Frieda," Margaret said, taking the girl's hand and trying not to smile. She and Frieda had developed a secret understanding, and she could always keep Frieda from the excesses of rebellious adolescence. "You shouldn't tease your mother right now. This matter is too serious to joke about."

"*Ach,* it's not so serious," Dvora said, taking out her cigarette holder and lighting up, her gestures broad and theatrical to needle her daughter. "Yudi will pay the man a visit so that she can report back to Mama, and that will be the end of it. As Frieda would say, it's no big deal."

"Big deal or not, I want to go as soon as possible," Yudi said, studying the slip of paper Sam had given her with fascination. "Shall we go tomorrow?"

"Shall *we* go?" Dov pushed back his chair and stood up. "Who said anything about *we*? This is your project, Yudi. You go."

Yudi blinked at him through the candlelight. "You mean . . . alone?"

Dvora exhaled a thin column of smoke. "I don't mind going with you. I'll admit to having a morbid curiosity about the man. I'll meet you at Longchamps, Yudi, about three. We'll have tea and then go beard the lion. He should be in his den by five or six."

"Yes, good. But you come, too, Dov, please?" Yudi insisted. "You *must.*"

Dov pushed in his chair so roughly that it banged against the table's edge. "I haven't the least intention of going. The whole subject of Avrum Gentz bores me. It always has."

Margaret, who'd been watching him closely, reached into the fruit bowl for an orange and began to peel it with studied casualness. "It might be good for you to go," she suggested quietly.

"Ah, another county heard from," Dov sneered. "And by what devious reasoning do you conclude that it would be good for me?"

She kept her eyes on the orange, but a slight tremor in her fingers showed what courage it took for her to go on. "Avrum Gentz has always been a presence in your life. Much more important than he should have been, and much more important than you're ever willing to admit. You've been looking for a father since childhood. From the little clues you've given me over the years, I think you latched on too tightly to your stepfather because of it, and you found all sorts of substitutes later on—"

"Substitutes, eh? What substitutes?"

"There was that man in Warsaw—what was his name? Mendel, wasn't it?—and the fellow you're always visiting on Essex Street, Mr. Okay Epstein. Even your friend Hersh Waksman plays a fatherly sort of role in your life." She put down the orange and clenched her hands in her lap. "I know you don't like me saying these things . . . interfering in your family decisions like this . . . but I think the problem is that this man has always been a phantom rather than a reality. Perhaps if you could actually *see* the reality, you'd be able to lay the phantom to rest."

"Beautiful," Dov said, his voice dripping irony. "That's a beautiful analysis. Just the right combination of Freud and Christian mysticism. And what will you have to suggest if the visit doesn't lay the 'phantom' to rest? A seance? We could sit around the table with a Ouija board and exorcise the spirit of Avrum Gentz. Would that be your next suggestion?"

"Hey, take it easy, Uncle Dov," Frieda protested, jumping to Margaret's defense. "I think Margaret makes a lot of sense."

"And I think, Frieda," her mother remarked, "that you should stay out of this. Mama used to say—funny how I'm beginning to quote Mama now that my own daughter is old enough to talk back to me—Mama used to say that one should never interfere in a quarrel between lovers or blood relations."

"No, Dvora," Yudi objected, "let the girl talk. I agree with her. Margaret knows our brother better than we do. Dov, you *must* come. The man's your father, not ours."

"Don't be a *narr,* Yudi," Dov snapped, reverting to his childhood language without even realizing it. "I don't consider the man my father and never have. Why should I care about him? Avrum Gentz be damned!" He strode out of the room and down the hall. A moment later they heard his bedroom door slam shut.

The women at the table were shocked into momentary silence. Then Dvora stubbed out her cigarette. "Well, Yudi," she said with her Viennese shrug—a shrug that said she'd seen everything and that nothing mattered very much, "it seems that it will be just you and me tomorrow."

Yudi nodded, too crestfallen to speak.

Frieda reached under the table and squeezed Margaret's hand. "He didn't mean it," she whispered.

"I know," Margaret said. She lifted her head and looked from Dvora to Yudi and back. "He thinks ghosts are Gentile," she explained with a mirthless laugh. "Well, maybe the Holy Ghost is Gentile, but there are other ghosts. You Jews have some ghosts of your own."

She stood up and started for the door. Dvora grasped her arm. "Damn it, Margaret, you're not going to him now, are you? After the way he spoke to you?"

Margaret smiled down at her and shrugged, a good imitation of Dvora's own mannerism. Then, without another word, she followed her lover down the hall.

The next afternoon, Yudi and Dvora met at Longchamps, as planned. It was one of those hot August afternoons that cause New Yorkers (at least those who can afford it) to desert the city in droves. The mountains, the beaches, the suburbs—anyplace was better than sweltering under the steel and concrete towers of Manhattan. Those who had to remain, to man the buses, the trains, the stores, the offices, and the factories, spent such afternoons mopping up their sweat with already-soaking handkerchiefs and drinking cold soft drinks so that they could sweat some more. Manhattan on a hot August afternoon was like a place baking in some vast cosmic oven. If you had to be there, the only way to live through it was to get out of the sun.

Inside Longchamps the air was comparatively cool. Yudi and Dvora, looking clean and pretty in their soft, sheer cotton dresses, ordered iced tea and pastry. They sat sipping the first and poking at the second without saying much. They pretended to be casual, but Yudi at least was shaking with nervousness.

They sat twirling the ice in their glasses until almost five. Then they went out and hailed a taxi. It was time.

They asked the driver to drop them at the corner of Avrum's street. Avenue C was not unlike the street on which Yudi lived. The block was made up of a row of tenement buildings that all looked the same—all five stories high and all bearing rows of iron fire escapes like scaffolding over their facades. Interspersed between the stoops were a few stores, their wares seeming to spill out onto the pavement on the wooden market stalls that the owners placed out front and covered with merchandise when the weather was fair. There was the R&G Hosiery Company (STOCKINGS AND SOCKS FOR LADIES, GENTLEMEN, AND CHILDREN), Peck and Baumgarten (DISCOUNT SHOES), and Herman's Produce (FRUITS AND VEGETABLES, ALL FRESH). Today some of the "fresh" vegetables were rotting in the heat and filling the air with a decidedly rancid aroma.

"Phew," Dvora said as she walked purposefully down the street, her high heels clicking on the pavement. She tried to keep as much as possible in the shade. "The hero of Ilinghovka hasn't come very high up in the world, has he?" Her little Viennese nose was wrinkled in distaste.

Yudi carefully examined each doorway to find the number. She soon spotted it, right in the middle of the block, on the opposite side of the street. A man was sitting on the stoop. He was in his shirt sleeves, the jacket of his seersucker business suit folded over one arm. "Dvora, *look*!" Yudi whispered, grabbing her sister's arm in excitement.

Dvora swung her eyes away from her revolted examination of a pile of brightly dyed anklets in front of the hosiery store to where Yudi was pointing. There on Avrum Gentz's stoop, waiting for them in the broiling sunlight with a hand shading his eyes and a sheepish smile on his face, was their brother Dov.

2

"*H*e's not home," the woman said, peering at them curiously from behind the small crack she'd opened in the doorway.

"Oh," Yudi said, uncertain as to what to do next.

Dvora stepped forward impatiently. She hadn't come all the way from the Bronx in this heat for nothing, nor did she intend to stand about in this dank, smelly little hallway a moment longer than necessary. "May we come in and wait for him?" she asked bluntly.

"Whatdya wanna see him for?" the woman asked suspiciously.

Yudi put a hand on Dvora's arm to restrain her. Perhaps it wasn't wise to tell this woman too much. If she were Avrum's wife (which seemed likely to be the case), how much did she know about his past? Yudi certainly didn't wish to make any unnecessary trouble for Avrum Gentz.

Both Dvora and Dov were having similar thoughts. They all exchanged glances, realizing that they hadn't considered the possible ramifications of this visit in nearly enough detail. Dov, with a slight oh-well-the-fat's-in-the-fire-now look at his sisters, took the foremost position at the door. "Are you Mrs. Gantz?" he asked the woman in the doorway.

"Who else?"

"Well, we're . . . er . . . relatives of your husband's," he said. "From the old country."

Both Yudi and Dvora approved of his judicious explanation. But the woman at the door was still suspicious. Her eyebrows rose in surprise. "Relatives?"

"Relatives?" The echoed word came from inside—a woman's voice. "Let 'em in, Ma. We never met anyone from Pop's family before."

The woman at the door shrugged her shoulders and stepped aside. Dov crossed over the threshold first, and his sisters followed close behind. The door opened right into the living room of an apartment almost as hot as the street. They found themselves in a good-sized but drably furnished room facing two windows that looked out on the tenements on the other side of Avenue C. The windows were wide open to catch whatever breezes might happen by, but their dingy curtains didn't stir. In front of one of the windows was a kitchen table at which sat a dark-haired, good-looking young woman of about twenty-five. She'd been polishing her nails but was now staring at them interestedly, the little brush from her nail polish bottle poised in one hand. The woman who had let them in stood off to one side, wiping her hands on her apron. She appeared to be in her fifties. She was gaunt, her skin marked with the scars of an old infirmity, and her gray hair, untidily wiry, was held back from her face by a number of mismatched combs.

The three visitors, standing in an awkward group just inside the door, felt uncomfortable, their unease heightened by the momentary silence. Dov tried to alleviate the awkwardness. "I suppose we should introduce ourselves," he said. "These are my sisters, Dvora and Yudi, and my name is Dov. Mr. Gantz is, we think, a relative of our mother's. Her name is . . . was . . . Mindel Rossner. Did Mr. Gantz ever mention that name?"

"Rossner?" The gray-haired woman, still suspicious, shook her head. "I don't think so."

"Well, sit down, sit down," the younger woman said, waving her little brush toward the chairs at the table. "That's my mother, Nettie Gantz, and my name is Rhoda. Are you from Pop's hometown? What was the name of that town again, Ma? It was in Russia, wasn't it?"

"Sure it was Russia," Nettie Gantz muttered, "but who can remember the name?"

Dov couldn't believe his ears. Was it possible that the name of the town in which Avrum had been a hero was not a household word in his own home?

"It was Ilinghovka," Yudi offered shyly.

"Aha! That was it," Avrum's wife declared. The identification seemed to dissipate the cloud of suspicion that had persisted in her mind. "Well, sit, sit. I'll go get some tea with a little ice."

She went to the kitchen through a door to their right. Yudi and Dvora took places at the table, and Dov perched on the windowsill behind them. While Yudi and Dvora studied Rhoda Gantz with interest,

Dov studied the room. It hadn't occurred to him, as it had to his sisters, that the girl at the table, so busily polishing her nails, was his half sister —as close to him in blood as they were. The thought would have appalled him. But he was, at that moment, more interested in discovering some signs of his father in this room.

At first there seemed to be nothing. The room was characterless, with a sofa, a few chairs, and a radio—as commonplace a set of furnishings as could be found anywhere in the city. But then his eye fell on a desk in the corner of the room opposite him. It was a rolltop desk, but its cover couldn't possibly have been rolled down without a major cleanup, so crammed were its cubbyholes with papers and so cluttered its surfaces. Every possible area of the desk that could hold them was piled with books. Even the top drawers were pulled out so that their edges could support additional mounds of books. From his place across the room, Dov could identify them: shabby, worn copies of scriptural texts and commentaries, volumes and volumes of the traditional works of Jewish learning. Although he hadn't seen these sorts of books in years, Dov recognized them at once. It wasn't only their dark bindings and the distinctive style of the gold lettering on their spines; it was the familiar smell they seemed to exude. The smell brought him back to the time of his *bar mitzvah* in Solitava, to his Great-uncle Nathan's study house. That musty old-book smell was an unforgettable part of his childhood.

There were additional piles of books on the floor beside the desk and even underneath. There were piles, too, of Yiddish-language newspapers and assorted periodicals. And mixed among them were notebooks, clippings, and sheets of handwritten notes. Avrum Gentz was evidently still a scholar.

Dov could discover no other signs of him in this room. The one easy chair held a number of embroidered cushions, making it too feminine to be the seat kept for the man of the house. And nothing in the room's Woolworth-style ornaments or in the pictures of movie stars hanging on the walls would have been chosen by a man of scholarship. Only that one corner seemed to be Avrum Gentz's place in the world.

Yudi and Dvora, meanwhile, looked closely at Avrum's daughter. She might have been beautiful, Dvora decided, if she had any taste. But she didn't seem to know how to leave well enough alone. Rhoda had enviably high cheekbones and a strong cleft chin, but she'd cheapened her looks with a too heavy application of lipstick and rouge. Worse than all the rest was what she'd done with her hair, which she'd carefully curled, fluffed, and teased to resemble Joan Crawford's in *Grand Hotel*.

Yudi could detect the scorn in her sister's eyes, but she herself did not feel scornful. She felt a pang in her heart at the similarity of some of Rhoda's features to Dov's. The girl had a little something of him in the configuration of her mouth and chin, but the shape of their eyes was almost identical. It was painful to realize that this stranger looked more like Dov than either Dvora or herself.

The girl was looking at them with interest, too. "Did you all come to America recently?" she asked. "All together?"

"My brother and I have been here many years," Dvora said. "Yudi is here only for a visit. She wanted to see your father before she returns."

"Oh. That's nice."

Since Rhoda had asked them a question, Yudi now felt free to ask a question of her own. "Has Mr. Gantz . . . your father . . . any other children?"

"Oh, yeah. I got a married sister. She married a furrier, very well off. They live uptown."

Poor Avrum, Dov thought. No sons to whom to teach scriptures.

Nettie Gantz came out of the kitchen with a tray of glasses of iced tea. "Here, take," she urged, handing one to each of the visitors. "A little bit cold tea wouldn't hurt in this heat."

"Thank you," Dov said as he took a glass from her. "When do you expect your husband home?"

"Soon, soon. He's usually home from work by five-thirty. He has to change and eat, y'know, and be outa here by half past six. To get to *shul* on time."

"Tonight?" Dov asked in surprise. "It's not Friday."

The woman snorted. "You're telling me? You think I don't know what day it is? Lissen, my husband goes *every* night to *shul*. By him it's a second home." Her voice dripped scorn, not pride. "He'd rather be in *shul* than home. A *yeshiva bucher* he was born, and a *yeshiva bucher* he'll die."

The manner in which she spoke puzzled her guests. How could the wife of Avrum Gentz, whom their mother had so adored, speak of him so disparagingly? If it weren't for the fact that Nettie Gantz had recognized the name of his hometown and that Rhoda seemed to have inherited some of the same features Dov possessed, they might have begun to suspect they'd come to the wrong place. "What does Mr. Gantz do for a living, may I ask?" Yudi ventured timidly.

"He works for the city," Rhoda answered, not looking up from her nails.

Nettie Gantz gave a bark of a laugh. "Ha! My daughter likes to make us fancy-shmancy," she said with heavy sarcasm. "She don't like to say that her father's a maintenance man in the subway."

Dov felt something grip him in the stomach—a knot of physical pain. Why? he wondered. If the so-wonderful Avrum Gentz, the hero of Ilinghovka, had ended up as a maintenance man in the New York subways, why should he care?

Yudi, too, seemed to be affected by what Nettie Gantz had said. She stared at the woman for a moment with eyes widened by pain and then put down her glass with hands that shook. "There's nothing wrong with that, is there, Mrs. Gantz? Of good, honest work no one should feel ashamed."

"Maybe not," Nettie Gantz retorted sourly, "but being a maintenance man ain't nothing to be so proud of neither."

"Ma never gives Pop the time of day," Rhoda remarked indifferently.

"Yeah, well . . . I gotta finish making supper." The older woman started back toward the kitchen.

She hadn't reached the kitchen door when a key was heard in the lock. "There he is," Rhoda announced.

The door was opening. Dov, without realizing it, rose slowly to his feet. His eyes, and his sisters', too, were riveted on the widening aperture in the doorway. All three were aware of their beating hearts, for each one of them was suddenly conscious of the many years, the many miles, the convolutions and crisscrossings of events and people that had brought them here together to this confrontation. Dvora almost spilled her tea.

The man who was pausing in the doorway and looking at them with mild curiosity was a very ordinary man. They would never have given him a second glance if they'd passed him in the street. He wore a workingman's plaid cotton shirt, open at the neck, and a pair of stained pants. There were huge patches of wetness under his arms, and beads of sweat dotted his face, which was grayish with fatigue. He carried a lunch pail in one hand and a Yiddish newspaper under his arm. He was very thin—as gaunt as his wife—and stooped in the shoulders. When he took a step into the room, to peer more closely at the strangers at his table, his step was leaden, as if his thick-soled workshoes were too heavy for his feet. He was a tired, aging, sweating, very ordinary man.

My God, Dov thought, he reminds me of . . . of *Leib*!

Didn't they always tell us that he was supposed to be so big and handsome? Dvora asked herself. He's so *small*!

Yudi wanted to cry. She'd heard him described so often that she felt she'd actually *seen* him in his youth, so it seemed to her that she recognized him now. She could see how age had changed him . . . weakened and diminished him. She wanted to run up and embrace him so that they both could weep for the Avrum that had been. But the old Avrum wasn't all gone. She believed she could still recognize something of him in the full lips, the still strong chin, and the intelligence of his eyes.

"Look who's here," his wife was saying in the sarcastic voice that the guests were beginning to believe was habitual with her. "Relatives of yours from Russia."

"What?" He put his lunch pail and newspaper on the nearest chair, withdrew a pair of eyeglasses from his shirt pocket, put them on, and looked at the visitors, puzzled.

"Not from Russia," Yudi said, standing up and holding out a hand to him. "From the Bukovina. From . . . Solitava."

Bewilderment seemed to freeze on his face. "Solitava?"

"Yes. I'm Yudi. Mindel's daughter."

"Mindel?"

Oh, my God, Dov thought, groaning inwardly. He doesn't remember her! She's made her life a shrine to him, and he doesn't remember her!

"Yes, Mindel Rossner," Yudi was saying gently. "She married Leib Weisenberg after you . . . left. We, my sister Dvora here and I, are their daughters."

"Aha. I see." He took a deep breath as if to steady himself. "Well, well. How do you do?" He took her hand and scrutinized her face intently. "Weisenberg, you say? Are there no Weisenberg sons?"

"No. Just the two of us."

He nodded and turned to give Dvora a similar scrutiny. "Two daughters. Like me. I also have two daughters. Beautiful girls, like both of you."

"Thank you," Dvora said with a touch of dryness. "But you haven't yet met—"

"Don't tell me." The man's bright eyes flicked to Dov's face. "I think I know who that is." He moved slowly around the table to take a closer look at the man standing so stiffly in front of the window. "You're . . . Dov?"

So this strange, detached, cool old fellow remembered after all. "Yes, I'm Dov."

"Aha." He seemed quite interested in the son who had materialized in his living room after thirty-five years, but not overwhelmed. He examined his son with the sort of concentration he might give to a specimen in a museum. "You live in America?"

"Yes. Right here in New York. For fourteen years now."

"Aha. You look like a professional man."

"Yes," Yudi said, watching them breathlessly. "He's an accountant."

"C.P.A." Dvora added.

"Nice," Avrum Gentz nodded. "Very nice." He took his eyes from Dov with an effort, turned, and removed his glasses. He pulled a handkerchief from his pocket and began to polish them. With his attention seemingly fixed on the task, he asked Yudi, "And your parents . . . they're still alive?"

"Papa died a long time ago," Yudi answered. "But Mama . . . Mindel . . . is alive."

"And well?"

"Fairly well."

He kept his eyes on the glasses in his hand. "In New York?"

"No, she's in Solitava. She had a stroke and can't travel."

"Aha." He seemed to be a bit relieved.

"But she wanted me to . . . to give you her best wishes," Yudi explained, suspecting that Avrum would have been as reluctant to face her mother as she'd been to face him.

"That was good of her," he said, putting his glasses back on with a sigh. "Very good of her. How did she know . . . where I was?"

"She only guessed. We had a hard time to find you."

He nodded appreciatively. "To take so much trouble . . . it was . . . good of you."

"Well, I didn't want to go back without seeing you." Yudi felt impelled to say something more, something to make him a little more aware of her mother's feelings for him. "Mama would have been so disappointed if—"

"Who *is* this Mindel, Pop?" Rhoda asked. "The way you're all talking, she sounds like an old flame."

"Old flame, ha!" Nettie hooted with disparagement.

Avrum blinked at his wife and daughter as if he'd just remembered their presence. Then he turned back to Dov. "So what do you think of this family you didn't even know you had, eh, Dov, my son? And you, Rhoda? Do you know who is this big, handsome, successful professional man? He's your *brother!*"

Rhoda gave a loud guffaw. "Oh, sure, Pop, sure. What a laugh."

Her father threw her a quick glance. "It's so impossible that your father could have had a family once before?"

"Oh, quit the nonsense, will you, Pop? A family we never heard of?" She began to laugh again. "Did you hear that, Ma? He's such a nut, your husband. Did you hear what he said? Why ain't you laughing?"

Nettie Gantz merely shook her head in disgust. "If he wasn't *my* nut," she muttered, "I'd laugh, too."

Dov felt his blood freeze in his veins. He'd heard those words before. Great-uncle Nathan's house . . . the Hanukkah party . . . Papa telling a story . . . and Uncle Shmuel laughing and saying to Mama, "Why aren't you laughing, Mindel?" . . . and Mama's voice, nasty, cold, and filled with contempt: *"If he weren't my fool, I'd laugh, too."*

He felt a rumble in his chest—a laugh of such great proportions that he didn't think he could control it. It was so *funny*! He began to choke with suppressed laughter. He had to get out of here. He clapped his hand to his mouth. "Excuse me!" he choked and stumbled across the room and out the door, shutting it behind him.

Yudi and Dvora exchanged looks of alarm. "My brother seems to have . . . er . . . taken ill," Dvora said. "I think we'd better go after him."

"Yeah, well, I got to get supper on the table," Nettie said, "so if you're not staying . . ."

"No, thank you," Yudi said. She took Avrum's hand again. "It was good to see you. Mama will be glad."

Avrum put his other hand on hers, the still-keen light brown eyes meeting hers with a look of complete understanding. "Yes," he said, "I'm glad, too. Give her . . . give her my best."

Out in the hall, they found Dov sitting on the top step, whooping with laughter. "What's the matter with you?" Dvora demanded. "Have you gone crazy?"

He shook his head and tried to talk, but he couldn't. His shoulders heaved and his chest shook with the tremors of laughter that he couldn't seem to control. His sisters stared at him bewilderedly until he was able to catch his breath. "Didn't you catch it?" he gasped, wiping his streaming eyes. "It's so funny!"

"What, for God's sake." Dvora demanded. "What's so funny?"

"Didn't you hear what she said? 'If he weren't my fool, I'd laugh, too.' "

"What's so funny about that? It's only an old Yiddish saying," Dvora pointed out.

"I know. I heard Mama say it about Papa."

Dvora frowned at him in impatience. "So?"

"So don't you see it? Didn't you notice it at all? Mama's wonderful Avrum is Nettie Gantz's *Leib*!"

3

*W*hen he said goodbye to his sisters and put them into a taxi, Dov told them he was going back to his office. It wasn't the truth. He didn't want to admit to them that he was going back to see his father. His need to talk to the man was so strong it felt like a compulsion. There were a couple of things he suddenly felt he had to know from the man who'd sired him.

He waited on a stoop across the street, keeping his eyes on the doorway of Avrum Gentz's apartment house. The sun had not yet set, although it had sunk behind the building at Dov's back. His father would have to be coming out soon if he intended to get to his synagogue before sundown. If Dov's recollection of the ritual was accurate, the *mincha* service (in which all nineteen benedictions were read twice) had to be performed before dark. From the look of the rapidly lengthening shadows on the street, Dov estimated that he didn't have very long to wait.

In a little while, Avrum emerged from his building. He had changed from his workingman's garb to a dark suit, under which Dov could see the gleam of his stiff white collar. Now Avrum Gentz looked more like the scholar Dov imagined him to be. Dov crossed the street swiftly and overtook the older man in a few seconds. "Mr. Gantz," he said, falling into step beside him, "I took the liberty of waiting for you. Do you mind if I walk along with you?"

"Why should I mind? What I mind is that a son should call a father Mr. Gantz."

Dov smiled wryly. "We're not much of a father and son, though, are we? You didn't seem to be much moved by my sudden materialization after all these years."

"I didn't? Well, my son, don't be deceived by appearances. I've learned over the years not to show my emotions in my face. I subscribe, partly anyhow, to the philosophy of Zeno and the Stoics."

"That true wisdom lies in being superior to one's passions? Is that what you believe?"

The father glanced over at the stranger-son with a small smile of approval. "So you're familiar with the philosophers? I didn't know they teach those things in accounting school."

"I've been to a lot of schools. Like you, I imagine."

"Aha. If you mean life's schools, yes, I've attended my share." He turned and looked his son over carefully. He noted the well-cut hair, the expensive shirt, the tailored jacket Dov had slung over his shoulder, the polished shoes on his feet. "You, my boy, don't seem to have had too bad a time of it."

"Don't be deceived by appearances," Dov retorted drily. "It hasn't been a bed of roses."

"Aha." Avrum nodded wisely. "And you blame me for it?"

Dov's expression hardened. "For some of it, yes."

"Interesting. I haven't been a part of your life for—how many years is it? You must be thirty-three, thirty-four—"

"Thirty-six."

"Thirty-six. And you weren't even one year old when I left. For thirty-five years I've been out of your life. And yet you believe that your troubles were in some way my fault?"

"Yes, damn it, they were!" The vehemence of the outburst surprised Dov himself. He wasn't sure where this astounding antagonism had come from. He knew it was ridiculous to maintain his old feelings of hostility to this modest, aging, battered old man, but he couldn't seem to help himself. "Did it ever occur to you, Mr. Philosopher, that an absence can have as great an effect as a presence? Sometimes a very pernicious effect? Can you imagine what it was like to grow up hearing about the great Avrum Gentz, the wonderful, brilliant, remarkable Avrum Gentz, the hero of Ilinghovka and the eternal beloved of Mindel Rossner Gentz Weisenberg, all the while trying to understand why this great man didn't think enough of the wife and son he'd left behind to try to come back to them?"

The old man's eyes were wide with shock. "*That's* how they talked about me? The great Avrum Gentz?"

Now Dov was taken aback. "You're surprised?"

"Surprised is not the word. Flabbergasted is more like it. I was driven out of Solitava like a whipped dog, with my tail between my legs and my nose sniffing on the ground. *That* was the great Avrum Gentz?"

"They never spoke of you as a whipped dog. You were described to us—to my sisters and me—in terms that were entirely in the superlative. Avrum Gentz, the cleverest, the handsomest, the wittiest, the strongest—"

Avrum's chortling laugh cut him short. It had a hollow, bitter sound. "Take a good look at me, my son. Do you see any of that in *this man*? Is it my fault you've let yourself believe a fairy tale?"

"A fairy tale?" Dov felt his anger recede. The man had a rather humble image of himself, and humility was not a characteristic he'd expected to find in his father. But he hadn't expected to find him a lowly laborer in the subway either. Life must have dealt very harshly with this man. Almost against his will, Dov let a surge of sympathy seep through the wall of his antagonism. He couldn't help it. Avrum seemed to have fallen very far from his bright beginnings. He wondered how his mother would feel if she knew. "It was no fairy tale to my mother," he said quietly.

"No?" Avrum shook his head in amazement. "Are you telling me that Mindel kept alive the memory of my old self all these years? Astounding. To have clung so long to something so unreal."

"It was the most real thing in her life. Didn't you think it would be? Why didn't you ever try to go back to her?"

"Aha. Now we have the real question, eh?" He peered at this stranger who was his son with piercing intensity. "Is this what you've come to me to find out?"

"Maybe it is. I'm not sure."

They walked on a while in silence. Then Avrum spoke, thoughtfully, hesitantly. "How can I explain such a thing? I don't know if you will be able to understand. When I first married your mother, I was someone else. It was another life."

"Nonsense," Dov cut in coldly. "Those are only words. Pretty words, maybe, but only words. 'Another life.' That doesn't *mean* anything. It was your life, just as this, today, is your life. I'm asking for truth—don't give me sophistry."

"Oho, it's truth you want, is it?" The older man stopped walking and looked at Dov mockingly. "Only truth? That's all? And where shall I find it for you, eh? You think I have it here in my pocket in a nice little package, all wrapped up in cellophane, maybe, stamped and labeled and sealed with a guarantee from the U.S. government: 'In Here Is Certified Truth'? Listen, mister, all I can give you is *my* truth, as it seems to me. I can't tell you it's your truth, or Mindel's truth or even God's truth. I can only say it's mine." His eyes glittered with a spirit Dov hadn't seen before. "My truth. You want it or not?"

Dov's eyes fell. "Yes, I want it. I . . . I'm sorry."

"Don't be sorry. I like it that you challenge me. It makes me feel less like a stranger to you." He resumed his walk. "So, where was I?"

"That it was another life."

"Yes, it was, whether you believe it or not. Tell me, Dov, don't you think it's possible for people to be different beings at different times in their lives? Just for instance, do you remember exactly where you were when you were twenty years old?"

"Yes, I do. I remember exactly."

"Well, tell me. Where were you?"

"I was in a prison camp in England."

Avrum looked at him with surprise. "In prison?"

"Yes, but let's not divert our attention from the point. Were you trying to prove that I was a different person then?"

"Weren't you?"

Dov tried to remember. Knockaloe . . . the desperation . . . the endless war . . . the attachment to Steigmuller, the Marxist, who'd been like a father to him (Oh, God, Margaret, another father figure!) . . . the uncertainty, the innocence, the feeling of having lost his grip on his fate. "I don't know. Maybe I was."

"So give me the benefit of the doubt. My truth is, I was another person. I think in my own mind I was, then, like a young prince. I believed I could do anything, accomplish miracles. I had very early won the respect of my parents, my teachers, my friends. I won the struggle with the rioters in the Ilinghovka *pogrom*. I even won your mother, which, believe me, was no small achievement. I remember believing that I held the future right here in the palm of my hand."

"Yes," Dov said softly, "I know that feeling."

"Aha." Avrum threw him a small, triumphant smile. "You had it, too. And lost it, no?"

"I lost it, all right. Life slaps down that pretension pretty early."

His father nodded appreciatively. "Then you will, maybe, understand how enormous was the change for me when life slapped me down. I left Solitava a different person. All of a sudden I had nothing, I knew nothing.

Something . . . how shall I say? . . . something basic, important, was gone from me."

Dov knew all too well what he meant. The grip on the future. It was shattering to the personality to lose it. He remembered those times in his own life when he became aware that his sense of being in control of his destiny had weakened. When Papa died. When they took him to Knockaloe. When the war ended and he'd felt directionless and lost. For him it had come little by little, step by step. But for Avrum Gentz it had come all at once, in one terrible, shocking blow.

His father had stopped walking. "There's the *shul,* down on the next block. We don't have much time for this now. I don't know, my son, if I can make you imagine my situation even if we had all the time in the world. But let me try to explain in a few words what those next years were like for me. I managed to find work—menial work was all I was good for—here and there. I scraped and starved and saved my pennies till I made it to America. America was going to be my salvation, where I would once again recover that sense of myself—the self I'd lost. Then, maybe, I could recover the rest. I would be a prince again. But when I got here, what did I find? I found I was a cipher . . . a zero . . . a nothing. What did I know but scriptures? And you know what was worse? There were thousands just like me . . . Jewish scholars with their heads in the clouds and no skills with which to earn a living. *Luftmenshen.* We would go from door to door offering to teach Hebrew to the children for a penny a lesson! Who needed Jewish scholars in America? We were a dime a dozen. Believe me, I was lucky to get a day's work hauling bricks for the bricklayers on a construction site. It began to seem that what I'd been before was a dream . . . that it had all been imagined in my head . . . a life that never was."

"But you knew it wasn't a dream, didn't you? You knew you'd left a real, living family behind."

Avrum sighed deeply. "In a way I knew. It wasn't so much that Mindel and the baby and Solitava had become unreal. What was unreal was the old Avrum. I couldn't anymore believe that I had ever been that princely fellow. And, more than that, I couldn't believe that *anyone else* had ever thought of me that way. I had become a nothing, and that was my reality. All the rest was illusion. So, as one does with dreams, I put the past out of my mind. Believe me, it was enough of a struggle to deal with the reality of my present."

Dov did understand. What had happened to his father was, after all, not so very strange. Dov could see that a man who'd lost his sense of himself had not wanted the woman who'd loved him at his best to see him at his worst. Yudi had said that Mama felt the same way now—that she didn't wish for Avrum to see how she'd changed. Each wanted to preserve in the mind of the other the unaltered vision of the past. It was a very human failing, to choose to preserve an illusion rather than to face the reality. He couldn't hate Avrum for it, or Mama either.

They resumed their stroll toward the synagogue. "Did I answer your question?" Avrum asked.

"Yes, you did. Thank you for it. It will help, I think."

"Help?"

"To lay my ghost. But never mind about that. Are you willing to answer another question? A more personal one?"

"Why not? What secrets should a man keep from an only son?"

"You said you put the past out of your mind. Does that mean you forgot my mother? Stopped caring for her?"

"No, no. How could I ever stop?"

"But you married again."

"Sure I married again. It was a different life, agreed? A different life."

"But if you still loved Mama—?"

Avrum smiled broadly. "Let me ask *you* a question, my son. You're not a married man, are you?"

"No, I'm not. How did you guess?"

"Because you talk like a romantic. A married man isn't so romantic about love. He learns that the pairings we make in life aren't so significant as they seem before we make them. When we're young, love seems to us something miraculous—so special, so important. But when we're married a while, even the miraculous becomes . . . well, everyday. By the time a man gets to be my age, he begins to see that most people are essentially lovable, at least for the purposes of everyday life. So, to answer your question, yes, I loved your mother when I married Nettie. But the fact that Nettie was willing to join herself to such a nothing as I was made me very grateful. So I loved her, too."

So I loved her, too. Just like that! Dov found the statement utterly amazing. Avrum hadn't been able to have the love he wanted, so he simply loved the one he had. How was it that he'd been able to do it while Mama couldn't? Was it just a question of lowered expectations? Had his diminished self-image made it possible for him to accept into his heart a lesser love, while Mama, whose self-image had remained intact, could not do it?

There were really two opposing views of love here, he realized—

his father's and his mother's. His father had said that even the "miraculous" love becomes mundane. What were his words? "A man . . . begins to see that most people are essentially lovable, at least for the purposes of everyday life." What he probably meant was that one couldn't really expect to find Paradise in marriage, or in any earthly institution. In fact, even a miracle marriage (like Mama's to Avrum) might begin to seem mundane after years of hurried breakfasts, crying babies, nasty in-laws, cold bedrooms, stale coffee, undone laundry, underdone roasts, overdue rent payments, short tempers, long silences, and all the rest of it. Avrum was probably able to wed his sour-tongued Nettie because he no longer expected a heaven on earth.

But Mama would not feel that way. Had Mama been, like Dov himself, too much the romantic? Had she built a romance in her head that was never real? Was the reason Mama had clung too strongly to her memories simply that her marriage to Avrum had not lasted long enough to become mundane, and she had therefore overvalued it? Or was it truly, for her, a love that was unique . . . a uniqueness that became, for Avrum, only an illusion. After all, illusion and reality weren't absolutes. What might be an illusion in one mind might well be reality in another. Maybe it was even possible that Mama's vision was more true than Avrum's. What, after all, was truth? As Avrum had said, it wasn't something solid that you could package and label with certainty. It was more like the wind—you might grab hold of a breath of it in your cupped hands, but you could never be sure how much you held or even if that little bit you'd caught had any significance at all.

He looked over at Avrum curiously. "This everyday sort of love you describe you feel for your wife . . . that isn't the same as what you felt for my mother, is it?" he asked.

"No, not the same. Different people, different love. You should know that by now. Thirty-six years old, you should have learned more."

Dov threw him a rueful grin. "I suppose I should. On the subject of love I seem to be a very slow learner."

Avrum patted him on the shoulder. "Don't worry about it, my son. You're still young, healthy, good-looking. You have time."

"Maybe. But say, speaking of time, you don't have much. Look how dark it's getting. Won't you be late?"

Avrum stopped in his tracks. "*Oy vay,* I even walked past the *shul*! I missed *mincha* for sure. It shows how a conversation with a long-lost son can distract a man. Come, it's only back this way a few steps. You'll see why we walked right past it. It's not much like Nathan's synagogue in Solitava."

Avrum's *shul* was not impressive. It turned out to be the kind that's housed in a converted store. The conversion was not complicated. They had simply painted the insides of the two glass display windows in front and marked the conversion by affixing a six-pointed star to the door. "No, it's not much like Solitava," Dov agreed.

"Would you like to come in?" There was something shy in the way Avrum made the request.

Dov hesitated. After their hour of intimacy, he felt unwilling merely to walk away. Yet his head was swimming with inchoate emotions, and he wanted very much to go home and sort them out.

Avrum was watching him from the corner of his eyes, his head cocked like a curious, uneasy bird. From his expression, Dov guessed that he, too, was unwilling to sever the intimacy of their brief meeting. It was the older man who spoke up. "Come," he urged. "Come take a look at what has become the most important part of your father's life."

Dov gave a nod of agreement and followed his father inside. There were fewer than twenty men in the long, narrow room. The afternoon service was evidently over, for the men were standing about in small groups or casually lounging on the benches reading or dozing. They were waiting for the official hour of sundown to begin their evening service. But they all looked up when Avrum entered, and it was immediately clear to Dov that, to them, someone important had come in.

"Ah, Gantz, there you are!"

"Abe! You missed *mincha*! I had to read the benedictions."

"And you know Endermann—how he mumbles the benedictions."

"Gantz, did you see the *Forward*? What do you think of what Mandelstam wrote?"

"Listen, Abe, we can't decide if we should write an answer. If we should answer, will you write it?"

He was immediately surrounded. Before he was borne off, he threw Dov a look of amused helplessness. "Sit down," he called. "Make yourself at home."

Dov nodded and signaled him to go ahead. "I'll be fine," he assured his father with a smile.

There was only a minute or two before the evening service, so everyone tried to get Avrum's attention at once. Even the man whom Dov took to be the Rabbi seemed to need his approval for something. Avrum looked contented and completely at home. Dov gazed around at the unadorned room with its Spartan benches and dirty walls. So it was here, he realized, on the lower East Side of New York, in a tiny, store-fronted synagogue among a handful of aging, shabby, displaced

Jews, that Avrum Gentz, the hero of Ilinghovka, had found his place.

The evening service, the *maariv*, began, and Avrum, wrapped in his prayer shawl, stood among his friends nodding and swaying over the prayer book as he recited the age-old prayers. Dov sat in the back, watching. He felt strangely tranquil. He had met Avrum Gentz, and there had been no thunder, no explosion, no emotional outpouring. Yes, there had been discoveries—even revelations of a sort—but they'd not been earthshaking. What he'd learned was surprising and not surprising: that the man was full of contradictions. A laborer and yet a scholar. Despised by his family, yet loved by them, too. Scornful of himself but respected by his peers. Sometimes sounding foolish, but often sounding wise. Ordinary and yet extraordinary. A man.

As Avrum stood there among the worshipers, he seemed to grow in stature and in dignity. Dov could see something of what his mother must have seen all those years ago. For so many years he'd hated his mother for loving this man. Now he felt forgiving. His mother had believed she'd had a great love and a great loss. Who was he to judge her or blame her? Her only mistake had been in deciding that loving anyone else would make her disloyal to that love. She'd withheld love from Leib Weisenberg, and that had been the cancer that had destroyed the family. The thing she'd failed to see—and that he himself had not realized until this moment—was that giving love was not a finite thing. One could give a full share of love to one person and still have a heartful left for another —for many others. Like the milk in the magic pitcher, the more you spilled out, the more you had. But if you *didn't* pour milk from the pitcher it turned sour. And the soul, too, turned sour when love was held back. That was the mistake his mother had made. But he couldn't hate her for it. Wasn't he guilty of the very same sin? He'd kept himself from caring for Avrum in his loyalty to Leib. And, most troubling revelation of all—wasn't he holding back from Margaret, too?

The service droned on, and the hour grew late. Someone had opened the door, and a breeze blew in from the street. It was cooler now, and the murmuring sounds of the prayer were soothing. Dov didn't want to leave. He felt so relaxed, and his spirit was at peace. He'd stay a while longer. He'd mingle with the men at the end of the service and let Avrum introduce him. He wanted to hear Avrum Gentz tell them proudly, "This is my son." He knew Avrum would feel proud. And he—oh, God, what a tremendous surprise!—he'd feel proud, too. That's what felt so good. He'd found his father.

Much later that night, he lay in bed remembering it all. Margaret, curled up beside him, had not spoken much that night. Her head was on his shoulder, and he was stroking her bare arm, but his mind was still savoring the details of the evening he'd just spent. The voices, the hand-shakes, the slaps on the back . . . "Rabbi, I want you should meet my son. Yes, really, my one and only son." . . . "So, Abe is your father? Isn't it wonderful? Such a miracle, that you found each other! . . . a fine man, your father, the finest!" . . .

"Dov?" Margaret's voice broke into his reverie, dissipating the sounds like a bell rung under a tree that scatters the birds into the air in a flurry.

"Hmmm?" He kept stroking her arm, long, smooth strokes that took forever to go from shoulder to elbow.

She lifted her head and looked down at him. "You went today, didn't you?"

"Went? Went where?"

"You know where! You went with your sisters to meet Avrum Gentz."

"Yes. How did you guess?"

"I don't know. Just a feeling. Well, tell me."

"Tell you what?"

She picked up a pillow and swatted him with it. "How was it? *Tell* me!"

"It was fine. I liked him."

Her eyes widened. "You *liked* him?"

"I liked him a lot."

"Oh, Dov!" She slipped both arms about him and buried her head in the curve of his shoulder. "I'm so glad!"

He laid his cheek against her hair. "You know, Margaret, I've been thinking." His hand resumed its slow, gentle stroking of her arm. "It's stupid of us to live like this . . . like we're holding something back from each other. We love each other, don't we? I think it's time you stopped stalling."

"*I* should stop stalling?" Her head came up again, and she peered through the dimness to read his face. "*I?*"

"Yes, you. It's shocking how you've avoided matrimony all these years. I think it's time you let me make an honest woman of you."

She drew in a gasping breath. "Dov! Lord, that must have been *some* meeting you had tonight."

"What kind of answer is that? I'm asking you to marry me, woman!"

"Oh, is *that* what you're doing? It's hard for me to be sure. The words are so damned unfamiliar."

"Well, I am. So what do you say? Are you just going to sit there staring down at me like I've turned into a frog? Or are you going to say yes, give me a kiss, and turn me into a prince?"

She dropped her face into her hands. "Oh, Lord! Yes, yes, *yes*!"

He pulled her hands away and drew her down to him. "Thank you, my love," he whispered. "I promise I'll be a better man to you than I've been."

She brushed back the hair from his forehead. "I don't wish to sound overeager," she murmured into his ear, "but when do you envision this unprecedented event will take place?"

"Oh, I'm not in any hurry. You probably have a lot to do . . . a special dress, a hat, and all those other wedding-type things. And getting the family together. And licenses and blood tests and arranging transportation to city hall. I'll give you all the time you need. What do you say to tomorrow afternoon?"

4

In the end, Sam, we all found our peace, except Mama. That's why I must go back to her. I can't buy my happiness if others will have to pay the price of it. I write this letter to make you see what that price will be. I hope it helps you to understand.

I have not written this with crying and unhappiness. Really, I am feeling a good measure of contentment. I've found my brother and sister, and that is a joy I never expected. I've seen Avrum and can tell Mama her message was delivered. And most important, I've experienced the kind of love that the poets sing of (as they did in our special Pelléas et Mélisande), *that not many people are fortunate enough to have. And even though I have to say goodbye to you, I'll always have the comfort of my memories. They will be always perfect, always young, always unspoiled. They at least are something to hold on to. And you can have them, too, if you don't kill them with anger and resentment.*

Goodbye, my dearest Sam. I shall never read a poem, listen to a piece of music, hear the word "America" without thinking of you. Je t'aime aussi.
Yudi

5

"My God, Sam, you look terrible," Dov exclaimed, leading his friend to a chair in his office. "Haven't you slept?"

"How can I sleep when the *Mauritania* sails in less than a week? I haven't been able to eat or sleep since I got Yudi's letter. She intended it to comfort me, but it only made things worse. If she leaves on that boat, it means a bleak life for both of us. That's why I sent you the letter, Dov. I thought it would help you see how I feel. Did you read it?"

"I did. Every word. It was some letter. I sent it on to Dvora. I hope you don't mind."

"I don't mind anything, except that Yudi's going. Did you talk to her, Dov? Did you try to reason with her?"

"No, I'm sorry. I haven't seen her since the wedding. I didn't even see the letter until yesterday, when I got back to the office from my honeymoon."

Sam, confused, gaped at Dov with red-rimmed eyes. "Honeymoon? When—?"

"We got married on Sunday. And I gave my bride a one-day honeymoon at the Waldorf. Did you every hear of anything so bourgeois . . . and *goyishe*?"

"You and Margaret?" Sam shook his head, envious. "It sounds wonderful to me."

"Do you want to hear something else that's wonderful? Guess who stood up with me, thanks to you."

Sam blinked up at him as realization of what Dov was hinting at slowly dawned on him. "You can't mean . . . not Avrum Gentz?"

"The very same." Dov leaned over and clapped Sam on the shoulder. "It was because of you, Sam. You, with your schoolteacher's intuition —you found me a father."

"I'm glad, Dov. Really glad for you."

Dov went back to his desk and leaned on it, sighing. "Yeah, but that doesn't help you with your problem, does it? I wish I could help you, Sam. I don't want Yudi to leave any more than you do. But she's adamant."

Sam dropped his head in his hands and groaned. "I know, I know."

"You won't want to hear this, Sam, but I don't think her decision is wrong. My mother needs her—she has no one else. I've thought about this a lot, especially after reading that letter, but I can't think of anything else to do. I'd move heaven and earth to get my mother here, but Yudi is sure she'd never come. So what other choice is there?"

"I don't know, but there must be something." Sam got up from his chair and paced about the office, awash in misery. "I tell you, Dov, I can't let this happen. Aside from my own desire to keep her here, I can't see permitting her to return to a Europe that countenances a Hitler. Who knows what's ahead for the Jews there? Dov, I can't let Yudi get on that ship!"

"Poor Sam," came a cheerful, feminine voice from the doorway. "But cheer up, *Liebling*. Help is on the way."

"Dvora," Dov greeted her, "what brings you all the way from the Bronx?"

Dvora floated in on a swish of silk voile and the scent of expensive perfume. "Yudi's letter brings me, what else?" She kissed her brother's cheek and turned to do the same to Sam, but his disordered appearance arrested her. She wrinkled her nose. "*Ach,* Sam, you're a disgrace to your profession. How can you expect to win your fair maid if you insist on looking like someone who sleeps in alleyways?"

"Never mind how I look," he said, his eyes eager. "What were you saying about help being on the way?"

"It's here, my dear. Right here. *I'm* going back to Europe in Yudi's place."

The two men stared at her, stricken speechless. With a trill of laughter at their shock, she lowered herself gracefully into the chair Sam had vacated and opened her bag for a cigarette while they gaped. "You're crazy," Dov said when he could find his voice.

"Why crazy?" His sister calmly fitted a cigarette into her holder. "Why must it always be Yudi who plays the *gute*? I'm Mindel's daughter, too."

Sam could hardly breathe. Though afraid to let himself believe in this new possibility, he couldn't prevent his stomach from flipping over in wild hope. "Do you mean you *want* to go?"

Dvora gave her expressive shrug. "Why not? I haven't laid eyes on my mother for twenty years. I've always wanted to go back, if I could return like a queen rather than a little drudge or a worn-out whore. After I read Yudi's letter, I realized not only how much I wanted to go but that I really *can*. My income isn't much to speak of here, but in Solitava it will get me the very best house in town. Mama and I will really enjoy it. We'll even be able to afford a couple of serving girls, which would be quite impossible for me here, I assure you. There, I can live like the nobility."

Dov sank down on his chair, utterly bewildered. "I can't believe my ears. Are you saying you'd prefer Solitava to New York?"

"What have I got in New York that's so wonderful?" She lowered her eyes to the unlit cigarette in her hands, her expression suddenly devoid of the theatrical excitement that had animated it since she arrived. "I live in a four-room flat over a store. In a month, Frieda will be going away to Radcliffe, and I'll be alone. What's so wonderful about that?"

"But Dvora . . . *Solitava*?"

"I dream of it, Dov, do you know that? It seems so beautiful in my memory. Peaceful and rustic and . . . innocent." She lifted her eyes to her brother's face. "I think I'd like to go back to that innocence again. Maybe I can make up to Mama for . . . some of the past. I'd really like to try. And, you know, I think I'd even like to see Eli again."

Dov rubbed his forehead, trying to take it all in. "Have you spoken to Frieda about this?"

"Of course. She thinks I'm being wonderfully noble. She says I remind her of Sydney Carton." She laughed and struck a pose with her hand on her breast. " 'It is a far, far better thing that I do—' "

Sam could no longer contain himself. He crossed the room, grabbed Dvora by the shoulders, and pulled her to her feet. Her bag and cigarette holder slipped to the foor unnoticed. "Are you really sincere about this, Dvora?"

"As sincere as I've ever been. Don't you men believe me when I say that I've really missed my mother?"

"Yes," Dov put in, "but this is more than a visit. It's a commitment for a lifetime."

"I know that. But you know, Dov, I've always been more European than American." She broke into her lilting laugh. "And when the *shtetl* atmosphere begins to irk me, I'll go off to Vienna for a week. So there!"

Sam pulled her into a bear hug. "Thank you, Dvora. With every cell in my body I'm grateful. I'll love you till my dying day for this!" He kissed her and turned away, too overwhelmed to let them see his face.

Dvora looked at his back with a fond smile. "I think Sam should be the one to break the news to Yudi, don't you, Dov?"

"Of course. Well, go on, slowpoke. What're you standing around here for?"

Sam looked up. "You mean it? You don't mind if I—?"

Dov pushed him to the door. "Go ahead, will you, before that ship sails with *both* my sisters aboard."

Sam paused at the door. He looked back at Dvora with a suddenly troubled frown. "I have to say this, Dvora, in good conscience. You have to know exactly what you're doing. You're going back to a Europe that is becoming a very dangerous place for Jews. Before you make your final decision, you must realize—"

"Are you going to start in about Adolf Hitler again? Do you men ever stop thinking about politics?"

"Damn it, it's more than politics—"

"Stop worrying, Sam. There have been Jew haters in Europe before, and we managed to survive. We'll survive this Hitler, too. Europe is a civilized place, you know. More civilized than America in many ways. So stop worrying about me. Go to your Yudi and tell her the good news."

Sam didn't wait for more. He spun around and raced out the door. "I'll never forget you, Dvora. Never!" he yelled back.

"Sam?" she called after him. "Before you see her, for God's sake, stop at home and *shave.*"

6

The pier was mobbed. Somewhere in the distance a band was playing lively English marches, but it was hardly heard over the din of voices and the traffic of departure. Porters pushed through the crowds with their dollies loaded with luggage of all sizes and descriptions, from huge steamer trunks to small paper boxes tied with string. Although there was still half an hour before sailing, paper streamers and confetti were already being tossed from the upper decks of the ship to the crowds on the pier below.

The day was bright, and a morning breeze was rippling the waters of the Hudson. The little wavelets sent back glints of morning sunshine, reflecting the sparkles of light to the roof and walls of the wharf, as if from thousands of tiny mirrors. The dazzles of light seemed to electrify the air. The chatter of voices, the faint strains of the martial music, the laughter, the excited movement, the color of the women's summer dresses, the twinkling glints of light from the water, the confetti—it was like a giant party. Not many in the crowd appeared to be feeling sad in the midst of all this exhilaration.

But Dvora's group, huddled together near one of the gangways, made an island of stillness in the midst of a river of movement. Yudi was leaning on Sam's shoulder, trying not to cry. Margaret was checking through Dvora's envelope of tickets and baggage checks, making sure everything was accounted for. Dov was holding Frieda's hand to give the girl reassurance that she wasn't being left alone. And Dvora, resplendent in a white straw hat, a white linen suit, and a long red-print scarf tied around her neck with its ends tossed over her shoulders in casual elegance, was looking from one to the other as if she wanted to be sure their faces were forever engraved on her mind. "Yudi, my sweet, don't look like that," she said, embracing her sister. "This is a *happy* day. We should be laughing like loons. After all this time, we're each getting exactly what we want from life."

Yudi held her sister close. "Be happy, Dvora, always," she whispered.

Dvora kissed her and then embraced the others. Frieda was last. Mother and daughter held each other tightly for a long moment. "Good-bye, Countess," Frieda said when they let go, trying to be flip but sounding choked with emotion. "It won't be forever, I promise you. Uncle Dov and I have a plan."

"That's right," Dov said, struggling with the tightness in his own throat. "We'll send Frieda on the Grand Tour when she graduates. We're starting a special fund for it today. In a few years time, you'll be able to show her all the magnificent sights of Europe."

"Won't it be wonderful, Mama?" Frieda said, smiling bravely. "Just you and me, touring all those places you've always told me about. Just think of it! You and me in Vienna again."

Dvora held the girl tightly. "Yes, *Liebchen,*" she said, trying to laugh. "And this time you'll be able to *talk.*"

The boat whistle blew a deafening blast. Dvora stepped away, waved, and walked toward the gangway. Yudi made a choking sound in her throat. Sam put an arm around her and held her close. Dov and Margaret moved nearer to Frieda, one on each side, and linked hands. Dvora, at the foot of the gangway, turned around for a last, close look. "For God's sake, smile, everyone," she ordered. "This isn't the last we'll see of each other. It's 1933, and we're all still young. We have all our lives ahead of us. Years and years and years!"

She waved once more and ran up the gangway. The others moved close to the barrier and waited for her to make an appearance on one of the upper decks. The ship's rails were crowded with smiling, waving passengers, holding glasses of champagne and throwing streamers.

It was Frieda who spotted her. "There she is! Right there, see?"

They could see her white hat and the brilliantly colored scarf blowing jauntily in the sea breeze. They waved and blew kisses until the ship began to move. "She's saying something," Frieda cried. "What's she saying? I can't hear a thing in all this noise."

But Yudi thought she caught an echo of her sister's voice on a passing puff of wind. ". . . all our lives, *Liebchen,*" the echo wafted down as the ship glided majestically along the length of the pier, ". . . years . . . and years . . . and years . . ."

About the Author

Paula Reibel was born and educated in New York City, where she earned degrees from Hunter College and City College of New York. She has taught English literature and drama at New York University and Dunbarton College. She now writes full time and lives in Annandale, Virginia, with her husband.